ALSO AVAIL/
CATHERINE COWLES

The Tattered & Torn Series
Tattered Stars
Falling Embers
Hidden Waters
Shattered Sea
Fractured Sky

Sparrow Falls
Fragile Sanctuary
Delicate Escape
Broken Harbor
Beautiful Exile
Chasing Shelter
Secret Haven

The Lost & Found Series
Whispers of You
Echoes of You
Glimmers of You
Shadows of You
Ashes of You

The Wrecked Series
Reckless Memories
Perfect Wreckage
Wrecked Palace
Reckless Refuge
Beneath the Wreckage

The Sutter Lake Series
Beautifully Broken Pieces
Beautifully Broken Life
Beautifully Broken Spirit
Beautifully Broken Control
Beautifully Broken Redemption

Standalone Novels
Further to Fall
All the Missing Pieces

For a full list of up-to-date Catherine Cowles titles,
please visit catherinecowles.com.

Beautiful EXILE

CATHERINE COWLES

Beautiful
EXILE

CATHERINE COWLES

sourcebooks
casablanca

Published by Sourcebooks Casablanca, an imprint of Sourcebooks
P.O. Box 4410, Naperville, Illinois 60567-4410
(630) 961-3900
sourcebooks.com

Cataloging-in-Publication data is on file with the Library of Congress.

Printed and bound in the United States of America.
LSC 10 9 8 7 6 5 4 3 2 1

FOR ANYONE WHO'S SCARED TO LET LOVE IN...
TAKE THE LEAP, EVEN IF YOU'RE SHAKING.
BECAUSE THE MOST BEAUTIFUL THINGS ARE ON
THE OTHER SIDE OF THAT FEAR.

PROLOGUE

AGE ELEVEN

DAD PULLED A CARD FROM THE PILE, STUDYING IT LIKE AN archaeologist trying to determine if it was some ancient artifact or just a knockoff. Mom and I shared a look, our own determining going on. He slid the card into the fan he held and reached for another, pausing.

Looking up, he glanced first at Mom and then me. His dark brown hair was just a little rumpled, not the perfect, slicked-back look he wore to court each day. And he was dressed in jeans and a polo shirt instead of one of those fancy suits. But it was the mischief in his green eyes that I loved—the kind that said he was up to no good and enjoying every moment of it. I hadn't seen it much lately. Not with how busy he'd been with case after case, stressed to the max. And maybe not seeing it as often made me love it more.

Dad held up the card, fluttering it for a second before discarding it face down. "Gin."

"He cheats," my mom accused, but there was only humor in her words, and the way she looked at him spoke of nothing but love.

"I do not," he shot back, stiffening his spine in mock affront. He laid his hand down for us to see.

He'd smoked us. Three aces. Three nines. And a four-card straight in hearts.

I slumped back in the overstuffed leather chair, tossing my cards onto the coffee table. "Definitely a cheater. That's three in a row."

My dad chuckled as he gathered the cards to shuffle. "Maybe this is the hand you'll trounce me in."

"At least you've won once," Mom said to me. "I haven't won a single hand."

"We could always switch to Scrabble. You'd kick all our as—" I halted at the look from my mom. "All our butts."

Mom's warning expression softened, a hint of humor playing around her eyes. "Nice save. And I say Scrabble after this hand."

This was always the way it went. Gin rummy, where Dad would win. Then Scrabble, where Mom would take us both. It was no surprise, given all the time she spent surrounded by books. Everyone who lived in our suburb outside of Boston seemed to have some charity they were hooked up with. Mom's was the library.

It was her favorite place to spend time, just like the one in our house was her favorite room. Which was why we always held game night in here. To me, it was too stuffy—all the dark wood paneling and floor-to-ceiling shelves. At least during the day, sunlight from the garden and surrounding woods poured in through the windows. But at night? It felt a little stifling. Like the walls and all the books were closing in around me.

"How about...if I win this next hand, I get to go call Claire?" I asked hopefully.

Mom sent me a look that told me my chances of that were slim to none. "Sheridan, it's family night. Give your poor mom her one win."

Dad chuckled. "She's eleven. She's getting too cool for us."

"Don't remind me," Mom said, sniffing exaggeratedly. "We'll be dropping her off at college before we know it."

I rolled my eyes and pulled my knees to my chest. "I think you're safe for a while. I gotta get through middle and high school first."

A phone rang. My dad shifted and pulled the device from his pocket. Mom sent him a look that would've had me rethinking what

I was about to do, but Dad just went right ahead and answered. "Hey, Nolan." A pause. "Sure. I've got it here." Another silence. "Let me pull it up, and I'll call you back." Dad moved the phone away from his ear and pushed to his feet.

"Robbie," my mom said, her voice managing to somehow be both soft and hard at the same time. "It's family night. You promised." Her gray-violet eyes—a color she'd passed on to me—pleaded with him.

"Nolan just needs some information about a case. It'll take five minutes."

But it was never five minutes. Dad would hole up in his office for hours when he got a call or someone stopped by. I got it. He loved being a judge and took it seriously. But the meetings and late nights seemed to be happening more and more.

"Five minutes," Mom muttered, shoving her blond hair back from her face.

"Blythe," Dad said, his voice going hard. "Don't start." And then he was striding out of the room.

I could picture the path he would take. Down the hallway and then the stairs, stopping in his office with its massive fireplace and more dark wood. When I had a house someday, it would be all light and windows—no stuffy rooms with wood paneling and wallpaper.

I glanced at my mom. She sat in a leather chair that matched mine, staring at the spot on the sofa where my dad had been as if it could give her the answers she needed.

Dropping my focus to my jeans, I wrapped a fraying thread around my finger. Mom hated these jeans. Hated that I wanted a pair with tears and rips in them. I pulled the string tight, cutting off blood flow to my pointer finger. "Are you and Dad gonna get a divorce?"

My gaze flicked up, wanting to see her reaction. I was pretty good at knowing when she was lying—her mouth would flatten out, and little lines would appear like parentheses around it.

Her eyes flared in surprise. "No. Of course not. Why would you think that?"

I pulled the string a little tighter. "You guys fight a lot now. And Dad isn't home as much."

Mom sighed, leaning forward and taking my hand. She quickly unwound the string from my finger and rubbed blood flow back into it. "He's had a lot going on with work lately. But he's trying to fix that. To be home more."

I nodded, not completely convinced. "Are you okay?"

Her entire face changed, her expression gentling. "My sweet girl." She pressed a kiss to my temple. "I'm just fine."

I knew that was a lie. She wasn't herself. Tonight was the first glimpse I'd gotten in a long time of how things used to be. But maybe she'd meant that she knew we'd get back there—to how things had been.

I couldn't imagine being with someone for as long as my mom and dad had been together. They'd met her first year at Yale when Dad was a junior. They'd gotten together then and had never broken up. When Dad graduated from law school, he'd proposed. There had to be ups and downs when you were with someone for that long. The only problem was that I had plenty of friends whose parents had decided the downs were reason enough to split.

The doorbell rang, the chimes' three-toned noise echoing through the old house. I couldn't help but stiffen. If another of Dad's colleagues interrupted game night, I knew Mom would be pissed.

She squeezed my hand. "Sheridan. We're fine. I promise. Nothing is going to change."

God, I wanted to believe her.

Dad's muffled voice sounded from downstairs, but an unfamiliar sound cut it off. It was somewhere between a crack and a pop, like a firecracker. But I highly doubted Dad was setting those off in a foyer full of priceless art.

As my mind tried to put the pieces together, I watched the blood drain from Mom's already pale face. I'd always been a mix of them. I had Dad's dark brown hair, and my skin had just a hint of tanned olive in it like his. But my eyes were all Mom, that gray-violet that could go stormy when I was mad or upset.

Mom's skin was like ivory silk, the kind that meant she always had to wear sunscreen. But it almost looked gray now. Another firecracker sounded, and Mom leapt to her feet, running for the phone discreetly tucked into a corner of the library. She lifted it to her ear, finger already punching a key on the pad. But then she stilled.

"Dead." She patted her pocket and cursed, a word she *never* used flying from her lips. "I left my cell in the kitchen..." Her words trailed off as she stood frozen for a moment. A beat of one passed. Then two. Three. When she moved again, she flew across the room, grabbed my arm, and yanked me up.

"Wha—?"

Mom clamped a hand over my mouth, cutting off my words. She lifted the pointer finger of her other hand to her lips in a *shhh* motion. Panic flared to life, zinging through my muscles like some sort of foreign energy.

She grabbed my arm again and hurried into the hallway. I heard voices below. Footsteps.

"Where the hell are they?" a voice snarled.

Mom's fingers trembled around my wrist.

"You've been paying him too much. This house is too big," another voice said, a hint of humor lacing the words.

"Well, I won't have to do that anymore, will I?" the first voice asked.

Mom hurried down the hall, abruptly stopping at one of the panels. Her fingers ran over the seam until she found the spot she was looking for. She pushed on the wood, and the panel popped open.

There were hidey-holes like this all over the house. Everything from secret closets to a dumbwaiter. It had made for the best games of hide-and-seek growing up, but this was something else. Something bad.

Mom pushed me into the space, where a tall duster and some other cleaning supplies were stashed for our housekeeper. The space was so shallow I didn't think she'd be able to close the panel with me inside. I grabbed her arm. "Mom, what are you—?"

"Stay here. No matter what you hear, do not come out. Do you understand me?"

"Mom—"

She wrapped her arms around me and hugged me tightly. "Love you to the ends of the Earth."

I gripped her sweater, fisting the soft cashmere. "Get in with me."

Mom peeled my fingers from her arm and shook her head. "I can't."

Footsteps sounded on the stairs.

"Mom," I croaked.

"Not a word." She quickly closed the panel.

The space was so tight it felt like I could barely breathe. It didn't smell like the rest of the house; in here, the scents of dust and cleaning supplies filled my nose. And it was dark. Pitch-black except for the tiny sliver of light from the seam in the wood.

"Blythe," a voice greeted. There was a smoothness to it that felt like a lie—the same way the lines around my mom's mouth gave her away.

I pressed my face to the wood, trying to see, and could just make out the hallway right in front of the panel: the antique rug that lined the gleaming hardwood floor, the oil painting opposite me.

I stared at the brushstrokes as I waited. Some looked angry and forceful, while others were peaceful and calm. It wasn't something I'd ever noticed before, even though I'd passed the painting every day for my entire life.

"What are you doing here?" My mom tried to keep her voice calm, but it had a shrill edge. "Where's Robert?"

A *tsk*ing noise sounded. "Now, Blythe. Don't play stupid. It doesn't suit you."

My mom went quiet for a moment before speaking again. "What do you want? Whatever you need, I'll gladly give it to you."

"I'm so happy to hear you feel that way. What I *wanted* was for your husband to do what he was instructed. Instead, he tried to renege on his promises. And, Blythe, I don't like it when people go back on their word."

I could hear my mom's breaths—short, ragged pants just a few steps from me. She was so close I should've been able to reach out and touch her. Squeeze her hand in the secret way we used to silently tell each other: *I love you.* But I couldn't. Not now. It was as if an ocean lay between us.

"Whatever he took from you, I'll make sure you get it. If we go to the computer, I can transfer it now."

"Blythe," the voice cooed. "That's so kind of you to offer. Truly. You always were so much classier than your other half."

The man spoke as if he knew my parents, but his voice was completely unfamiliar. I searched my memory for something—*anything*—that would pull a name free. A face. But there was nothing.

"Please," my mom begged. "Don't hurt us. We have a daughter."

A few steps sounded, muted as if the man were moving closer on the carpet. "And where is that daughter now?"

My whole body began to tremble. It was like I'd been struck by lightning, and these were the aftershocks.

"She's at a sleepover. A couple of girlfriends from school," my mom said, her voice trembling like my body.

No one spoke for a beat or two. "You wouldn't be lying to me, would you, Blythe? I don't take kindly to liars."

Tears tracked down my cheeks as I again reached for that loose thread on my jeans. I wrapped it so tightly around my finger that I knew it likely drew blood.

"I'm not lying," Mom whispered.

The man made a humming noise, and a shadow covered my mother. I pressed my face harder against the door's seam, trying to see better. The tip of a single shoe moved into the frame. I couldn't take my eyes off that sliver of an image.

Leather. Dark brown with intricate stitching. It formed a shield of sorts with a lion. Words in Latin were above it, but I couldn't make out the exact phrase.

"You know? I believe you," the man said. "You always were more respectful than Robbie. But I'm afraid it's too late. What he owes me is a blood debt. But that's been paid. Unfortunately, because of your traitor of a husband, you'll need to pay, too."

The shoe disappeared from view, and another of those firecrackers sounded. Only now, I knew it wasn't that. It was something so much worse.

My mom jerked, disappearing from my line of sight for a moment before stumbling back into the frame. She clutched her chest and then crumpled to the floor, blood spreading and seeping through her light purple cashmere sweater—the one that had felt so soft beneath my fingers.

Black spots danced in front of my vision. *Breathe.* I needed to breathe.

I sucked in short bursts of air. It was all I could manage.

My mom's gray-violet eyes—*our* eyes—went wide and then froze, unblinking. Her hands went limp against the antique carpet—the one she always told me to be careful not to spill on.

But *she* was the one spilling now, her life force draining onto the dark mix of woven colors.

A shadow slid over her body again, and then a man moved into the frame. He looked like he belonged. Like someone who lived at one of the properties a few acres away. Someone we'd see at the club or church. He wore khakis and a button-down shirt, his light brown hair just a little shaggy and unkempt.

But his hands showed he was different: the black gloves he wore, the gun in the hand closest to me.

My whole body trembled, and I felt liquid sliding down my legs, soaking my jeans.

"Check her," the other voice said—the one that had taunted my mother. The one who'd ordered the spilling of her blood. The one with the Latin lion shoe.

The man in front of me crouched, careful not to step in the blood—Mom's blood. He pressed two gloved fingers to her neck and then turned, looking at the man I couldn't see. "She's gone."

My knees nearly gave way. *Gone.* My mom. The black dots were back, almost taking me under.

"Good riddance," the other man spat. "Search every room in this house. I want to make sure that brat really is at a sleepover. If not, she's dead." His voice began to fade as he stomped down the hall, but his words reverberated in my ears.

Sleepover… My mom's story was saving me, telling the beautiful lie that I was gone.

Only it wasn't the *gone* my mom was. Or my dad. My chest burned as I slid to the floor, my body contorting to fit the space. But I couldn't stay upright anymore.

All I wanted was to slip into that *gone* right along with my parents.

CHAPTER ONE

Arden
PRESENT DAY

I STARED AT THE PAINTING, FRUSTRATION SWELLING, SWIRLING in inky tendrils as I assessed the image and brushstrokes, the angry beat of heavy metal blaring from the speakers. It wasn't working. Something was missing. Perhaps it was too similar to pieces I'd done in the past. Or maybe it felt just the slightest bit false.

I worked in various mediums: metal for sculpting, oils for canvases, even the occasional pastel or charcoal piece. It was my way of processing and dealing with the darkness. Letting it come and then expelling it onto some surface.

Some would think it was healthy. The foster family I'd ended up with on the opposite side of the country certainly did. But the truth was, the darkness and I had never really come to an understanding. We constantly battled, but I never won the war—even now, at age twenty-five.

Which was why my workshop, nestled in the mountains of Central Oregon, was currently ablaze with light. It was my way of casting out those shadows, the same as I did with my art. Ironically, while my fear of the dark had remained, my creativity came alive at night.

Maybe it was the darkness's way of keeping its hooks in me, tempting me to see if I was brave enough to face it. I stared harder at the canvas. The image was haunting; I'd give it that. Dark, tunneling trees beckoned you to come closer. But something was definitely missing.

I let out a growl of frustration that had Brutus lifting his head from where he lay in the dog bed in the corner, his gray ears twitching. The massive cane corso was always checking up on me. He was another weapon in my arsenal against the darkness.

"I'm fine," I grumbled, heading to the sink on the far wall. Pouring some solvent into a dish, I began the process of cleaning my brushes.

The routine was a meditation of sorts—one of the few I could muster. Because sitting on a pillow while soft music played wasn't really my thing. I needed something active, punctuated by the raw anger of hard rock and various kinds of metal. I found it in art and jujitsu.

Both were gifts in their own way. Ones given to me by the family I'd found in a place I'd least expected. After months of foster care and then witness protection in Boston, they'd finally placed me far from that world and with a family who knew nothing about Boston society or judges who'd taken bribes to throw cases a certain way, ultimately costing their family everything.

As that familiar mix of anger and guilt swirled in a noxious stew inside me, I took a steadying breath and remembered where I'd landed.

With the Colsons.

A family that was a mix of blood, adoption, and foster bonds but closer than any I'd ever known. But maybe it was the element of choice that made it that way.

Nora Colson's choice to continue to bring children into her home after losing her husband and one of her sons in a car accident. But not just any children. She took the toughest cases, the most broken ones. So, it hadn't been a surprise that I'd landed on her doorstep, barely verbal and scared of my own shadow.

But she and her mom, whom we called Lolli, had brought me out of my shell and helped me heal the best they could. Just like they had for everyone who came across their threshold. They had Cope and Fallon, Nora's birth children; her adopted son, Shep; and Rhodes, Trace, and Kyler, her fosters.

We were a patchwork family full of different threads and fabrics, but it created something that never would've been otherwise. Something more beautiful.

But that didn't change the fact that I sometimes felt like I didn't fit. I was just a little too odd. Not especially good with people. I was better with my paints, metals, animals, and sparring—all the things that didn't need words.

I dropped my brushes onto the towel, spreading them out to dry. My fingers were still twitchy since I hadn't gotten the outlet that painting provided tonight. My gaze flicked to the massive windows along my workshop's back wall. I could just see the beginnings of the sun peeking over the ridge of the Monarch Mountains to the east and knew it would cast its rays across the golden faces of Castle Rock before long.

The view from these windows was breathtaking, and one my brother, Cope, had given me out of generosity: a home and a studio on his massive property. He liked to couch it as him needing a property manager since he spent so much time on the road with his hockey team, but I knew the truth.

He wanted to make sure I was safe. Sequestered from the world as much as possible. Behind fences and gates with cameras and alarm systems. It didn't matter that it had been almost fourteen years since anyone had tried to harm me. My siblings would always want me safe.

Laying out the final brush, I arched my back to loosen the muscles. I'd need a good soak in some Epsom salts later—the curse of being on my feet for too many hours straight. But first, I needed to move.

I glanced at my watch. Just a few minutes past five. My gaze moved to Brutus. "Want to go to the gym?"

Brutus let out a deep woof and was on his feet instantly. He loved Kye's mixed martial arts gym, not because of the building itself, but because of all the attention he got there.

My lips twitched. "You're going to be bummed when you realize it's too early for anyone else to be there."

Brutus simply panted in response.

I grabbed my gear bag from the beat-up leather couch along the far wall and switched off the music. The sofa was storage, bed, and sometimes dining table all rolled into one since I spent more time here than in my small guesthouse next door. But it was everything I needed. And it wasn't like sleep came easily in an actual bed.

Ducking into the small bathroom, I quickly changed into workout gear and headed for the door. Brutus was at my side in a flash, my mostly silent companion.

As I headed outside, the automatic lights flicked on, bathing the gravel parking area in light and illuminating my most prized possession: my 1979 red Ford F-150 pickup. Her exterior had seen better days, but her guts were perfect.

She was the first thing I'd bought myself with the proceeds from my art. Thanks to the hefty trust fund my parents left behind, I could've bought a vehicle when I turned sixteen, but I couldn't help seeing it as blood money. The reason my parents were no longer here.

Sure, some of it had been hard-earned, coming from my father's job as a lawyer and then a judge. But when the FBI dug into my parents' case, it was clear that someone had been bribing him. They just didn't know who.

The FBI commandeered those funds, but I couldn't help but wonder if more had flown under the radar, or help but feel like the bribes had tainted the rest of it.

So, I'd left the money in the account and never touched it. I only knew how much was in there because I'd had to move it from one bank to another a few months ago. The amount had been staggering—so staggering, I'd gotten physically ill afterward.

But keeping it apart from my life now had been a gift. Because earning the cash I needed for Wanda made the purchase even sweeter. My brothers were always on me to sell or fix her up, but I thought her dents and rust spots gave her character.

Sliding the key into the lock, I opened the driver's side door and motioned Brutus inside. He leapt in with grace and power—things that kept me safe, right along with his years of personal-protection training.

Brutus had been a gift from my eldest brother, Trace. The most safety-conscious rule follower of all of us. But given his upbringing, that wasn't a surprise. Just like it wasn't a shock that he had ended up as the sheriff of our entire county.

I started Wanda, and she purred to life, the rebuilt engine humming perfectly. My headlights cut into the early-morning darkness, illuminating roads I knew by heart now. And with those headlights, the dark didn't feel so ominous, more like a blanket of quiet. I craved that just as much as turning my beloved music up to eleven.

Silence or deafening chaos, there was no in-between for me.

The benefit of heading to the gym at five a.m. was that the streets were completely clear. Even though it was August and the height of tourist season in Sparrow Falls, this was too early, even for the hikers. So, I made the drive in two-thirds of the time it usually took me.

As I pulled into the parking lot behind the building on the outskirts of town, more lights flicked on. Yet another way my siblings took care of me. Kye had put extras in the moment I started coming to Haven in the early-morning hours or late at night.

Shutting off the engine, I slid out of the cab and glanced at Brutus, who waited patiently, but his quivering muscles gave him away. My lips curved into a half smile, one that would've turned full had my wasted night at the easel not still hounded me. "*Komm.*"

At the German command, Brutus leapt out of the vehicle and stuck right by my side. I should've had him on a leash. If Trace saw us now, he'd write me a ticket faster than I could blink. But what he didn't know wouldn't hurt him.

My gaze automatically scanned the lot as I walked, feeling the switchblade I always carried pressed into the pocket at my waist. Some might think me paranoid, but safe and wary was a hell of a lot better than dead.

As I reached the gym door, I punched in the lock's code. My skin was already humming with the need to move, to feel the contact of my fist against the punching bag. Sparring would've been even better, the give and take of going up against someone else, but Kye would've murdered me if I'd tried to get him out of bed for a workout before the sun rose fully.

I stepped inside, flicking on the lights to illuminate the massive room. The space was a mix of black and gray, except for two walls covered in elaborate murals I knew Kye had painted himself. I could study the intricate designs in their vibrant colors for hours and not get bored. He was an artist. And while his medium and aesthetic were so different from mine, it only entranced me more. I understood why people traveled from all over the country and even the world to have him ink permanent pictures on their skin.

Pulling my phone out of my bag, I ignored the endless stream of notifications and texts and moved to my music app instead. I opted for something to drown out the noise swirling in my head. The moment the attacking riffs spilled through the gym's speakers, some tension bled from my shoulders.

I moved through my warm-up routine of jumping rope, then pulled on fingerless MMA gloves for the portion of my workout I was dying for. The heavy bag. Its weight was exactly what I needed— something strong enough to take whatever I unleashed. Something I couldn't hurt with all the anger and darkness still living inside me.

Rolling to the balls of my feet, I lifted my hands to a guard position in front of my face. I gave the bag a few testing jabs before giving myself over to the full force of my strikes. I lost myself in the music and movement, the meditation that was mine and mine alone. It was one of the few times I could be fully me without judgment or worry; one of the two places I could let loose everything that lived inside me.

That otherworldly state and the single-minded focus that caused my distraction meant I didn't hear anything until Brutus let out a low warning growl. My heart skipped a single beat, but that was all I allowed it to do. One tiny moment of fear and weakness.

My fingers curled around the hilt of my knife, pushing the button to release the blade. I whirled, pressing it to the stranger's neck, freezing him in place. When I was sure of that stillness, I looked up, up, up into the face of the most beautiful man I had ever seen. But I'd learned once before that looks could be deceiving. You never knew what lay below the surface. So, I kept my blade pressed where it was as the man's hazel eyes widened in surprise.

"Who. The. Hell. Are. You?"

CHAPTER TWO

Lincoln

GOD, SHE WAS FUCKING GORGEOUS. SHE HAD A WILD, POWERFUL kind of beauty. The kind you could never control. The type you could never cage.

I'd stood in the shadows like a creep, watching her: the way she moved, her long, dark brown ponytail swinging with each punch. Her tan skin pulling tautly over lean muscle. She was on the petite side, but you'd never know that, given how much force she put behind her blows.

It was clear the woman had training, and the fact that she currently had a blade pressed to my carotid told me she wasn't afraid to use it. Amusement was my first reaction, that the tiny powerhouse was so full of fire.

She pressed the blade harder against my skin, not enough to slice me open but enough to prick my flesh. The sting took hold the same way her beauty had.

"I asked who you were," she gritted out, her gray-violet eyes flashing.

The fierceness there had all amusement fleeing from my system.

Because there was only one reason someone defended themselves with such ferocity: they'd been hurt before.

Fuck.

I slowly lifted my hand, revealing a key ring with the Haven gym tag I'd picked up yesterday dangling from it, one coded to let people into the gym any time after six. "New gym member."

The woman didn't show any signs of retreat. Her bewitching eyes simply narrowed on me, looking for all my secrets. "It isn't open yet."

I kept my hand where she could see it, not wanting to risk further injury but also not wanting to frighten her more. I wanted to kick my ass for that as it was. "I was told it opened at six."

Her gaze flicked to the large clock on the wall, and then she cursed, finally pulling the knife away from my neck. "Of course, Kye's late," she muttered.

So, she knew the owner. An owner who happened to be the brother of my best friend, the one who'd gone on and on about the best place to train in Sparrow Falls. A prickle of something unfamiliar slid through me. Were the two involved? No part of me liked that idea. Which was ludicrous, given the fact that the only things I knew about this woman were how quickly she could pull a knife and that she looked like a walking temptation when taking on a heavy bag.

The massive gray dog next to her let out another low growl. Her gaze flicked to him. "*Beruhigen.*" She spoke as easily as if she'd been born speaking German. For all I knew, she had.

The dog eased but still watched me carefully. I had a feeling he'd lunge if I made even one wrong move. But I was glad she had that.

She watched me closely as she slowly closed the switchblade and stepped back. She wore leggings that hugged every inch of her lean, muscular legs and a black tank top that dipped just enough to hint at what was under it—something that was none of my business. But as my gaze swept over her, I noticed something else.

Her tan skin was dotted with something. Paint. Gray, black, deep purple, and blue. The pattern had no rhyme or reason, but I found I wanted to search for every last speck of color.

She cleared her throat, annoyance evident in the sound.

My gaze flicked up to her face and the swirling irises that had held me rapt a moment ago. Those gray-violet orbs were siren's eyes. Ones that could cast a spell and make you crash your ship against a rocky shore.

One of the paint splatters on her cheek fluttered as she scowled. "What are you staring at?"

"You aren't going to apologize for nearly cutting my jugular?" I challenged, trying to shift the conversation from my fast-growing obsession.

The woman arched one dark brow at that. "You're the one who broke into a gym without permission. You're lucky you're still breathing."

Those siren's eyes flashed a brighter violet as she spoke, and I thought I fell just a little bit in love with her fire.

"Vicious," I muttered, but there was only admiration in my tone. "Though I don't know if it can be considered *breaking in* when the door was unlocked, and I called out. But it's hard to hear over this… noise."

Annoyance flickered across the woman's features as she bent and snatched a phone from the mat. She tapped the screen a few times, and the music cut off. "It's not *noise*, it's *Cradle of Filth*."

My lips twitched. "You said it, not me."

She rolled her eyes. "It's the band's name."

"I think calling that a *band* is a stretch."

"Toh-may-toh, toh-mah-toh," she said, then winced, heading for a stack of towels. "Sorry about your neck."

I moved to follow her as if she'd cast some sort of spell on me, but the gray beast stepped into my path, baring his teeth. "Is your dog going to rip out my throat?"

The siren chuckled, and the sound had a husky tone that wrapped around me, causing all my nerve endings to stand at attention. "Not if you stay where you are," she said as she grabbed a couple of paper towels and crossed back to me.

She glanced down at her dog, grinning at him. "*Freund*, Brutus."

The moment she spoke the words, the tension in the dog's

muscles eased, but his gaze stayed fixed on me as if he didn't trust me yet.

"Brutus knows German."

The woman shrugged as she handed me a towel. "That's how he was trained."

"Guard dog?" I asked, curiosity piquing as I pressed the paper towel to my neck.

A hint of wariness slid into her expression. "Personal protection. Lots of people have protective dogs around here. Ranches and all."

But that hit like a lie. A person didn't bring their ranch dog into town if they weren't worried about something. I had the bizarre urge to push for more. To learn all this woman's secrets.

That wasn't me. I'd built an empire through patience and tenacity. I didn't rush. Didn't let a single soul know I was eager for something. Because they could take advantage. And I'd learned the hard way never to let someone know what I really wanted. Or how much I cared.

The woman headed for a duffel by the shelves stocked with gloves, jump ropes, and other equipment. Swinging it over her shoulder, she straightened. "Enjoy your workout. Try not to steal anything. Even if it would serve my brother right for being a lazy ass."

I stilled, my hold on my keys tightening. "Your brother?"

"Kye. He owns the place. He's also notorious for sleeping through alarms."

Kye. As in Cope's brother. And if Kye was Cope's brother, then…
Hell. My siren was my best friend's sister.

CHAPTER THREE

Arden

I HATED HOW MY HANDS TREMBLED AS I CLIMBED INTO MY TRUCK. That tiny flickering motion gave me away as I twisted my key in the ignition. I'd moved fast, my training and instinct kicking in, and that was a good thing. I could've ended the too-handsome-for-his-own-good man in a single heartbeat.

His face flashed in my mind. Dark brown hair, just a little wild and unkempt. Stubble coating a strong, angular jaw. Hypnotic, gold-green eyes. He hadn't looked like a killer. And it turned out he wasn't one. Just a new gym patron. One who probably thought I was more than a little unhinged.

My fingers tightened around the wheel, making the leather creak and groan as embarrassment flooded my system.

More than thirteen years.

Yet it sometimes felt like I was still that broken little girl who'd arrived on the Colsons' ranch scared of her own shadow. But I wasn't. I knew how to protect myself now. Keep myself safe. If that meant people thought I was a freak, so be it.

I reminded myself of that all the way home as the sun rose,

casting glittering pink and gold across the landscape. There were already a couple of vehicles at Cope's place, and I knew it was because he was headed back to Seattle with his girlfriend, Sutton, and her son, Luca.

A pang lit in my sternum. It wasn't that I didn't like solitude. I did. It was simply that, after all they'd been through in the past month, I liked the reassurance of knowing they were safe. Especially Cope. When you almost lost someone, it took a while to trust that they weren't going to fade away in front of your eyes. And when you saw someone you loved disappear into the gone, it took even longer.

I flexed my fingers around the wheel, forcing them to relax slightly as I turned toward the guesthouse. I knew sleep wouldn't find me now. I had too much brewing after the encounter at Haven. Instead, I opted for a shower and coffee.

Once I'd cleaned up, caffeinated, and dressed in my barn clothes, I headed outside, Brutus on my heels. The August sun beat down on me as I headed for the small, two-horse barn. The deeper into summer we got, the earlier in the day the blistering heat arrived. I was just thankful that being nestled in the mountains of Central Oregon meant the evenings were cool.

The peaks also made for a beautiful backdrop that made me feel like I could breathe. I stopped for a moment, pausing to turn and really take in the landscape surrounding me. The snowcapped Monarch Mountains to the east and the golden faces of Castle Rock to the west. It was a breathtaking place to call home. Even if it wasn't truly *mine*.

Cope would hate it if he knew I thought that way. My brother had done everything he could to make me feel like this place was mine, from building a barn for Whiskey and Stardust to constructing a massive art studio beside the guesthouse to hold my pieces.

A heavy weight leaned against my thigh, and I glanced down to take in my shadow. Brutus was one hundred pounds of pure love but would gladly take out someone's jugular at my command. My hand lowered to scratch his head. "Your breakfast is next. Don't worry."

Sweat already threatened to gather at the small of my back from the combination of the August heat and the thought of mucking out the stalls. If I was smart, I'd start earlier, when it was more civilized. But a morning person, I was not. Because when sleep did manage to find me, I held on to it with everything I had.

My girls greeted me with snorts and whinnies as I entered the barn. They were already waiting at their stall doors. They knew the drill. The routine was a balm to all of us, and I was grateful that I'd managed to find two mares who didn't begrudge my later start times.

"Sorry I'm late," I said as I ducked into the tack room that also housed their feed. Filling a bucket, I headed back out and down the aisle.

I stopped at the first stall, bending to press my forehead to the dappled gray's. Her coat was like a scattering of light and shadow. Some days, it looked like the light would win, and others, the shadow. It was the same sort of battle I felt warring inside me. I stayed there for a moment, soaking in the contact and the grounding sensation it gave me. Stardust stayed, too, as if she sensed I needed extra today.

Finally, I forced myself to straighten and poured half the grain into her bucket. I moved on to the buckskin. She was all tan body and dark mane, tail, and legs. I gave Whiskey a scratch between her ears the way she loved, relishing how she pressed into my hand, searching for more. The trust in that movement was the same gift it always was. I pulled my hand back and poured the rest of the feed into her bucket.

My girls didn't wait; they dove right in. And I knew Whiskey would be begging for more in a matter of minutes. I wasn't wrong. A whinny sounded, and when I turned around, she blew air between her lips.

I couldn't help the laugh that bubbled out of me as I grabbed a lead rope. Sliding the stall door open, I hooked it to her halter. "You know treats are for the evenings or after a ride. You have to earn it."

The mare snorted as if she understood every word I said. I led her into the pasture and then did the same with Stardust. I poured some kibble into a bowl for Brutus and got to work on my barn chores. An hour or so into mucking out and sweeping up, Brutus let out a bark.

As I turned, he quivered next to me. Over the seven years I'd had him, I'd learned to decipher his barks. There were warnings and alerts, but there were also happy ones like this. Those that told me someone he loved was near.

I wandered to the edge of the barn, my hand shielding my eyes to take in the figures climbing out of the familiar SUV. The moment Luca's feet hit the gravel, a wide grin on his seven-year-old face, I gave Brutus the command for release. *"Freigeben,"* I said, patting his massive gray booty.

Brutus didn't wait. He bounded over to Luca, who crouched to get right up in the dog's face. Sutton laughed as she joined them, bending to give him all the rubs and whisper sweet nothings. They were effusive with their praise of my pup, and I wondered if he wished I were more like that. But our bond was a quiet one built during endless days in my studio or on long walks and rides in the wilderness. Still, I hoped he knew how much I loved him, even if that love lived in the silence between us.

A new flash of movement caught my eye as Cope slid from the SUV. He no longer moved as if every step was painful, but I didn't miss the strain around his eyes and mouth as his feet hit the ground. The urge to scream at him to stop moving was strong. The image of him in the hospital after a bullet had torn through his chest and collapsed a lung flashed in my mind.

My hands fisted, fingernails biting into my palms. As the sting of pain flared, the image retreated, but not before Cope caught my look. Pain was back in his expression, but for a whole new reason now. *Fucking hell.*

Cope forced a smile as he ruffled Luca's hair. "Why don't you and your mom go say goodbye to Whiskey and Stardust?"

Luca pushed to his feet, sighing. "I'm gonna miss them. Think they've got horses in Seattle?"

Sutton's expression softened. "I'm sure they do. But I know what they definitely have…"

Luca gave her a wide smile, revealing his new permanent tooth growing in. "Hockey!"

Luca was hockey-crazed, so it felt like destiny that his mom had fallen for my professional-hockey-playing brother. As soon as Cope fully rehabbed his injury, the three of them would be surrounded by all things ice.

Sutton laughed as Luca took off toward the pasture. She followed but stopped to give me a quick squeeze. "I'm going to miss you."

I'd gotten used to having her company and admired the hell out of her strength and tenacity. "You'll be back before you know it."

"We will." Her gaze lifted to Cope. "And this is important."

I knew it was. Cope needed one more chance to play hockey his way—a healthier way—now that he had Sutton and Luca in his life.

As Sutton followed her son into the barn, Cope made his way toward me. I grimaced at the way he still guarded his steps. "Are you sure you should be doing this much walking around?"

"You've been avoiding me." This was the new Cope. No hiding behind jokes and straight to the point.

My hand dropped, and my fingers found a loose thread on my jeans to twist. "You've been busy."

Cope pinned me with a droll stare. "Oh, yeah, super busy watching endless movies and doing my hundred-yard walks every couple of hours."

I winced. "I suck."

He moved in closer, ducking his head so his dark blue eyes met mine. "Don't talk shit about my sister. Only I get to do that."

A half laugh, half scoff left my lips. "Brings up stuff…you getting shot."

It had stirred my ghosts and demons. Maybe that's why I'd overreacted to the poor guy at the gym this morning. Somehow, I doubted he'd keep his membership.

Cope muttered a curse. "I'm sorry, A—"

"You ask to get shot?"

His lips twitched. "No."

"Then don't be dumb. It's not your fault. But I like your egotistical ass, so I'd rather you not get dead. Think you can work on that?" It took everything I had to make light of what had happened—an obsession that had turned deadly.

Cope nodded. "Sutton's going to make sure I only have boring days ahead."

"I heard that," she yelled from the pasture.

This time, I did laugh. And it helped. It released some of the tension that had been building in my chest.

Cope turned his focus back to me. "You going to be okay?"

I nodded. "You know me. I like my alone time."

Cope winced as his gaze pulled toward a vehicle in the distance.

"What?" I asked, dread pooling in my stomach.

"You won't be alone. Not *exactly*."

"Explain, Puck Boy," I growled.

Cope scrubbed a hand over his face and glanced back at the SUV getting closer. "You know Linc, the owner of my team?"

I nodded slowly. I knew *of* him but hadn't actually met the man, even during the camp Cope had hosted in Sparrow Falls and in the aftermath of his attack.

"He's been looking for a spot to build a vacation house."

"Billionaires," I muttered. I might not have met Lincoln Pierce, but I'd heard plenty. Merciless when it came to protecting his various holdings. Innovative when it came to his approach to business. And if what I'd been told was right, a bit paranoid about giving his trust.

Cope pinned me with a hard stare. "He's not like that. Linc's a good guy and is going through some stuff. So, go easy on him."

That piqued my interest, but I didn't bite. I just eyed him warily and waited for him to explain.

Cope sighed. "I told him he could stay at my place while Shep started the build."

"You didn't." The look I sent my brother should've had him ducking for cover. I didn't do well with strangers, as evidenced by this morning's gym outing. The last thing I needed was someone to be awkward around when Cope wasn't here as a buffer.

"It's only a few weeks here and there. Just at crucial parts of the build. His life is in Seattle," Cope protested.

"Unbelievable," I muttered, scowling at the approaching vehicle.

"Could you try not to look like you're being tortured when you say hello?" Cope mumbled.

I flipped him off. "Strangers make me grumpy. You know that."

Cope chuckled. "Yeah, he said you already almost killed him."

Everything in me stilled. The door to some overpriced SUV slammed, and my spine jerked straight at the sound. But more than that, at the sight. Those swirling hazel eyes. The thick, dark hair my fingers itched to run through. The jaw sharp enough to cut glass.

Oh, hell no.

One corner of that beautiful mouth kicked up. "Hey, Vicious."

CHAPTER FOUR

Lincoln

I WATCHED THOSE PERFECT BERRY LIPS PART IN SHOCK AS I climbed out of my SUV, the mental dots connecting as I strode toward the woman who, through a process of elimination, I now knew was Arden. And then the heat settled in—that smoky flare of fire in her gray-violet eyes. Anger might have put it there, but that didn't make the burn any less beautiful to watch.

"You knew who I was," Arden accused.

I held up both hands in mock surrender. "Not at first. I was just going to the gym—one my good friend here always talks about." I glanced at Cope. "Thanks for that, by the way."

He tried to cover his laugh with a cough. "Sorry."

"He snuck up on *me*," Arden defended.

Cope pinned her with a stare I recognized: a big brother exasperated with his little sister. "And how loud was your music?"

Pink hit the apples of Arden's cheeks, and it somehow made her look even more beautiful. "Not *that* loud."

"Not sure it qualifies as music," I added.

She glared in my direction, and Cope chuckled as he shook his head. "Pierces your eardrums, huh?"

"Like someone took an ice pick to my skull," I agreed.

"You two clearly have no taste." Arden turned to her brother. "I need to get back to work, and you need to get off your feet."

Cope's face twisted with a hint of annoyance. "I'm fine."

"And I will be, too." She moved into his space, stretching up onto her tiptoes to press a kiss to his cheek. "Be safe, please. I like you in one piece."

"I'll do my best," Cope said. "But you might want to know something first."

"What's that? You gave the other half of your house to the starting line of Seattle's football team?" Arden called, walking backward away from us both.

"Sutton's going to marry me."

It was like some invisible force hit Arden, causing joy to slide over her features. But it was joy laced with pain. And I couldn't figure out where the pain had come from.

"You're gonna have a beautiful life, Copey," she called and then turned, jogging away, her giant dog trailing behind her.

I couldn't take my eyes off her as she headed toward what I assumed was her art studio. Cope never shut up about the sister who lived in the guesthouse on his property and made captivating art that people clamored over. But he'd conveniently left out the fact that she was the most stunning human being on the planet. Figured.

Finally, I forced my gaze away from where she'd disappeared and glanced back at my friend. "Big news, huh, *Copey*?"

"Oh, fuck off," he muttered.

I chuckled. "Seriously, I'm happy for you, man. You more than deserve this."

Cope's gaze moved from me to the pasture that currently held the two people he loved most in this world. "I didn't always believe that. But thanks to Sutton, I'm starting to."

Hell, if that didn't hit me right in the solar plexus. I honestly wasn't sure I'd ever known a love with the power to create change like that. I loved my little sister, Ellie, fiercely, but it was a protective love. My mom had done her best, but the tyrant who ran our household had crushed her spirit over the years. The beautiful memories I had of her were coated in an acid that made them hard to endure. And the man I should've called *Dad* sure as hell didn't love anyone but himself.

"Linc? You okay?"

I blinked a few times to clear away the memories that felt like a combination of smoky tendrils I couldn't quite grasp, and shards of glass I couldn't clear away fast enough. "I'm good. Just happy you found this."

His expression eased a fraction. "Then maybe that will put you in a good enough mood to do me a favor."

"Cope. You're letting me stay in your house while I work on building mine. I'll do whatever you need." The moment he'd offered up his stunning mountain oasis, I'd jumped at the chance. Not that I couldn't afford to rent something while we got the project started, but whatever I found wouldn't be this close to the siren's orbit.

Cope paused for a moment as if choosing his words carefully. "Watch out for Arden while I'm gone?"

Tension wove its way around my muscles, tightening every strand of sinew. "She in some sort of trouble?" Between the knife this morning, the hulking guard dog, and Cope's request, I didn't have a good feeling.

"No," he said quickly. "It's not like that. She just…my getting shot was hard on her. I wouldn't mind someone being around for a while."

Everything started to fall into place. Her need to protect herself. Being extra jumpy. But something still niggled. A piece of the puzzle didn't fit, and I wanted to figure it out. Only the desire was bordering on need at this point.

"Of course. I'll make sure she has my number, too. Just in case."

"Thanks, man," Cope said, one corner of his mouth kicking up. "Try not to get stabbed, though."

"You just worry about getting my star player back on the ice,"

I shot back. But it was so much more than that. I wanted my best friend to truly *heal*.

"Yeah, yeah," Cope muttered. "I think you've still got a little scab right there from my little sister kicking your ass."

I couldn't help but laugh. "Thanks for the reminder." I started heading toward the art studio as Sutton and Luca ducked through the fence rails. "Travel safe."

"Thanks for letting us use your plane," he called back.

"Anytime." I turned, moving with a single-minded focus now. The guesthouse and studio perfectly complemented the main house with their mixture of reddish wood, stone, and glass. The design made me eager to work with Cope's brother, Shep, who had executed the builds here.

But I couldn't stay focused on that, the properties I'd be viewing tomorrow, or the meeting with Shep to talk about the design. Because my mind wouldn't let go of thoughts of the woman with the haunted eyes. The walking juxtaposition. Hard and soft. Quiet and loud. Light and dark.

Those opposites in one human being tugged at me and made me want to know how both resided so fully in one person. But more than that, it made me want to know *why*.

As I rounded the guesthouse, a retro truck came into view. A red Ford F-150, likely dating back to somewhere in the late seventies. The paint job was rusted in spots, and there were more than a few dings, but it somehow only gave the vehicle more character. And I only became more intrigued with its owner.

I walked up the workshop steps, and as I lifted my hand to knock, I noticed a camera tucked into the eaves. *Interesting.* I knew Cope had plenty of security on his property, so it made sense for him to extend that to his sister's place. Still, something gnawed at me. Something didn't quite fit.

My knuckles connected with the door three times. There was no answer. Nothing but angry strains of music from within the space.

This time, I tried the doorbell. I thought I heard a deep woof from inside, and then the music cut off. I waited, some phantom energy starting to buzz through my muscles.

The door flew open, and I was met with an adorable scowl. "Yes?"

Something about her expression only made me want to grin more. "Wanted to give you my number."

The violet in those siren's eyes flashed brighter. "Why would I need that?"

"Oh, I don't know. In case you want me to kill a spider. Or fight off an axe murderer."

Arden let out a sound somewhere between a laugh and a scoff. "I relocate the spiders outside, and if an axe murderer shows up, I'm offering you up as a sacrifice."

I only smiled wider. "You're brutal."

She lifted a shoulder and then let it drop. "The truth hurts."

I slid a card out of my wallet and handed it to her. "In case you want to give me over to any axe murderers. Or need help with your horses or something."

Arden arched a dark brow. "You a secret cowboy?"

I chuckled. "You never know. Either way, I'm good with grunt labor."

Arden tapped the card against her thigh. "I'll keep that in mind." When I made no move to leave, she sighed. "What else do you need, Lincoln?"

Hell.

The way she said my name… There was a slight grit to her voice, a realness I couldn't get enough of.

"You mean besides medical treatment from my eventful morning?" I asked, amusement lacing the words.

Arden's cheeks flushed pink, and *fuck,* it made her look even more beautiful. I wanted to follow that blush and see what I could do to make it spread.

"You won't sneak up on me next time," she shot back.

My gaze flicked from her to the dog behind her and back again. "Definitely not."

Arden didn't look away, and our gazes locked, held. "Lincoln—"

"Linc," I corrected. "My friends call me Linc."

"And me almost impaling you on my switchblade makes us besties?" she asked.

I fought the smile that wanted to stretch across my face. "We've definitely got a bond." My fingers lifted to touch the tiny scab on my neck. "Cemented in blood."

The blush disappeared from her face in a flash, her skin taking on an almost gray hue.

I muttered a curse. "Sorry. Squeamish around blood?"

"Something like that," she muttered, taking a step back. "What do you really want, Linc? I'm working."

The moment she uttered my nickname, I found I missed the sound of the full thing on her lips. The way her tongue caressed each syllable. I cleared my throat, trying to get a hold of myself. "I wanted to see about buying one of your pieces."

Surprise lit in those hypnotizing eyes. "You know my art?"

"Is that really so surprising? You've built quite a name for yourself, and your brother won't shut up about how talented you are. I looked up your site a while ago. Been meaning to reach out about an acquisition."

That wasn't the entire truth. It had started as simple curiosity and then grew into an obsession. Her artwork was like nothing I'd ever seen: haunting and captivating all at once. Looking at it felt like staring into a beautiful nightmare, but something about it made me feel seen somehow. As if she'd plucked my demons from my mind and put them on canvas or sculpted them out of metal. Even her charcoal drawings felt three-dimensional somehow.

I'd found myself bookmarking the page, checking back time after time. I'd memorized every piece of information on the site, but all it left me with was a mystery that never released its hold. The bio was purposely vague, not even giving her actual location. There was no photo of Arden. Only her art. But I was like a man starved for any morsel I could get.

It had been a jolt this morning when I realized that the woman who held me spellbound at the gym was the same one whose art had long held me in a choke hold. Somehow, meeting her only added to the mystery.

Arden stared at me. "If you've seen my site, you know I sell through a gallery in town. They're your best bet for purchasing."

"What about a custom piece? My new house. I'd like something that fits perfectly in that space." I was pushing and knew it, but I was greedy for even a few more seconds with her.

Annoyance flashed across Arden's expression as she shoved my card into her jeans pocket. "The billionaire's building yet another house. Color me shocked."

Interesting.

I knew from my friendship with Cope that the Colsons weren't exactly struggling. But I also had no idea what had brought Arden to live with them. Maybe she'd struggled growing up and had something against those who carelessly threw their money around.

But I knew better than anyone that money didn't guarantee happiness. It didn't protect you from pain or loss. It *did* create ease that came in handy. And I wasn't about to apologize for that.

"Consider it my way of helping the local economy," I said, watching as she stepped back and turned to face the canvas.

Strands of her dark brown hair were starting to spill from her bun, showing hints of the ferocity she clearly had at times. "I don't do commissions."

Even more interesting.

"Name your price." The words were out of my mouth before I could stop myself. Tipping my hand yet again.

Arden whirled around, her eyes flashing pure violet. "I'm not for sale."

Oh, hell.

"I wasn't suggesting you were."

"Weren't you?" Arden pressed. "No rules apply to you, do they? You think you can flash your money, and the answer will always be *yes*."

"Arden—"

"My art isn't something to be controlled. *I'm* not something to be controlled." She tapped the screen on her phone, and ear-splitting rock filled the speakers again. "You know the way back to the main house."

Arden turned back to the canvas, dismissing me entirely. And I didn't blame her. I'd royally stepped in it.

I glanced down at the gray beast standing between us. The dog glared up at me as if to say, "*Get moving, pal.*" I didn't blame him.

Sighing, I stepped into the late-morning sun. It was already at least eighty and would soon be tipping even hotter. My phone buzzed in my pocket, and I slid it out.

> **Philip Pierce:** *We have not received your RSVP for your sister's wedding. Please rectify this immediately.*

The slap of the text was a visceral thing. Far worse than the sting of Arden's blade against my neck. My back teeth ground together as I stared at the words. It was a jerk on an invisible choke collar, and we both knew it.

The DNA donor known as my father was used to getting what he wanted by any means necessary. It was why he'd cut me off at age eighteen when I refused to follow in his footsteps. It was why my sister bowed to his every whim, even down to choosing the man she was set to marry in a matter of weeks. And it was why my mom no longer drew breath.

It didn't matter how much I loved Ellie and wanted her to know I was there for her no matter what. I couldn't spend a week at our estate in the Hamptons pretending I didn't hate Philip Pierce with every fiber of my being.

I locked my phone, shoved it into my pocket, and breathed deeply. The scent of pine trees and fresh air filled my lungs. As I looked around at the place Cope had carved out for himself in the world, I understood why he'd chosen to build here.

The vastness and wide-open spaces reminded me to breathe, which was exactly why I was going to build my next chapter here. Away from the pressures of the city, my father, and everything else.

CHAPTER FIVE

Arden

I SCOWLED AT THE CANVAS AS STRAINS OF ONE OF MY FAVORITE bands pounded through the speakers. Usually, I could count on an old favorite to get me into my creative headspace. But not this time.

The canvas stared back at me, its blank spaces taunting me. It was all Lincoln Pierce's fault. He'd come to my studio yesterday looking more like some dark, avenging angel than a billionaire business magnate. When I tried to focus on work, all I could see was his stupid smirk and how it made a dimple pop in his cheek.

My phone buzzed on the table for the dozenth time. I let out a growl of frustration, slammed my brush down, and picked up the device. Sliding my thumb up the screen, I unlocked it and tapped the text icon with twenty-three alerts. *Twenty-three.*

I hit the sibling group text chain, reading the first message. *Kye has renamed this group My Organ Donors.* It was a constant battle between us to one-up each other in renaming it. Well, it was mostly Cope and Kyler. But that wasn't a surprise. Those two had gotten into more trouble growing up than the rest of us combined.

> **Kye:** *Too much? Your bullet hole still leaking water when you drink, Copey?*

> **Fallon:** *That's not funny, Kyler.*

I wasn't surprised that our most tenderhearted sister had jumped in to reel Kye back from the inappropriate edge. She was the only one he'd listen to anyway. He'd come to live with the Colsons at sixteen, furious at the world and two seconds from imploding. Fal had seemed to be the only person who could reach him, and their bond had remained.

> **Kye:** *Hey, I helped his ass to the bathroom for a week after surgery. I have earned these jokes.*

> **Cope:** *No one cleans out a bedpan like you, buddy.*

I didn't want to admit the relief I felt at just seeing Cope's name in the chat, cracking jokes like always. I could pretend that he was in hockey preseason instead of at some fancy physical therapy place Linc had set him up at.

> **Me:** *I thought I had you idiots on silent. Who turned this chat off do not disturb?*

> **Rhodes:** *I might've made some adjustments when I stopped by the other day.*

> **Kye:** *That's cold, A. Muting your siblings. The people you love most in this world.*

> **Me:** *I'm turning my phone on silent now. Byeeee.*

> **Trace:** *No, you aren't. Because it's a security risk.*

Of course, the eldest and most overprotective of our bunch would point that out. He was more than just the sheriff of this county; he'd also taken it upon himself to be law enforcement in our patchwork family.

I lifted my phone, took a selfie of me sticking out my tongue at him, and hit send.

Kye: *Don't worry, Arden can kick everyone's ass on this chain except for me.*

Me: *Including you.*

Shep: *In case you were looking for photographic proof.*

A second later, a photo appeared of me putting Kye on the mat in an armbar hold. It made me look like a badass, but as good as I'd gotten, I knew Kye had let me have that one. He'd been training for years longer than I had, and his style had an edge that mine didn't. The kind that came from struggling to stay alive when no one had your back.

Kye: *Come spar with me tonight, Bob the Builder. We'll see how you feel then.*

Fallon: *You know Thea will cut off your balls with her garden shears if you give Shep another black eye.*

Shep's girlfriend had not been pleased when he came home rocking a shiner after their last session.

Kye: *Scratch that. Thea scares me. How about we throw a dayger at Cope's mega-mansion while he's out of town? Gotta use that pool while we can.*

Cope: *You try to throw a party while I'm out of town, and I'll pour peach schnapps all over your precious truck.*

Kye: *You play dirty, hockey boy. But just remember, I have photographic proof of you streaking down Cascade Avenue the night before graduation.*

Cope: *And I have photographic proof of you letting Keely give you a makeover.*

Fallon: *Nope. I've got that one.*

She sent a photo of Trace's six-year-old daughter biting her lip in concentration as she swept gobs of blush over Kye's cheeks. He might look like a cross between a mountain man and a tattoo god, but he was putty in his niece's hands.

Kye: *I'm letting Keels paint all over Cope's walls with those glitter markers she loves so much.*

Cope: *Don't you dare.*

Rhodes: *You're just tempting him by saying that.*

Cope: *I've got Linc staying at the house. He'll protect it from a glitter attack.*

I stilled, every nerve ending in my body going live. Just reading Linc's name sent images of him dancing through my mind: those vibrant hazel eyes pinning me to the spot with questions I could never answer, the twist of his lips when he smiled, that damn dimple.

My fingers flew across my phone's screen.

Me: *Thanks for the chaperone, by the way.*

Kye: *Uh-oh. You really pissed off the princess of darkness now.*

Cope: *Linc needed a place to stay while he looks for property in Sparrow Falls and Shep works on a house design. It was the least I could do.*

I didn't need the reminder. I was happy living in denial land. The thought of Linc *staying* within a two-minute walk from my house? *Moving* to Sparrow Falls, even part-time? *Nope. Nope. Nope.*

Me: *I'm helping Keely douse your walls in glitter. You deserve it.*

I flipped the notifications on the chat back to *Do Not Disturb*, frowning at the fact that Rhodes had switched it off in the first place. More evidence that she was worried. Or maybe it was simply because she'd found happiness and healing and wanted the rest of us to, as well.

My lips twitched at the image of our sunshiniest sister ending up with the broodiest guy I could imagine—one all but allergic to color. But the grumpy ex-FBI profiler had turned out to be the one for her. And she was the one for Anson.

An uncomfortable sensation slid through me. An ache that reminded me of the growing pains that woke you up as a kid. I shook off the feeling, placing my phone face down on the table. No more distractions.

I stepped back, trying to take in the canvas with fresh eyes. Something about it *still* wasn't working. Over the years, I'd found that the painting would never come together if I didn't get the first broad strokes right. But that didn't mean all was lost. Not yet.

The canvas had paint in some areas, and pencil marks that were supposed to be my map in others. I tried to erase the sketch lines in my mind and let go of the plan I had to see the endless possibilities. The spark of something lit. It was just an ember of an idea, but I gently blew on it, letting it grab hold.

I quickly moved to my paints, my fingers flying over the rows of options before stopping on perylene red. It was a deep cherry red. Not a color I used often, but exactly what I needed today. I crossed to my palette and pressed some out of the tube.

As the music and my vision took hold, I lost myself in creation. First, in the darker colors I'd started with—the purples, greens, and blues. Instead of trees, I painted thorny brambles, a tangle you'd never be able to escape.

But then the red came—slashes of color against the darkness. They were messy and imperfect, just like Linc invading my space with his charm, vitality, brash humor, and challenge. I smeared the blooms across the dark canvas in an unmeasured way, some of the edges darkening with the deeper colors around them. Until Brutus let out a loud bark.

I jolted, just then realizing someone was pounding on the door. I reached for my phone, ignored the countless notifications, and turned off my stereo. The knocking stopped as soon as the music did.

I stilled. The security alarm for the property hadn't gone off. It could've been Linc at my door or an axe murderer like he'd suggested. Honestly, I thought I'd take the axe murderer over someone who had me painting fucking flowers.

My fingers flew over my phone's screen until I reached the app for the security cameras. Cope had an elaborate system covering his property. He always said it was because of his hockey-star status, but I knew the truth.

When I finally moved off the Colson Ranch property, my siblings, Nora, and Lolli all wanted to make sure I was safe. Their need for me to be secure felt stifling at times but like a warm embrace at others.

As I tapped on the screen for the camera above the door to my studio, I had to admit the system came in handy at times. Denver looked up at the camera, grinning the second it came on and flashing a peace sign. I couldn't help the snort that left me when I saw his attire.

He'd gone a bit over the top with his hippie-chic outfit. His long, light brown hair hung loosely around his shoulders, a few thin braids among it with feathers at the ends. He wore a flat-brimmed hat, a white tee with countless turquoise necklaces, and dark-washed jeans with paint splatters that I knew were put there by some designer and not by working on a piece. Because while my art dealer and manager of the gallery space I owned appreciated art, he didn't have the patience to master it himself.

I sighed and headed for the door, giving Brutus a hand signal to be at ease. The moment I yanked it open, Denver strode in. He never waited for an invitation or worried he was disrupting my flow.

"Have you seen a doctor about your potential hearing loss yet?" he asked, making a beeline for the painting.

I fought the urge to go stand in front of it and try to block it from view. I was never crazy about people seeing works mid-progress, but this was different. More. Something about the piece felt far too personal to have Denver staring at it and assessing every brushstroke.

The thought didn't make sense, not when I was used to displaying my darkest moments on canvas or in sculpture. I bled into my art, each piece carrying a piece of my soul. So, why was this one so different?

"Den," I called, trying to get him to turn away from the painting.

He studied it for a few more seconds before turning. "I could hear every scream in that godawful stuff you listen to from the main road."

My lips twitched. "Not the mystic chants you're used to?"

"Hey," Denver said. "Don't knock it until you try it. Maybe it'll clear the storm cloud hovering over your head all the time."

"But then what would I make art about?" I challenged.

"Good point." He turned back to study the painting. "This is good. Really good. A little different. I like it. It'll be a good match for the auction."

"I'm not sure it's going in the auction," I said quickly. I might hold on to this one for myself, and I rarely did that.

Denver glanced at me, his eyebrow lifting. "Shouldn't you be focusing on pieces that *will* be part of the fundraiser?"

"You know it doesn't work like that for me. I have to go where the creativity leads."

He was quiet for a moment, studying me the way he had the painting. I fought the urge to squirm. Finally, he seemed to see something he needed and released his gaze. "All right. Don't forget we have a meeting next week at The Collective."

I groaned. "Do you really need me there?"

Denver just shook his head, looking exasperated with me. "This whole thing was your idea. The show, the auction. For a good cause, remember?"

I knew it was: raising funds to expand art programs for youth in the Sparrow Falls community, after-school programs and training with teachers in a variety of mediums. I was good with the work that needed to go into it, less so with the socializing.

"Fine," I mumbled. "I'll be there."

Denver moved in closer, dropping his hands to my shoulders and crouching slightly so we were eye-to-eye. "We would have a much larger turnout if you'd agree to give an interview."

Alarm bells rang out in my mind, and every muscle in my body stiffened. "No."

"Arden—"

"No," I said, dipping out of Denver's hold. "You know interviews are a no-go for me. Not my thing."

They were so much more than a no-go. They were the kind of thing that could get me dead. The witness protection guidelines swirled in my mind. Even though I'd opted out of the program over seven years ago, the rules were still branded on my brain.

No contact with people from your old life.

That one was easy. My parents were gone, now nothing more than names on tombstones on the other side of the country. I had no other relatives except for a cousin on my father's side who'd declined to assume custody of me at the time. And I was a distant memory to the childhood friends I'd left behind.

Don't tell anyone about your past.

That one got a little murky. The Colsons knew bits and pieces now, but I trusted them with my life. They'd proven themselves over and over again. But I hadn't told a single other soul.

Don't have your picture anywhere public.

I ran into issues with Denver on that one. He constantly wanted me to do interviews or create social media profiles where I *showed my personality*. Only by personality, he meant my face.

"Arden, I know attention isn't your thing, but—"

"No." I tried to put as much finality into the word as possible.

Denver sighed. "This arts collective is your brainchild. You're the one who wanted to create a place for all artists in the community to have a home. Space to create and share those creations with the world."

I shifted uncomfortably. He wasn't wrong. Art had given me an outlet I desperately needed at the worst time in my life. I just wanted to make sure others had access to the same if they wanted it.

"I'll come to the meeting. I'll make sure you have paintings and sculptures to auction off to the highest bidder. I'll even smile at every deep-pocketed douchebag who wants to tell me what he thinks my art means while staring at my cleavage. But no interviews."

Denver's lips twitched. "Who are you kidding? If some d-bag stares at your boobs, you'll break his arm."

I choked on a laugh. "I'd give him a warning first."

"I need to check on the gallery's insurance policy."

I grinned at my friend, but it slipped slightly as worry niggled. "I'm sorry. It's just—I can't."

A muscle fluttered in Denver's cheek, but he nodded. "It's okay. I can probably get Hannah to do one. Maybe Isaiah or Farah."

The other artists in our little collective would likely jump at the chance. And they deserved it, too. They were all incredibly skilled with interesting perspectives and outlooks. "Thanks, Den."

He pinned me with a stare. "I just want the world to know your art. You're ridiculously talented. You deserve to be known more widely."

"I'm good with my little corner of the universe," I promised him.

And that wasn't a lie. But it wasn't the whole truth either. The truth was, I couldn't afford the risk.

Because when someone put a hit on you when you were eleven and living in foster care, you didn't take chances. Not when your life depended on it.

CHAPTER SIX

Lincoln

I STARED OUT ONE OF THE MASSIVE WINDOWS IN THE OFFICE COPE had let me commandeer as mine. I was pretty sure my staff back in Seattle thought I was losing my mind, but it wouldn't be the first time. I'd purchased more than a couple of companies where they'd doubted my sanity. Just like how people thought I was headed into some premature midlife crisis when I bought the Seattle Sparks hockey team. But all of that had worked out just fine. This would, too.

A flicker of movement caught my attention—one of Arden's horses grazing in a far field. I wouldn't lie to myself and deny that I'd hoped for a flash of mahogany hair in the distance or an appearance of those gray-violet eyes on my doorstep. I'd gotten neither.

I hadn't seen any hint of Arden since she'd all but slammed her studio door in my face days ago. And I didn't blame her. But it also made apologizing difficult. The last thing I wanted to do was invade her space without her permission, and if I texted Cope and asked for her number, it would give far too much away.

"Linc?"

Shep's now familiar deep voice pulled me out of my swirling

thoughts. I turned to face the contractor, a sheepish smile tugging at my lips. "Sorry, losing myself in possibilities."

Shep chuckled, tapping a construction pencil against the desk. "I get it. Starting from scratch is always a little overwhelming."

"But there's something rewarding about it, too. Taking something that only exists in your mind and bringing it to fruition."

He nodded. "It's my favorite thing. Creating a vision of what will meld best with the surrounding landscape."

It was one of the reasons I'd chosen Shepard Colson to design and build my home here in Sparrow Falls. He wasn't the kind of designer who went for flash. His creations felt like art in and of themselves, and the surrounding land was his canvas. He always made sure the two came together in the perfect blend. And it didn't hurt that he was Cope's brother, which meant I trusted him. And trust didn't come easily for me. Not anymore.

"I'm looking forward to seeing what you come up with."

One corner of his mouth kicked up. "Then let's pick your spot."

I'd spent the past two days looking at parcels of land in and around Sparrow Falls, taking in the views and listening to a realtor talk about all the benefits and pitfalls of each. The woman had been no-nonsense and a straight shooter, which I appreciated. Especially when I'd dealt with more than one realtor who simply tried to sell me the most expensive thing on the market.

Shep gestured to the eight listings he'd laid out across my desk. "I went by each of them earlier this week just to make sure my instincts were correct."

"Appreciate you taking that time," I said.

"It'll save us in the long run. Picking the right build site is half the battle."

The right spot to call home. Just thinking the word had me shifting my weight from one foot to the other. I didn't feel like I'd ever had one of those. Not really. The penthouse on Central Park West had been more like a museum. With an endless list of rules of what you couldn't touch and where you couldn't run.

My only escape had been the park. Charging over grassy knolls and around walking paths with Ellie as our nanny watched. Racing around the Peter Pan statue and across countless bridges. Central Park had been the one place I'd felt like I could breathe growing up. And I'd been determined to search out and find that for myself ever since.

I'd come close with my place in Seattle. On the water. Plenty of space. But it ended up feeling empty half the time with nothing to fill it but too many nights caught up in endless hours of work.

"I'm not sure these three are right." Shep cut into my thoughts, tapping his pencil against the three listings on the right. "This one's too close to Castle Rock. The ground is full of lava rock and cinder. Thanks to all the excavating we'd have to do, it'd take twice as long. It would be worth it if the views were something you couldn't get elsewhere…"

"But other properties have better ones," I finished for him.

Shep nodded. "These two are so close to that ridge line, you'll have a higher risk of forest fires in the vicinity."

I sure as hell didn't want that. "Scratch those three."

"You know, for someone with a reputation as a controlling bastard, you're being pretty damn agreeable."

My lips twitched as I grabbed the three we'd nixed and threw them in the trash. I knew I had a reputation. One that suggested I could be hard to deal with. But the truth was, I didn't play games or manipulate. I said exactly what I wanted and was never afraid of a little hard work. I'd done more than my share to get where I was today.

"I'm not a tyrant."

"Tell that to *Forbes*," Shep shot back.

I rolled my eyes. That damn article would haunt me forever. "Maybe you can write a letter to the editor. Tell them how agreeable I am."

"I'll put that on my to-do list."

"Appreciate it."

Shep turned back to the listings. "Any of these would make great build sites. They all have pros and cons, but I'm curious if any spoke to you."

I scanned the remaining papers on the desk, bringing the images printed on them to life in my mind. But I already knew the answer. It was likely the least practical of the five: farther outside of town and nestled in the foothills of the Monarch Mountains. But there was something about the spot.

The property had the sort of quiet that meant you could hear your thoughts. No neighbors in sight. A creek that ran through the land and made wildflowers spring to life around it. Endless meadows that shifted into forests, which melted into staggering mountains. It felt like you were so close you could reach out and touch them.

Something about the vastness reminded me that anything was possible. And more than that, it reminded me to stop and breathe. To appreciate the simple beauty that lay around us.

I lifted the piece of paper that read *Meadowlark Lane*. "This one."

The grin that spread across Shep's face was like a kid's at Christmas. "You know it's a good thirty minutes outside of town, and you have the potential of getting snowed in come winter."

Even that sounded like heaven. No one able to get to me. The ability to turn off my phone and simply be unreachable. "I don't mind that. But you'll have to run through what I'll need. I grew up back east, so I'm familiar with snow, but something tells me Manhattan snow and Sparrow Falls snow are slightly different."

Shep outright laughed then. "How do you feel about getting a truck with a plow setup?"

It was my turn to grin. "I'm in."

"I'd recommend solar panels that feed a storage battery. But you might want a generator on top of it, just in case. You'll be on well water, so you're good there. Are you thinking a guesthouse or any other outbuildings?"

A vision of Arden's workshop flashed in my mind: the windows facing that gorgeous view, and an endless array of paintings and sculptures scattered around the space. It was a bizarre thing to pop into my mind. It wasn't like I had a secret art hobby I needed a home for. Maybe it was simply that she'd taken over so many of my thoughts the past few days.

There was just something about her. A fiery honesty I'd had too little of in my life. But more than that was the thirst for survival I admired the hell out of.

I shook myself of those swirling thoughts, pulled under by gray-violet eyes yet again. "A guesthouse would be good. Pool for sure." After sparring, swimming was my favorite workout, the only one that truly cleared my mind. "I'm not sure about others. Can we start there?"

"Of course," Shep said, gathering up the other listings and tossing them into the wastepaper basket. "I won't get started on an official concept for the main house until you close on the property, but I might doodle some preliminary ideas to see what you like and don't. Is there anything else you want to cover today?"

"I think we're good for now," I said, setting down the Meadowlark Lane listing and running offer figures in my mind.

"All right, then. I'll get to work," he said, starting for the door.

"Shep."

He turned, waiting for whatever I was about to say. I cursed myself but kept on going. In for a penny, in for a pound.

"What's the story with your sister Arden?"

Shep's easygoing demeanor shifted in a heartbeat. Gone was the slight grin and open expression. In their place were hard eyes and a mouth set in a grim line. "That's a no-go zone. You wanna get laid, you look elsewhere."

My spine straightened as a prickle of suspicion skated down it. I should've been insulted by the idea that Shep thought I would use his sister to get off—that I would treat *any* woman with such callous disregard. But I couldn't be bothered to even consider that when I was too focused on the reasons why.

Why was Shep this protective of Arden? It made sense that he would look out for a younger sibling, but this stark flip in demeanor and intense reaction...didn't make sense.

"Not how I meant it," I said, assessing the best approach. I was used to that sort of thing in business. How to get the information I needed without showing my cards to my opponent. But Shep wasn't my opponent, and I wouldn't lie to him. "Just curious. I hit up Kye's gym early the other morning." A smile tugged at my lips. "Think I might've startled her because she held a knife to my throat."

Shep stared at me for one beat, then two. Then he barked out a laugh, running a hand through his rich brown hair. "Shit, Linc. I'm sorry. She turns that music up to ear-bleeding levels and can be a little trigger-happy."

"Please, tell me she doesn't actually have access to firearms. I'd definitely be missing a little of my ear."

Shep shook his head and sighed. "No guns. But definitely knock and wait to be invited in. Kye's trained her in jujitsu. She's pretty damn good."

"She's not half bad with a switchblade either."

"I'm going to give her shit about that one," he said, amusement filling his expression.

Something about the pleasure Shep got out of hearing about the interaction and the clear affection he had for his little sister had a pang taking root in my chest, worry rising alongside it—concern that *my* sister, Ellie, had gone so far down a road she couldn't come back from it, and worry that I might lose her to a world we'd always sworn we would never be a part of.

I shook that off, refocusing on the conversation at hand and finding out what Arden's story was. "Is there a reason she's so quick with a blade?"

A shadow passed over Shep's expression a split second before he donned a mask. I was good at reading those defenses. A childhood spent trying to figure out people's motives or determining when they would snap had trained me well.

He shrugged, the motion meant to be read as careless, but I could see the tension winding through Shep's shoulders. "We've all got stories. Hers isn't mine to tell," he said.

Fuck.

I'd been right. This was about more than Cope's attack. Something had happened to Arden. Something bad. Something I didn't have any right to know about. But that didn't stop me from wanting the information.

I bit the inside of my cheek until the coppery taste of blood filled my mouth—whatever it took to keep from pressing Shep for more and stop myself from showing him every damn card in my deck.

"Understood," I said, my fingers twitching at my sides. I needed to spar or go for a swim. Maybe hike into those beautiful mountains where I could breathe.

Shep held my gaze for a beat longer than was typical. "She likes her space. I recommend giving it to her."

I understood that, too. Heard the warning that lay beneath his words. I lifted my chin, a gesture that said I heard him, but I didn't give him the words that said I agreed to his terms. Because they would've been a lie.

Arden's ferocity and vitality pulled at me. It was the sort of thing that grabbed you by the throat and never let go, forcing you to wake up and pay attention.

"I'll walk you out," I offered, already heading in that direction as if Shep didn't know the way far better than I did.

"I'll shoot you a text when I've got something for you to look at," Shep said as he headed outside and toward his truck.

"Sounds good. Thanks for taking this on."

He shot me a grin. "Kind of fun to work on a project with no budget."

I chuckled. "Just no gold toilet seats, okay?"

"Aw man," Shep mock complained.

"You'll live," I called over my shoulder as I headed back inside.

Just as I closed the door behind me, my phone rang. I pulled it from my back pocket, tapping accept as I read my second-in-command's name.

"Hey, Nina," I greeted.

"We've got a problem." Right to the point, like always. I appreciated her lack of pretense and bullshit. But we'd lost the need for that long ago. When you knew someone for almost two decades, hand holding wasn't required for bad news.

Nina and I had met at Stanford, both struggling to balance classes and as many part-time jobs as possible while determined to make the most of the opportunities in front of us. We'd both continued on to get our MBAs at the university, specializing in entrepreneurship. The moment I secured enough capital to make my company a reality, I'd asked her to join me. We'd been running Gardien—the company I'd named using my mother's native French—together ever since.

"On a scale of french fries in your milkshake to pineapple on pizza, how bad is it?" I asked, knowing that she hated both with a passion, but that there was nothing worse than the sacrilege of pineapple on Italian food to her.

She snorted across the line. "The best thing about you being gone is that I don't risk coming across any leftover Hawaiian atrocities in the kitchen." She paused for a moment, and I knew I needed to brace. "We lost Ice Edge."

My fingers tightened around the phone, annoyance and confusion sliding through me. The company produced a variety of hockey gear and was one of the few with manufacturing operations in the United States. They'd been struggling for the past few years, and I saw a way to turn that around. The fact that I owned a hockey team that could put new eyes on the gear and brand didn't hurt either.

"How?" I growled.

"I don't know, but I'm working on finding out. Mike went into negotiations today, and the owner said they'd gotten another offer last night and were taking it. He already signed."

I cursed. I hated losing deals, but this one bothered me a little more than normal. I'd liked the owner, Shawn. I'd thought he understood how we could take his company to the next level. But it was also something more. I'd seen how he was with his son. Had witnessed the bond they shared through hockey. It was something I'd never had with my father, and I'd wanted to support that more than anything.

"Who?" I asked. It wasn't unusual for other companies to try to swoop in and disrupt our deals. I'd gained a reputation for wisely choosing fledgling companies, and others wanted in on that. But we'd kept this one under lock and key. Only four or five people even knew about it.

"Don't know that either, but I'm working on it."

"Text me the second you know more," I snapped.

"Don't get growly at me, Linc," Nina barked. "I wanted this deal as much as you did."

"Sorry," I muttered.

"That's better."

"Gonna get off this call before you ground me."

Nina laughed. "Go for a swim. Clear your head."

She knew me too well. "Will do. Talk to you later."

I hung up before she could say anything else. If she took pity on me, I'd feel even worse.

The moment the call cleared, I saw I had a new text.

> **Philip Pierce:** *Always wanted to take a trip to Minnesota. Just long enough to sell them for parts.*

Beneath the text was a photo of a signed contract between him and Ice Edge. My gut twisted. Shawn had no idea what he'd done. My father had likely promised him the world, but his company was about to be no more. And for what? To get at me? To prove he was the apex predator?

Another text appeared as I stared at the screen. It gave me all the answers I never wanted.

> **Philip Pierce:** *There will be more if you don't come home for the wedding. I won't have you embarrass this family any further.*

CHAPTER SEVEN

Arden

WRAPPED MY HANDS AROUND MY MUG AND STARED OUT AT THE mountains. Breathing deeply, I took in the scent of coffee mixed with pine as I watched my girls graze. Brutus lay on the patio, his favorite spot when the sun had baked the stones for hours.

It was beautiful, my little spot in the world. But it sometimes felt like a beautiful exile—the one place in the world where I was truly safe. But that safety could lock you in a place.

Not today.

In a few minutes, I would grab my bag and drive to Kye's gym. I would make the choice to leave these invisible walls. Because it was a *choice*. One that required tamping down the fear stoked by over a decade of warnings to be careful, cautious, and not let anyone truly know me.

That sort of endless refrain had a price. One that meant an echo of fear still lived in my head. It also meant I wasn't especially good at peopling.

Brutus lifted his head, his gray fur shimmering in the afternoon light. A second later, I heard the sound of an approaching vehicle. My muscles tensed, the way they always did. The stiffening was slight, a mixture of preparedness and not wanting my solitude interrupted.

Brutus pushed to his feet just before a door slammed. He positioned himself between me and the path someone would take to round the house. His muscles quivered with the same tension I had.

But the moment the figure appeared, he let out a happy bark, his entire body wagging. "Freigeben," I told him, giving Brutus the command for release.

He bounded over to the woman whose gray hair was wild, like the creature herself. She wore a workout set with cropped and flared leggings that were tie-dyed in various shades of pink, purple, and blue. Her T-shirt was tied in a knot at her hips and read *I know my CBDs* with a large, bedazzled pot leaf across the center.

"My big, beautiful beast," she greeted Brutus, bending to give him all the pets.

A smile tugged at my lips. God, I loved this woman. Lolli was the first of the Colson clan to reach me when I arrived in Oregon. She'd come to live with her daughter, Nora, after Nora's husband and son passed away in a car accident, leaving her to raise their two biological children, adopted son, and foster kids herself.

But Nora hadn't once considered no longer fostering. She was one of the strongest people I'd ever met, and you could see she'd gotten that strength from her mom.

Lolli glanced up at me as she kept giving Brutus his rubdown, endless bracelets jangling. "And how's my Little Gremlin? I'm surprised you're even awake."

I grinned at her. "It's after two."

Lolli straightened, crossing to me and pressing a kiss to my cheek. "But my girl is like a bat. Prefers to hunt at night."

I snorted. "I'm not exactly hunting."

"Okay, fine. My girl likes to create at night."

That much was true. My creativity flowed best after the sun went down or first thing in the morning. Sleep never came easily to me, so I figured I might as well get some work done.

"How's the new piece coming along?" Lolli asked.

Her asking about my work never bothered me because it never felt like pressure. Maybe because she was the one who'd given me the gift of art in the first place. I'd never forget her setting up two easels in front of the horse pasture and inviting me to paint with her.

Weeks passed where we simply painted together. She never asked me questions or pushed me to speak. She simply let me open up in my own time.

It was Lolli I talked to about my fears: that the man with the gun would find me, too; that I'd never be safe.

And it was Lolli who encouraged me to take all that fear and put it onto a canvas. From that day on, I hadn't stopped. And I had her to thank for it.

"I'm not sure," I admitted, the dark bramble painting with its deep red blossoms flashing in my mind. Right on that image's heels came Linc's face: his sharp jaw covered in a thick layer of dark brown scruff, his hazel eyes pinning me to the spot.

"That bad, huh?" Lolli asked, amusement lacing her words.

It was then that I realized I was glaring at the grass in front of me, only it wasn't the grass that had gotten under my skin. It was Lincoln Pierce. I tried to dislodge the image from my mind, the memory of the hints of cedar and bourbon that clung to him. But shards of both had dug in deep.

"Not bad, just different," I muttered, taking a sip of coffee.

Lolli was quiet for a moment as she studied me. I wondered if she'd press, sensing there was more to the story. But, understanding me like always, she didn't. Instead, mischief danced in her eyes. "Want to see *my* new piece?"

I turned to her, grinning. "Of course." Lolli had never been a professional artist. She was a true hobbyist, trying out every medium under the sun. The second she got bored, she moved on to the next. But she'd been firmly settled on one for the past year or so.

Diamond art.

Like paint by numbers but filled in with tiny gemstones. Only Lolli created her own images. And they were always…unique.

Lolli slid her phone out of her pocket and moved closer, showing me a photo. "It still needs some finishing touches. I'm calling it Elf Queen."

It was a good thing I hadn't taken a sip of coffee because I would've spewed it all over the screen. "Is that—I mean—are those elves...?"

"Doing a little Eiffel Tower action on their queen?" she asked innocently as if she hadn't constructed an elaborate elven three-way.

I chuckled and took a sip of coffee. "Definitely gift that one to Trace." I could only imagine the shade of red his face would turn.

Lolli made a humming sound. "He could use a reminder to let loose a little."

I grinned down at my coffee. I couldn't wait to see this gift-giving in action. "Please, do it when I'm there."

"This weekend. Family dinner," Lolli said.

I winced. "I've got several pieces I need to finish for the fundraiser and—"

Lolli pinned me with a stare she only used once in a blue moon. "My girl. It's time for a command performance. If you don't come, Nora will be over here hovering. Stocking your fridge, cleaning your house, poking into your business."

I did a mental tally of the last time I'd done a family dinner. It had been a while. It wasn't that I didn't want to spend time with my family or didn't adore them. I did. It was just that when we all got together, especially since half of them were partnered up now, it was a crowd. And crowds weren't my thing.

Add to that the fact that all my siblings were a touch overprotective and constantly worried about me, and it felt like I was on display at times. But I didn't want to be a source of concern for any of them. They all had their own stuff to deal with and didn't need me burdening them.

I studied Lolli for a moment. "Did I make you worry?"

It wasn't uncommon for her to make the drive out here, but it wasn't a regular occurrence either.

Lolli's mouth pulled into a smile, the wrinkles on her cheeks deepening, showing just how easily her lips made the move. "I missed my girl."

Guilt niggled, and I quickly wrapped her in a hug. "Sorry, Lolls. I'll do better."

"You don't have to do anything. You're perfect as you are. But you will need to put up with these old bones checking on you once in a while."

I released her and stepped back. "Who are you calling old?"

Lolli cackled. "Damn straight. I'm trying to get the girls together for another night at the cowboy bar. You in?"

I shook my head but did it smiling. "You know that's not my scene."

"I could do some of that goth face paint, and we could go to one of your murder band shows."

I snorted. "I'll keep that in mind." I pulled out my phone to check the time and cursed. "I gotta run. Sparring with Kye."

Lolli shooed me toward the house. "Go. Kick that boy's ass. It's good for him."

"I'll tell him you said that," I called over my shoulder.

By the time I grabbed my gear bag and Brutus's leash, Lolli had already taken off. I motioned him into Wanda's cab and climbed in behind him. The leather seats were warm from the sun but not too hot, and I let the feeling skate over my skin as I started her up.

I drove into town a little faster than was strictly legal and hoped like hell one of Trace's deputies didn't pull me over. If they did, I'd never hear the end of it.

Downtown Sparrow Falls was the sort of picturesque you'd expect of a small town. Aged brick buildings held a mixture of restaurants, galleries, tourist shops, and other retail businesses. The town prided itself on the elaborate flower beds that dotted every corner of the main drag: Cascade Avenue.

Kye's businesses weren't on that main street. He'd chosen a spot off the beaten path in a slightly less perfect part of town. It felt like a conscious choice, part of how Kyler saw himself despite finding incredible success as a tattoo artist.

The fact that he also owned the mixed martial arts gym next door was less of a well-known fact. He liked to stay under the radar there, which made sense given what he'd gotten mixed up with in his teens. Kye also didn't want the world to know what a tender heart he hid beneath all the ink. Which meant he didn't advertise the fact that he also ran a youth program out of the gym.

I pulled into a parking spot next to a couple of motorcycles and Kye's souped-up black truck with shadow detailing along the sides. I grinned at the difference between our vehicles. He *hated* that I hadn't fixed Wanda up.

I grabbed my phone out of the cupholder and saw a flurry of new texts.

Shep has changed the group name to Arden's Next Victims.

I scowled at the screen. What the hell had I done now?

Shep: *Apparently, Arden nearly made poor Linc bleed out on the floor of Kye's gym.*

I dropped my head, pinching the bridge of my nose. I'd thought I was safe from Linc spreading that little story around since it didn't paint him in the best light, but apparently, he didn't care about people knowing he'd gotten his ass handed to him by a girl.

Rhodes: *You didn't.*

Cope: *Kye, you need to up your umbrella insurance policy. I already called about mine.*

Kye: *We'll never be able to afford enough coverage for Arden.*

I let out a little growl of frustration and typed out a text.

Me: *He barely even bled, you guys.*

Fallon: *YOU CUT HIM?!?!*

The chat devolved into a series of stabbing GIFs, and I locked the screen, shoving the phone into my bag. Linc would pay for this. I wondered if there was a way for me to sabotage the hot water heater. Or maybe put pink dye in his showerhead.

A smile tugged at my lips at that image. Turning off my engine, I hopped out and grabbed my bag, motioning for Brutus to follow. He loved going to the gym during regular business hours because he was a ho for all the pets he got. And everyone here loved him.

I slung my duffel over my shoulder and shut the door, locking it behind me. Then I headed for Haven. The moment I hauled open the door, the music hit me. I wasn't talking about the rock playing over the speakers; the *true* music was the sound of gloved hands hitting bags and mitts. It was a rhythm that managed to both soothe and excite. A familiar buzz lit in my muscles as I stepped farther inside.

The moment I moved deeper into the gym, Kye greeted me. "Way to go, killer," he said, his lips twitching beneath his dark brown beard.

I flipped him my middle finger. "You guys are the worst."

He smiled fully then, and I saw why women fell at his feet. The combination of the ink, the muscular frame, and that devastating grin were potent. "You mean the *best*?"

"Keep telling yourself that."

Someone let out a hoot, and I turned. It only took a second to see why. Mateo was sparring with someone in one of the practice rings. Usually, Kye was the only one who could give him a run for his money. And it made sense; Mateo was working his way up the pro circuit in MMA. But whoever he was sparring against now had him struggling.

I couldn't make out who it was. They didn't look familiar from the back. All I could see was a bare torso, broad, muscular shoulders with intricate ink wrapped around them, and a head of dark hair. But everything about the man's body was toned. Lean muscles that had been honed into a weapon.

The man's fist snaked out lightning-quick, clipping Mateo on the chin. But he didn't rest on his laurels; he went for a double-leg takedown. Mateo hit the mat in a flash. *Oooooh*s filled the air at the smacking sound.

But his opponent didn't stop there. He quickly moved into a triangle choke hold, the movements fluid, graceful, and almost beautiful in their restrained brutality. I couldn't help but stare in fascination.

The moment Mateo tapped the mat, the man released him and

jumped to his feet, offering Mateo a hand. As he pulled Mateo up, he turned, and I saw his face. There was no stopping the way my lips parted on a silent but sharp inhale.

Linc.

His eyes were darker than the last time I'd seen him, the green deepening and drowning the gold as if shadows were doing battle there. There was also a hardness to his features that seemed in direct opposition to the teasing man I'd first met. I studied every detail of his beautiful face, trying to understand the changes.

Dark, avenging angel was the perfect description for him. Even more so now because he was battling something. I couldn't tell if something had happened or if this was simply his outlet for the things that haunted him, the way my art was an outlet for me.

He pulled out his mouthguard, tucked it into his case, and grabbed some water. I watched as he reeled whatever it was in, tucking it away and hiding it from the world. He turned as Mateo asked him something about the takedown. Linc gestured, demonstrating the angle of his body during the approach, but I just kept staring, trying to see a glimmer of those shadows that felt so familiar. Because the same ones lived in me.

Kye bumped his shoulder against mine. It was about as affectionate as he got. "You've got a little drool right there."

"Fuck off," I muttered, annoyance flaring to life.

Linc slipped between the ropes, sliding his feet into flip-flops. Those hazel eyes flashed the moment they landed on me, a grin tugging at his lips as he crossed the space. "Have you checked her for weapons?" Linc asked Kye.

"You trying to get me killed?" Kye challenged.

Linc chuckled as he glanced down at Brutus. "Hey, big man."

Brutus's tail thumped twice, which only served to piss me off more.

"Can I pet him, or will he rip off my hand?"

I looked down at my dog. "He'll only do that if I tell him to."

Linc's dark brows lifted at that. "And are you going to tell him to, Vicious?"

I glared at the man opposite me. "You could've easily disarmed me the other day."

Surprise filled Linc's expression. Maybe at the abrupt turn in the conversation or perhaps my statement. But I knew it was true. It only took a matter of seconds to see that he was ten times better than me in the ring—actually, at hand-to-hand in general. But he'd stood there and let me press a blade to his throat. Let me *cut* him.

Linc shrugged, seemingly without a care. "So?"

"Why didn't you?" I ground out.

He stared at me for a moment, his gaze sweeping over my face. "I don't ever want a woman to feel powerless because of me."

And with that, he walked away.

CHAPTER EIGHT

Lincoln

MY WORDS ECHOED IN MY HEAD ON THE WAY HOME. *"I DON'T ever want a woman to feel powerless because of me."* But I knew the truth beneath the statement.

I didn't want to be my father.

I gripped the steering wheel tighter and headed back to Cope's property. I'd caught sight of Arden on my way out, moving around the ring with Kye. She was good. Better than good. Probably could've worked her way into the professional circuit if she had half a mind.

Her movements were like the rest of her: brash and bold, never coloring between the lines. It was fucking hypnotizing. Which was why I just kept walking. Out the door and behind the wheel of my Range Rover I'd driven down from Seattle.

I rolled the windows down, hoping the fresh air would turn around my completely sour mood. It didn't. All I could think about were the people about to lose their jobs simply because my father had wanted to make a point. Wanted me to bend to his will.

But that was always his way. Philip Pierce needed to know that he could break every single person in his orbit. That he could control them like a master puppeteer.

I pulled to a stop in front of Cope's house, taking in the gorgeous blend of wood, stone, and glass. I didn't miss how both the wood and stone had the same reddish-gold hue as Castle Rock to the west. Turning off the engine, I slid out and headed inside.

Angry energy still hummed in my muscles. The sparring had helped, but maybe not enough. Just as I thought about going for a swim, my phone rang.

I pulled it out of the pocket of my joggers and grinned when I saw Ellie's face on the screen. The photo showed her with a ridiculous expression, sticking her tongue out to one side while crossing her eyes.

I tapped the screen and accepted the video call. "Hey, El Bell."

She made a face. Not quite as extreme as her contact picture, but annoyed little sister through and through. "I know how to play that game, ConCon."

I chuckled at the old nickname. At thirty-seven, I was eleven years older than Ellie. And when she started speaking, she couldn't quite wrap her tongue around Lincoln, opting for ConCon instead. Mom thought it was adorable. Dad despised it, expecting his daughter to have a perfect grasp of the English language from birth.

"How are you?" I asked, walking through the foyer and into the open living space.

"Pretty good," she said, running her hand through her long hair. Everything about Ellie was lighter than me. Her hair was a mix of light brown and blond, her eyes were a pale green that almost looked gray in some light, and her skin was just a few shades fairer. "What about you? How's life in the middle of nowhere?"

One corner of my mouth kicked up as I pulled one of the sliders open and stepped out onto the back patio. "See for yourself."

I flipped the camera around so she could see everything I was looking at. Cope had made the outdoor portion of his massive spread a showpiece. The terraced patio had three levels. An outdoor eating area with a firepit and lounge seating up top, a second level with an array of gardens, and a third with a stunning pool that melded into the natural landscape beyond.

Ellie's lips parted on a gasp. "Look at those mountains. Toto, you are not in Kansas anymore."

"No, I'm not," I said as I moved to sit on the outdoor sofa and flipped the camera back to me.

Ellie stared at me for a moment, studying my face intently. "You like it there."

"I do. There's something about the stillness. It's like I can hear my own mind for the first time in years."

Ellie got quiet as she pulled her knees up to her chest and sank back in the overstuffed chair in her apartment's living room. "Make any friends yet? Don't want my big brother getting lonely."

Arden's stunning face flashed in my mind. Those tiny freckles that were only visible in the brightest sunlight. The way her lips were stained the same shade as sun-ripened raspberries.

Ellie jerked upright. "Did you meet a girl?"

I barked out a laugh. "I feel like that level of shock at me possibly meeting someone should be an insult."

She made a *psh* sound. "Excitement, not shock. You need someone in your life. So?"

"I don't know if you can call being held at knifepoint *meeting* someone, but it was certainly memorable."

Ellie's eyes widened. "You got *mugged*?"

The laughter came more easily this time. "No. I surprised her one early morning at the gym. She just reacted. No permanent damage done."

My sister's brows raised. "Good for her."

"Hey," I clipped. "Your favorite brother could've been seriously injured."

She rolled her eyes as she leaned back in her chair. "You're my *only* brother."

"That doesn't stop me from being the favorite."

Ellie flashed an easy, familiar smile. "I wish I could meet this mystery girl."

"Arden."

"I like her name."

"Me, too."

Those pale green eyes twinkled, but there was also sadness there. The type that had my gut churning. "Miss you, ConCon," she whispered.

Hell.

"You could come out," I suggested.

She shook her head, her loose waves shifting around her shoulders. "There's too much to do for the wedding."

The muscles in my shoulder blades tightened, making me sit up straighter. When I didn't speak, Ellie hurried on. "Dad said you're coming back for it. I'm really glad. I can't imagine getting married without you there."

My back teeth ground together. "El…"

Her face fell. "You're not coming."

"I can't. You know it wouldn't be good." I could deal with my as-shat of a father for Ellie, if she were marrying someone I knew she was head over heels in love with. But Bradley wasn't that. He was the son of a longtime family friend who worked for his father's hedge fund. I wasn't sure they had a single thing in common.

Ellie had started dating him after our dad's none-too-subtle nudging. When she tried breaking it off, Dad made his displeasure clear, and she'd caved in a matter of weeks, going right back to Bradley.

"I know he's a hard man," Ellie said softly. "But he's the only parent we have left. Losing Mom was bad enough. I don't want to lose him, too. Or you."

White-hot pain lit along my sternum. If she only knew the truth. But it carried a weight I didn't want Ellie to shoulder. So, I said the only thing I could. "You'll never lose me. Never."

"It feels like I already am."

Each word was a blow. One she didn't realize inflicted the worst kind of pain.

"El, I love you more than anyone on this planet, but I can't be a part of that world for you. It was killing me."

Everything about it had slowly strangled the life out of me. Dad was a huge part of that, but it was more. The oppressive weight of expectation, the pressure of perfection, and the quest for more. More money. More power. More prestige.

It was part of why I'd founded my company, Gardien. I was looking for a way to do business that enabled me to help people while still succeeding. I'd needed to prove to myself that it was possible. That you didn't have to tear others down to get ahead.

Pain flashed across Ellie's features. "Sorry, ConCon. I know. I just… I miss you."

Fuck.

"Tell you what. How about after the wedding and honeymoon craziness, we do a sibling trip? Just the two of us."

She grinned at the screen, her eyes lighting. "You going to take me to Disney World like I always wanted?"

I laughed. "I think I'll pass on endless lines and rides that are bound to make me hurl."

"You always did have a sensitive stomach."

I shook my head and scrubbed a hand over my stubbled cheek. "You really show no mercy."

"That's what little sisters are for."

"So glad the stork dropped you on our doorstep."

Ellie flipped her hair over her shoulder in an exaggerated motion. "As you should be." The video cut out for a second. "Sorry, that's Bradley. I need to jump. Love you, ConCon."

"Love you, too, El Bell."

And then she was gone.

I stared at the screen for a long time. The background image was the same one the phone had come with. No photos of a wife or kids to personalize the device. Not even a damn dog.

As I stared at the endless array of apps, a sense of loneliness settled over me as if I had some gaping hole in my chest that would always be empty.

But it was more. There was a sense of true fear. Because the person I loved most was diving deeper into the shark-infested waters. And I worried she'd never get out.

I shoved to my feet, locking my phone and stalking inside. I made my way to the guest room Cope had given me and quickly changed into swim trunks. Grabbing my goggles, I went straight for the pool, diving in with no pretense or easing into it.

The cold water was a shock to the system, but it would be when I hadn't bothered with the heat. I welcomed the brutality of it and gave as good as I got, attacking the water as I swam. Back and forth, lap after lap. When my muscles burned, I kept right on pushing.

Until I saw a pair of feet dangling beneath the surface at the far end. The toes were decorated with a dark purple polish, and some part of me just knew who they belonged to.

When I reached the end, I popped up and tore off my goggles. Arden stared back at me, not a care in the world. "You done doing battle with the devil?"

CHAPTER NINE

Arden

I'D HOVERED ON THE STONE PATIO AROUND THE POOL FOR TOO long, simply gazing at the man in the water. No, the *beast*. He was warring with his demons, and I couldn't stop watching like some kind of stalker.

When I slipped my feet into the water and felt how cold it was, I knew he had to be truly tortured to put up with those temperatures. But studying him now, his bare chest heaving and muscles and tattoos on display, I knew he didn't feel it. Not one bit.

Water slid down the planes of his chest, and my fingers itched to trace each droplet. But more than that, his tattoos. The ink was a work of art. Thorny vines, not unlike the ones in my painting, curved over Linc's sides and up his chest. One pec had the word *truth*. The other, *trust*. The combination packed a punch. And the fact that it lined defined muscle with a dusting of dark hair only made the effect headier. *Dumb, dumb, dumb.* I was not going there.

Linc stared up at me, those gold-flecked green eyes still the slightest bit stormy. "What are you doing here?"

Wasn't that the million-dollar question? I fought the urge to squirm on the pool's edge. With my luck, I'd end up tumbling right into the water. Instead, I lifted my chin, defiance sliding through me. "*I* live here. What's your excuse, Cowboy?"

His lips twitched, the scruff coating his cheeks and jaw moving with the motion. "I live here, too."

"*Temporarily*," I shot back.

Linc chuckled, and the sound was just like the man: surprising. It was all warmth coated in grit. The kind of sound that had all my nerve endings waking up. "Fair enough." His gaze roamed over me like the featherlight caress of fingertips. "What do you have there?" he asked, inclining his head toward the white bag next to me.

I instantly regretted my decision to search Linc out. To make sure he was okay. But I couldn't change my tack now. "The best chicken pesto sandwich ever created."

Linc arched a brow. "That's a bold claim."

"I know how to back it up."

"Seems kind of cruel to brag about the best chicken pesto sandwich ever created when I just swam for a good hour and am starving."

"I brought you one." *Dumb, dumb, dumb.* I should've left Linc to his demons. He was obviously doing just fine in the world. But I was a sucker for shadows, and he had them in spades.

A smile spread across Linc's face—no, a grin, and a cocky one at that. "You brought me dinner?"

I kicked water at him. "Don't get too excited. It's an apology. For being a bitch the other day."

His grin fell. "Arden, the last thing you are is a bitch. I got pushy. It wasn't cool."

I shook my head, strands of hair tickling my bare shoulders with the movement. "You weren't. You asked for what you wanted. I could've said no in a nicer way." I plucked up a loose string from my jean shorts and twisted it around my finger, pulling it as tightly as I could. "I'm not the best with new people. It takes me a little while to get used to them."

I didn't hear him move. And I sure as hell wasn't looking at him. So, I didn't see Linc until he appeared right in front of me. My knees were just a breath from his chest. One slight shift, and I'd know what that skin felt like.

Linc's hands lifted out of the water. He gently took mine and slowly unwound the thread from my finger. "I think you're doing just fine, Arden."

I let out a scoff as my eyes lifted to his. Fine wasn't how I'd describe my people skills. But what did you expect when you'd been hidden away for most of your life? Nora had homeschooled me through middle school, and I'd tried our public high school for all of two weeks before begging her to let me take online classes.

The story Nora gave people was that it was to give me more time with my art. People thought I was some sort of prodigy. In reality, I just jumped at every little thing. That had changed with Kye's arrival. He'd seen my timidness and asked if I wanted to learn how to protect myself.

Nora had been skeptical at first, but when she saw my confidence growing, she'd ordered us gym mats for the basement. But as much as training in jujitsu had helped me no longer be fearful, I still wasn't crazy about crowds or new people. It felt like I didn't have the full set of instructions on social cues.

Linc released my hand, and I instantly missed the contact. People didn't touch me very often. Something about my awkwardness made them think I didn't like it. And I often found myself missing the casual affection of a hug or the squeeze of my hand. But Linc's fingers? They were so much more. I could still feel the rough pads and how they dragged over my skin, leaving a warm trail behind.

"You say what you mean. What you need. There's not a damn thing wrong with that," Linc said, his voice lowering to a growly tenor.

"Maybe," I muttered. "Do you want a sandwich or not?"

One corner of Linc's mouth pulled up. "Tell me the truth. Is it poisoned?"

I flipped him off and lifted my feet out of the water. "I'll just take it back to my house. Don't think I can't eat both. Or Brutus will help me."

Linc's gaze flicked to the grass where Brutus lay, soaking up the last bits of sun for the day. "Brutus would never eat my sandwich."

I scoffed at that, but the sound got lodged in my throat as Linc hoisted himself out of the water. Broad, tanned shoulders flexed as his biceps tightened, the inked designs dancing. My mouth went dry as I took in the wall of abs. I was so totally screwed.

Linc grabbed a towel and wrapped it around his shoulders, disrupting my view. "I'll risk poisoning for the best chicken pesto sandwich ever created."

I cleared my throat. "It's worth death."

"I'll be the judge of that." Linc sat on the edge of the pool, his feet gliding through the water as he did. He was close but not too close, seeming to respect that little hint of truth I'd given him: that I struggled with new people. New *anything*, honestly, but he didn't need to know that.

I slid my feet back into the water and opened the bag. I pushed one wrapped sandwich over to Linc and grabbed the other for myself. "I didn't know what kind of soda you drank, so I just got you a Coke."

He took the drink nearest him. "Coke's good. Dr Pepper would've been even better."

I wrinkled my nose. "Seriously? You like the taste of eighty-two different drinks in one?"

"You don't know what you're missing. It's delicious," he argued. I made a gagging noise, and Linc laughed as he unwrapped his sandwich. "The moment of truth."

He took a bite and then closed his eyes, groaning as he chewed. "This might just be heaven in a sandwich."

"Told you." I didn't bite into mine because I was too busy staring at Lincoln chewing his. The pure pleasure on his face took root somewhere deep inside me.

Finally, his eyes opened. "Thank you."

I struggled to swallow. "It's nothing."

"No, it's not. I had a shit day, and you made it a hell of a lot better."

I studied him for a long moment. I wanted to ask what had made it such a bad day, but I couldn't, not when I wouldn't answer questions in the same vein. So, I opted for something else. "This is how you work out what's bothering you?"

He lifted his chin in the affirmative. "Hell of a lot healthier than some of the alternatives."

I unwrapped my sandwich, staring down at the perfectly toasted bread. "You're not wrong there."

I felt Linc's gaze on my face as I bit into my sandwich, but I refused to turn, letting him know I was that attuned to his attention. "Is that why you train with Kye?" Linc asked finally.

"No."

"Please, stop talking. It's too much."

I broke off a piece of bread and threw it at him. "I like to know how to protect myself."

We were edging in on the danger zone, but I couldn't help it. I wanted to give Linc the answers he wanted—the ones he seemed to *need*.

"You're obviously good at it."

"Not as good as you."

Linc shrugged, the towel shifting with the movement and revealing a bit more of the tan skin below. "I've been training for a long time. Been lucky to work with some pretty incredible teachers."

"Those billions come in handy sometimes."

"Sometimes," he echoed, his gaze moving to mine. "How do you deal with your demons?"

My heart hammered against my ribs. "My art. It's always how I've gotten out what I need to."

"And it's why you don't do commissions," he surmised.

I nodded. "It's always been such a personal process. The medium, the vision, all of it. I put a piece of my soul into every single creation. I can't control that. I wouldn't want to."

Linc stared at me for a moment, not speaking. "It needs to be wild, just like you."

Those words hit. Every single one. But they managed to be a caress, too. A balm. "Yes," I whispered.

"Well, they're incredible. After Cope showed me a picture of one of the pieces in his house, I'm pretty sure I scoured the internet for every piece I could find. There was a fair amount about your work but not so much about the creator behind it."

My ribs constricted, making it hard to breathe.

"Kind of surprising, given some of the exhibits you've had."

"I don't like the spotlight," I croaked, trying to keep my breaths even and measured.

"Fair enough."

Linc's eyes were on me again. But this time, panic took hold. I'd taken a risk sitting here with him. Answering questions I shouldn't have. Letting him peek behind the curtain.

I stood quickly, gathering up my sandwich. "I need to go."

I was already moving as Linc called my name, slipping my feet into flip-flops and making a beeline for my guesthouse, whistling for Brutus as I went. I heard Linc call for me again, but it was too late in so many ways.

I was already gone. And it was better that way.

CHAPTER TEN

Lincoln

THE URGE TO RUN AFTER HER WAS STRONG. SO DAMN STRONG it took everything I had to keep myself in place, feet in the freezing water, sandwich on my lap. Arden had left her drink behind. That would be the perfect excuse. I could bring it to her guesthouse or studio.

But I knew she wouldn't welcome me there. I mulled over the events of the past twenty minutes. What had sent her running?

I played back snippets of our conversation. We'd been talking about her art when she stiffened, her spine going ramrod straight. I frowned at that. Maybe it was simply because she'd shared a little of what happened behind the curtain, what inspired her art.

The conversation and Arden's reaction swirled round and round in my brain, and then everything stilled. I'd said I had looked up everything I could find about her.

I was moving before I'd even consciously given my body the order. I wrapped up my sandwich and grabbed both drinks. I wanted to go straight to Cope's office, the one he'd let me take over for the duration of my stay, but I knew he wouldn't be pleased with me if I ruined his desk chair with wet swim trunks.

No longer hungry, I ditched the food in the kitchen and went straight for my room. I made quick work of grabbing a shower and changing into some joggers and a tee, then headed right for the office.

My fingers itched to be at the keyboard, figuring out what the hell had Arden so damn spooked. I slid behind the desk and flipped open my laptop. I ignored the staggering number of emails in my inbox and opened a search engine.

I typed in her name. *Arden Waverly.*

It was interesting to me that some of Cope's siblings had taken the Colson last name, and others hadn't. I was sure that was a complicated thing to contend with—whether or not to change a fundamental part of yourself.

It fit that Arden hadn't. She seemed to set herself apart from her siblings. From everyone, really.

A few dozen search results popped up, all having to do with Arden's art. There was her website and another local site I'd seen before but hadn't dove into called The Collective.

I clicked on that link. The homepage was artfully done, and the site read, *A home for the arts in Sparrow Falls where all are welcome.*

Something about those words hit. They landed in a way that made me long for that kind of sense of belonging. There were countless photos of gallery showings and classes, even what looked like a mural project in downtown Sparrow Falls.

I clicked on the tab that read *Artists in Residence.* There were four. Hannah Farley, Isaiah Reynolds, Arden Waverly, and Farah Whitman. It looked like they all showed there, and some had studio space at The Collective, as well.

It looked like an amazing community center of sorts, but one specializing in art. A banner on the site caught my eye. *Save the Date. A Fundraiser for Youth Programming at The Collective.*

I clicked on that next. It looked like they were planning a show and auction to raise money for expanding their programming for young artists. I quickly typed the date into my phone and made a mental note to stop by the gallery and check it out.

Exiting out of The Collective's home page, I moved on to the next hit. There was article after article about Arden's creations, but they were all eerily similar. None had a photo of her or even an interview. They called her a reclusive artist who refused every interview request.

I went through about two dozen of the same sorts of articles before my eyes started to burn. I leaned back in my chair and glared at the screen. It wasn't as if Arden had Banksy-level fame, but her art was getting picked up by bigger and bigger galleries, even some important collectors. I recognized the names from my mom's involvement with the art world.

Just thinking it had a burn flaring in my sternum. She would've loved Arden—her talent and her fire.

But Arden's art wouldn't give me the answers I needed. I tried to think back to what Cope had shared about his siblings over the years. He'd walked me through how they'd all come to be with the Colsons: he and Fallon by birth, Shep by adoption, and Rhodes, Arden, Kye, and Trace, through fostering. I knew Arden had come to live with them at a fairly young age.

Twelve. I was almost positive that was how old she'd been. I plugged in new search parameters, setting the years to a few before and after that twelve-year mark.

Endless results popped up, but none of them were my Arden. *Mine.* It was such a ridiculous thought. She could barely spend fifteen minutes with me.

I combed through the search results a second time. Nothing. I tried slightly different terms. Still nothing.

Finally, I broadened the search window and found an article in the *Sparrow Falls Gazette. Art Show by Local Youth Phenom.* I clicked it, quickly reading the piece. It talked about the local gallery that was putting on a show for fifteen-year-old Arden Waverly. But again, there was no picture, no interview, and barely any identifying information about her.

I sank against the leather chair. Nothing. There was absolutely nothing about Arden Waverly before this article.

She was a ghost.

And that begged one question.

Why had she needed to disappear?

CHAPTER ELEVEN

Arden

MY TRUCK'S ENGINE PURRED AS I SLID TO A STOP AT ONE OF the three traffic lights in Sparrow Falls. I remembered Boston traffic, not well, but it was there in the recesses of my mind. How my dad would complain about getting stuck in it for hours on his way into and out of the city. And now I complained when there were three cars in front of me.

I liked the simplicity of life here. The way no one seemed to be in too big of a rush. My gaze flicked to a man walking down the street, a camera around his neck. He wasn't familiar. My brain automatically tried to place him, attempting to flip through memories to see if he was someone who'd tried to hurt me or worse.

I was constantly playing that game. It got harder during the summer months with the influx of tourists. Instead of recognizing a good seventy-five percent of folks in town, it went down to fifty at best. And I was left assessing every new face I came across. The only problem was that the man who'd pulled all the strings was still a faceless ghost. Only his voice haunted my nightmares.

A short honk sounded behind me, and Brutus let out a

grumble of annoyance. It was the polite version of honking because the light had most definitely changed. I eased off the brake, giving Mrs. Peterson behind me a wave of apology.

My stomach twisted. Just one more thing to add to the pile of evidence that my brain was a messed-up place. Always playing tricks on me. It was the same reason I'd bolted from having sandwiches with Linc like a scared doe.

The twisting sensation shifted to annoyance and then anger. That wasn't me. I didn't run away. Not since that night almost fourteen years ago. That was the point of the endless training with Kye, the reason I had Brutus, so I didn't have to be afraid.

I drove past Sutton's bakery, The Mix Up, and my stomach rumbled. I'd be stopping there on the way home, even if it would feel a little bittersweet now that she and Luca were in Seattle with Cope. I passed The Pop on my right and made a plan to get a burger tomorrow. It was good to know what food was coming next.

Just before I reached the edge of town, I flipped on my blinker and turned left. The Collective was set back two blocks from Cascade Avenue, but it was still close enough for tourists to meander into the gallery. And that two-block distance from the main street meant it had been a hell of a lot more affordable, even for such a large space.

And we needed large. A gallery space with plenty of natural light. Studio space for the artists. Studio space for classes. And I had a vision for making it even larger, but we needed an influx of cash first. I was fine funding the lion's share of it from my art's proceeds, but to be sustainable on a larger, community-wide scale, we needed more donations than I could provide. I just hoped the fundraiser was the start of that.

As I turned onto the side street, I saw that most of the parking spots were already full. *Tourists.* I hoped like hell they were at least purchasing some things from the gallery to offset my parking issues.

I fist pumped to the drumbeat of the song blaring from my speakers as I spotted someone pulling out of a spot up ahead. I quickly snagged it and hopped out of my truck. Turning to face Brutus, I held up the leash. "You know the rules, buddy."

His head dropped as he gave me a disdainful look.

"I'm sorry. But you know Trace will write both our asses a ticket if we don't follow the rules." As if I'd summoned my siblings by words alone, my phone buzzed in my pocket. *Kye has changed the group name to We Know What You Did.*

> **Kye:** *Spoiler alert. Not only did Arden almost slice Linc's carotid, she also threatened to have Brutus rip off his hand.*

I scowled at the screen.

> **Fallon:** *Uh, A? Do we need to go over those play-nice-with-others lessons again?*

Jesus. My siblings would never lay off me now. I was going to kill Kye.

> **Kye:** *Oh, she wants to play REAL nice with Linc-y Linc. Especially when he's sparring shirtless.*

Oh, hell. A flurry of texts appeared all at once.

> **Shep:** *Is he making you uncomfortable, Arden?*

> **Trace***: Do you need me to talk to him? Explain things?*

> **Cope:** *I'm going to kill him.*

I opened the camera app, took a picture of myself flipping the bird, and sent it to the group chat.

> **Me:** *That was for Kyler and Kyler alone.*

> **Rhodes:** *Shit. She formal-named you. Duck and cover.*

> **Me:** *For the rest of my 82 million big brothers, I can take care of myself. Big dog, brown belt in jujitsu, always has a knife or Taser. Remember?*

I didn't wait for an answer, I simply flicked the phone to silent and shoved it into my pocket. I could hear Trace's warnings about a silent phone being a security risk ringing in my ears. But I didn't care. I'd left WITSEC at eighteen for a reason: to live. But I wasn't sure I'd actually done that.

It was time.

Squaring my shoulders, I lifted Brutus's leash and motioned for him to hop down. He did as I instructed but sent me baleful eyes as I hooked the clip to his collar. "I know, buddy," I said, giving him a pat. "I'll give you some turkey when we get home."

That had his tail wagging and booty shaking. Turkey and hamburgers were his favorite.

Wrapping his leash around my hand, I headed for The Collective. Brutus was great in town, happy to be at ease with new things to sniff and people to see. Unless someone made a move on me, he would behave just like every other happy-go-lucky pet. But some people gave him a wide berth anyway. I got it. He was massive, but he was also the sweetest dog you'd ever meet.

As we walked up to The Collective, I frowned and checked my watch. It was two minutes before noon, but there wasn't a soul inside. Annoyance flickered when I opened the door and called out. "Denver?"

No answer.

Apparently, I was rocking a murder list today. First, Kye. Now, Denver, for leaving the gallery unlocked and unattended. I moved through the space, checking the walls and spaces for sculptures. Everything seemed to be in place.

I saw Hannah's beautiful and delicate watercolor landscapes, Farah's brightly colored, mixed media masterpieces, and Isaiah's earthy and sultry sculptures. Plus, my pieces. Mine were a mix of mediums: oils, pastels, charcoal, acrylics, metal, and the occasional clay piece. But one thing tied it all together...darkness.

For the first time in a long while, that had me shifting uncomfortably. I'd come to terms with my battle with the darkness, feeling like my art was an honest expression of the human condition. Now, I wondered if I was missing something.

The bell over the door jingled as it opened, and I whirled, suddenly feeling naked at the flash of self-doubt I'd felt. A tall, muscular man just shy of a decade older than me strolled into The Collective, his black hair shaved on the sides but done in twists on top. He grinned, his white teeth flashing against his dark skin. "Ardy."

It was the mischievousness in the nickname that had me fighting a grin. "Isaiah," I greeted.

He moved into my space, not worrying about Brutus at all. He bent to hug me, kissing both of my cheeks. "I missed you like crazy. Why are you always breaking my heart?"

I snorted as he released me. "I doubt you'll be heartbroken for long." He was too gorgeous, talented, and charming for that.

Isaiah's grin widened. "You know I don't like the silence."

"Or an empty bed," I muttered.

"You know me too well."

The bell rang again as Hannah walked in, looking flustered. Her red hair was piled in a wild bun atop her head, and she wore a sundress with spaghetti straps adorned in wildflowers. "Arden, hey. We weren't sure if you were coming."

Guilt churned. I'd been in art and family world lately and not all that present at The Collective. "I made it. Where's Denver? I want to ream his ass out for leaving the gallery unlocked while no one was here."

A scoff sounded as someone walked in from the area of the back door. Farah's lips twisted in a wry grin as she entered, her black hair cut in an angled bob and dressed in her usual artist's black. How the newest member of our crew had ended up in Sparrow Falls was beyond me, but I adored her angry honesty.

"He's off passing out flyers for the fundraiser and kissing some reporter's ass," Farah mumbled, dropping a stack of flyers onto the desk in the corner.

My mouth went dry. "Did you say *reporter*?"

The bell jingled yet again as Denver entered, a man with salt-and-pepper hair next to him. Denver instantly winced. "Hey, Arden."

I scowled at him. "Something you want to tell me?"

Denver's throat worked as he swallowed. "Yeah. It just all

happened so fast. Sam Levine is a reporter for *Aesthetica*. He's doing a big piece on community art programs. Came all the way from New York."

I didn't miss how Denver had stressed *all the way*, as if warning me not to be an ass. There weren't that many print art publications, and *Aesthetica* was the best of the best. If he wrote a piece about our community program, it could be huge for us.

But it could also put me in the crosshairs. *Again.*

CHAPTER TWELVE

Arden

I LOOKED FROM DENVER TO THE REPORTER, TRYING TO FIGURE out how to play this. Brutus sensed my unease and pushed against my side, assuring me that he was there and asking if I needed him. I scratched him behind the ears, trying to reassure him, but it did nothing to settle *me*.

My gaze swept over Sam Levine. He looked like the quintessential reporter in his mid-forties: black-framed glasses, a scruffy, slightly unkempt look as if he'd been staying up way too late to finish a story and existed on coffee alone. But I knew looks could be deceiving. The man who'd killed my parents looked as if he could've been seated next to us at the country club.

"Did Denver tell you that I don't do interviews or photos?" I asked.

The man pushed his glasses up the bridge of his nose. "I'm aware of your media aversion, Ms. Waverly."

Isaiah snickered. "Dude, don't call her that. She'll put you on your ass."

The reporter's eyes widened a fraction. "What do you like to be called?"

"Arden. Call me Arden." The name tasted sour on my tongue because it felt like a lie. Even though it was exactly who I was now, it wasn't who I'd been. But I sure as hell didn't feel like a Sheridan either. Sometimes, I felt like no one at all.

"All right, Arden. Why don't I put you on background? Nothing you say will be quoted, and I'll make sure you aren't in any photos," Sam said.

He was being kind, more accepting than most reporters I came across, but I still couldn't help the unease and anxiety. But then I thought back to my promise to myself. To live. And living meant doing things that made me happy. Like working with kids in our art program and knowing we gave them a safe place to land whenever they needed it.

My back teeth ground together as my gaze flicked to Denver. I saw pleading in his brown eyes. Even if this was partly so he could get his ego stroked, I also knew he was doing it because he cared. Because he wanted the program to succeed.

"Okay," I muttered.

Denver rocked to the balls of his feet and clapped his hands, making countless turquoise bracelets rattle in the process. He and Lolli could go shopping together; she just went for the more bedazzled versions of his attire.

"Thank you, thank you, thank you." Denver hurried over to me to give me a hug but came up short at Brutus's low growl. "Uh, I'll just thank you from over here."

I patted Brutus's head. "Freund, Brutus. Freund."

The growling instantly eased.

"Your dog speaks German?" Sam asked, his gray brows lifting.

Shit. This was why I didn't like reporters being around. I didn't need any information about my dog getting out. "His trainer was German," I lied. But ole Sam would probably get even more suspicious if he knew these dogs were trained in a variety of foreign languages to keep most people from understanding their commands.

I sent Denver a pointed look.

But it was Isaiah who rescued me. "Sam, why don't I walk you out? I know you have that interview with one of the families with kids in the after-school program."

"I'd love to stay for your meeting," Sam began. "Hear about your fundraising efforts."

"Next time," Isaiah promised.

A time when I would be conveniently absent.

The moment Sam disappeared from sight, I whirled on Denver. "Seriously?"

His cheeks reddened. "What's the big deal?"

"The big deal?" I asked, my frustration rising. "I told you flat out that I didn't want to do any interviews, and you just go behind my back and ambush me?"

"Sam is here to write about the program, not you," Denver huffed.

"Den," Farah said, her voice completely deadpan. "You know you were hoping she would cave under pressure, and that shit isn't cool."

"Farah has a point," Isaiah agreed, crossing back through the space.

The red on Denver's cheeks deepened. "I'm just trying to make this fundraiser a success."

"And it will be," I argued.

"But think about how much bigger it could be if we got national attention," Denver pressed.

My palms started to sweat. It was always an invisible equation. How much attention on my art was okay? How much was too much?

I'd turned down shows at some top galleries because they required me to be in attendance for the openings. It felt like giving away pieces of a dream in the quest for safety. Not that stuffy parties were my thing, but they might've been worth it.

"Denver's just trying to help," Hannah said softly. She hated when we fought, and artists could have fiery tempers.

"All I'm asking is that you give me a heads-up," I said, pinning Denver with a hard stare.

He squeezed the back of his neck and sighed. "I'm sorry. I should've warned you so you could've avoided him."

"Thank you." I bent and unhooked Brutus's leash since we were inside. "We should see about setting up a phone bank for the auction.

That way, people who aren't local can bid. Might come in handy if we get national attention."

Denver stared at me for one beat, then two, before a huge grin spread across his face. "Think we could get in with that Upper East Side socialite crew?"

I tried not to let that one land. How many times had my parents talked about the new pieces of art they'd bought or ones they had their eyes on—art purchased with money that had cost them their lives? And for what?

Farah blinked at Denver a few times. "Upper East Side socialite crew? What are you, Gossip Girl?"

The two of them devolved into bickering like siblings, but Isaiah moved to my side, bumping my shoulder with his. "You okay? I can throw a fit and refuse to let any reporters be in your presence if it will help."

I chuckled. "Thank you. But I'm okay. And it'll be good for the auction to get some attention."

"As long as you're sure."

"I'm sure." I glanced down at my watch. "Come on. Let's get this show on the road. I have a tomato and burrata panini from The Mix Up calling my name."

Farah smirked. "When isn't a panini calling your name?"

"Never," I shot back. "Because I'm smart."

We all grabbed seats that Denver must've set out earlier and began working our way through tasks: music, staffing, the phone bank, show layout, and finally, food.

"I volunteer Arden as tribute," Farah said. "She's obviously very food motivated."

I flipped her off. "I'm happy to tackle that. I can talk to Sutton and see if her crew at The Mix Up would be willing to cater."

"I do love those devil's food cupcakes," Hannah said dreamily.

"Gotta find me a woman who looks at me like Hannah looks at devil's food," Isaiah muttered.

She flushed instantly and ducked her head. Hannah was the

youngest of all of us at twenty-three and easily scandalized by Isaiah's comments.

"Chocolate over men, every single time," I muttered.

As if I'd tempted fate, the bell over the door jingled, and a man stepped inside. But not just any man. One with dark hair and hazel eyes whose broad shoulders and muscular chest were practically on display in the pale gray T-shirt he wore the hell out of.

"Why are you stalking me, Cowboy?" I growled.

"He can stalk me anytime he wants," Farah mumbled as Hannah choked on a laugh.

I shot Farah a glare. "And what would your boyfriend say about that?"

She waggled her eyebrows at me. "Welcome to the bedroom?"

Linc chuckled. "Thanks, I think."

Brutus, the traitor, jogged right over to him, tail wagging. Linc crouched to greet him with rubs and scratches. Brutus licked his cheek, and Linc laughed, the sound so damn beautiful.

"Holy hell. I'd lick him, too," Farah muttered.

"Hey," Isaiah snapped, affronted.

She leaned over and patted his cheek. "Don't worry. You're still my favorite nude model."

"That's a little better," Isaiah huffed.

I pushed to my feet and crossed to Linc and my traitorous pup. "What are you doing here?"

He looked up at me through lashes that were too gorgeous for his own good and only seemed to accentuate the deep green in his hazel eyes. "Haven't you heard? I'm building a house."

"So?" I ground out.

"So…I'm going to need art for that house. Thought it would be nice to have some of it be local. *Someone* told me this was the place to find it." Linc's gaze flicked behind me, hardening a fraction as he pushed to his feet.

"Billionaires," I muttered.

Then I felt it. Heat at my back. I glanced over my shoulder and saw Denver standing far too close. He extended a hand to Linc, his arm brushing mine in the process. "Hello. I'm Denver Wick, manager of The Collective. I'd be happy to show you around and suggest some pieces."

"Lincoln Pierce. Thanks for the offer, but I'd just like to wander and see what grabs hold." His gaze flicked to me and held for just a beat too long.

And in that beat, my skin heated, and my nipples pebbled, lips parting just slightly with my sharp intake of breath. It was official. My body was an idiot.

Linc's gaze zeroed in on my mouth, registering my quick inhale, and his hazel eyes flashed a bit more gold. "Maybe you can tell me about the artists, Vicious."

"If you don't, I will," Farah called from our meeting spot.

Heat flashed somewhere deep and felt alarmingly like jealousy. I knew Farah was joking; she was happily coupled up with a local mechanic. But I still didn't like the idea of her being the one to show Linc around—to be close enough to smell his cedar and bourbon scent.

"We're in the middle of switching over displays, so we only have a few pieces up at the moment," I said, hoping Linc would simply go. That would be easier. Less complicated. But even just thinking that was a lie.

Linc's gaze didn't move from my face as if reading every thought that passed through my head. "It'll still give me a chance to get a feel for the artists, don't you think?"

"Sure," I grumbled.

"We need to finish our meeting," Denver said, his voice tight.

I glanced at my manager, taking in the tightness around his eyes. He'd normally be jumping at the chance to gain a rich patron.

"Why don't you just piss a circle around her?" Farah called. "Might save us some time."

Denver's eyes flared, the brown color lightening to almost amber. "I'm just pointing out that we weren't finished. We still need to figure out who's handling the music for the fundraiser."

Isaiah pushed to his feet, saving me yet again. "That's all me, boss man." His gaze flicked to me, a mischievous smile playing on his lips. "Lord knows we can't put Ardy in charge of that."

A chuckle sounded behind me. "As someone planning on attending that fundraiser, my ears thank you," Linc said.

Isaiah barked out a laugh, then crossed to us and extended a hand. "I'm Isaiah. That wildflower queen with the red hair is Hannah, our resident watercolorist. That coffee-black-just-like-her-heart dream is Farah. She does the mixed media pieces you'll see around here."

Linc took Isaiah's hand, his expression warm. "You must do the clay work." His head inclined to a sculpture in the corner. "Bold. And damn captivating."

"Appreciate it," Isaiah said, releasing his grip.

Surprise lit through me. "How did you know it wasn't one of mine?"

Linc's gaze moved back to me. The focus made me want to squirm. "I know your art. Know its style. What it makes me feel."

Farah reached for a few flyers from a stack and began fanning herself. "Good God, I need a cigarette."

My mouth went dry, and the urge to reach for something to drink was so strong I only managed one word. "Oh."

Isaiah chuckled. "This is going to be so much fun."

I turned in his direction, pinning him with a glare that should've had him rethinking his words.

He held up both hands but only laughed harder. "What'd I say?"

"I'm leaving," I muttered, pulling my keys from my pocket. "You guys have fun."

Annoyance flickered through me, but I knew the emotion was a lie. It hid something else. Something that felt a lot like a mix of shame and hurt.

I knew my people skills were more than a little lacking. The few relationships I'd had were more like short-lived encounters or situationships, and always with people who were temporary. An artist I'd met on a retreat in Sedona. A photographer in Sparrow Falls for a month shooting wildlife. They were never invited into my spaces. My walls remained firmly intact.

It wasn't normal, but then again, nothing about me was. That had never bothered me before. Until now.

I snapped my fingers, beckoning Brutus to follow me. He did instantly, reading my mood. I snapped his leash back on and was out the door and halfway down the walk before Linc caught up with me.

He didn't make a move to grab me or stop my forward progress; he simply matched my steps. "You okay?"

"I'm fine," I lied. "Go back and look at the art. I'm sure any of them would be happy to show you around."

My stomach twisted at the thought of any of them being the one to catch Linc's eye. Getting close enough to bask in his light. *Dumb, dumb, dumb.*

"I don't want any of them to show me around. I want to hear about the art from the woman who creates pieces that grab me by the throat and refuse to let go. Who creates work that haunts you long after you've looked away. Art that makes you confront the dark places inside."

I stumbled over nothing; his words were like beautiful punches. Linc caught my elbow to steady me, and I looked up into his face, searching for some sort of deception. How could he know? How could he have plucked exactly what I wanted my art to do to people from my head?

"Okay." It was all I could get out, but it seemed enough for Linc. He beamed like I'd just given him a puppy.

"You name the time, and I'll be there."

"After all the new pieces are in. But they're ones that are going in the auction, so you'd better have your checkbook ready if you want one."

The grin on Linc's face only widened. "I think I can handle that."

I let out a small scoff. "Billionaires."

Linc barked out a laugh. "We're the worst."

I started walking again, Linc following on one side while Brutus walked on the other. "You said it, not me."

"At least you know that when you take me for all I've got, it'll go to a good cause."

I couldn't help the smile tugging at my lips. At least he was being a good sport about it all. "It is. The after-school and summer programs here give many kids a place to go when they need it. And an outlet for everything going on in their lives."

I felt Linc's gaze on my face, gently probing. "The way art is an outlet for you."

Fighting the urge to squirm, I tightened my grip on my keys, feeling the metal tines bite into my palm. "If I can give even one kid the outlet that was given to me, it'll be worth it."

I couldn't resist glancing up at Linc, needing to know if he understood. His expression had softened, the green in his eyes paling just the slightest bit. "I bet you've given it to more than one, Arden."

Something about him saying my name made it feel like it fit me more. Like it wasn't a lie.

"I hope so."

"I know so."

Something about that felt too intimate. The feeling of Linc understanding me was so overpowering I needed some distance. When my truck came into view, I breathed a sigh of relief. "I'll text you when all the pieces are in."

"Sounds good," Linc said, not crowding me as if he could read that I needed the space.

I stepped off the curb and moved toward my driver's side door. One of the flyers for the auction and fundraiser had been tucked beneath my windshield wiper. I automatically grabbed it, but something caught my attention. A flash of red.

There hadn't been any red on the flyers we'd created as a team. We'd designed the image as a mixture of all four of our art styles with a headline in deep blue, and the date, time, and location in green at the bottom. But this flyer had boxy red writing at the top. Angry slashes that had my breaths picking up speed and blood roaring in my ears.

I KNOW WHO YOU REALLY ARE.

CHAPTER THIRTEEN

Lincoln

COULDN'T STOP STARING AT HER. IT WAS A PROBLEM. I WAS USUALLY so much better at keeping my cards close to my chest and not revealing a damn thing. But I couldn't seem to do that with Arden.

Something about her pulled honesty out of me. Raw and real, no hiding.

And I was addicted to the feeling. Just like I was addicted to staring at her. Watching how the breeze caught her dark brown hair. How the bright afternoon sun hit the apples of her cheeks, revealing those hints of freckles. The way her mouth curved in the most tempting way.

And how she moved. It was just like her: bold, no holding back.

She stepped off the curb, and I knew I was going to lose her. She'd climb into her truck and disappear. I wanted to hold on to her for as long as I could. Hold on to the way she made me feel. But I knew I had to let her go. It was the only way she'd come back to me.

As she snatched the flyer off her windshield, my gaze stayed fixed on her, soaking up every movement. But then something changed. Her muscles tensed, and her hand began to tremble. The color drained from her normally tan face.

Panic shot through me, and I was moving before the conscious thought entered my head. "What is it?" I barked.

Arden trembled harder, but it was as if she didn't hear my voice. Brutus let out a low growl at her side, obviously reading his human's unease.

I peered over her shoulder at the flyer she stared at so intently. Angry, red letters had been scrawled across the top of it. *I KNOW WHO YOU REALLY ARE.*

"What the fuck?" I snarled.

Arden still stared at the note, completely frozen. Clearly terrified.

What the hell was going on?

I might not have the answer to that, but I had enough rage coursing through me that I wanted to end whoever had put this kind of fear into Arden. It took everything in me to gentle my tone.

"Arden, I'm going to take the note, okay?"

She didn't show any signs of reaction. I pulled the paper from her, careful to only touch the very corner. Arden simply stared at the spot where it had been.

Fuck.

"We need to get you into the truck. Can you help me?" I laid a hand on her shoulder, and Brutus let out another low growl. My back teeth ground together. I was damn glad Arden had him looking out for her, but I also didn't need him going for my jugular for trying to help. "Arden, I need you to tell Brutus it's okay if I help you."

She blinked a couple of times but didn't speak.

"Tell him I'm a friend," I encouraged.

"Freund." Arden's voice was more rasp than word, but Brutus eased a fraction.

"That's it." My hand wrapped around hers, gently uncurling her fingers so I could take the keys from her hand. "We're gonna get you home, okay?"

She didn't move, and I fought the urge to punch something. I moved to the driver's door, then unlocked and opened it. I motioned Brutus inside, but he didn't move. "Come on, pal, help me out. I'm trying to get her home."

The dog's head cocked to one side, and then he leapt into the cab. I let out a breath of relief. I didn't want to think about what it would've taken for me to get him into the vehicle if he hadn't wanted to obey.

I set the flyer on the dash and moved back to Arden. My fingers curled around her shoulders and I turned her to face me. "We're gonna get you in the truck. Can you help me with that?"

She was looking right at me, but it was as if she didn't see me at all. As if she were in some other place completely. Finally, she nodded.

I guided her toward the door and helped her inside. She slid into the center seat automatically. I quickly climbed in after her and started the engine. Glancing over, I registered her still pale complexion, and my hands tightened on the wheel.

Maybe I should be taking her to a doctor or hospital, but all I could think about was getting her home. Safely.

Slamming the door, I threw the truck in reverse. I made the drive in half the time it normally took, glancing over at Arden every couple of minutes as if she might disappear in front of my eyes—into whatever alternate reality she was looking at as she absently stared out the windshield.

Because it was closer, I went to Cope's house instead of Arden's. I pulled to a stop in front of the massive structure, then eased Arden out of the vehicle, Brutus instantly following behind. It only took me a few seconds to hit the code for the door's lock and get her inside. But when we reached the living room, she wouldn't sit. She simply started shaking her head.

"Talk to me." There was a pleading tone to my voice. Like I was begging. But I didn't give a damn. I needed to know that Arden would be okay.

She blinked a few times, a little awareness coming back. "I froze."

"You froze?"

Her hands fisted in my tee, twisting the fabric. "All my training and I just froze."

A sick feeling slid through me. "What were you training for?"

Arden's gray-violet gaze fully focused and collided with mine. "What to do in case they try to kill me again."

CHAPTER FOURTEEN

Arden

THE TRUTH SLID OUT SO EASILY IT WAS SHOCKING. ESPECIALLY given the fact that it was a truth I'd guarded with my life for over thirteen years. But I gave it to Linc as if it were nothing. As if he had earned the right to all my secrets. And maybe he had. Or perhaps there was simply something about him that made me want to lay myself bare.

That in and of itself should've had me running for the hills. But it didn't. I stayed and watched as the words hit him and realization dawned.

Those hazel eyes turned thunderous, the sort of stormy that threatened retribution of the highest order. "Who. Hurt. You?"

I could feel the war within him, the battle to keep his hold on me gentle, and the fight to not scare me. But I wasn't frightened. Somehow, his anger was a balm. I knew I shouldn't tell him—my family were the only ones I could truly trust—but I found myself speaking anyway. It was like my voice belonged to someone else, as if I were listening right along with Linc.

"My parents were killed when I was eleven," I began. "I saw it.

My mom, at least. She'd hidden me in a secret closet, but there wasn't enough room for us both."

Acid surged up my throat, burning it. The older I'd gotten, the more I recognized her sacrifice. "I watched as a man taunted her and then ordered his hired hand to kill her. All because my father was greedy. Because he wanted more."

I'd realized with time that my mom must have known what my dad was up to. The mastermind had known her. Had called her by name. But I couldn't stop replaying the conversations of that night all those years ago in my head. How my mom had told me things would get better, and Dad would be home more. Either she'd known and had convinced my dad to stop taking the bribes, or he'd grown a conscience and decided to stop all on his own. But none of that changed the fact that his greed had set the series of events in motion.

I let out a shaky breath, anger mixing with my fear. "As if we didn't have enough. Our house was bigger than we'd ever need, his car was top of the line, and his clothes were impeccable. But it wasn't enough."

Confusion swept over Lincoln's face. "He stole something?"

I shook my head. "He was a judge. He accepted bribes."

Linc muttered a curse.

"Apparently, there came a time when he wanted to stop."

"And they didn't want him to," Linc surmised.

"No," I whispered. "They didn't. So, I watched from the pitch-black of a hidden closet as they shot my mom in the chest. I watched her take her last breath. Watched as her blood spilled out onto one of our antique rugs. I watched her *life* spill out. I waited, locked in the dark for hours until a neighbor saw our open door and called the police. But even then, I was too terrified to step into the light. They had to sedate me to get me out of there."

"Fuck," Linc bit out, and then his arms were around me. He engulfed me in a hug that nearly drowned me—in the best way.

For the first time in over a decade, I felt truly safe. As if no one could get to me because the embrace would protect me. I let all that was Linc drown my senses. Let that bourbon and cedar scent wrap around me and seep into my skin.

He held me for a long time. So long, I thought the sun might've sunk lower in the sky. But it wasn't long enough. As he pulled back, he lifted his hands and framed my face. His palms and fingertips were callused—a fighter's hands. And those made me feel safe, too.

"Tell me they got them. Tell me those bastards are rotting in jail."

I wanted to say yes. Wanted to know I'd never have to worry about those men again. But I couldn't. "One is." I swallowed hard. "I only really saw the man who shot her, not the one who ordered him to. But my description led the police to the shooter. My testimony put him away."

Linc's thumb stroked the apple of my cheek. "So damn strong."

I wasn't, not really. I was still terrified of the dark. Still held myself back from all the people in my life. But I didn't tell Linc any of that. Instead, I gave him a different truth. "They never found the mastermind—the one calling all the shots. The hired gun never flipped on him, and all I saw was his damn shoe. Only heard his voice taunting my mom before he killed her and said he'd find and kill me, too."

Linc's hold on my face tightened infinitesimally. "Fucking hell."

"The cops tried to put the pieces together and link him to my dad or the hired gun. But the money trails they found disappeared in Switzerland."

"Hiding his tracks," Linc muttered.

"Yes. And he used that anonymity to try again. He didn't want to take any chances that I might've seen something more."

Linc released me then as if he didn't trust himself not to hurt me somehow. He ran a hand through his hair, tugging hard on the ends of the strands. "What do you mean *try again*?" he spat.

I swallowed hard. "They put me into foster care after my parents were killed. I only had one distant family member, and they weren't equipped to take custody of a young girl. So, I lived in a house with a handful of other kids. One night, someone broke in. Apparently, they hacked CPS to find my location."

Linc's hands fisted as he let out a sound that resembled a snarl.

"The woman who ran the foster home, Mrs. Dearborn, saved my life. She must've heard something because she came out of her bedroom and surprised the masked person outside my room." No, not a person. A hit man. A hired gun. Someone contracted to kill *me*. "She screamed for me to run and got knocked unconscious as a result. But she did it anyway. Saved my life, just like my mom had."

I let out a shuddering breath as my throat burned. "I was so scared. I slid out my window and ran as hard and fast as I could. I didn't even have shoes on, but I pushed until I couldn't go any farther. I didn't know what to do."

Tears pooled in my eyes as the memories hit me one after the other. "Finally, I came to a church. My family wasn't religious, but I thought I might be safe there until morning. I hid in the back pew. I must've fallen asleep because the next thing I remember is a nun waking me up and asking if I was okay."

Linc stared at me, unmoving, pain and fury splashed across his face.

"The police came and brought me to the station. That's when they put me into witness protection."

Linc's eyes flared in surprise. "Witness protection," he echoed.

"They placed me far away, across the country. Even Nora and Lolli didn't know where I'd come from or what had happened to me. They just knew I was traumatized and needed them. They were so patient. Never pushed, were just there, my steady rocks. I'll never be able to repay them for what they did for me."

Linc moved again, back to me, engulfing me in that embrace. "You're safe now." I sensed the words were as much for him as they were for me. And I wanted to believe them. But I wasn't sure I could.

"The note," I croaked.

Linc pulled back but kept his hands on me. "You think someone knows about your past."

"*I know who you really are.*" I recited the red scrawl.

He muttered a curse. "You need to call your case agent."

"I don't have one. Not anymore. I opted out of the program when I turned eighteen."

Linc's eyes hardened. "Why?" he gritted out.

My spine stiffened. "You have no idea what it's like. Endless rules of who you can tell what to. Feeling like people are constantly watching you. Like the small sliver of life you've managed to carve out for yourself is constantly under a microscope. I wanted the freedom to live."

I might not have seen that through in all the ways I wanted to yet and might've let fear keep me from reaching for certain dreams, but at least it was *my* choice, not that of some case agent looking over my shoulder twenty-four-seven. And I could take the baby steps I wanted to whenever I was ready.

Like today. Telling Linc. Hell, that was way more than a baby step. It was a monumental leap. One I'd taken because of all he made me feel.

His shoulders released some of the tension as he pulled me back into his arms. "I'm so fucking sorry. I can't even imagine."

I shuddered against him, my fingers twisting in the fabric of his soft tee once again. I needed that tether right now. Something to hold me to the here and now so I didn't slip back into those awful memories.

"Who knows?" Linc asked.

"The Colsons, a handful of people at the bureau, and the marshals."

He let out a long breath. "We need to call Trace."

It was my turn to pull back. "I don't know—"

"Arden." He cut me off. "This is serious. If someone knows who you really are…"

My life could be in danger. My stomach twisted. "Call him."

Even though I knew this was how I'd lose my freedom all over again.

CHAPTER FIFTEEN

Lincoln

I N THE FIFTEEN MINUTES IT TOOK TRACE TO GET TO COPE'S house, I watched as all the fight bled out of Arden. Instead of being fiery and full of life, she looked…defeated. I fucking hated it.

The front door flew open, and Trace's boots hit the hardwood, eating up the space. "What the hell happened?"

I moved on instinct, stepping between him and Arden, holding out a hand in a gesture for him to calm down. "Take a breath," I growled. Brutus moved to my side and let out a warning growl of his own.

Trace's dark green eyes flashed in surprise. But that shock was enough to break through the worry, fear, and anger so he could get ahold of himself. He looked around me, his gaze running over his sister as if checking for injury. "You're okay?"

Arden nodded and said, "I'm fine." But she sounded resigned. "*Ruhig*, Brutus. Komm." The dog quieted and trotted back to her, leaning against her leg.

"This is what happened," I said, handing him the flyer I'd put into a Ziploc bag using cleaning gloves so I didn't get prints on it.

Trace's brows lifted. "You a secret ex-profiler, too?" he asked, referencing Rhodes' boyfriend, who had a past with the FBI.

I wanted to grin, but I couldn't quite get there. "The extent of my knowledge comes from the handful of *Criminal Minds* episodes my little sister has forced me to watch."

That had Trace grinning, but the smile died the moment his gaze hit the flyer. The fury and fear were back, and his attention cut to Arden. "You call—?" His focus flicked to me for a moment before returning to his sister. "Your contact?"

"Linc knows, Trace. I told him."

His eyes went comically wide. "You told him? Everything?"

"Everything," Arden said, exhaustion in the single word.

Trace studied me as if seeing me in an entirely different light. "All right. Did you call the marshals?"

She shook her head. "I'm not their problem anymore. You know that."

A muscle in Trace's jaw fluttered. "That doesn't mean they wouldn't want to know about this."

"So they can...what?" Arden challenged. "Offer me a chance to start over *again*? To lie to everyone in my life all over? No thank you. I'm not doing that."

Trace's fingers tapped his leg as if he were struggling not to fist them. "I'll call my contact at the bureau and see if they know anything."

Arden simply shrugged and bent to scratch Brutus between the ears.

Trace watched his sister for a moment before turning to me. "Walk me through it."

I glanced at Arden before speaking, hating everything about her demeanor and wanting to do something to change it. But I was powerless. "I went by The Collective to check out the art. See if there were pieces I wanted to purchase for my new build."

"When you went in, were flyers already on the vehicles?"

Good question. I mentally traced my path from my parking spot to the art gallery, trying to remember. "Yes. There were."

"Denver, Hannah, Farah, and Isaiah distributed them a little before noon," Arden said, her voice completely flat.

Trace's jaw tightened. "I need to know which one of them left the flyer on your vehicle."

Arden's back teeth ground together. "They went out as a group. I highly doubt any of them could've written that note without someone else seeing. Not to mention the fact that, if one of them wanted me dead, they've had ample time and opportunities to off me."

Trace's hand fisted then, fury grabbing hold. "This isn't something to joke about."

"I'm not joking. It's a simple fact." Little lines formed between her brows as she mulled that over. "A note like this doesn't even make sense. If someone knows about my past and wants to harm me, why warn me? Now, I'll be on guard. If they really wanted me gone, they'd have simply done it."

Her words had a sick feeling churning in my gut. What was it like to forever wonder if you were in someone's crosshairs as you simply tried to live your life? But Arden also had a point. "This doesn't feel like the threat of a professional killer."

Trace sighed. "No, it doesn't. But until we know *what* it is, we need to take precautions."

That had Arden sitting up straighter. "I won't be kept under lock and key. Not again."

Trace made a placating gesture. "I'm not saying you can't live your life. But I think you should come stay with Keely and me."

Arden's eyes flashed, the violet engulfing the gray, and damn, it was good to see a little of her fire back. "I'm not staying with you."

"Why not?" Trace pressed.

"It's away from my workspace, my horses, my home. And if a psycho killer really is after me, do you honestly think I'd put Keely in that kind of danger? She's never going through what I did. Never."

Pain slid over Trace's expression. "I'm sorry, Arden. I—"

"It's fine. I'm sorry I bit your head off."

Trace's shoulders relaxed a fraction. "You could stay at the ranch for a while. You know Mom and Lolli would love to have you."

Arden pushed to her feet. "Don't you dare tell either of them about this. Or anyone else. You know it'll make them sick with worry. And for what?" She ran a hand through her hair, tugging on the dark strands. "The more I think about the words…it was probably some prank. Kids getting their rocks off with some I-know-what-you-did-last-summer sort of jazz."

That was certainly possible. Kids pulled knuckleheaded moves like that all the time. But it didn't put me at ease. I wouldn't be able to relax until whoever had put Arden in the crosshairs all those years ago was rotting in a cell where they belonged.

Trace scrubbed a hand over his stubbled jaw, suddenly looking exhausted. "Fine. But I'm not about to leave you alone out here. I'll see if Leah can take Keely for a while, and I'll stay."

"No," Arden said instantly. "I'm not stealing your time with Keels. You don't get enough as it is. I'll be fine."

The pain lacing Trace's expression told me custody of his daughter was a sore spot. "Arden—"

"I'll stay with you." The words were out before I could consider the wisdom of them. There were a million reasons why I shouldn't spend any more time with Arden than necessary. But I couldn't stay away. Not before I knew what kind of danger she'd faced, and sure as hell not now.

Hell, I'd build her a goddamn army if I had to. Whatever it took to keep her safe.

CHAPTER SIXTEEN

Arden

I WAS PRETTY SURE MY BRAIN WAS SHORT-CIRCUITING, OR MAYBE I was having some sort of stroke. "You're going to what?"

"I'm going to stay with you," Linc said as easily as if he'd stated he was going to get a glass of water.

"There's only one bedroom." The words tumbled out of my mouth on instinct, anything that would keep some distance between me and the walking temptation that was Lincoln.

He simply pinned me with that swirling hazel stare. "Then stay here."

I shook my head. "I can only sleep in my room."

That was a stretch. Sleep *never* came easily to me. Even in the bedroom that had been mine for years. But at least I felt safe and secure there. It wasn't like I thought someone would take me out if I stayed elsewhere, but I felt at ease in my space because it was *mine*. There was comfort in the routine of what I knew.

A look of understanding settled into Linc's features—one I didn't want to look too closely at. "Then I'll sleep on your couch. You do have one of those, don't you?"

"Yes, I have a couch," I snapped.

I opened my mouth to tell him it was lumpy and uncomfortable and certainly not suited for a billionaire likely used to the best beds money could buy, but Trace cut me off.

"Are you two done? I need to go get this note processed."

I snapped my mouth closed, but annoyance still swirled, and guilt came fast on its heels. Because they were both being overbearing because they cared. But it still felt like control of my life was being wrested out of my hands. "I'll walk you out."

I stalked toward Trace and Linc but kept right on walking, assuming Trace would follow. Stepping outside, I breathed deeply, letting the fresh pine scent in the air slide through me. It was different than the evergreens back in Boston.

Even now, I could still grab hold of those hints of memory. Playing in my backyard surrounded by tall trees. The crisp air as the leaves began to fall. The air there had been sharper somehow. But maybe that was my imagination simply because *life* had been sharper. Harsher.

"Arden?" Trace's hand gently landed on my shoulder, and I fought the urge to move away.

The impulse had tears burning the backs of my eyes. Why was it always my instinct to retreat from those who cared about me when I was hurting? As if I needed to crawl back into my shell to protect myself from the possible pain.

Trace's hand dropped away as if he could read those thoughts as clear as day. But he was the sibling best at that: reading below whatever surface we painted with any sort of lie. "We're going to figure this out."

My hand dropped to my side, fingers twisting around a loose thread on my jean shorts. "I know."

"I'm here if you need to talk. Always."

Pain burrowed deep in my chest. Trace was too good. Every single member of the Colson crew was. And I couldn't help feeling that I didn't deserve any of them. "Thank you," I whispered.

He pulled me into a quick hug and dropped a kiss to the top of my head. "Do me a favor and don't kick Linc to the curb. You do, and I'll be sleeping outside your house in my truck."

I sighed, knowing Trace wasn't kidding. "You know I can handle myself. You've seen it."

"I know you can. But I also like knowing someone has your back, and Kye said the guy can handle himself."

An image of Linc in the ring filled my mind: the way he moved with a brutal grace, how every move was both strategic and wild, tightly corded muscle bunching and flexing, revealing just how much power lay beneath the surface. And then there was that surprising ink. The kind that told me he was anything but what I'd expected.

"Is that silence agreement?" Trace pushed.

I blinked a few times, trying to clear the images from my mind, but I knew it would do me no good. Those memories were burned into me. "I'll let him stay."

Tension seeped from Trace's shoulders, which only sent more guilt sliding through me. "Thank you," he said. "I'll call you as soon as I hear anything."

"Okay." I watched as Trace climbed into his SUV and drove away. I stayed there for one moment, then two, the pressure in my chest intensifying. It was as if I were being crushed under an endless mountain of bricks, making it hard to breathe.

I was so lost in the sensation and trying to work through it that I didn't hear Linc until he was right at my back.

"Tell me what you need." His voice was low—not gentle, but not forceful either. And it bled kindness, understanding.

That simple act had the burn behind my eyes returning. "I need to paint."

"Then paint. I'll walk you."

My gaze flicked up to him. "I don't need—"

"Just because you don't *need* it, doesn't mean I won't give it to you anyway. Not taking any chances. Not with you."

I swallowed, trying to clear the emotion clogging my throat. I reached for something, anything to lighten the mood and stop the foreign feeling from trying to invade. "Don't think you're getting food or sex just because you're staying with me."

Linc's lips twitched, and those green-gold eyes danced with amusement. "I'll keep that in mind, Vicious."

Then he walked me to my studio and checked every nook and cranny before allowing me inside. And I let him.

The music blared from the speakers, wrapping around me, pulsing through me. It was hard, screaming metal tonight. A sad, raw rage coursing through my stereo system. And it fit my mood.

I took a step back from the painting. *Almost done.* But it needed something else. One last piece of the puzzle.

That happened sometimes. I could think a creation was finished, but then I would realize something wasn't quite right. That it needed one last element to bring everything into focus.

I studied the canvas and the way the thorny brambles clawed at the fabric, looking like they could reach out and ensnare you. But those deep red blooms gave it something else. Hope. The realization that a flower could bloom despite its circumstances.

It was the message I needed to tell myself. The thing I needed so desperately to believe. So, I'd put it down on canvas.

But what was it missing?

I studied it for another beat. It needed the realness. The authenticity. The part of me I was afraid to show anyone.

My gaze flicked to my palette, and I studied the paint options. None of them were right. Snatching up some ultramarine blue, I dabbed it onto my palette, mixing it with the perylene red. A deep purple erupted as the result.

I picked up a brush and didn't allow myself to hesitate. I went straight for the center of the canvas, the middle of that tunnel of brambles. There, I painted a heart. Not cutesy but realistic. One with all four chambers.

Switching out my brushes, I went back for the perylene red and gave the heart a dripping look. Bleeding. Because there was a cost for blooming in the darkness, and you had to be willing to pay it.

I took a step back and tilted my head. Studying the painting made me uncomfortable, like my skin no longer fit my body. Uncomfortable was good. It meant a new level of work.

Brutus let out two sharp barks. I reached for my phone, ignored the countless notifications, and switched off the music. A knock sounded at the door.

"It's me," Linc called.

A shiver of *something* skated over my skin. Anticipation? Excitement? The combination was foreign. Nothing I'd ever experienced before.

I crossed to the door in a handful of strides. "What's the password?"

A soft chuckle sounded through the wood. "Cheeseburger."

My lips twisted into an amused grin as I opened the door. "Cheeseburger?"

Linc held up a bag with a familiar teal and red logo with a retro vibe that read *The Pop*. "It's almost ten, and I'm pretty sure you haven't eaten since breakfast."

"I had an energy bar," I argued, but my stomach growled as if to call me a liar.

"So, should I take this cheeseburger with caramelized onions, cheese fries, and a strawberry shake back to the house with me then?" Linc challenged.

My jaw went slack. "How did you know my order?"

"I asked Cope before I called them."

My spine stiffened. "Please, tell me you didn't share what happened today."

Linc's brows pulled together. "I didn't, but you should."

I ushered him inside, shaking my head. "You don't know my family. If they think something is going on, they'll all move in. I'll never have a second alone."

"And that would be a bad thing?" Linc asked, making his way to the leather couch on the far wall and setting the bag and drink holder on the beat-up, paint-splattered coffee table.

I picked up the brushes I'd been using and carried them to the sink. "It's not that I don't like having them around. I do. I just—I need my alone time."

Linc studied me as I cleaned my brushes. "You're not much for groups, are you?"

One corner of my mouth kicked up. "What gave that away?"

He chuckled. "I get that. But you do have to consider how they'll feel when they find out what happened and learn you didn't tell them."

I winced as I lay the brushes flat to dry. "Maybe they'll never know. I've thought about it a lot, and this note doesn't read like a professional killer. They wouldn't want a trail."

"You might be right there. But someone wanted to scare you at the very least."

Sliding my hands under the water, I washed them thoroughly. "We don't know that it was specific to me. Could've been a very unfunny prank, and they didn't care who got the note."

Linc watched me as I crossed the space to the couch, his gaze like a heat-seeking missile. "Possible. I hope like hell that's the case. But we take care in the meantime."

We.

I didn't miss that one tiny word. I'd never been a *we*. Not even before my father's greed ripped my life apart. I'd always simply been *me*.

Something about being a part of something larger was nice. Even if just for a handful of moments. I didn't feel quite so alone.

"I'll be careful," I muttered, reaching for the white bag. Brutus was already sitting politely, a little drool gathering at the side of his mouth at the prospect of a french fry or a bite of burger.

Linc snatched the bag just before I could get it. "Promise me."

My jaw went the slightest bit slack. "Are you holding The Pop's delicious, caramelized onion cheeseburger over my head?"

His brow arched as a mischievous grin spread across his face. "I'm not above using food to get what I want."

"Of course, you're not," I mumbled. But Linc showed no signs of handing over the goods. "Fine. Fine. I promise I'll be careful. I won't even turn my phone on silent."

Linc lowered the bag and handed it to me. "That's better."

I fished my burger out of the bag. "You play dirty."

"No, I play to win."

Goose bumps rose on my skin at the promise of his words, but I shoved the awareness down, reaching for something—anything— else. "I'm surprised you left poor little defenseless me alone to go pick up dinner."

"I didn't."

My gaze lifted to Linc's face. "They don't deliver way out here."

That mischievous grin was back, the one I was growing addicted to. "They do if you offer to pay the driver a hundred bucks."

A laugh bubbled out of me as I rolled my eyes. "Money doesn't solve everything, but I guess it does when it comes to cheeseburgers."

The smile I was coming to adore slipped from Linc's face. "Doesn't solve everything. Not even close."

CHAPTER SEVENTEEN

Lincoln

SOMETHING ABOUT HOW SHE SAID, *"MONEY DOESN'T SOLVE everything,"* hit. But right along with that came another blow I wasn't expecting.

Doubt.

I wondered if I tossed cash around with too much callous disregard—just like my father.

Arden lowered her burger and set it on the coffee table. "I was just joking. I didn't mean—"

I waved her off. "It's fine."

Her expression hardened, and that stubborn fire blazed to life. "It's not."

I opened my mouth to speak, to let loose some sort of brush-off, but Arden cut me off.

"Don't lie to me." Those gray-violet eyes were pleading now. "You don't have to talk about whatever put those shadows in your eyes, but don't lie. Not when I told you about the hardest moments of my life."

A curse slipped free. She was right. I'd be a bastard of the highest order if I fabricated some elaborate alternate reality for why her words had tripped my trigger. But laying that shit bare? That wasn't in my nature.

When you laid it all out there, it meant people could use it against you. Just like my father had.

My gaze moved to the painting in the center of the room. It grabbed hold—like Arden's art always did. But this one was different somehow. Even more honest. More raw.

I stared at the bleeding heart. The brambles could be protecting it or imprisoning it. Or maybe they were simply an allegory for the harshness of the outside world. But then there were the flowers. Blooming despite it all.

"It's beautiful," I whispered.

Arden's gaze followed mine, and she stared for a long moment. "I think I like it."

I glanced back at her. "You don't always like your work?"

She shook her head, some dark brown strands falling free of her bun, more than a few splatters of paint decorating them. "No. But this one...it makes me nervous."

"And that's good?" I wanted to know more, wanted to know *everything*. How her beautiful mind worked in all the ways, but especially when she created. And wasn't that fucking unfair? Here I was, keeping all my secrets locked away while demanding hers.

"Nervous, uncomfortable. It means I'm feeling. Art should always make you feel." Arden stared at the piece. "Sometimes, when I'm lucky, the pieces align, and I find real truth."

My heart hammered against my ribs. "And what is this one's truth?"

"Sometimes, you need to bleed to bloom." Her voice wasn't a whisper, but it held a quiet strength, coated in a rasp that resembled the brambles in the painting.

Those words painted themselves over the ones from earlier, coating them so thickly it drowned out the ones from before. And they made me reckless.

"My dad killed my mom." My truth. My blood on the canvas.

With that sort of shocking statement, I expected a jolt, maybe a gasp. But not from Arden. She simply watched me and took in my truth. And then she waited. She didn't give me any of the countless platitudes I'd heard before.

"I'm so sorry for your loss."

"She's with the angels now."

"She'll always watch over you."

It was nothing as simple as that for Arden. She let the silence do the talking. And in that quiet was acceptance. One that invited me to keep going. To share a little more of my bloody truth.

"He didn't put a bullet in her brain or a knife in her heart. But he killed her just the same."

Arden gave me words then, and with them, more acceptance and understanding. "There are countless ways to kill someone."

My fingers tightened, curling around my kneecaps and digging into the denim there. "There are. And my father is an expert at not leaving any evidence behind."

Arden simply met my gaze and waited, pools of understanding in her irises.

"He has a pathological need for power and control. To know that he can exert his will over everyone around him." Images of his face flashed in my mind, that stone-cold calculation. "He built the perfect trap for her, promising her forever and a beautiful life. Then he locked her in a tower while he cheated on her daily, belittled her, and made her feel like she was worth nothing. That she was nothing more than expensive window dressing."

My mom's tower had been that Upper West Side penthouse. The one that overlooked the park and held the promise of forever. But forever had become a prison.

My hands gripped my knees so tightly my fingers started to go numb. "He choked the life out of her little by little, snuffed out her light. She tried to fight it. There were times when she fought. Took my sister Ellie and me out of school and surprised us with a trip to Coney Island. Let us stay up late, eating all the junk our dad never let us have while bingeing *Goonies, E.T.,* and *Hook.* Read us stories and made all the voices."

My words caught, tying in a knot at that last memory. I could still see her, clear as day, reading *Where the Wild Things Are* and making me laugh until my sides ached. "She tried to leave," I croaked. "He found out the moment she talked to a lawyer. Dropped a file of so-called evidence in her lap, showing what an unfit mother she was."

There was a fire in Arden's eyes now, the violet flaring to life. "He was threatening to take you away from her."

"Ellie doesn't remember much. Doesn't remember how she simply faded. She was breathing but no longer living. She didn't play as much or create the voices when she read. She slid into a bottle and never came out."

I didn't see Arden move. Didn't know she had until slender fingers wrapped around mine. But those fingers weren't delicate; they were far stronger than they appeared—like the woman herself.

She slid them under my death grip, forcing me to hold on to her instead. In that moment, I could feel everything about her. The strength of steel. The gentle kindness. The flecks of paint on her skin, marking her with the price she paid to create art that reached people. That reached *me*.

I stared down at our joined fingers. Another type of art. "She drove off a bridge upstate when Ellie was six and I was seventeen. Her blood alcohol level was twice the legal limit. Dad played it off to everyone as a horrible accident and painted himself the grieving widower. But there were no skid marks at the scene."

Arden's fingers tightened around mine, holding on to me as tightly as I held on to her. "Loss and theft."

My gaze lifted from our hands to her face, questions in my eyes.

"It's a tangled web," she rasped. "The grief of losing her. The anger that part of you feels like she didn't fight hard enough for you and Ellie. The fury at your father for his cruelty, his killing."

"A tangled web," I echoed. "Just like your painting."

Her mouth curved the barest amount, those berry pink lips just starting to part. "True."

"I'm not good at sharing this sort of stuff."

"Seems like you're doing a pretty good job to me."

I let out a breath, finally exhaling fully and releasing some of the oxygen that had been held hostage in the deepest recesses of my lungs. "Sometimes, you need to bleed to bloom," I said, repeating her words.

"Sometimes," she agreed. "I find it's what you do with the pain that matters the most. What do you turn it into? Something that brings light, or something that brings the darkness?"

"You bring the light."

A genuine smile spread across Arden's face. "Not everyone would say that. Not when you look at my art."

I shook my head. "Then they don't see it. Don't see *you*. Facing that darkness is exactly what brings the light."

"That's what I like to think. And you can't have one without the other."

No, you couldn't.

"I know that tangle, Linc." My nickname on Arden's tongue was a sensuous stroke. "I know what it's like to miss someone and despise them in the same breath. I'm not sure I'll ever be able to forgive my father for what he cost us all. Not sure I'll be able to forgive my mother for possibly being complicit. But that doesn't stop me from loving them both."

Each word was like a blow to the chest. Because I felt that same battle when it came to my mom. I forced myself to release Arden's hand, even though it was the last thing I wanted to do. Shifting, I pulled out my phone, tapped in my code, and opened the photo album to the very last image.

"She's both. The darkness and the light," I rasped, turning the phone around so Arden could see the screen. I'd memorized the photo. If I'd had any sort of artistic skill, I could've etched it on paper without even looking at the original image.

I was twelve in the photo, and Ellie was only one. I held one of her hands while my mom held the other as we walked over the grass in Central Park. Ellie beamed up at us with a gummy smile, and my mom was so *alive*. Her hair was the same mix of light blond and brown as Ellie's, but her eyes were a gray that none of us shared.

"She was beautiful," Arden whispered.

I didn't reply, simply swiped my finger across the screen to the next photo. It was a formal portrait from five years later, just a month before she died. There was no life in it; not even in six-year-old Ellie perched stiffly next to my mother—a woman whose eyes had gone completely dead.

"So much pain." Arden's voice was barely audible. "And rage," she said as her gaze moved to my father with his perfectly styled dark brown hair so much like mine. And those dark hazel eyes.

"I look like him, and I hate it," I muttered.

Arden's gaze flew to me. "The hell you do." Her hand lifted, fingertips grazing the skin beneath my eyes. "There's light here, life. There's nothing in his. You couldn't look more different."

Something shifted inside me, a recalibration I had no control over. "Thank you," I whispered.

Her hand dropped away. "Thank you for giving me that."

We stared at each other for a long moment, and then I forced my gaze away. "Not sure you'll be thanking me when your burger's cold."

She chuckled. "I've eaten much worse than a lukewarm cheeseburger."

I popped the top off my vanilla shake and dipped a french fry into it. "At least this won't be ruined."

Arden looked on in horror as I popped the fry into my mouth. "You did not just do that. French fries dunked in a *milkshake*?"

I barked out a laugh. "You sound like I'm putting liver and onions over ice cream or something."

"You might as well be," Arden accused.

"Have you ever tried it?" I challenged.

"I don't need to try it to know it's gross."

I plucked up another fry and dipped it in my shake. I held my hand under the concoction as I extended it to her. Arden shook her head, making a face.

I just grinned. "Chicken."

That had the fire lighting again. Arden opened her mouth, and I slid the fry inside. Her lips closed around it, and I watched, transfixed as she chewed. Slowly, her brows lifted, and her expression shifted into delighted surprise.

"Good?" I didn't know what it said that everything hung on her enjoyment of my favorite eccentricity.

A smile stretched across her face as she shook her head. "Damn you, Cowboy. Now, I'm a weirdo who likes dunking my french fries in milkshakes."

"I think you'll survive." I leaned forward, my thumb swiping across her bottom lip where a speck of milkshake remained.

Arden's lips parted as she took a sharp breath. Our eyes locked, and need swirled in hers, making the violet deepen to nearly black. My thumb stilled, resting on that perfect swell of her mouth, relishing the delicate silkiness beneath my callused fingertip.

Arden leaned in, and my hand slid along her jaw, fingers tangling in her upset hair. God, I needed to taste her, to know if it would grab hold the same way her art did, showing no mercy. Closer. So close our breaths mingled.

Brutus let out a demanding bark.

Arden startled, jerking back and out of the haze we'd both been lost in. She let out a laugh, her cheeks heating. "He's mad. I've usually given him a fry by now."

I sent Brutus a frustrated stare. "I'm not sure he deserves one," I mumbled.

Damn dog was a cockblock.

CHAPTER EIGHTEEN

Arden

A WHIRRING SOUND CHIPPED AWAY AT MY SKULL LIKE AN ICE pick. I blinked against the mostly darkened room, trying to get my bearings and figure out what the hell the sound was. I stared up at my ceiling, awareness seeping into me. Most people would think it was weird, my thick emerald blackout curtains cutting out any glimmer of sunlight, only to have a nightlight in the corner. But it worked.

Swinging my legs over the side of the bed, I sat up, and Brutus lifted his head from his dog bed. My eyes burned, and I fumbled for the drops on my nightstand. The sensation wasn't new. My typical lack of sleep meant that I bought the drops in bulk. Only last night, my lack of sleep wasn't due to nightmares.

I'd tossed and turned, replaying that *almost* kiss in my mind. The way Linc's thumb felt as it grazed my lip. How the roughened pads of his fingertips skated across my jaw. The way my skin heated as his hand slid into my hair.

My nipples pebbled beneath my worn tee, the buds tightening

against the soft fabric. *Fucking hell.* I shoved to standing, annoyance sweeping through me. I needed to get a grip.

The whirring, grinding sound intensified as if to call *bullshit.* Striding across my bedroom, I threw open the door and stalked down the hall, Brutus trailing behind me. But I came up short as I reached the kitchen and living area.

The house wasn't large, but I didn't need it to be. Even though it was smaller, the open-concept design, along with the massive windows, made the space feel larger. Inviting. And the sage green walls complemented the view, giving the space a peaceful air.

But there was nothing peaceful about what greeted me now.

Linc stood at my island, hand braced on a blender, the sleeves of a blue button-down rolled up, exposing tan, muscular forearms. His hair was darker, almost black now, making me realize it was damp from a shower. My mouth went dry as my gaze dipped, taking in the dark-wash jeans that hugged his hips and worn boots that didn't feel like something a god of money would wear.

But that was Linc. A series of unexpected surprises. Always keeping me on my toes.

The blender cut off, and I glared at the man in my kitchen. Glared for so many reasons. But most of all because he was making me *feel.* "Do you know what time it is?" I growled.

As if he'd already known I was there, Linc didn't look my way. Instead, he glanced at his watch—an antique gold piece. Not perfect, but full of dings and scratches that told a story, just like my truck did. "It's almost eight."

"That's practically dawn," I muttered. "Some of us were *trying* to sleep." I gestured to Brutus, who simply trotted over to Linc for pets. Traitor.

Linc's lips twitched as he scratched behind Brutus's ears. "And some of us have been up for hours. Did some work. Fed your horses. Got some supplies from the main house since all you had in your fridge were energy drinks and eighty-two condiments. Oh, and some leftover Chinese that was questionable at best."

My scowl only deepened. "You never know what kind of hot sauce you'll need."

He chuckled and reached for the blender pitcher. "Fair enough."

"And you fed my horses?" I asked, a little shocked.

Linc poured a green concoction into two glasses. "Cope told me how, and, shockingly, I do know how to measure."

I fought the urge to squirm. Something about the familiarity of that, the effort to help, hit a little too close to center mass. "What is that?" I asked, nodding at the goop Linc was pouring.

Linc grabbed one of the glasses and held it out to me. "Green smoothie. I made you one. It has four different kinds of veggies. Six fruits. Vitamins. Protein powder."

My nose scrunched as I studied the glass, but I didn't take it. "Thank you, but I think I'll pass. That looks like something I muck out of Whiskey's and Stardust's stalls."

Linc barked out a laugh. "Not a morning person, are you?"

"What about me suggested that I enjoy rising before the sun?"

That devastating grin stretched across Linc's face. "Grumpy and fucking cute. Even the shirt is cute."

Cute wasn't a descriptor often used for me, and Linc using it now did something to my insides. I glanced down, not remembering what tee I had put on. It was black cotton but with a unicorn over a rainbow. Below, it read *Death Metal*. My cheeks heated. "It's my favorite."

"Adorable," Linc muttered, setting my glass on the counter and moving in closer. "But what I'm really partial to is these shorts." His fingers skimmed along the hem of my short-shorts, grazing my skin with the barest of touches.

I sucked in a breath, my whole body tightening at the contact, which was barely anything. It was as if everything intensified when Linc touched me. It was *more* than any other contact. It made me greedy for that *more* and terrified of it in the same breath.

I stared at the man opposite me as he waited. Linc should've considered giving professional poker a try because he had the kind of patience that meant taking home the whole pot. I opened my mouth to speak, unsure what might come out. A blow-off, or a plea for him to take me right here on the counter?

But my doorbell cut off both.

Brutus went on alert, instantly coming to my side. It was Linc who scowled now. "Dogs and doorbells," he muttered, annoyance lacing his words.

That little glimpse of humanity, proof that Linc wasn't a god, had a smile tugging at my lips. "I'll get it."

"*I'll* get it. We don't know who's there."

I let out a long sigh and leaned a hip against the counter. "If you get my phone, I could pull up the camera feed, but I really don't think assassins ring the bell or have the gate code."

That only had Linc's scowl deepening and those green-gold eyes darkening like storm clouds. *Note to self, don't mention assassins.*

"Better to be safe," he ground out as he started for the front door.

I couldn't deny that Linc was hot when he was pissed off and protective, but I still felt the walls closing in and the freedom I'd found disappearing from my grasp.

Linc pressed his face to the door to look through the peephole. When he pulled back, there was still a hint of pissed off in his expression, but it was more annoyance than anger now. He unlocked the door and opened it.

I peered around him to find Denver standing there, blinking up at Linc in surprise. He had different colored feathers in his hair today to match the stitching on the western-style shirt he wore. His jeans had that artfully distressed look, and his cowboy boots were the kind that never actually touched manure.

"What are you doing here?" Denver asked, more than a little hint of demand in his tone.

Linc's expression hardened. "Not sure that's any of your business."

Oh, Jesus. Someone save me from male pissing contests.

I tried to move around Linc, but he shifted slightly as if he didn't want Denver to get a good look at me. I smacked Linc's arm. "Enough. I highly doubt Den is hiding a bazooka in his boot."

Linc's gaze flicked down to me, and I noticed a tightness around his mouth that had a flicker of guilt taking root inside me. He was genuinely worried. I squeezed his arm. "I'm fine. Promise."

He lifted his chin in assent, shifting slightly the other way so I could have an actual conversation with Denver. But when I met Den's gaze, it was to find his face twisted in a scowl, too.

This was what happened when you tried to people before eight in the morning.

"What the hell is going on, Arden?" Denver demanded. "Trace shows up yesterday, wants all of our prints, wants to know if we saw anyone around your truck. I call, you don't answer. I text two dozen times, you don't message back."

I winced. "I'm sorry. The day got away from me."

Denver scoffed. "Looks like you were just fine shacking up with moneybags here. But you don't have two seconds to get back to your friends?"

"Watch your tone," Linc ground out.

"I'm not talking to you," Denver snapped.

"Maybe not, but you'll *only* be talking to me if you don't watch what you say."

Denver puffed up his chest like a gorilla about to charge. "What? You've been here for like two-point-five seconds and get to dictate who she talks to?"

Linc moved forward in two long strides, forcing Denver back onto the front steps. "It's not about *dictating* anything. It's the fact that I'm not going to let *anyone* speak disrespectfully to Arden in my presence...*ever*. So, try again."

Normally, I found it oppressive when someone stepped in like this. It reminded me too much of my family's overprotectiveness. But something about Linc in this moment felt anything *but* oppressive. For the first time in a long while, I felt like I could breathe. Like I was safe. It was the same as when he wrapped his arms around me.

Denver glanced nervously between Linc and me, then sighed, running a hand through his long hair and getting his fingers stuck in the feathers. "Sorry, A. I was just worried."

I stepped out onto the front patio. "I'm sorry, too. I was painting all afternoon and night. Then I crashed."

That had interest lighting in Den's eyes. "You finish it?"

One corner of my mouth kicked up. All was forgotten if new art had been created. "I did. It'll take a couple of weeks to fully dry, but—"

"It can cure at The Collective. We can still hang it for the show."

A pang lit in my sternum. I wasn't sure I was ready to give this one away. Something about it was just a little too personal. Or maybe it was that I still needed the message that lay within the layers of paint. "I don't know—"

"Come on, A. We need as many pieces as possible for the auction."

Linc's jaw hardened, a muscle fluttering along the curve, but he stayed silent.

"Okay," I said. "I'll bring it in later." I wouldn't have been able to ship it for weeks, but I could lay it in the bed of my truck and drive it into town. Denver was right, we needed everything we could get for the auction.

Denver beamed. "You're the best." His smile dimmed a fraction. "You going to tell me what happened with your truck?"

My fingers found the drawstring of my shorts, and I curled the cord around them. "Just a stupid prank. But you know Trace doesn't like anyone messing with his little sister."

Denver chuckled. "Some poor kid is going to end up pissing himself when Trace corners him. That dude is scary when he wants to be."

It was true. Trace had a gentle, easy, approachable demeanor most of the time. But when someone flipped that justice switch, it was best to steer clear.

"Hopefully, it'll be a couple of days before he finds them. He'll chill by then." *Maybe.*

Denver nodded and quickly glanced at Linc. "All right. I'm heading back into town. Call me if you need help unloading the painting. I'll be in and out of the gallery all day. I set up a bunch of interviews for Sam."

Denver let that last sentence hang, and I knew why. He wanted me to offer up an interview with the reporter. But that wasn't happening.

"Good luck. I'll text when I bring the painting in." What I didn't say was that I'd also be texting Isaiah or Farah to check if the coast was clear and reporter-free. I wouldn't put Hannah in that position. She was too nervous about hurting anyone's feelings.

"Sounds good. See you later." Denver gave me a salute that was a little ridiculous and studiously ignored Linc as he went to climb into his Subaru hatchback.

Linc watched him the whole way, not taking his eyes off him and then his vehicle until both had vanished from sight. Then, he turned slowly, his gaze dipping to mine. "I don't like him."

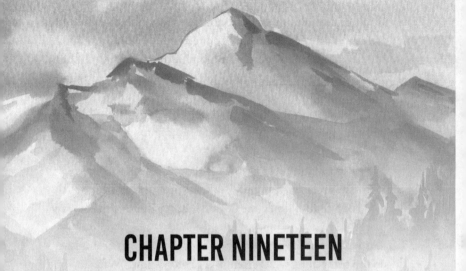

CHAPTER NINETEEN

Lincoln

ANGER AND ANNOYANCE SWIRLED, EACH ONE BATTLING FOR dominance. Denver Wick was a prick. The fact that his last name rhymed with the word was only greater proof that the two were intertwined.

He didn't give a damn about Arden. Or rather, he cared a hell of a lot more about what her art could get him than her well-being. And his sheer disrespect of her only had my anger mounting.

Arden's berry-colored lips pressed together but fluttered as they did, as if she were desperately trying to hold in a laugh. "You don't like him? What are you, five?"

A scowl twisted my face yet again. "No, I'm not five. But I *am* annoyed as all hell by his disrespect."

Arden rolled her eyes. "It's just him. He's got a single-minded focus when it comes to The Collective. And he's not used to seeing me with, uh, guys."

That piqued my interest. "Not the relationship type?"

God, I hoped that wasn't true. I had no interest in one-night stands or shallow flings. I'd gotten that out of my system in college. It wasn't for me. I craved real, true connection.

Arden lifted one shoulder and then dropped it, her T-shirt sliding down and revealing tan skin and the absence of a bra strap.

Fucking hell.

"Told you," she said, her voice dropping. "Not really good with the whole people thing."

"Bullshit."

Those gray-violet eyes flashed. "Excuse me?"

"You're great with people. When you want to be," I challenged. "But that doesn't mean connection doesn't make you uncomfortable."

Arden pulled the drawstring of her shorts tighter around her finger, the tip turning white from lack of blood flow. "Why do you have to see so much?" she asked, her annoyance clear in her tone.

The corners of my mouth tipped up in a half smile as I moved in closer, gently unwrapping the cord from her pointer finger. "I spent a lot of my life trying to figure out what makes people tick. Might've learned a thing or two."

Arden looked up at me, searching for something. "You tried to work out why your dad was the way he was."

My body stiffened. I tried to catch the reaction, knowing it gave too much away, but I couldn't. "Yes," I admitted. I wouldn't lie, not to Arden.

"Did you ever figure it out?" she asked softly.

I didn't release her fingers, couldn't make myself. "No. But he's the master of walls and subterfuge."

Arden gave me a sad smile. "Sometimes, understanding why helps, but it still doesn't change what they did."

"No. It doesn't." I forced myself to release my grip on her. "What do you know about Denver? *Really* know?"

Arden arched a brow. "Change of subject much?"

"It's important."

"I'll let that one slide," she said, a hint of amusement in her tone. "What do you mean what do I *know* about Denver?"

"His history. Relationship ties. All of it. Maybe he's the one who left the note," I suggested. There were more than a few things I wasn't crazy about with the dude.

Arden's face transformed with a full grin. "He's been my art dealer for almost as long as I've been selling pieces. Born and raised a couple of towns over and only a handful of years older than me. I highly doubt he was involved in murder for hire in Boston."

She snapped her mouth closed at the last statement, her skin paling a fraction.

The reaction was like a knife to the gut. How hard would that be? To hide every part of your past twenty-four-seven? "That's where you're from?" I asked gently.

Arden rolled her lips over her teeth but nodded quickly. "No one's supposed to know." A little of the fear left her then, a hint of mirth lighting those captivating eyes. "But I guess you make me break all the rules, Cowboy."

Fuck.

She slayed me. I wanted to break every rule with her. To smash down any walls between us. To pin her against one right now and take her. To lose myself in her body and brand myself on her bones.

"I won't tell a soul."

Arden looked at me for a long moment. "Maybe you will. Maybe you won't. But I'm tired of hiding. Of guarding every word I say. It's exhausting."

I didn't have her trust. Not yet. But I would. I brushed a strand of dark hair out of her face. The color seemed to have a golden edge in the sunlight. "I would give anything for you to be free of that."

She searched my face as if looking for a lie. "I'm done waiting for it. I'm claiming it for myself. No more fear. It's a choice. And I'm making it."

God, she was brave. So damn strong. "Okay."

"That's it? No trying to tuck me away from the world?" she challenged.

"Not going to try to lock you up, Arden. It would suffocate

you. But I will ask you to be safe and cautious while you grab that freedom."

Arden studied me for a long moment. "Deal."

One corner of my mouth tugged up. "That easy acquiescence makes me think I should've pressed for more."

Arden laughed, and the sound was light and easy, musical. It grabbed hold the same way her art did. "Did I outmaneuver the business tycoon?"

"Not surprised at all, Vicious." My fingers slid deeper into her hair, soaking up the feeling of the silky strands as I moved closer. The heat of her body poured into mine, and I wanted more. I wanted to know what it would feel like to have all of her pressed against me. To sink into that scalding heat.

My fingers tightened in Arden's hair, and I tipped her head back. And then my phone dinged. Once. Twice. A third time.

I muttered a curse and pulled it out of my pocket.

> **Ellie:** *Where are you?*
>
> **Ellie:** *8 a.m., hmm? Gym? Already in a meeting?*
>
> **Ellie:** *???*

I frowned down at the screen and began typing.

> **Me:** *I'm at Cope's. Are you okay?*
>
> **Ellie:** *Where at Cope's? Open the gate.*

She sent a compass emoji that had me chuckling.

I sent her a pin to my location. Maybe she was having something delivered but they'd have to buzz the gate to get in. Staring down at my phone, I waited, but Ellie didn't respond.

"Everything okay?" Arden asked.

"My sister," I muttered. "I'm pretty sure she probably had some bagels airlifted from New York or something, and I didn't answer the buzzer up at the house."

Arden grinned. "Sounds like she's trying to take care of you."

Movement in the distance caught my eye. A vehicle. The SUV

picked up speed, spitting gravel, but slowed as it approached the guesthouse. The engine cut off and then a figure jumped out.

"ConCon!" Ellie shouted, a smile stretched across her face. Then she halted, her gaze jumping back and forth between Arden and me. "Oops. Did I just ruin my big brother getting some?"

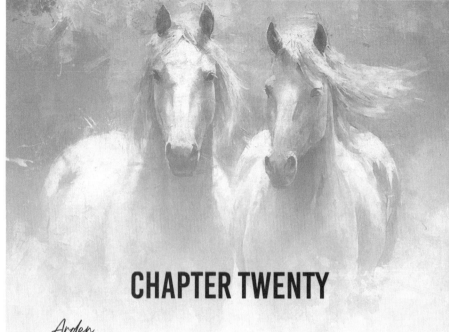

CHAPTER TWENTY

Arden

THE WOMAN STANDING IN MY DRIVEWAY WAS A PICTURE. She'd obviously just gotten off a plane but looked like she was about to walk a runway. She wore wide-leg, cream pants I would've stained in two seconds flat, a thin brown belt with a gold H clasp holding them in place. A figure-hugging, wide-strapped tank was tucked in, and a blue-and-white-striped sweater curled around her shoulders. To complete the outfit, a handful of gold necklaces ringed her neck.

And you couldn't miss the *massive* diamond on her ring finger. But the only thing that didn't fit was the worn, navy blue Yankees cap on her head. It had history. Not the kind of wear artificially put in place by a designer. This was *real* wear. The kind that came from donning the cap countless times for hours on end.

"El Bell," Linc chastised.

"What?" she asked with mock innocence. "I would never want to be accused of being a cockblock."

Linc barked out a laugh, and Ellie flew at him. He caught her in the air, swinging her around as she laughed loud and free. The sound hit me square in the chest, making an ache take root there.

Their bond was as clear as day. It was borne of a lifetime of history and deep affection. I wished I had that lifetime with my siblings. Sometimes, I wondered how different I would be if I'd been born into the Colson family instead of placed there at age twelve. Would I have been more normal? Would I have fewer demons? I bet I would sleep a hell of a lot better.

Linc set Ellie on her feet, her chunky-heeled boots kicking up dust. "What are you doing here?"

She grinned up at him, but I saw a hint of shadows in her pale green eyes. "Can't a girl surprise her big brother?" She glanced at me, her smile still just as warm, and the shadows now hidden. "He wouldn't shut up about this place. I had to see it for myself."

"Welcome. I'm Arden." I glanced down at myself and winced. "And I need to get dressed."

Ellie giggled. "No need to get out of pj's on my account. Besides, I'm kind of obsessed with your T-shirt." Her eyes lit. "And your big, beautiful dog. Hello, love of my life," she cooed.

Brutus's tale thumped against the patio stone in answer, but he didn't go to her.

"Freund, Brutus. Freigeben," I said, releasing him.

Brutus went straight to Ellie, who crouched low, all but throwing her arms around him. "Aren't you just the most handsome love? And so smart, speaking German."

Linc glanced from his sister to me. "Ellie loves dogs."

"Do you have one at home?" I asked.

She glanced up at me, a hint of sadness playing over her features. "Not yet. Maybe when we get a place outside the city."

Linc's mouth thinned into a hard line. I guessed he wasn't a fan of the fiancé, and I couldn't help but wonder what the story was there.

"Come on in," I said, heading inside. "I'm just going to change real quick."

I was already darting for my bedroom, and not just because I was in my pajamas. I was unsettled and needed to get my bearings. Linc was throwing my routine existence out of whack, making me realize the palette I'd been painting with was all shades of gray while he splashed a vibrant rainbow across my canvas. It was beautiful but unsettling, and I needed a second to regain my equilibrium.

Grabbing clothes, I ducked into the bathroom to brush my teeth and change. I quickly donned my favorite deep green cargo pants and a gray tank. It would do for taking care of the horses and hauling my painting to The Collective. I pulled on thick socks, even though it was already hot out. I'd need them when I slid my feet into boots.

As I straightened, I stared at the door, the hint of voices filtering through it. I took a deep breath. I couldn't hide in here forever. My fingers curled around the knob, and I twisted. The voices got louder as I made my way down the hall.

When I stepped into the kitchen, Ellie looked up, a smile still on her face. "I miss the death metal unicorn, but I do love those pants."

I laughed, surveying the space. "I'd offer you food, but I don't really have that around here. Your brother tried to force some sort of health drink on me, but you don't look like someone who favors poison either."

Ellie laughed, that same full-of-life sound filling the air as she turned to Linc. "I like her."

His lips twitched. "Glad you approve."

"You should be. I have impeccable taste," Ellie said, flicking her light brown hair over her shoulder.

"You *sometimes* have impeccable taste," Linc challenged.

Ellie's jaw dropped in mock affront. "Excuse me? Who helped design your company logo? *And* gave you feedback on the Sparks mascot reboot?"

Linc's eyes danced in amusement. "But who *also* used to dip grapes in ketchup and call it the height of cuisine?"

"I was five!" Ellie exclaimed, throwing her hands wide.

"My taste buds will never forget," Linc muttered, but there was clear affection in his eyes.

That shifting and rearranging sensation took flight in my rib cage. I could see the image as clear as day as if it were actually playing out in front of me. A teenage Linc dipping grapes in ketchup just to please his little sister. There was something about a boy who would do that. And he'd grown into a man who was the same at his core. Making sure I was fed. Staying with me on the off chance someone wanted to stir up trouble.

Lincoln Pierce was a good man. The best kind. And it scared the hell out of me.

"While you two argue the culinary worthiness of grapes and ketchup, I'm going to go let my horses out and head into town."

Ellie whirled in my direction, her pale green eyes lighting. "You have horses?"

Her excitement was almost childlike. Even though she was probably a year or two older than me, I felt the bizarre urge to look out for her. "I have two. If you stick around, I'll take you for a ride."

Ellie let out a little squeal. "That would be amazing."

I glanced at Linc, who was frowning. "What? No horses?"

He shook his head. "I'm not sure you should go into town alone. We can come with you."

I tried not to let his concern wrap around me like a warm hug, but it did anyway. Which was exactly why I shouldn't let him go with me. "I'll be fine. Just a quick trip there and back. Trace already made me turn on that damn find-my-device setting on my phone, so he'll know my whereabouts at all times."

"Arden—"

"I'm good, Cowboy. A stupid prank, that's all."

"We don't know that for sure."

"No bogeyman sends you notes before they strike. And I'll be careful. Promise."

As Linc stared at me, I knew he didn't believe me. And the worry in his hazel eyes put me on edge. Not because it meant he cared, but because I knew what it was like to lose that care after having it. Knew what it was like to have your world ripped out from under you with no warning. And I never wanted to feel that again.

Wanda bumped along the gravel road as I headed into town. My windows were rolled down, letting the summer breeze blow through the cab. Brutus was in heaven, his head out the window, ears flopping in the wind. I reached over and gave his hind end a scratch, making his tail thump.

This was it. All I needed. The fresh air. My dog. My truck. My work.

I didn't need dark, avenging angels who woke things in me that were terrifying beyond measure. Even if every cell of my being came alive at his touch. Even if he was the only person who'd made me feel completely safe for the first time in over a decade.

Just thinking about how Linc made me feel had annoyance coursing through me. How dare he waltz into my life and flip it on its head? How dare he make me realize everything I'd been missing with my walls sky-high?

My phone rang just as I turned onto Cascade Avenue. As I pulled to a stop at the first light in town, I plucked it from the cupholder. At the sight of the name on the screen, I hit accept, putting it on speaker and dropping it back into the holder.

"What can I do for you, Sheriff?" I asked.

Trace grunted in response. "Want me to tell Mom you're sassing me when I'm just trying to look out for you?"

I chuckled. "Sassing? I'm not your six-year-old, remember?"

"Sure are acting like her," he shot back.

I stuck out my tongue at the phone, even though he couldn't see me.

"You're either flipping me off or sticking out your tongue."

My spine snapped straight as the light changed. "Did you put cameras in my truck or something?"

Trace laughed, and it was damn good to hear the sound coming from my eldest brother. He didn't do it much anymore. I wasn't sure if it was the weight of his divorce, managing Keely on his own when he had her, or maybe simply the heaviness that came with his career path. He'd always been more serious than the rest of us, a rule follower. But this was more.

"If you were Keely, I'd have you doing extra chores for that sass," Trace said, humor lacing his words.

I guided my truck down the main road through town, taking in the flower beds at each corner with their brightly colored blooms, and the tourists already moseying down the streets to peek in shops. "I already mucked out stalls this morning. Can we call it good?"

"I guess." Trace paused for a moment, and I braced. "Got a call late last night. Mrs. Henderson said some kids were playing ding-dong ditch in those creepy *Scream* masks. Checked this morning, and we had a few other reports of the same."

I pumped a fist in the air. "Told you. Stupid kids playing pranks."

"There were no other reports of notes."

"Trace," I said, gentling my tone. "If I hadn't been through what I have, I wouldn't have reported the note either."

He sighed. "I guess you have a point there. Still, I talked to the agent at the FBI who has your case." I sucked in a breath, holding on and not letting go. "She said there has been no movement as far as she can tell. Grady Ellison gets exactly one visitor in prison. His mother. She comes once a month. He doesn't use the phone or email. There's no way he was behind this."

Just hearing the name Grady Ellison sent a shiver down my spine. The man who had so carelessly killed my mother, father, and countless others. All for a little extra cash.

"That just fits with the prank line of thinking," I said, flipping on my blinker to make the turn toward the gallery. I swallowed hard, steeling myself. "They say anything else?"

"They still have no idea who paid him and why. No idea exactly what cases your father threw beyond the few they were able to pin down early on. If they had a wider picture, they might be able to track it back to whoever was behind the hits."

I gnashed my back teeth together. "If they haven't found out any new information, it doesn't make any sense that whoever was pulling the strings would suddenly come after me all these years later. It's not like I remember anything beyond what I already told them."

And that ground at me. I'd played the voice over and over in my head, trying to place it. But nothing ever fit. If I had heard it before, it hadn't stuck. The police had found the shoes, a high-priced loafer with waiting lists and thousand-dollar price tags, but they'd never been able to match the recipients of the shoes in the Boston area with any persons of interest.

Trace sighed across the line. "Okay, okay. I'll let up."

"Thank you."

"I still want you being cautious in case we have this wrong. I've got Cope's place on the deputies' drive-by route, and I want you to keep that location app and ringer *on*."

I made a grumbling noise in response.

"Arden," Trace warned. "Do not make me get Nora and Lolli involved."

"Cruel and unusual punishment," I shot back.

"Desperate times call for desperate measures."

"Yeah, yeah. I promise."

"Thank you. Where are you now? I hear your truck."

"Detective on the case," I muttered. "I'm dropping off a painting at The Collective, then heading back home. Think I'm feeling a sculpture calling my name today."

"All right. Just don't forget about dinner tonight. And I invited Linc."

I cursed. I'd forgotten all about Lolli's request for a command performance. Her visit felt like it'd happened a lifetime ago. And having Linc there would make it that much harder. He saw too much. "I'll be there."

"Good," Trace said, then paused. "We just care about you. You know that, right?"

My throat constricted, a burning sensation igniting there. "I know. Sorry I don't always make it easy."

"Screw that noise," Trace clipped. "You make caring about you as easy as breathing. Even when you're being prickly."

My mouth curved the barest amount as I turned into the alley behind The Collective. Trace was being too easy on me, too kind. Which meant I hated myself more for not being able to give any of them the words and tell them I loved them. It was like if I did, I would know just how much pain I'd be in if I lost any of them.

"You're the best brother," I whispered. It wasn't enough, but it was all I could give him for now.

"I'm gonna tell Cope that."

I barked out a laugh. "You trying to get me kicked out of my house?"

"I'd never," Trace said, humor lacing his words. "I gotta get back to work, but call or text if you need anything."

"Will do," I said. "Be safe out there."

"Always am." And with that, Trace hung up.

I tried to shake off the conversation as I pulled into an empty spot near the back door of The Collective, but the conversation still clung to me. As I put the truck in park, my phone dinged twice. Lifting it from the cupholder, my lips twitched.

Your group name is now Arden's Favorite & the Other Ones.

Trace: *Arden finally admitted it today. I'm her favorite.*

Kye: *Someone check on A. Trace might be torturing her if she lied like this. We all know I'm her favorite.*

Cope: *The fuck you say? I'm the only one Arden allows to keep Brutus when she has to go somewhere without him.*

Rhodes: *You mean you're the most convenient one since you're a five-minute walk away?*

Cope: *Harsh, Rho Rho. That was uncalled for.*

Shep: *You can all stop now. I built her art studio, so I'm obviously the favorite.*

Fallon: *You're all being ridiculous. I know exactly who Arden's favorite is. It's Lolli.*

Kye: *That's not fair. Lolli's probably bribing her with pot brownies.*

I snorted out a laugh.

Me: *I wouldn't mind the brownies minus the pot. From everything I heard about Rho getting accidentally dosed in college, I'm steering clear.*

Fallon: *You mean this??*

She sent a video we'd all seen countless times, but it never got old. Rhodes was wandering through Lolli's flower garden, singing and talking to all the flowers.

Rhodes: *You said you got rid of that!!! TRAITOR!*

Fallon: *Sorry. I lied. This is too golden not to keep forever.*

Kye: *Fal is tiny but fierce. And she has way too much blackmail material on all of us.*

Fallon: *And it would do you all good to remember that when I ask you to volunteer at our back-to-school event in a few weeks.*

There were some texts of protest, but everyone mostly agreed. When your sister worked for Child Protective Services, how could you say no?

Shutting off my engine, I slid out of the cab and motioned for Brutus to follow. Since we were heading straight into the gallery, I didn't bother with a leash and swore my pup looked up at me with gratitude.

The moment I slammed the door, a familiar head of dark hair poked out of the back door. Isaiah grinned as he stepped outside. "How's the love of my life?"

I made a face. "Just fine, heartbreaker."

He strode over to me, crouching to give Brutus some scratches. "I don't know. I hear you're the heartbreaker. Had Daddy Warbucks at your place this morning."

Isaiah waggled his eyebrows to accentuate the point, and my face flamed. "It's not like that," I muttered.

"Suuuure, it's not."

I flipped him off, and Isaiah just laughed.

He pushed to his feet, and I saw the clay smeared across his worn tee. "Heard you were bringing in a new piece. Need help?"

Gratitude swept through me, not at the offer of help, but because Isaiah was letting it go. He might like to needle me, but he also always had my back. "That would be great. It's not fully dry yet, so we need to be careful."

Isaiah gave me a two-finger salute and headed toward the back of my truck. I'd had a cover designed for the bed for situations just like this one. There were times I needed to transport pieces I couldn't risk getting wet in snow or rain—or in this case, getting dirt or other debris on a still-tacky surface.

Isaiah started the dance we'd done countless times before, rolling back the cover and reaching into the bed. But he stopped just shy of the painting, glancing up at me. "Ardy. This is incredible."

My face heated again. "Thanks. It's, um—"

"Different," he finished for me.

I nodded. "Makes me twitchy."

Isaiah grinned over at me. "If it makes you feel like you're standing naked in front of a crowd, you know it's good. Important."

"Says the man who loves being a nude model."

He barked out a laugh. "Fair enough. Come on. Let's get her in to dry. People are going to freak over this baby."

That had my stomach flipping. I hoped people would connect to it, but I also wasn't sure I wanted to give the piece up. And that was a problem.

We navigated our way to the back door, careful not to run into any vehicles or other roadblocks on the way. When she saw us, Hannah hurried to the screen door. "I've got it."

"Thanks," I said, glancing over my shoulder to make sure I didn't run into anything.

We got the piece inside and onto an easel Denver had left out.

I was sure he wanted to photograph it before he moved it into one of the studios to dry.

"Wow," Hannah said, her voice going soft. "This is stunning."

"Thanks, Hanny," I said.

She sighed, running a hand through her tangled red waves. "I need to get moving on my piece. I'm behind."

When I looked at Hannah this time, I really studied her. There were dark circles under her eyes, and paint dotted her fingers. "You doing okay?"

She sent me a half-hearted smile. "I'm struggling with this one."

God, did I ever know that feeling. "You want me to take a peek? We could talk it out. I hit a wall with this one, too, but it finally all came together."

"I can help, too," Isaiah offered. "I know I'm a clay man, but art's art, right?"

Hannah beamed at us as if we'd just offered her a bag of diamonds. "That would be amazing. Thank you."

The bell over the door jingled, and I glanced over to see Denver leading another man inside. It wasn't the reporter from the other day. This man had *slick* written all over him. And money.

He wore shiny shoes that made zero sense in the mountains with black trousers that were perfectly pressed and creased. He'd tucked a crisp white shirt into them and finished the look with a watch rimmed in diamonds. Even his black hair was slick—gelled into artful waves.

The man's gaze swept over us but then went to the painting, staying there. "Tell me this is her newest work."

"It is," Denver said, a grin on his face that looked like a cat who'd snagged a canary.

Brutus pressed against my side, a silent check-in and assurance that he had my back. My hand fell to his head, reassuring him.

"Arden, this is Quentin Arison. He wanted to get a look at our offerings before the auction," Denver said, his grin still in place.

The man's gaze cut to me with a sharpness that had me wanting to take a step back. Brutus let out a low growl, and I did nothing to stop it. Quentin's dark brown gaze stayed locked on my face, showing no fear of my dog as he should have.

"Arden Waverly. Such a beautiful, young woman creates such dark work. Interesting." He began walking toward me, his steps long and languid.

Brutus's hackles rose, and he let out another warning growl, louder this time.

Quentin's gaze flicked to my dog. "An interesting choice of companion, as well."

"He's protective," I said, not lowering my gaze. We were surrounded by people, yet my fingers itched to palm the switchblade in my pocket.

Quentin arched a brow. "And if I reached out to take your hand?"

"He wouldn't like it," I gritted out.

"Fair enough." Quentin's focus shifted, studying the painting. "I like it. I'll need it. The blood...it calls to me."

A shiver ran over my skin as nausea settled in my stomach. I did not want my precious painting in this man's hands. Especially when he missed the point of it altogether.

He turned back to me. "Let me take you to dinner. You can tell me about my piece."

The fact that he spoke of my painting like it was already his had anger flickering to life in me. "I'll pass."

Annoyance and more than a little heat surged to life in Quentin's eyes. "I am quite the collector. I think you'll want to reconsider that."

"Not worried about collectors," I told him honestly. You either got my art, or you didn't. I wouldn't waste my breath trying to explain what I created to people who only wanted to judge it.

A muscle ticked in Quentin's cheek. "I could open a lot of doors for you, Arden. You don't want to lose that opportunity."

I opened my mouth to tell the douchebag to get bent but didn't get a chance because a new voice cut through the air. One that held a fury so cold it burned. One I recognized.

"I believe she said *no*."

CHAPTER TWENTY-ONE

Lincoln

FURY COURSED THROUGH ME IN RIPPLING WAVES SO COLD IT was a miracle I wasn't spitting ice. That was the thing about me when I got angry. I didn't erupt. Didn't rage. I got ruthless. Because if you harmed someone I cared about, there was no going back.

The smarmy bastard turned in my direction, holding up both hands in mock surrender. "My apologies, I didn't know the lady was spoken for."

"I'm not," Arden ground out, purple fire blazing in those hypnotizing eyes. "But that doesn't mean I want to go to dinner."

The man chuckled, but I didn't miss the bite to it. Or the way his eyes narrowed on Arden in a manner that said he didn't care for her rejection. "A challenge. I can respect that."

"Not a challenge. A final answer," Arden corrected, squaring her shoulders, fingers fluttering at her side.

A smile stretched across my lips because I knew she was debating pulling her blade. God, I wanted her to. Wanted to watch this stunning woman put that bastard on his ass.

The man simply made a humming noise.

"Enjoy your tour," Arden muttered, turning away from him in a clear dismissal.

Damn, she was a show all on her own. The most entertaining one I'd ever encountered.

The man's eyes flashed in anger, but Denver stepped in to coddle him. The gallery manager gestured toward the hallway. "I'd love to show you the studio space and the pieces we have stored for the auction."

For a second, I thought the man wouldn't go. Thought I might have to step in and remove him. But he finally followed Denver, the two disappearing down the dark hallway. I glared after them until clapping started.

I glanced over at my sister, who was grinning as she gave Arden a standing ovation.

"You are a thing of beauty," Ellie said.

Arden turned back to face us, wisps of hair falling from the bun piled atop her head. "Not a fan of creeps." Then she glanced at me. "What are you doing here?"

There was a wariness in the question, a challenge. She wanted to know if I was checking up on her. I wouldn't cross the line she'd drawn, not when I knew how much Arden's freedom meant to her. "Ellie wanted to see the gallery and some of your work."

Arden's shoulders relaxed a fraction, but I could tell she was still on edge. The urge to go to her and pull her into my arms was almost too strong for me to bear.

Isaiah shot a grin in my sister's direction. "Ellie, is it? I could give you a tour. I'm the *true* artist of this bunch."

She let out a soft giggle but flashed her hand with the ring on it. "I'm afraid I might make your *tour* more boring than you typically like."

Isaiah sighed. "It's just a day of rejection all around. I guess I'll have to settle for best friend status. Looking between you and Mr. Chiseled Jaw, I'll Break You If You Look At Arden Wrong, I'm guessing you're related?"

"He's my big brother," Ellie said with a grin.

"Well, welcome to Sparrow Falls and The Collective." Isaiah moved in, offering Ellie his arm. She took it, and he began leading her around the room, talking about each piece on display.

The fair redhead glanced at Arden. "Are you okay?"

Arden sent her a reassuring smile. "I'm good."

The woman studied her for a moment as if making sure, then nodded. "I'm going to take another stab at my painting. Just holler if you need me." And then she was gone.

Arden stared at me for a long moment. "No assassins. Only douchebags."

I wanted to smile, to give her that, but I couldn't. "No one should be pushing you for something you don't want to give. Making you feel uncomfortable in your place of work. Thinking they can buy you."

And as I spoke, I realized that's what Arden had thought *I* was trying to do that day in her art studio. The knowledge made me sick.

As if she'd read my mind, Arden crossed the space in four long strides. "You are *nothing* like him. Never were. I just—he's not the first person who has thought their money could buy more than my art."

I bit down on the inside of my cheek so hard I tasted blood. But it was the only option I had. If I didn't, I'd be demanding to know the name of every bastard who'd suggested as much. And coming up with some very creative ways to *ruin* them.

"Breathe, Cowboy," Arden whispered. She reached out, her fingers sliding through mine and squeezing. "I'm just fine. And I have flipped someone on their ass for crossing the line. You don't need to worry about me."

My free hand lifted, ghosting over the side of her face. "Just because I don't *need* to worry about you doesn't mean I won't."

Ellie leaned into the buckskin, pressing her forehead to Whiskey's and breathing deeply. My little sister shouldn't look like she belonged in the mountains of Oregon, on a property that looked more ranch than anything else, but she did. And more than that, she looked more at peace than I'd seen her in years.

That knowledge had a grinding sensation picking up in my sternum. I wanted that peace for Ellie, not just for a few fleeting moments but always. She pulled back from the horse but scratched beneath Whiskey's chin.

"Okay, after the full Sparrow Falls experience, I get it. I can see why you love it here." There was a wistfulness in Ellie's voice that only had the grinding sensation intensifying.

"You could stay," I offered.

Ellie's brows rose. "There's too much to do for the wedding, and Bradley needs me for some business dinners."

I couldn't help the scowl that twisted my mouth.

"ConCon," Ellie whispered, a pleading note in her voice.

I met my sister's gaze and finally asked her the question I'd wanted to since the moment they'd gotten engaged. "Do you love him?"

"Yes," she said instantly. But there was no joy in the word. So, I asked another question. Possibly the most important one.

"Are you happy?"

Ellie's gaze shifted away from me and back to Whiskey. "I don't think anyone's happy all the time."

"That's fair. Are you happy most of the time? Is your life what you want it to be?"

Ellie's pale green eyes glittered as tears filled them. "I don't know."

"El Bell." I moved into her then, wrapping her in a hug like I'd done countless times before. "You deserve to have the life you want. Whatever that is."

She sniffed, trying to rein in the tears. "I don't know what I want. And it feels like I hurt someone with every direction I move."

I gripped her tighter. "Ignore everyone but yourself, just for a minute. What would make *you* happy?"

Ellie pulled back. "I can't just ignore them. Their happiness is linked to mine. And whatever steps I take could mean some of those people aren't in my life anymore."

"If you're this uncertain, do you really think you should be getting married in a few months?" I asked, keeping my voice as gentle as I could.

Ellie's spine straightened. "It's just cold feet. This is a big life change. It's understandable that I'm nervous."

"Sure, it's natural to be nervous, but I want to make sure you aren't doing this just because Dad wants you to. This is *your* life." And God, I didn't want her to waste it on anyone who didn't deserve her.

Ellie brushed some dirt off her pants, evidence that perhaps this wasn't her world. "It is my life. And it's important to me not to lose my dad when I already don't have a mom. *And* it's important to me not to lose you."

I saw it then, what this trip really was. Ellie wanted to know that she wouldn't lose me when she submerged herself in the life I'd run from. She was doing whatever she could to hold on to everyone, even at great cost to herself.

"Told you, El Bell. You'll never lose me. *Never.* I promise."

Her shoulders sagged in relief. "Thanks, ConCon."

Ellie's relief was an ice pick to the chest. Just like it would be when she walked away tomorrow and headed back to that vipers' den. And all I would be able to do was pray that her path didn't take the same route as our mother's.

CHAPTER TWENTY-TWO

Arden

I SAT IN MY TRUCK, STARING UP AT THE HOUSE I'D SPENT HALF MY life in. The large, rambling farmhouse was still in impeccable condition. Nora wouldn't have it any other way. But it wasn't in a quest to be perfect, the way I often felt my mother had been. This was an appreciation for everything she had.

Nora was a caretaker, through and through, from plants to buildings to human beings. She nurtured everything that crossed her path. And I'd been no different.

But something about that nurturing made me twitchy, the need to run fast and far humming beneath my skin. And I knew what fueled it.

Fear.

Because the more I let the nurturing, care, and love in, the more I had to lose.

So, I sat in my truck, staring at the farmhouse: its white siding and massive front porch—boards carrying generation after generation of stories. Countless heart-to-hearts in those rockers or on one of the porch swings. Losses and triumphs. Pain and joy. All of it mixed together in the most beautiful painting I'd ever seen.

Gravel crunched beside my truck, and my hand instantly went to the blade at my belt.

"Can I keep my neck intact this time?" a deep voice asked.

My fingers released the handle of the switchblade. "You know, your stalker tendencies are really showing."

Linc chuckled, the rasp of it sending a delicious shiver through me as he shifted to look down at me. "I was just innocently taking a call but couldn't help but wonder if you were going inside or planning to just stare at the house all night."

Annoyance flitted through me at the challenge of Linc's words and the fact that he'd seen me as I'd done silent battle with a damn house. "Just needed a minute."

That had Linc's demeanor changing instantly. "Are you okay? Did something happen?"

"Breathe, Cowboy," I said as I glanced up at him, Linc's concern wrapping around me like an echo of his embrace. It wasn't quite as good as one of his hugs, but it didn't suck. "I'm just not the best with big groups."

Linc studied me for a moment. "So you said. You going to be okay?"

"I'm fine," I muttered. The problem was that my family knew me best. They saw things I could usually hide from the rest of the world. And there was no denying that the events of late had me rattled. That reporter. The note. But most of all…Linc.

"Pulling on a mask?" he asked. His voice held no judgment; there was simply a desire to understand. I appreciated that.

"More like trying to find inner calm. I like spending time with them, I do. It's just…"

"It's a lot coming at you all at once," Linc suggested.

I nodded, one corner of my mouth kicking up. "It is. But it's affectionate chaos."

Linc chuckled. "Been here fifteen minutes, and I can already tell that." His fingers curled around my door handle. "You ready?"

There was something about the question and gesture. It was as if Linc would wait here all night with me if I needed him to. But it was also more. It was the fact that I had someone to walk into the farmhouse with and wouldn't have to deal with the wave of people alone. It helped.

"Ready as I'll ever be," I mumbled, pulling my key out of the ignition.

Linc opened the door and held it for me and Brutus. The moment Brutus was out, Linc bent to give him a scratch behind the ears. "You been keeping her in line today?"

I let out a soft scoff. "Tried and failed, most likely."

Linc's gaze lifted to me. "Can't rein her in, too wild for that. But that's how you were meant to be."

That twitchy sensation was back, and it wasn't just because Linc saw me. It was because he saw who I wanted to be. "Tell that to Trace. I'm pretty sure he wants to inject me with one of those tracker things."

Linc barked out a laugh. "That's one way to play it."

I started toward the house, and he fell into step beside me. The gravel drive was littered with my siblings' vehicles: SUVs, trucks, Fallon's hatchback. The only one I didn't see was Trace's. My gaze slid over them to the ranch lands spread out around us and the beautiful view.

I took a second to remember the peace this place had always given me. The safety. And sent up a silent thanks to whatever greater being had put me here.

Glancing over at Linc, I knew that had tugged him here, too. That feeling of peace. The quiet beauty.

"Where's Ellie?" I asked as we walked up the front path.

A smile tugged at Linc's beautiful mouth, surrounded by scruff. "Already inside, making your family her new best friends."

That tracked. In the handful of minutes I'd spent with Ellie, she seemed like pure sunshine. And I was sure she was already being brought into the fold. But as I looked at Linc, I saw something in those bewitching, green-gold eyes. I saw pain.

My steps faltered. "What's wrong?"

Linc shook his head. "Nothing—"

"Cowboy," I said, pinning him with a stare. "Don't insult my intelligence."

Linc scrubbed a hand over his face. "She's not happy."

A lead weight settled in my stomach. "What do you mean?"

"She's living for everyone's happiness but hers. Her fiancé's. Our dad's. Mine. I'm worried she's caging herself in a world that will bring her a lifetime of living for others."

I could hear the anxiety and pain swirling in Linc's words—the concern for his sister. That care made a home in my chest, digging in deep. "You're worried she's going to put herself in the same position your mom was in."

It was a guess, but when Linc's head lifted, his hazel gaze had gone stormy, and I knew I was right. The storm clouds swirled in Linc's eyes in a mixture of agony and fear. "I don't want her to live in a prison of her own making. She deserves so much better than that. She's the most giving and kind person I've ever known. And I don't want them to change her. Or worse, make her fade away."

I moved into Linc's space then, sliding my fingers through his and holding tight. "I've only been in your sister's presence for about twenty minutes, but I can tell she's a fighter. She's not about to let anyone steal that light. But you need to give her the freedom to figure it out on her own. All you can do is be there when she needs you."

Linc's hold on my hand tightened as if I were his lifeline. "I know. I just...it's so fucking hard. And it brings up ghosts."

I moved again, tugging my hand free so I could wrap my arms around his waist. I wanted to give Linc a little of what he'd given me when I got that nasty note. I wanted to give him the feeling of safety. Of not being alone. I might not be the best at finding the right words, but I could give him this.

Linc's arms wound around me as he pulled me tighter against his chest. I breathed deeply as he held on. "Cherries," he muttered.

"Cherries?"

"You smell like cherries and a touch of jasmine. Best damn scent I've ever smelled. You could bottle it and make millions."

I tipped my head back so I could look up at Linc. "The billionaire *would* be looking at business opportunities, even now."

One side of his mouth kicked up in a crooked grin. "Never going to ignore an opportunity when it's presented." His hand lifted and brushed some hair out of my face. "Thank you."

Linc's hand stilled, his fingers tangled in my hair as his thumb grazed the side of my face. The rough pad of it sent shivers cascading through me. My gaze locked on his, and I felt my whole body lean in, craving more. As my lips parted, I swore I could taste him on my tongue.

Just one tiny move and his mouth would be on mine. The slightest lean in, and I would know if Linc tasted as good as I imagined. One moment, and—

"Well, what do we have here? My girl finally gettin' herself some?"

CHAPTER TWENTY-THREE

Arden

MY FACE FLAMED WITH HEAT AS LOLLI'S VOICE CUT THROUGH the early evening air, but Linc made no move to let me go. I tugged myself out of his arms, instantly missing the warmth that was only his—a feeling more grounded and real than anything I'd ever felt before. And that scared the hell out of me.

"Now, don't you two stop on my account," Lolli said, a grin spreading across her face. "Can I recommend the barn for a little horizontal tango? The hayloft is surprisingly comfortable."

"Lolli," I hissed.

"What?" she asked innocently, throwing up her hands and making the bracelets around her wrists jangle. She wore a hilariously adorable outfit: a brightly colored floral skirt paired with bedazzled sandals with little mushrooms on them. They complemented her T-shirt perfectly. The top had an array of rainbow mushrooms and read *M.M.I.L.F.* in big, blocky letters, while smaller script spelled out the acronym. *Magic Mushroom I Like to Forage.*

"You *know* what," I chastised. "Did Trace lose his mind at your shirt?"

Lolli's lips twitched. "My stick-in-the-mud grandson was not a fan, but I just reminded him that psychedelic mushrooms are legal in Oregon now. He needs to open his mind."

Linc chuckled. "You growing your own?"

Lolli beamed at him. "Interest without judgment. I knew I liked you."

"I try," Linc said, grinning at her.

"No mushrooms for me, but I do have twelve different strains of marijuana. I could set up a taste test for you—"

"Lolli," I cut her off, warning in my tone. "Let's go inside."

She sent a scowl in my direction. "I didn't think you'd be the one to ruin my fun." But she hauled open the door and headed into the house.

Linc dipped his head to whisper in my ear as we climbed the steps. "Buzzkill."

I choked on a laugh but smacked his stomach with the back of my hand. "You wouldn't be saying that if you accidentally got dosed. Happened to Rhodes in college, thanks to Lolli's pot brownies. She ended up rolling around in a field of flowers and declaring she was meant to be a daisy, not a girl."

Linc's laughter was full-out this time, the kind I wanted to grab hold of and never let go. "I'll keep that in mind. No brownies from Lolli."

"Smart choice."

As we headed inside, Brutus trotting along beside us, the sound of beautiful chaos rose. Conversations, and the shrieks of Keely's laughter. As we stepped into the living room, all eyes were pinned on us. I hated the attention, but gritted my teeth, knowing it would pass.

A hand found the small of my back, strong and steady. The heat from Linc's palm bled into me, letting me know he wasn't going anywhere. And, God, I wanted to sink into that reassurance and let someone be strong for me for once.

"Auntie Arden," Keely squealed, making a beeline for me. When she was a few steps away, she launched herself.

I caught her with an *oomph* and spun her in a circle. "Did you grow on me?"

She giggled. "I don't think so. But Dad only measures me on my birthdays so we can put the mark on the wall."

God, Trace was a good dad.

"I bet there'll be a big jump this year."

Her dark brown pigtails with big bows on the ends bobbed in a nod. "I'll be able to go on so many more rides at the fair." She glanced up at Linc curiously. "Are you my Auntie Arden's boy toy?"

Kye let out a strangled sound and then started coughing as he straightened on the couch. Fallon leaned over and started patting his back. "Careful, wouldn't want you to choke to death."

Shep sent Lolli an amused look from where he and his girlfriend, Thea, sat curled in a massive, overstuffed chair. "You know Trace will kill you if she starts calling kids *boy toys* in the first grade."

Lolli shrugged. "It's better than bleep buddy."

Kye started coughing all over again.

Rhodes grinned at Lolli. "You're going to off Kye if you're not careful."

She frowned at her grandson. "Never expected you to have such a delicate disposition."

Keely's gaze pinballed around the room. "What's a bleep buddy?"

"Oh, Jesus," Shep muttered. "Someone tell Trace I had nothing to do with this."

I pressed my lips together to keep from laughing. "It's nothing, Keels. Now, tell me. Who did these beautiful braids for you?"

Trace had worked hard to master simple braids and a couple of other hairstyles, but nothing he did was this fancy. These were intricate. Something I had no idea how to do either. But Keely beamed up at me and cast her arm wide, pointing to the kitchen. "My new bestie, Ellie."

Linc's sister stood in the kitchen next to Nora, where it appeared she was chopping vegetables. She waved. "That's me, bestie extraordinaire." She gave Keely a wink. "Never pass up an excuse to make a girl feel like the queen she is."

Keely giggled, then wiggled to be let down, making a beeline for her new friend. Something about it made my heart ache. My niece was the sweetest kid known to man and deserved someone who would give her those over-the-top braids whenever she wanted.

"So," Kye said, kicking his scarred motorcycle boots up on the coffee table and glancing at me. "Try to kill Linc lately?"

All my siblings burst into laughter, but a concerned Nora crossed the space, looking between us. "Kill Linc?"

Heat hit my cheeks, but it was Linc who stepped in. "Just a little innocent mishap. I hardly bled at all."

"Bled?" Nora gaped, her eyes going wide.

Rhodes just grinned from the arm of the couch as Anson gazed up at her adoringly. "I gotta admit, I feel safer having Arden around, even if she is a little violent."

"Says the woman who threatens to de-ball anyone who even sends a scowl in the general direction of someone she loves," Anson said, amusement lacing his words.

She stuck out her tongue at him. "I only threaten castration to those who *really* deserve it."

Anson shook his head. "I really am going to have to build you a murder shed, aren't I?"

She leaned over, giving him a quick kiss. "You might."

Lolli frowned at the two of them. "Now, why would you want to get rid of a perfectly good set of balls?"

"Lolli!" a chorus of voices shouted.

Nora covered her face. "I'm so sorry, Linc, Ellie. I'd like to tell you she isn't normally like this, but it would be a complete lie."

"I love it," Ellie called from the kitchen. "Lolli's my girl."

"Danged straight," Lolli called back. "You want to hit up the cowboy bar with me later?"

Ellie laughed. "I don't think I could keep up with you."

"But you'd have fun trying," Lolli singsonged and then looked at

Linc. "You know, I think you'd look pretty good in a pair of Wranglers and a cowboy hat. What do you say?"

Linc looked slightly terrified at the prospect of Lolli dressing him up and taking him out. I patted his chest. "Don't worry, I'll protect you."

He glanced down, amusement dancing in his hazel eyes. "I do feel safer knowing you've got that switchblade."

"Oh, that won't save her," Lolli called back. "I've been getting Kye to teach me on the side."

Lolli took up an elaborate fighting stance that didn't look like any martial art I'd ever seen while calling out some sort of battle cry.

Kye dropped his face into his hands. "Please don't tell anyone I'm your trainer."

"Rude," Lolli huffed, then eyed Linc again. "Okay, you're not ready for the cowboy bar. How about a little one-on-one sparring?" She waggled her eyebrows.

Linc grabbed my shoulders and moved me so my body was in front of his. "You said you'd protect me, right?"

A laugh bubbled out of me, light and free. "I don't know now. Pretty sure Lolli could kick my ass."

Movement caught my attention, and I looked over to see Nora with her hand hovering over her mouth, her eyes misty.

My stomach sank. "Are you okay?"

She shook her head, waving a hand in front of her face. "I'm fine," she croaked. "It's just—I haven't heard you laugh like that in a long time."

My insides twisted as guilt dug in. I'd worried her, the woman who'd given me everything. I hated myself a little for that.

Nora's hand lifted to my cheek. "I'm happy. Love seeing you like this."

I swallowed, then nodded quickly.

"Lincoln," Lolli called, breaking the moment and saving me from an overload of emotion the way she often did. "I want to make you a welcome-to-Sparrow-Falls gift. What do you say?"

Linc eyed her warily. "As long as it's not *special* brownies, I'm in."

"I want special brownies!" Keely yelled from the kitchen.

Nora pinched the bridge of her nose. "Trace is never going to leave her with me again."

"Where is he?" I asked.

"He got a callout. Break-in at the clinic. I think they were looking for pain medication."

I winced. Dr. Avery would not be pleased about that.

"Excuse me," Lolli cut in. "Lincoln and I have artistic vision to discuss. I specialize in diamond art."

A series of groans lit the air from my siblings, except for Rhodes, who looked positively giddy. "Don't let these cynics get you down. You know I love my dick flower."

"Yeah, you love it so much it hangs over our mantel," Anson muttered.

Linc coughed, trying to clear his throat. "I'm sorry, did they say *dick flower*?"

Thea grinned from next to Shep. "They did. I got a penis gourd painting."

"Don't forget Sutton's phallic pile of pastries," Fallon added.

"I think this scares me more than one-on-one sparring with her," Linc said, lowering his voice.

Kye leaned forward, cupping his mouth in a stage whisper. "It should."

"Oh, don't be such a prude," Lolli snapped. "So, Lincoln. What speaks to you more? A fairy throuple vibe, or perhaps I could do something interesting with hockey pucks…"

"Don't forget the elves doing it on horseback option," Kye offered.

"What's a throuple?" Keely asked in her most innocent voice.

Everyone froze, silence blanketing us. And then the room erupted into laughter.

Linc dropped his head to my shoulder, covering his laughter with my body. "I gotta tell you, Vicious. I love your family."

I did, too. But more than that, I felt like I belonged for the first time in a while. Somehow, Linc made me feel that way.

I stood at the fence, waiting as my favorite mare made her way over. Sunny was just what her name suggested, a ray of sun in animal form. She'd been born on the ranch not long after I arrived. She'd help you round up cattle or take you on the gentlest trail ride, whatever you wanted, as long as you asked nicely. And she was the one who'd taught me about horses.

Sunny moved toward me slowly, letting out a sound I was sure meant: *Where the heck have you been?* The moment she was within reach, I stretched out to stroke her face. "I'm sorry, girl. I'll make it a point to stop by more often."

I bent down and pressed my face to hers, letting our connection bleed into me. Even if tonight had gone better than I ever could've hoped, it was still a lot for me. I needed these moments of quiet to recenter. Calm.

And the horses always gave me that. Animals, in general, helped, but horses most of all. They had a wisdom you couldn't find in any other creature. An emotional astuteness that made you feel like they could see right into your soul.

"She loves you."

I turned at the sound of Ellie's voice, my mouth curving. "We've known each other since she was born."

Ellie moved to the fence line with the same grace she'd had when she arrived at Cope's. She wore a sundress with elaborate stitching, half a dozen gold necklaces around her neck, and delicate gold sandals. But her hair was tied into a messy bun atop her head, and I saw a smudge of dirt on her shoulder from the after-dinner game of hide-and-seek Keely had talked her into.

Ellie was artful beauty and I-don't-give-a-damn authenticity. It was a mixture completely unique to her, and I admired the hell out of it.

She slowly lifted a hand, offering it to Sunny. The mare sniffed one, twice, and then leaned into Ellie's touch. Ellie stroked the horse's face, reading each reaction to see what the creature liked and didn't.

"You're good with them. Some people come on too strong. But you wait for them to come to you."

Ellie's mouth curved slightly. "Maybe I was a cowgirl in another life."

I studied her for a moment. "Why can't you be one in this life?"

Ellie went quiet as if some battle was playing out inside her. "Do you ever feel like your life has been laid out in front of you, and there are no moves left to play?"

My muscles stiffened, tightening around every bone in my body. "There are *always* moves left to play."

Ellie kept her gaze locked on Sunny, continuing to stroke. "Not for me, there's not."

The grief of that hit me square in the chest, and I could see what Linc was terrified of now. He worried this bright light would be dimmed—or worse, snuffed out entirely. "If you think there are no moves left, then topple the damn board. Start fresh."

Ellie's eyes lifted, her gaze finally meeting mine, a sad smile lining her lips. "Just that easy, huh?"

"Just that easy."

She shifted and glanced up at the farmhouse. "It's nice that you have this. Linc and me, our family, it was never even close to this."

That twisting sensation intensified. "Sometimes, having the hard, painful, and the lack makes us appreciate when we find the good. It allows us to value it. To hold on and never let go."

Ellie's eyes misted. "I'm glad you found that."

I reached out and squeezed her hand. "You'll find it, too. You just have to step into the darkness."

Her throat worked as she swallowed. "I don't know if I'm brave enough for that."

"Maybe not today. But one day, you will be. You just need to keep trying until you're ready."

Ellie nodded, then looked out at all the horses. "One day."

I glanced back up at the house, and that's when I saw him standing in the shadows of the darkened evening, watching. Worry and pain swirled in those hypnotic eyes. And I knew Linc was battling those demons tonight.

CHAPTER TWENTY-FOUR

Lincoln

I KICKED BACK IN ONE OF THE CHAIRS ON COPE'S BACK PATIO AND stared into the night as if it held all the answers to my problems. And maybe it did if I stared long and hard enough. If not, that's why I had bourbon.

My fingers curved around the glass as if it could reassure me. I lifted it, tipping back a sip and letting the flavors of plum and cinnamon play on my tongue. The heat tracked down my throat, warming me from the inside. And that was a good thing, given the cold set in once the sun sank behind the mountains.

But the cold helped, too. It numbed the edges. Just not enough. And the bourbon wouldn't either, not even if I downed the whole bottle.

I didn't hear her until she lowered herself into the chair next to mine. Brutus instantly sat at her feet as she switched off a small flashlight. The moon was almost full, casting Arden in a glow that any artist would kill to paint. She eased into the chair, pulling her knees up and curling her body. "Whatcha got there?"

She voiced the words without looking, simply staring out at the horizon.

I wanted to chide her for walking over here in the dark, even with Brutus and her training, but I couldn't stop staring. I took in how the moonlight danced across the apples of her cheeks, revealing the scattering of tiny freckles there and the way her body curved like a goddamn sculpture, one I wanted to trace with my fingers and tongue.

Fuck.

"Bourbon," I rasped.

Arden's gaze came to me then, a small smile playing on her lips. "Didn't take you for a bourbon drinker."

"What'd you think was my drink?" I was suddenly curious what she would peg me with. But I was curious about everything she thought. Every wild thing that swirled in her beautiful mind.

Her smile widened a fraction. "I don't know. Champagne? Some ridiculously expensive scotch?"

I took a sip, letting the flavors swirl and heat again, then set the glass on the arm of my chair. "If it makes you feel any better, this is ridiculously expensive Kentucky bourbon."

Arden laughed, the sound wrapping around me and digging in. "It's a comfort to know I'm right about some things."

She reached over and took the glass. Lifting it to her lips, she tipped it back. The sip wasn't small, but she wasn't shooting it either. She wanted to experience everything the bourbon had to offer. I could admire that approach.

I watched as she swallowed, her throat working on the action. A hint of wetness remained on her lips as she pulled the glass away. I'd never been jealous of an inanimate object before, but damn, I was jealous of the bourbon in that moment.

She set the glass back on the arm of my chair. "So, you want to tell me why you're glaring into the dark?"

I didn't look away from her, couldn't if I tried. "Only if you tell me why you went looking for me there."

Arden stared back at me for a long moment as if she could read every thought in my head. "Saw shadows in your eyes tonight. Ones I recognized. Didn't want you to be alone with those demons—at least not if you didn't want to be."

God, she was a kick to the solar plexus. Her brash honesty. Her authenticity. Her kindness. "You were right earlier. I'm worried Ellie will end up like my mom."

Just saying the words out loud was both freeing and agonizing. Because once they were out there, it was as if there was more of a chance of them coming true.

Arden shifted, her whole body turning to face mine. "Does she know what your mom went through? What your dad put her through?"

Right to the heart of the matter. Always picking up on the most important details.

My fingers curled around the rocks glass. "No."

Arden's mouth thinned. "Why not?"

I'd thought about it more times than I could count. It might fix some things, but it would break far more. "She was so young when it happened. Too young to really remember a lot of the bad times."

"Are you sure about that?" Arden asked.

I braced, my fingers tightening around the glass. "What do you mean?"

She shifted slightly and glanced up at the main house as if looking for Ellie, checking if it was okay for her to share. But there was nothing but moonlight. "We talked a little tonight. She seemed to know that her family life growing up—and now—were lacking."

An invisible fist ground into my sternum. I'd worked so hard to protect Ellie and give her a safe place to run to whenever she needed. "It wasn't enough."

Arden's brow furrowed. "What wasn't?"

"Me." The pain of that one word was almost too much to take.

Pain swept through Arden's eyes, but quick on its heels was heat. "That's bullshit."

"Excuse me?"

"You heard me. That's bullshit. It takes two seconds of seeing you two together to know you're her safe place to land. She feels safe with you."

"Then why the hell won't she stay? She's going back to New York tomorrow. Back to that dick weasel, Bradley, and our dad."

Arden's lips twitched. "I'm sorry, did you just say *dick weasel*?"

"Maybe I should ask Lolli for *that* painting," I muttered.

Arden choked on a laugh. "That would be a sight."

We were quiet for a moment, but neither of us looked away. And there was comfort in the simple connection, the contact of it.

"I've looked after her my whole life. It kills me that I can't protect her now. Shield her," I said, the words quiet in the night air.

Arden's face softened. "You've been more father than brother."

"Maybe."

"But at some point, you have to let her fly. Test her wings. She's stronger than you think. She'll figure it out."

I knew Arden was right. Knew I couldn't make these decisions for Ellie. She had to find the path herself. But I worried about the wolves lining it. Ones who could twist her life into something unrecognizable.

"I just keep seeing my mom's accident over and over in my head," I admitted.

Arden hugged her knees to her chest. "I know that feeling. It's like you can't escape it, no matter what you do."

I lifted my chin in agreement. "Ran ten miles in Cope's gym tonight. Didn't even touch it."

"Do you think telling Ellie might help?" she asked softly. "This is a lot to hold on your own. A lot to pretend you don't know. Holding it in is eating you alive. I saw that when you were sparring in Kye's gym."

My back teeth ground together, annoyance and frustration swirling. Because she was right. I knew it was eating me alive. This infectious secret tainted everything around me. But giving voice to it felt like I'd be blowing Ellie's world sky-high.

"I'm scared of the dark," Arden said suddenly.

I blinked a few times, pulling those pieces together, understanding why that was. Being locked in a hidden closet while watching your mom slip away right in front of your eyes and being powerless to help her, feeling the terror that you were going to die along with her... That would cement fear in anyone. Now I knew why there were lights everywhere in Arden's orbit. Night-lights. Automatic lights outside her house and workshop. Flashlights in the junk drawer in her kitchen.

"But here's the thing about the dark. It's only scary until you turn on the light." She pulled a set of keys from her pocket and flipped on what was a surprisingly bright mini flashlight.

She flipped the beam off but didn't look away from me. "Pull everything out into the light. Maybe it'll feel like less to hold if you trust Ellie to carry it with you."

Arden pushed to her feet but didn't retreat like I expected her to. Instead, she moved deep into my space, walking right up to my chair, her legs bracketing mine. She placed her hands on the arms of the chair and bent. All I could do was watch and wait as my fingers itched to grab her. To pull her onto my lap or take her against the chair. All I knew was that I wanted to drown in Arden.

Her hair tumbled around us, the strands teasing my chest. I smelled cherries and the promise of all that was *her*. I didn't breathe, didn't move. Wouldn't risk a damn thing until I knew which way she'd tip.

Her lips pressed to the corner of my mouth in a featherlight touch. It was the barest contact, yet my body went wired. Every nerve ending stood at attention, yearning for more of the drug that was Arden.

She straightened slowly, her eyes never leaving mine. It was as if I was losing her and getting it all at the very same time. Pleasure and pain warred with each other, just like in her painting.

"You're not alone. Not if you don't want to be." And with that, she walked away, flashlight on and Brutus trailing after her.

But I was still frozen to the spot. Gripped by a touch that was barely a kiss. My tongue flicked over the place where Arden's lips had been, needing more of everything that was her. A groan slipped free. That taste: sunshine, bourbon, and cherries on the darkest night.

Arden might've told me to turn on the lights, but she didn't know that she'd already done that for me with her presence alone.

CHAPTER TWENTY-FIVE

Arden

ANGRY VOICES SCREAMED FROM THE SPEAKERS, SO LOUD I could hear them above my blowtorch. But more than that, I could *feel* them. And I needed that. It was as if the music and art were outlets for feelings I wasn't ready to process.

Feelings that were springing to life because of Linc.

And I was pissed as all hell about it. But I still wanted more. And that craving scared the crap out of me. So, I'd done what I did best. I avoided.

I took Whiskey and Stardust for long rides, locked myself in my studio, and helped Denver prep for the auction and show. If I saw Linc anywhere in my vicinity, I went the other way.

I was a chicken. And I knew it. All because of one single kiss.

Switching off the blowtorch, I stepped back and lifted my mask, studying the piece. Something about using scrap metal as both canvas and paint spoke to me, connected on a primal level. Because in many ways, entering the system had felt like I was carelessly tossed-away trash. Until the Colsons took me in and showed me what I could truly be.

The same could be said for the woman currently being cast out of the rubble. I could see the strains of the past few weeks in her. I could see notes of Ellie, Linc, and me. She was a blend of all of it.

Her head tipped back in an open-mouthed scream as a hand stretched up, reaching toward the light, trying to break free. But chains and locks held her feet, keeping her imprisoned. It wasn't a piece I could picture sitting in anyone's foyer. It was anything but peaceful.

It was haunting. Vicious. Real.

Brutus leaned against my leg, and my hand dropped to scratch his head. I set the blowtorch down and reached for my phone, switching off the music. My ears rang from the echoes of the angry melodies, and I winced at the countless unread texts on the screen.

I tapped on our sibling group chat, noticing it had a new name today. *Look What the Stork Dragged In.* I snorted as I scanned the messages.

> **Cope:** *Has anyone checked to make sure Linc hasn't burned down my house?*

> **Fallon:** *I heard he did some redecorating. Glitter pink walls all the way.*

She dropped a glitter explosion GIF.

> **Trace:** *Don't talk about glitter. I'm still scarred from the glitter bomb you detonated in my truck.*

> **Fallon:** *Sorry, broski. But honestly, ancient history, right?*

> **Trace:** *Not when I'm reminded of it every time Keely wants to do an art project.*

> **Kye:** *Pretty sure I saw pink glitter in your hair when we sparred this morning.*

> **Rhodes:** *I think pink glitter could be a good look for you, Trace.*

> **Shep:** *Pretty sure he's got pink glitter polish on his toes right now.*

> **Trace:** *I told you that in confidence. Remember this when my deputies write you that next speeding ticket.*

Shep: *It's only Cope who has to worry about speeding. Maybe Arden. I play by the rules.*

Cope: *Hey, don't throw me under the bus. I'm reformed. Precious cargo and all.*

Cope sent a photo of Luca in a Seattle Sparks jersey, holding a puck signed by a couple of players.

Rhodes: *Watch your back, Copey. Luca's coming for your spot on the team.*

A mixture of feelings swirled inside me, each one battling for supremacy. Happiness for Cope and what he'd found. Longing for it for myself. And a hollowness, knowing it would never be mine.

Cope: *He's got what it takes. Hey, Arden. Proof of life, please.*

I shook off the haze of emotions, doing my best to sock them away until I could bleed them into my art again. I sent a quick selfie of me sticking out my tongue, mask still flipped up.

Me: *Some of us work for a living. We can't be attached to our phones 24/7.*

Kye: *Burn, A. That wasn't very nice.*

Me: *Says the guy who put a massive fake spider in Shep's gym bag the other week.*

Kye: *He ratted me out about missing family dinner to hit the bar with the guys.*

Shep: *I didn't know you told Mom you were working. If you're going to lie to one, lie to all.*

Kye: *At least I didn't miss last week. Lolli hitting on Linc is going down as a favorite family moment.*

Rhodes: *What do you think she's diamond painting him right now?*

Fallon: *I got a little peek the other day, and it might be her best work yet.*

Kye: *I hope it's elves fucking again. Always a classic.*

Cope: *Jesus. I can't believe he's still there after all of this.*

Something about that text had pressure mounting in my chest. Linc's time here was temporary. He'd get the house going and then head back to Seattle, only coming here on holidays or the odd weekend. I hated the idea that I wouldn't be running into him at Haven, around the property, or in town. I'd been doing nothing but avoiding him for the past week, but I couldn't stand the thought of him going.

Cope: *How's he seem, Arden? I know Ellie came to visit.*

This felt like a test. Did he know I'd kissed his best friend? That I was still dreaming of the taste of bourbon on his lips and the scent of cedar swirling around him?

Me: *He's fine.*

Cope: *Please, stop. Too much text to read. I'll never get through it all.*

I sent him a middle finger emoji before anything else.

Me: *I haven't seen him much lately. But your house is still standing.*

All of that was true. But it still felt like a giant lie.

Fallon: *Surprising you haven't seen him. You two seemed pretty tight at dinner last week.*

Rhodes: *Agreed. Lolli might've slipped and said she saw you two more than a little…close.*

Texts came through in rapid-fire succession.

Cope: *What does she mean, close?*

Shep: *Is he hitting on you?*

Trace: *I can get you a restraining order.*

Kye: *Get yourself some, Little Killer!*

The fact that I knew Trace was only half-kidding had me groaning and my fingers flying across the screen.

> **Me:** *Retract all claws and weapons please. My virtue is safe. You know Lolli sees sex everywhere.*

> **Shep:** *Even in gourds. I'm reminded every time I walk into the greenhouse and see that damned diamond painting.*

That had me stifling a giggle. Poor, by-the-book Shep having a penis gourd painting in his and Thea's greenhouse brought me more joy than it should've.

> **Cope:** *Just tell me if you need me to have a word.*

> **Me:** *Perfectly capable of speaking for myself.*

> **Kye:** *And wielding knives.*

True enough.

Glancing at the time in the upper left-hand corner of my phone, I cursed. I was going to be late if I didn't move. Locking the device, I shoved it into the pocket of my shorts and quickly put away my supplies.

"Want to go to town?" I asked Brutus.

His tail thumped enthusiastically.

"I'm taking that as a yes."

I grabbed my keys and headed for the door. Yanking it open, I came up short at the massive man filling the space, hand raised to knock. Linc's green-gold eyes stared down at me, a wariness there that had my stomach churning.

"Hey," I greeted lamely.

He didn't waste time or mince words. "You're avoiding me."

I stepped out onto the front stoop, trying to avoid Linc's broad body. "Just been busy."

"Bullshit."

I winced. If I'd called bullshit on him, it was only fair that he call it on me. I licked my lips; they suddenly felt like they were as dry as a desert. "I'm on a new project. Got the show. Things at The Collective. Family stuff."

Linc just stared down at me, but then a gentleness slid into his expression, one that slayed me in the worst way. Because even though I'd been avoiding him, it was as if he understood. "Arden. Why are you avoiding me?"

The use of my name was worse. The way his tongue curled around the syllables. How he used my actual name instead of some silly nickname. The vulnerable honesty of the question.

"I'm scared." The two words were out before I could stop them—accidental vulnerability.

Linc's gaze only softened further; the deep green swirling with lighter flecks caught in the sunlight. "Talk to me."

My mouth went dry, words lodging in my throat. I didn't know how to explain. But I'd try. He deserved that. "I'm not good at this stuff. Emotions. Relationships. I can't even tell my family I love them without all but having a panic attack."

He was quiet for a moment, seemingly taking that in. Then he shifted and moved closer, his large form towering over me. But his hand moved slowly, giving me every chance to back away or stop him.

But I didn't.

Linc's thumb skated along my jawline until his fingers tangled in my hair. "I know a little something about that. The urge to lock everyone out because you know what it's like to lose the people you love most."

"But you don't. I've seen you. It's as easy as breathing for you. With Ellie. With Cope."

"It's a choice," he said, fingers tightening in my hair. "It doesn't mean it doesn't scare the shit out of me at times. You saw me the other night. If I'd shut Ellie out, maybe it wouldn't hurt so much to worry about her."

Everything twisted inside me, knotting and tangling because I knew he was right. My eyes burned. "I keep messing it up."

Linc's thumb stroked across my cheek. "You're doing just fine."

I battled the tears that wanted to fall, but I knew if they started, they'd never stop. "I hurt you. And you're the last person I want to do that to. Sometimes, it feels like all I do is bring hurt and pain into people's lives. Worry."

"Arden," he whispered. "I know my worth. I can take it if you have a little freak-out. I'm still gonna be here. Waiting for us to fix it. And that's what we're doing. It's the only thing we can ask for. Perfection is impossible. Mending broken pieces isn't."

My fingers found a thread on my cutoff shorts, and I absently wrapped it tightly around one, the bite of discomfort helping me hold back the tears.

"You bring so much more than hurt, pain, worry." Linc reached out, gently unwinding the string from my finger. "You bring insight, understanding, kindness, and so much fire. Don't sell yourself short. It pisses me off."

I let out a choked laugh. "Sorry."

"You should be," Linc said, amusement coating his words.

He tipped my head back. "You are nothing less than miraculous, okay?"

I swallowed. "I—"

But my words were cut off as if Linc knew what I was about to say and wasn't about to let it reach the air. Instead, he stole them, swallowing them whole as he took my mouth. The kiss was both gentle and powerful, comfort and fire. A potent and surprising mix that was all Linc.

His tongue slid against mine, stroking and teasing. I leaned into it, pressing my body to his, needing the contact, the strength. I moaned into his mouth as he took.

Linc's hand moved under my ass. I ground myself into him when he lifted me, feeling him harden against me and wanting more. Wanting it all.

Brutus let out two sharp barks, and I tore my mouth from Linc's, glancing down at my pup.

"That dog," Linc ground out, still holding me to him. "He's lucky I like him because he's a fucking cockblock."

I burst out laughing, burying my face in Linc's neck.

"Love that sound. Your laughter."

I pulled back, peering into those hypnotizing eyes. "Thanks for letting me fuck up."

"Thanks for letting me call you on it," he said with a grin.

"Do you want to do something with me?" I asked, a bit of hesitancy bleeding into my voice.

"Vicious, I want to do *a lot* of things with you."

I pressed my lips together to keep from laughing. "Sorry to disappoint, Cowboy, but we won't be naked for this particular activity."

"I can get creative with our clothes on," Linc challenged.

My nipples tightened into sharp, almost painful peaks. "You're not helping me right now."

"And you think you're helping me? The fact that I can feel your heat bleeding into me, practically burning me alive, knowing how close I am to sinking into you, how close I am to knowing exactly what you feel like, taste like…" He groaned.

A shiver racked me. "Linc."

"Fuck," he muttered, setting me down. "I need some distance from you. You're more addictive than cocaine."

My lips twitched. "Sorry?"

"You should be." Linc sighed. "All right, where are we going… not naked?"

I grinned up at him. "It's a surprise. But I think you'll like it."

CHAPTER TWENTY-SIX

Arden

THE DRIVE INTO TOWN WAS QUICK, BUT I DIDN'T MISS THE occasional scowl Linc sent poor Brutus, who sat between us on the bench seat. I tried to stifle a laugh but couldn't quite get there.

"It's not funny," Linc muttered. "If you're taking me somewhere in public, I'll probably be arrested for walking around with a hard-on."

This time, my laugh wasn't stifled at all. "Sorry about that."

"You're not sorry at all," he shot back.

"No, I'm not."

"Vicious," he muttered.

I glanced over at him. "Would you wish away that kiss not to have blue balls in this moment?"

Linc's eyes flashed that brighter green. "Wouldn't wish away a single second with you, even if it meant agreeing to a lifetime of torture."

"Good."

"Blue balls, it is," Linc muttered.

Brutus turned and licked his cheek.

Linc chuckled. "A little solidarity. Finally."

"I don't know about that. Brutus hasn't had balls for a long time."

Linc covered the dog's ears. "Don't remind him. That's just cruel."

I laughed as I pulled into an empty spot a little bit down from The Collective. "Come on." I hooked Brutus's leash to his collar, and he looked up at me balefully.

"And now you add insult to injury," Linc said, shaking his head. "I'd never do this to you, B."

I rolled my eyes. "Then you'd get a ticket from Trace."

"I can afford it."

"Billionaires," I muttered, shutting the door behind me and Brutus.

As I started toward The Collective with Linc at my side, he peered down at me, confusion in his gaze. "I've already been to The Collective."

"Yes. But you haven't been to one of our art camps. They're my favorite."

The confusion melted into something else, and whatever the emotion was, there was a tenderness to it. "Thanks for letting me into your world, Vicious."

"You're welcome, Cowboy."

Brutus wagged his tail as we walked up the path to The Collective. There was a table set up in the gallery space, where I knew parents would check their kids in for the day. Behind it stood Farah with a shit-eating grin.

"Well, look what the cat dragged in. A reclusive artist and the man who looks like he needs to be climbed like a tree."

I choked on a laugh. "Farah."

She held up both hands. "I just call 'em like I see 'em. Can't be helped."

"Well, try to refrain from any tree climbing, would you?"

Farah waggled her eyebrows. "I can't make any promises."

"I swear, between you and Lolli, it's a miracle I don't have gray hair," I muttered.

Linc dipped his head to kiss my temple. "You'd look cute rockin' the grays."

"Oh, Jesus," Farah mumbled and started fanning herself. "Get outta my sight before I combust."

I laughed and led Linc down the hall. I pointed out the different studio and storage spaces as we went. We saw works in progress from Hannah, Isaiah, and Farah. And it looked like Hannah's watercolor that she'd been struggling with had found its stride.

The Collective's building formed a U shape with the gallery on one side and the storage and studio spaces in the other two. But what lay in the middle was my favorite part.

I slowed before a set of French doors, the sounds of voices and laughter on the other side filtering around me. I glanced up at Linc. "Welcome to one of my favorite places."

Opening the doors, I gestured for Linc to pass through. I tried to take it in through his eyes. The courtyard had a magical feel to it, as if it were a land that could be home to fairies. Fig trees were scattered around, their branches wrapped in lights. And the entire space was oriented with the best views of the mountains.

But there currently wasn't a whole lot of peace to be found in the space. A little girl screeched as she leapt over one of the planters teeming with flowers. A little boy held up a paintbrush like he was about to duel with someone. Half a dozen miniature tables covered in art supplies had been set up.

"Who knew this was hidden away back here?" Linc said, taking it all in.

"We can open some doors in the gallery for events. It makes for a nice spot for cocktails and hors d'oeuvres."

He arched an eyebrow. "And are you one for cocktails and hors d'oeuvres?"

I made a face. Stuffy parties were not my thing. "Sacrifices must be made for a good cause."

Linc's gaze roamed over my face, taking me in. The movement felt like his fingertips were grazing the skin, making every nerve ending stand at attention. "Let me guess. Never for personal gain but always willing to fall on your sword for the kids."

One of said kids let out a battle cry as if to punctuate Linc's point.

The corner of my mouth kicked up, and I shrugged. "They're worth it."

"They are. But there's more."

Of course, Linc would see that there was a deeper motivation for me, a clawing need to give to others what had been given to me. "I didn't talk when I came to live with the Colsons."

Pain streaked across Linc's expression. I tried not to let it land— the fact that he cared so deeply about my agony—and pushed on. "I was scared all the time. So sure those men would find me again. Kill me this time."

"Arden," Linc rasped.

"But things changed. It was gradual and a multi-person effort, but it all started with paint and Lolli."

A little of the sadness and pain lifted from Linc's eyes. "I hope she wasn't doing dick art with you when you were twelve."

I choked on a laugh. "No. She was in her oils and landscape phase then and would set up two easels for us in the backyard every day. She'd talk some but never expected me to answer. She taught me the basics and told me to let out whatever I needed to."

A muscle fluttered along Linc's jaw. "It's how you started letting out the darkness."

I nodded. "There were other things, too. Nora taught me about horses, and I discovered their healing powers. When Kye came to live with us, he taught me how to protect myself and feel strong. And slowly but surely, I found my way through. It wasn't back to the girl I'd been because she was gone, but I'd become someone better. Someone more real."

Linc moved in then, crowding me. His fingers slid into my hair and tipped my head back. "So fucking strong."

"Because others helped me find that strength, the healing. I want to make sure I give that outlet to anyone who needs it."

"You're killing me, Vicious." Linc's head dipped, his lips brushing mine with a featherlight touch.

Then, a tiny but very angry voice broke into my Linc-haze. "*Why are you kissing my girlfriend, mister?*"

CHAPTER TWENTY-SEVEN

Lincoln

I PULLED BACK FROM ARDEN, THE TASTE OF CHERRIES STILL clinging to my lips and stared down at the little boy. He looked about seven or eight, but his stance was decades older. He had his arms crossed over his tiny chest and glared at me.

"Your girlfriend, huh?" I asked.

"Yes," he huffed. "Miss Arden has my painting on her fridge, and I let her have half my cookies at lunch break."

I glanced at Arden as she pressed her lips together to keep from laughing. "Painting and cookies? That sounds serious. More than I can compete with," I said.

The boy let out something that sounded almost like a *harumph* an elderly man would make in a cartoon as he pinned me with a warning stare. "You should remember that. I'll be watching you." He stalked away.

I couldn't help it, I laughed. "You didn't tell me you were already involved."

Arden let out a laugh that was more giggle than anything, and something about the lightness of it eased some of the weight of our earlier conversation. "I'm sorry. Would you believe it slipped my mind?"

"Vicious. Now, I need to start working on a painting and find some damn cookies," I muttered. "It's hard to keep up."

Arden laughed harder.

"You got the smackdown from Benny, didn't you?" Isaiah asked as he strode up, his eyes dancing with humor.

"Oh, I'm dead in the water."

Isaiah barked out a laugh. "He kicked my a—" Isaiah glanced around. "My, uh, butt for bringing Ardy coffee one day."

Arden rolled her lips over her teeth, trying to stifle her remaining laughter. "What can I say? I've got high standards."

Isaiah shook his head. "Heartbreaker. Just leaving a trail of trampled shards in your wake."

"Hey," Arden argued.

"I don't doubt he's right, baby," I said. "You have no idea of your power."

"She really doesn't," Isaiah said, shaking his head.

Arden's cheeks reddened as she glared at Isaiah. "Don't you have something important to do?"

He just grinned at her and then clapped me on the shoulder. "Yeah. I gotta put your boyfriend through his paces."

Boyfriend. The term was ridiculous for a thirty-seven-year-old man, but I couldn't deny that I got a surge of pleasure from any link to Arden. Any claim. Because the truth was, I'd do anything to be hers.

I sat at the ridiculously tiny table, my knees coming up so high they were practically at my ears. It was a miracle the minuscule chair I sat on hadn't simply given way under my weight, but the three kids at my table had no such issues.

The little girl to my left had brown hair and freckles, her lip tugged between her teeth as she went after her paper with a gusto I admired.

There was no hesitancy in her at all, no second-guessing. Isabella was ready for whatever came her way; no challenge was too big.

To my right was a girl named Gracie. She was much more timid. Her dark hair hung in a way that mostly hid her face from view, and each brushstroke she made was thoughtful and deliberate. Her worn clothes and shoes made my heart clench. Suddenly, I knew I'd be asking Arden if there was anything I could do to help.

There was nothing timid about the energy coming at me from across the table. Benny glared at me with a hatred fueled by a thousand blazing suns. He only moved it away to paint little pieces of his creation at a time.

I studied my piece. The assignment had been to paint something that made us happy. I'd wanted to paint Arden, but I didn't think ole Benny would be too happy about that. Plus, my art skills were fairly limited. So, I'd gone with a simple landscape: the view from the plot of land that had officially become mine two days ago.

I leaned slightly to my right and peeked at Gracie's paper. "That's so pretty."

Her head lifted for the barest moment, just long enough for her to give me a hint of amber eyes before it ducked again. "Thank you," she whispered.

That invisible fist ground against my sternum again as I studied the picture. It was of three people in front of a Ferris wheel. "Is that your mom?" I asked, pointing to the tallest figure.

Gracie shook her head. "That's Hay Hay. My sister."

"And who's this?" I asked, pointing at the second tallest.

"My other sister. Mom doesn't like the fair."

Something about that set me on edge. I got that fairs and carnivals might not be someone's thing, but you sucked it up and did it anyway if your kids loved them. Memories of escapes to Coney Island with Ellie and our mom swirled in the back of my mind in smoky tendrils I couldn't quite grab hold of.

"Looks like you had fun," I said softly.

Gracie's head lifted again. This time, I got a smile. It was brief but dazzling. "It was my best day."

"I love best days."

Benny made a sound of protest opposite me.

I turned my focus to him. "What's your painting of?"

He grinned, and there was a cocky air to it, even at age seven or eight. He held up a portrait of a woman with dark hair and purple eyes. "Miss Arden. She makes me happy."

That little shit was one-upping me.

Benny's grin only widened in challenge. "What's yours?"

I help up my landscape. "The mountains."

Benny's face screwed up. "Mountains make you happy? Dumb."

"Benny," Arden's voice cut in, a sternness to it I hadn't heard before. "We don't talk to others that way. What's our motto around here?"

Benny ducked his head, his cheeks flushing. "Everyone's art is beautiful. Everyone has their own path."

"That's right." She patted his shoulder. "And yours looks awesome."

Any embarrassment disappeared as he lifted it to her. "It's you."

I swore Arden melted. *Dang that kid for stealing my moves.* "I think that's the sweetest thing anyone's done for me."

My gaze cut to her. "Better than cheeseburgers when you haven't eaten all day?"

Arden choked on a laugh. "Just a little."

Benny sent me a smirk and mouthed *sucker*.

I pushed to my feet, stretching as Arden encouraged each tiny artist, giving them pointers as she made the rounds. When she got to me, she stopped and glanced into my eyes. "Let's see what you've got, Mr. Pierce."

Fuck.

My dick twitched, and now was so not the time. I thought about the disgusting smell of a hockey locker room after a game, sweaty gym socks, anything but Arden's sultry voice calling me Mr. Pierce.

I snatched up my painting and handed it to her, waiting for her assessment.

"He needs to work on his shading," Benny said from across the table.

Arden looked up at me, her eyes dancing with mirth.

"Everyone's a critic," I muttered.

"He's not wrong," she said, pointing to an area of the mountains. "If you add some shadow here, the mountains will look more three-dimensional."

I leaned in closer as I took the painting back. "I'll work on it, Miss Waverly."

Arden's lips parted on a sharp inhale, those berry-stained pillows just crying out for a kiss.

"What about mine, Miss Arden?" Isabella demanded, thrusting her paper out. "It's fireworks."

The painting was like the kid: wild and full of color. The paint was layered on so thick the paper had wrinkled and curved in places.

"Izzy," Arden said, grinning at her. "I love it! I think it's your best one yet."

"Yes!" Isabella did a little boogie in her chair, fists and painting raised.

"Show-off," Benny muttered under his breath.

Isabella's gaze narrowed on him. "Just because Miss Arden got a new boyfriend doesn't mean you get to be all grumpy."

"She didn't," Benny yelled.

I might not have kids, but hockey players were kind of like overgrown toddlers at times, so I knew the start of a brawl when I saw one. I went for redirection. "Who can help me make my mountains not suck?"

All three pairs of eyes came to me, their tiny jaws dropping.

I winced, glancing at Arden. "Is suck a bad word now?"

She struggled not to laugh. "It's borderline. But we don't talk about our work that way. Right, guys?"

"Right," Benny said quickly.

"Mm-hmm," Isabella agreed.

Gracie just nodded.

"But it's always okay to ask for help, right?" Arden pressed.

Another round of agreement.

"Who can help Mr. Linc?" she asked.

Everyone volunteered. Even Benny.

As I eased back in the chair that would likely leave me permanently injured, all three mini artists dove in with suggestions. But my gaze followed Arden as she wove between the tables. She had a way with the kids. The crowd of tiny humans didn't seem to faze her. It was the adults she was wary of.

Denver strode out of the gallery doors, crossing the space and heading straight for Arden. My teeth clamped down, and annoyance rose. I didn't like him. It wasn't altogether logical, but the man irritated me. Likely because of how he looked at her.

There was an attraction for sure, but it was more. He appraised her like a blank check, just waiting to be signed.

He bent and whispered in her ear. Arden's expression turned hard as she shook her head.

"Mr. Linc," Isabella prodded. "Are you paying attention?"

I was not.

"Sorry, Isabella," I said, trying to refocus.

Benny glanced over his shoulder and scowled. "I don't like him either."

Suddenly, I was united with my little nemesis.

"He looks at Miss Arden wrong," Gracie whispered, darting a glance at Denver before turning back.

The quiet ones usually saw more, and Gracie was definitely that. But the fact that she could pin down the wrongness made me edgy.

My annoyance burned brighter as someone new entered the courtyard. Quentin Arison, the douchebag from last week. He strode directly toward Arden, looking ridiculous in his tailored suit and dress shoes when it was over eighty degrees outside. His over-the-top watch peeked out from under his sleeve, and the diamond ring on his pinky finger was absurd.

"I *really* don't like him," I muttered, pushing back my chair and stalking toward the douchebag.

CHAPTER TWENTY-EIGHT

Arden

I WASN'T SURE WHO TO GIVE MY BEST BENNY GLARE TO, DENVER or Quentin. Quentin was a douchebag for sure, but it was Denver who kept allowing him into my space.

"Arden," Quentin practically cooed. "It's so kind of you to spend your time teaching these…little ones." He said *little ones* as if it tasted bad. "But shouldn't you be focusing on your work?"

My annoyance shifted into anger territory. "You say that as if you have any say in how I spend my time."

Denver started coughing, his face flaming. "Arden," he hissed.

I sent him a scathing look that had him shutting his trap immediately.

Quentin simply laughed. "Such fire. Would be interesting to find out what it takes to break that spirit."

I gaped at the man opposite me. He hadn't seriously said that, had he?

"You know what I think would be interesting," a low voice said behind me. It was a voice I recognized, but it was completely devoid of emotion.

Quentin's gaze flicked up to Linc's. "What's that, Mr. Pierce?"

He'd obviously done his homework on Linc—and likely me. That made me uneasy. More than that. It freaked me the hell out.

Linc moved so he stood beside me, his arm pressing against mine, telling me he was there without suggesting I needed his protection. "I think it would be interesting to find out just how quickly I could snap your arm in two. Perhaps break a finger or three."

Quentin chuckled, but there was no humor in the sound. "You know, Mr. Pierce, I heard that someone's trying to dismantle your empire. I don't think you need another enemy."

I stiffened. *What the hell did that mean?*

But before I could say anything, three tiny figures stomped into our circle. Benny was first, crossing his arms and glaring up at Quentin and Denver. Izzy was next, her little fists balled as she scowled at them. And finally, Gracie. She was nervous but didn't let it stop her, and I admired that most of all. Brutus followed behind, baring his teeth at Quentin.

"You make Miss Arden mad. Leave," Benny demanded.

Linc chuckled next to me, and Benny turned slightly at the sound. Linc held out a fist. "My man."

Benny gave him a knuckle bump.

"This camp has a no-meanies-allowed rule, and you're meanies," Isabella informed them.

It was my turn to start coughing as I tried not to laugh.

A hardness settled into Quentin's eyes, one I didn't like one bit. "Clearly, your parents have neglected to teach you manners."

"You mean yours didn't," Benny shot back. The kid had a point.

Quentin's gaze flicked to me. "I'm going inside to make a bidding strategy. I can't wait to have your pieces in my home, Arden."

Nausea swelled. Him owning my art felt like him owning a piece of me. And that was almost more than I could take.

Quentin turned and strode inside. Denver turned to me, and I saw the anger stewing below his normally placid expression. "We'll talk about this later."

Fire surged, and I knew my eyes blazed as I glared at him. "You'd better believe we will."

Then Denver went hurrying after his meal ticket. My nausea intensified. Because as much as it sucked that Quentin was here and being creepy, it sucked more that Denver was throwing me to the wolves.

A hand curved around my elbow, a gentle reminder that I wasn't alone. "You okay?"

I sighed and looked up at Linc. "I don't want that creep to have my art in his house."

A muscle in his jaw fluttered. "Understandable."

"And I think I'm going to have to fire my friend."

Linc's expression softened. "Is he really your friend if he'd put you in that sort of situation?"

That was a good question.

Tiny arms went around my waist, and I looked down to find Gracie hugging me. "I'm sorry, Miss Arden. But it's good you have Mr. Linc to protect you. He's real big."

One corner of my mouth kicked up. "I am lucky, aren't I?"

Benny sighed. "I guess he's okay."

Linc grinned at the little boy. "Does that mean we're besties now?"

"Too far," Benny grumbled, stalking away.

Isabella smiled at Linc. "Don't worry. Sometimes, he just needs a snack. He'll get over it."

Linc glanced at me. "Get that boy some cookies before I end up with a shiv in my spine."

I burst out laughing, and Brutus barked happily at the sound. "Cookies, it is."

Everything hurt. I swore even my hair felt a little abused. And I was in shape. I trained with Kye weekly. I rode my horses almost daily.

And my work was physical on top of it. Yet there was nothing like an entire day wrangling tiny kiddos.

Hands landed on my shoulders as I stretched, kneading the knots there. "You okay?" Linc asked.

"I will be if you keep doing that forever," I mumbled.

"I could be convinced."

"I'm not above a little sexual coercion."

He chuckled. "Good to know."

"It's exhausting, isn't it?" I asked, looking around at the destruction left in the kids' wake. Hannah, Isaiah, and Farah were getting them off to their parents while Linc and I were handling clean-up duties.

"I think this has convinced me I don't want six kids. I think three is good."

I whirled, gaping at him. "You want six kids?"

"Want*ed*," he corrected. "I'm good with three now." He paused for a moment. "What about you? You want kids?"

My palms instantly started to sweat as my heart rate picked up. "I'm not sure," I croaked.

Linc studied me in that assessing way of his, the kind of look that peeled back the layers in search of understanding. "Not sure or scared?"

My fingers went in search of something—anything—to hold on to. They found one of the threads on my favorite jeans and began to twirl it. "Why do you have to see so much?"

He shrugged. "I pay attention to the things that are important. And you're important."

I pulled the string tighter, cutting off the blood flow to my pointer finger. "I don't know if I'd be good at it. I can't even tell my family I love them. I freak out about weird things. I don't know if it's fair to saddle a kid with that."

But it didn't change the fact that I wanted it. I wanted a chance to do things differently than my parents had, to focus on the *right* things, and make sure my kids knew that happiness didn't come from having *more* but from the people you surrounded yourself with.

Linc reached out, taking my hand and unwrapping my finger.

"I watched you today. You have a gift when it comes to children. You reach them. You make them feel seen. If you decide you want to have some one day, they'll be the luckiest kids in the world because you're their mom."

My throat constricted, a burning sensation surging. "Thank you." The words were barely audible, but they were there.

A throat cleared.

I jerked at the intrusion into such a private moment. When my gaze found the reporter hovering in the courtyard, my annoyance doubled.

"Yes, Mr. Levine?" I clipped.

He didn't seem put off by my tone. "You've been avoiding me."

He wasn't wrong, but that was my prerogative. "I told you I don't do press."

Sam's eyes narrowed. "You said you'd go on background."

"No, I said you could hang around if I was on background. There's a difference."

He huffed out a breath. "This article won't be half as good without your involvement."

I shrugged. "Oh, well."

"You'd chance fewer donations because you're shy?" Sam challenged.

I barked out a laugh. "Mr. Levine, I'm a lot of things. Shy isn't one of them."

That had him assessing me with new eyes, and I almost cursed. This was why I didn't like having reporters around. There was always the chance that I'd slip up, and they'd see something they shouldn't.

"I think Arden has made herself clear." Linc stepped in, gesturing Sam back toward the doors that led to the gallery.

"Crystal," Sam said, the single word tight as he sent Linc an annoyed look. "I know the way."

I sighed as he stalked away. "What is it with grown men having tantrums today?"

Linc wrapped his arms around me. "I don't know, but I think I'm on that list, too."

"You?" I asked, tipping my head back.

"Vicious, you've ruined me. I think I was jealous of a seven-year-old today."

A laugh bubbled out of me. "I promise you don't have to worry about Benny."

"Losing it over you," Linc whispered.

I stared up at him, taking that in. Knowing I wasn't alone helped somehow. "I feel the same way. You freak me out, Lincoln Pierce."

He grinned down at me. "I'm taking that as a compliment."

I rolled my eyes. "You would."

He patted my butt. "Come on. Let's clean up and get out of here. Otherwise, I'm pretty sure I'm going to deck the next person who's rude to you, and I don't need to get sued."

My lips twitched. "Fair enough."

We got to work restoring the courtyard to its original glory. It took us over an hour, but doing it together made it fun. By the time we made it to my truck with Brutus in tow, we were both starving. We decided to go for more burgers, and after a pit stop at The Pop, we headed home.

I tried not to let it freak me out that it felt more like home with Linc there. As if he had some sort of grounding force. I shoved all those feelings down and punched in the gate code to Cope's property before heading toward the guesthouse. "I need to check one thing in my studio."

It was a lie. I just needed a minute to catch my breath and still my rapidly beating heart.

"Sure," Linc said easily. "I can get dinner set up."

It was so normal. So not me.

"Okay," I said. "The code's the same." I didn't want to look too closely at the fact that I hadn't changed it after the night he'd stayed on my couch, or that I felt comfortable with him having it.

I pulled to a stop between the house and the workshop. Linc slid out and whistled to Brutus. "You wanna come with me, boy? I've got your burger."

Brutus looked between us, and I smiled at him. "Go on."

I watched as they headed for my house. They fit, the two of them. And they were clearly fond of each other. That only made me more nervous.

It was as if I was at war with myself, wanting more yet being terrified of it.

I headed for the studio. I'd just take a second, a moment to reel it all in and stuff it away until I could paint it all out. Punching in the code, I stepped inside and flicked on the light.

I froze. Not a single breath or movement. Maybe my heart stopped, too.

And then I screamed.

CHAPTER TWENTY-NINE

Lincoln

ARDEN WAS TWITCHY. NOT IN A SKITTISH WAY, BUT IF I GOT too close, she put some distance between us. She thought I didn't know that's what she was doing, but she was wrong. Only I found it didn't bother me this time. It was honestly adorable.

Because the thing Arden didn't realize was that, even amid the push/pull of each interaction, I still ended up closer. To her scent. Her feel. Just *her*. And that was worth any price.

"Come on, Brutus," I said, punching in the lock code to the front door. "I want you to know I got you a double patty. No singles for you. Think that means you won't cockblock me next time?"

He looked up at me with eyes that said he thought I was ridiculous. He was probably right. I *was* having a full-on conversation with a dog.

A scream tore through the air like a lightning strike, hitting my ears like a bolt slamming into the ground. I was running before I could think twice. The food and drinks fell, spilling out over the front stoop.

The run to the workshop was quick, barely a couple of seconds, but it felt like a lifetime passed in those beats. A million what-ifs swirled. Countless fears.

Brutus pulled ahead, snarling, barking, and charging into the studio. A place where Arden stood frozen. I scanned her quickly, checking for injuries, but I didn't see any. Then my attention moved to the room, looking for an intruder. No one.

But that's when I saw it.

Arden's workshop had been all but destroyed. Supplies were strewn across the room, broken and smashed. Canvases had been slashed by what must have been a knife. And the metal statue Arden had been working on was toppled to the ground. Whoever had done this wasn't just angry.

They were enraged.

But it was more than that. Because beyond the destruction was the blood. Splashed on the walls, across the floor, coating her statue and the sliced canvases. And written on the far wall...

YOU CAN'T HIDE.

Fury coursed through me. It was as if whoever had done this had infected me with their rage. I moved into Arden's space and pulled her against me. My hands slid over her body, searching for reassurance—for her, for me, for us both. She trembled, and that slight movement, so unlike Arden, only stoked the fury coursing beneath my skin.

"You're okay." My voice didn't sound like mine. It was as if some robot had spoken the words.

Arden just shuddered against me in response.

Fuck.

"You're okay." I spoke the two words again like they would miraculously work this time. "Let's get you back to the house. I'll call Trace and—"

"The horses." Arden jolted, ripping herself from my arms and taking off at a run.

I cursed, quickly running after her, Brutus right by her side. We didn't have the first clue if whoever had done this was still around, getting his rocks off by watching. Or worse, waiting to strike.

"Arden," I barked. "We need to get to the house. We need cover and to call the fucking cops."

She sent me a look that should've had my skin blistering. "They are mine. They save me over and over, just like my art. I'm not leaving them alone."

Hell.

I didn't argue. I simply pulled out my phone and hit Trace's contact as I scanned the surroundings. He answered on the second ring. "Everything okay?"

"No."

"Talk," he clipped, but I could hear him already moving through the station.

"Someone trashed Arden's studio. Left behind a threatening message and a lot of blood." I didn't want to think about what that blood could be from.

"Get her somewhere safe and lock yourselves in. I'm on my way and sending units."

"That might be a problem," I muttered.

Arden rushed to the fence line, slipping between the rails and into the pasture. Her two horses moved to her instantly, and I watched as her shoulders sagged in relief at the sight of no visible injuries on the animals. She pressed her head to the gray one's as the tan nuzzled her neck.

It was only then that Arden's shoulders began to shake. She made no noise as the sobs broke free, but the force of them racked her whole body.

And I wanted to kill whoever had done this.

"Linc," Trace growled.

"She wants to stay with the horses," I said quietly.

"Of course, she does," Trace muttered as a door slammed, then sirens flared to life. "Don't leave her."

"I'm not going anywhere." The call disconnected, and I followed Arden into the pasture. But I didn't move into her huddle. I knew the creatures she was with now gave her something I couldn't. The only thing I could do was stand guard, making sure no harm came to any of them.

I scanned the forest and the buildings in an irregular pattern, over and over until Arden finally broke away from her horses. She was facing away from me, but I still saw her putting the armor back on. Her spine straightened, her shoulders squared, and she breathed deeply. Then, she turned.

Arden's eyes were red and a little glassy, but those were the only signs of her tears as sirens sounded in the distance. She crossed to me, a hardness settling into those gray-violet eyes, the gray taking over now. "If you tell anyone I cried, I'll put ex-lax in your coffee."

I wanted to smile but couldn't quite get there. "Noted. Now, come here."

Arden shook her head, wisps of deep brown hair falling free of her haphazard bun.

"Vicious," I warned.

She came then, stopping when we were toe-to-toe. I stared at her for one beat, two. Then I pulled her to me. She nuzzled in, letting me hold her, giving me what I needed: to know she was okay. Or at least that she would be.

The sirens grew louder, and a parade of sheriff's department vehicles kicked up dust. The horses whinnied and shied away from the sound, put on edge by the intrusion. I kept hold of Arden as most stopped at the workshop and guesthouse. One squad car and an SUV came toward the barn.

Trace was out of the vehicle in a flash, striding toward us with a fury I'd never seen before on his face. "Is she okay?" he barked.

Arden pulled back. "I'm fine, but my horses won't be if your deputies don't cut their sirens."

Trace sent something over the radio. Slowly but surely, all the sirens silenced.

Arden let out a long breath. "Thank you."

Trace ducked between the fence rails and moved to his sister, giving her a quick hug. "You sure you're all right?"

"Better now. Finding my mad."

One corner of Trace's mouth kicked up. "You always did do better when you found your mad."

Her lips twitched. "I find out who did this; they're likely to lose a ball."

"Just one?" I asked, a hint of humor finally bleeding into my voice.

"I'm not a monster," Arden said, brushing hair from her face.

Someone in uniform jogged toward us from the workshop. Trace's gaze tracked them instantly. The deputy, who looked a few years younger than Trace, slowed, his tan complexion a little sallow as unease slid over his features. "It's bad, boss."

"Talk to me," Trace ordered.

The deputy's gaze flicked to Arden and then back to Trace. "Never seen anyone that mad. It's like he was slaughtering her studio."

So, what did that say about what he wanted to do to Arden?

CHAPTER THIRTY

Arden

THERE WERE PEOPLE EVERYWHERE. AND MY HOUSE WASN'T exactly equipped for lots of company. I was starting to realize that maybe I'd done that by design.

And I was running out of excuses to avoid them all. I needed to change. I needed to get Brutus water. I needed to check the horses *again*.

Nora filled my vision, crouching low like I was twelve years old again. "I made some soup. Do you want some? Or maybe some tea?"

"Only if you add a strong dose of whiskey," Lolli called from the opposite side of the room as she watched the deputies combing the property. She glanced my way. "Or I brought my brownies. One or two of those, and you won't even know what day it is."

"Don't tell Trace you brought them," Fallon muttered from her spot at the kitchen island where she'd been put to work chopping vegetables for some other thing Nora was making.

Lolli turned back to the window. "I don't know. Maybe I should tell him. Wouldn't mind being cuffed by a few of those new recruits."

Kye choked on a laugh. "Please, tell Trace that. But warn me before you do. I want to get it on video."

Nora pushed to her feet and pinched the bridge of her nose. "Lolli, I really don't think this is the time—"

"This is *exactly* the time." She sent me a wink.

I appreciated her rescue attempt. Normally, I would've gotten a chuckle out of the back-and-forth, but the walls felt like they were closing in around me today. Fallon and Rhodes in the kitchen. Nora hovering. Lolli catcalling at the window. Kye's massive form taking over my armchair. The knowledge that Trace was walking a crime scene with Anson right now to get his profiler take.

It was all too much.

A loud knock sounded on the front door. Linc squeezed my knee and then stood. "I'll get it."

I was pretty sure I'd sent him a panicked look because I wanted to bolt. Too many people. Too many possibilities for what this all could mean. He sent me his best reassuring glance, but it didn't do much good.

A second later, voices rose, and someone was stomping down the hallway. Shep appeared, his Colson Construction hat still in place and jeans dusty from a jobsite. "What the hell happened?" he barked.

Linc stepped in front of him in a flash. "You need to rein it in. She's been through enough today."

A mixture of anger and respect flashed across Shep's expression, but he struggled to take a breath. Then Thea was by his side. She squeezed his arm. "Linc's right. You storming around all caveman-like isn't going to help anything."

Shep's gaze dipped to her. "Caveman-like?"

She shrugged, a small smile playing on her lips. "If the shoe fits."

He lowered his head to give her a quick kiss. "Thanks, Thorn."

My chest tightened at the tenderness, the back-and-forth, the give and take. They were so in tune with each other. But what would become of either if something happened to one of them?

The walls closed in a little more, and my breathing grew shallow. Tiny dots started dancing in front of my vision.

I shoved to my feet. "I'll be back," I mumbled, bolting for the front door.

A handful of family members called my name, and I thought I heard Linc's voice saying something. Maybe telling Brutus to stay? But the ringing in my ears was too loud to know for sure.

Tumbling outside, I tried to breathe, but people were everywhere out here, too. More pressure. No space.

I started walking, just trying to get away from everyone, everything. Someone fell into step beside me, not touching me but there. "Follow me," Linc ordered.

His voice wasn't gentle or harsh, but I heard the command in it. And that cut through the fog. My body listened on instinct. Apparently, it was an idiot. But I didn't have it in me to come up with another plan.

So, I followed.

It took me a couple of minutes to realize that Linc was leading me toward the main house. "Aren't Trace's people up here?"

Linc shook his head. "They cleared it. No one got in. Camera feeds were checked, too."

Camera feeds.

One of the things that was supposed to keep me safe. But they hadn't this time. It was as if someone had known the system. They'd climbed a spot in the fence around the property where we had fewer cameras. They'd worn a dark hoodie and jeans that made it difficult to make out any distinguishing features beyond broad shoulders. But the creepiest part had been the mask.

Whoever it was had looked straight up and into the camera with a mask that only had dark holes for eyes and a mouth. It was the sort of thing that could give a person nightmares. And that's exactly what they were trying to do.

Anger surged to the surface. Whoever this was wanted to terrorize me. And they were succeeding.

Linc plugged in the code to the front door, then opened it and ushered me inside. The moment I stepped into the cool quiet, I breathed a little deeper.

"Come on," Linc said, leading me farther into the house. He moved to the door that led to the basement. There were only two things down there: a gym and a screening room. If he thought going for a run right now would soothe me, he was dead wrong. And if he thought I could focus on a movie, he wasn't as bright as I thought he was.

"What are we doing?" I protested.

Linc didn't stop until he reached the gym. "Talking it out doesn't help you. You need to *do*. You don't have access to your art studio, and you can't go for a ride. But you can fight."

He flipped on the lights, illuminating the space. The fact that my brother was a professional athlete meant that he had a ridiculous setup in his gym. Half a dozen cardio machines, countless pieces of weight training equipment, and a whole boxing and martial arts setup.

There was a punching bag, a speed bag, a kickboxing bag, and, of course, fight mats. Linc moved toward those. I just stared after him as he slid off his shoes. Even the man's feet were hot.

Linc crossed to a cabinet with a variety of gear. Pulling out two sets of hand wraps, he tossed one to me.

"You're wearing jeans," I said dumbly. I had changed into loose shorts and a sports tank, but Linc was still in the same pants and tee he'd worn to The Collective.

"Maybe it'll give you the upper hand," he shot back, wrapping the fabric around his hands.

I scowled in his direction, but it died as he moved around the circle on the mat, loosening his muscles. My mouth went dry. Even in those simple movements, he had a grace I couldn't explain. It pulled me in and held me captive.

"Come on, Vicious. You need to let it out."

Warmth and annoyance warred within me, and over the same thing: that he understood me so well. But I started moving because I worried that I'd combust if I didn't. Was afraid I'd snap and bite someone's head off who didn't deserve it.

I quickly donned the wraps and began swinging my arms in warm-up moves that brought new blood flow into them as I kicked off my flip-flops. My thighs and calves warmed, the tension there easing. Linc slowed and moved to the center of the mat. I did the same.

As I met him there, I realized just how much bigger Linc was than me. He dwarfed me in every way. And that should've put me on edge, but my jujitsu training was the great equalizer, allowing me to use someone's size against them.

"Gonna give me all you got, Vicious?" Linc challenged.

Everything heated in a new way, the buzz of what was to come mixing with the knowledge that Linc was such a beast in the ring. I arched a brow at him. "That depends. You gonna hold back because you think I'm breakable?"

The gold in those hazel eyes flashed brighter. "Would never disrespect you in that way."

And the funny thing was, I believed him. Linc might be the only person who wouldn't hold back. My brothers, the guys at the gym, they all restrained themselves in some way. And it annoyed the hell out of me. The only thing that eased it was when I handed one of them their ass.

I lifted my hands, closing them into fists as I settled into a fighting stance. Then, I waited. Linc studied me for a moment as if checking whether I was ready. Then his knuckles bumped mine.

The tap was featherlight, and then Linc was moving again, his panther-like grace in full effect. We circled each other, and he was surprisingly light on his feet for his size. Each of us sent out a few testing jabs and the occasional kick. We were studying each other's defenses.

While we'd each watched each other spar once, that was different than being in the ring opposite someone, seeing how they moved up close, and feeling how much heat they could put behind their blows. And Linc was a beast of beauty.

He moved in with a sneaky uppercut, a punch I wouldn't have expected, given how much larger he was than me. That punch required a lower angle, one that meant he needed to get down. But Linc had it all, apparently. Quickness, power, and flexibility.

My skin tingled, a combination of the rush of the bout and feeling way the hell turned on by all that was Linc.

He sent another punch in my direction, but I didn't let this one connect. I ducked under the blow and took advantage of his open side. My fist connected with his ribs, and Linc sucked in a breath.

But I was already moving out of the retaliation strike zone. Some alpha males at the gym couldn't handle me getting in good hits, or God forbid, kicking their asses. But Linc just grinned at me, a little too widely. "Damn, Vicious. That was good."

"You look like one of those freaky clowns at a carnival. You know, the ones where you shoot out the teeth? It's creeping me out."

Linc chuckled. "Can't I appreciate good form?"

"Only from the mat," I shot back, moving in to attempt a foot sweep. There was just one problem. While I could potentially use Linc's size against him, he was too damned centered. His balance was something I'd need to study.

I only had a second to curse mentally before he flipped me onto my back. I hit the mat with a smack but rolled away before he could pin me. I was on my feet in a flash, circling away to regain my balance.

"Nice try, Vicious," he goaded.

My eyes narrowed. "You're like some Zen giant. It's annoying."

"Good," Linc shot back. "Maybe it'll annoy you enough to let go."

I saw it then. The way his moves were designed to make me snap. To release everything that was pent up inside me. And that *did* uncork the anger.

I moved without him expecting it, grabbing his wrist and twisting it behind his back. He bowed as he made a sound of protest. I expected him to fold, but he didn't. He pulled some sort of spin move, extricating himself from the hold and leveling a kick to my side.

Pain flared. Not bad but present, and it stoked the embers I'd buried beneath the coals of trying to hold it all together. I moved quicker this time, and with more power. My body tilted, hitting Linc in the shoulder with a roundhouse kick. I would've gone for the face if we'd had mouthguards and headgear.

Then again, that face was way too pretty to damage.

Linc stumbled back a few steps but quickly rallied. And then we truly began our dance. Back and forth. We were almost evenly matched but in ways completely unique to ourselves.

Sweat beaded and glided down my spine. My muscles strained in their search for more. More of what? I wasn't sure. More contact. More pain. More release.

That moment of distraction was my undoing. Linc moved in with a single-leg takedown, and my back hit the mat with enough force to steal the air from my lungs. This time, I wasn't quick enough to escape.

Linc was on top of me in the blink of an eye, his big body straddling my hips as he pinned my hands above my head. I bucked and writhed, but it was no use.

I knew my grappling game was weak. If my opponent got me on the mat, that was always my downfall. But I couldn't find it in me to give up now or let him win.

"Tap out," Linc growled, his face hovering over me.

"No," I snarled.

His eyes flared, surprise making a home there.

"It's not enough," I admitted. "I need more." I needed to fight until my muscles gave out. Until I was starved for breath. Until I could finally forget about the events of the day.

Linc's gaze searched mine. "Tell me what you need."

I tried in vain to unseat him, twisting my hips and bucking against him. It was no use. "I don't know!" The words were half yell, frustration, anger, and fear stewing inside.

And then Linc's mouth was on mine.

Everything about it was domination, the promise that he was in control when it felt like everything in my life was spinning wildly out of it. His weight pinning me. His hands holding my wrists. His tongue invading.

I moaned into his mouth, but then I sparked alive, ready to duel. Fighting for that dominance. Feeling the power spark to life inside me.

Linc stole his mouth from mine, his lips trailing across my jaw to hover at my ear. "Tell me what you want, Vicious. Tell me you want me to make you come. That you want me to shatter your body so it'll never be the same."

I shuddered under him, the promise of his words digging in. My nipples tightened, beading beneath the light cotton of my bra.

"Fuck," Linc swore. "I can feel those perfect nipples. Wonder if they're the same berry pink as those lips I've been dreaming about wrapped around my—"

I bucked with everything in me, rolling so I was the one straddling him, even though he still gripped my wrists. And then I felt it, his hard length pressed against the apex of my thighs, making a home against my core. My body moved on instinct, rocking against him. I couldn't help it. A moan slipped free.

Linc's eyes flashed, the green brighter in the sea of gold. "What are you going to do now?"

A dare laced his words—a challenge I was more than ready to meet. My hips rocked again, and Linc swore.

"Pure sin on a fight mat," he growled.

I grinned down at him. "Is that so?" But my words cut off as Linc's hips angled up, hitting me right between the legs. The friction and pressure were almost too much. A whimper slipped free, and it was all Linc needed.

He released my wrists and pulled a wrap off. I wasn't even aware of them hitting the mat until his fingers were tangled in the strap of my tank and bra. His eyes collided with mine. "You tap out; this all ends."

My free hand slid through his hair, fingers tightening in it, tugging just enough to bring a flicker of pain. Heat. "*You* tap out; this all ends."

Linc grinned—the kind that knocked me senseless. And this one almost did, literally. He didn't miss his opportunity to get the upper hand, rolling us so I was beneath him again. Only this time, he settled between my legs. Had our clothes magically disappeared, this man would be primed to slide inside me.

And holy hell, did I want that.

Linc ground against me, sending flickering sparks dancing

through me and forcing a mewl from my mouth. He nipped my lip. "Those sounds. Like a kitten purring, all pliant and perfect."

I'd never been described as *pliant*.

I bucked against Linc, making him harden more, then curse. But he did it with a grin. "Okay, maybe she has claws."

My neck strained as I reached up to nip his lip. To give as good as I got. Linc's tongue drove in. Demanding. Dominating.

His fingers moved back to my tank, and he tore his mouth from mine as he pulled down the straps of my tank and bra. "Don't make me miss this show."

I sucked in a breath as my back arched, not in any sort of fight tactic but welcoming him, beckoning him closer.

"Fucking perfect. Like those nipples were dipped in cherry juice. Wonder if they taste like that, too." Linc's head dipped, and he pulled the bud into his mouth.

My body bowed. I was the puppet, and Linc was the master, pulling every string in perfect synchronicity. I whimpered but didn't give a damn as Linc's tongue worked my nipple, tugging so hard I felt it in my clit.

My mouth opened in a silent cry as I rocked against him. "Linc," I whispered. "Need you inside me."

Linc's lips released my nipple with a pop, his face coming to hover over mine. "The first time I'm inside you, it's not going to be after a day from hell or in search of something to take the edge off. It will be because you want nothing and no one but me. Your body will weep for me, and you'll beg me to take you. And you can be god-damned sure I'm going to take my time."

My lips parted on a silent inhale as an argument rose. I wasn't above begging right fucking now.

Linc stilled my words, putting two fingers over my mouth. "That doesn't mean I'm not going to take care of my girl. Gonna let you spill all that darkness pooling inside you into me. Gonna take it all. Everything you have to give."

Normally, someone shushing me would've guaranteed a knife to the throat, but I was too caught up in Linc's words, his promises.

Wetness gathered between my thighs as my tongue darted out, wrapping around Linc's fingers and pulling them into my mouth.

I sucked deeply, taking in the slightly salty taste of sweat combined with Linc's natural flavor. I swore he even tasted like bourbon.

He groaned and rocked into me. More sparks spread, my core tightening around nothing, crying out to be filled. I arched into him. This time, Linc cursed.

His hand moved, sliding between our bodies to the hem of my shorts. He stroked me through the thin cotton of my underwear, and I whimpered, shuddering at the tease.

"Fucking soaked, but we can do better," Linc growled.

His fingers slipped beneath my underwear, gliding over my slit, back and forth as if he were in no hurry. My hips rose to meet the caress as Linc's other hand tangled in my hair. I tried to move in search of more or quicker, but Linc wouldn't let me play that game.

I let out a snarl of frustration.

He only grinned down at me, those strong fingers tightening in my hair. "My vicious girl. Love that fire."

His words had me stilling, fear striking out, but I was already gone. Lost to this man and his touch, his understanding.

At my stillness, Linc slid two fingers inside. His eyes fluttered closed as if he were memorizing the moment. "Fucking perfect."

His eyes opened, and his fingers began to move, in and out in an alternating pattern I couldn't ever quite pin down. Sometimes it was a twist. Other times, a drag against my walls. Occasionally, a stretching glide.

And through it all, I never lost him. Couldn't take my eyes off his.

"You're doing such a good job. Taking exactly what I give you. Feeling it all."

My walls trembled around his fingers, ready to break.

"Not yet." Linc's fingers tightened in my hair again, that bite of pain helping me hold back my orgasm. "That's my girl. Breathe. Take it all."

In and out. Twist. Drag.

Sweat dotted my brow. My nipples tightened to the point of pain. It was too much.

Linc's face hovered over mine, his lips a mere breath away. "When you're ready. Let me see. Let me feel it. Let it all into me."

Each thrust cracked a tiny piece of my resolve like a chisel strike to stone. Until Linc's fingers twisted again. One last strike.

I shattered.

Glass fractured, and everything I'd been holding back flooded out. Waves of pleasure and pain coursed through me as my body bucked against Linc. My eyes closed, and my body bowed, moving in wild, nonsensical ways as I let it all free. The fear, the anger, the agony.

I let Linc have it all.

And as I slowly came back to myself and blinked against the light, Linc was there, still hovering over me.

His smile was gentle now, a little lazy. "How do you feel?"

My mouth curved. "Well, your fingers are still inside me. So, pretty damn good."

Linc barked out a laugh, the vibrations of it coursing through me and setting off aftershocks of all he'd given me in all the ways. "My girl has a point."

Hearing him call me that—*my girl*—told me I was more than in danger. I was in the red zone. And there wasn't a damn thing I could do about it.

CHAPTER THIRTY-ONE

Arden

I STOOD AT THE THRESHOLD TO MY WORKSHOP. THE BRIGHT yellow crime scene tape felt like a permanent stain in the form of a massive X across the door. Anger swirled, building on itself. Whoever had done this was probably pleased as punch about that.

My fingers curled around one piece of the tape. I tugged it free and balled it up before doing the same with the other piece, thinking I'd like to burn it. Steeling myself, I punched in the code to the door.

Then I stepped inside.

As I turned on the light, my gaze swept the studio space—a place that had felt more like a home than any other place had. It didn't feel that way anymore. I couldn't even let Brutus inside with all the damage and debris littering the floor. That only had my anger burning brighter, which was intensified by my stubbornness. Whoever this asshole was didn't get to win.

I stormed back onto the stoop and picked up the stack of cleaning supplies. I'd need to refill them before long, but at least this would get me started. It wasn't that people hadn't offered to help. All my siblings had, so had Nora and Lolli. And of course, Linc. Cope had even offered to hire a team to come in.

And it wasn't that I didn't appreciate the offers. It was that I *needed* to do it myself.

Three days.

Three days since someone had infiltrated my safe space and smashed it all to hell. Three days since someone had tried to scare the hell out of me.

My gaze moved to the writing on the wall. *YOU CAN'T HIDE.*

I wanted to scream at the person who'd written it. Rage. I wasn't hiding. That part of my life was over. I was living. And I wouldn't let them stop me.

I'd erase them from every inch of this place and then go right on with my life. Moving around the room, I opened every window and propped the two doors open, as well. It wasn't like I was at risk.

A patrol car was parked between my house and the studio—it or another was present since the day I'd discovered it all. I hadn't slept in an empty house since then either. My siblings had offered to slumber party it, right up until Linc said he would stay. Lolli had *loved* that idea.

"Woo-hoo. The broody billionaire bites the dust. I can't decide, is he stoic in the sack or wild? Each would have their benefits."

A few shouts, Rho's laughter, and Shep gagging had stopped her from saying more. I'd wanted to crawl under a rock. Linc had just grinned at her and winked. *"Wouldn't you like to know?"*

But Linc hadn't made a move. I'd waited as he showered, my breath catching when he came out shirtless and in nothing but gray sweats—basically lingerie for men. Only, all he'd done was turn out the lights and hold me.

Each morning, I woke with my face pressed to his throat and more turned on than ever. Linc would mutter something about needing a cold shower and then disappear. If this studio destroyer didn't take me out, my blue lady balls would.

Pulling out the paint tray, I filled it with baking soda and then poured a little hydrogen peroxide in. I swirled it together to form the paste my research had told me was good for removing blood from surfaces—research I was certain had gotten me on some sort of watch list. I was just glad it hadn't been human blood.

Trace had sent a sample off for testing and it had come back as pig's blood. They were now canvassing butchers in the area to get a list of people who had purchased the stuff. The thought made my stomach churn.

They weren't going to win.

Flipping on my music to some mind-numbing decibel, I got to work. I lost myself in the rage-filled riffs and angry refrains of song after song. It helped. It bled out all I wanted to but wasn't quite ready for.

I started with the walls and worked in a circle, leaving the paste to sit. Then I got out the industrial trash bags Fallon had picked up for me. I threw away ruined tools and paints and countless other supplies. But when I got to the statue in the center of the room, the real heartbreak set in.

The woman reaching out wasn't a picture of hope now. She looked as if she'd fought a battle and lost. The metal was covered in blood, pieces of her face were smashed in, and the hand was broken. As I studied her more closely, I saw that it looked like someone had taken a bat or some other solid object to her. *Bastard.*

My music switched off, and I whirled, automatically assuming a defensive stance. Instead of some hired hit man, I found Trace glaring at me with Anson and Linc behind him. My brother prowled forward, carefully restrained rage coursing through him. "Someone breaks into your studio, leaves what is very clearly a threat, and you think it's a great time to blast your music with all the doors and windows open?"

"Trace," Linc warned, his jaw going hard.

"I know she's been through a lot, but I'm not about to let her be an idiot about her safety," Trace shot back.

Linc moved then, getting in Trace's face. "I know you're tweaked and scared as hell something's going to happen to her. But you *do not* get to speak to her like that. Not ever. But especially not in front of me."

Trace's eyes flared in surprise as he took in Linc with new eyes. "This serious?"

"If Vicious wanted to share that information, she would."

My heart stutter-stepped as a wave of fear hit me hard. *Serious.* We hadn't even slept together. As if that would keep Linc out of my goddamned heart. He was like a ninja, sneaking into places without me even noticing he was there.

Trace looked from Linc to me and back again. "Fuck," he muttered.

His use of the curse word meant he was at the end of his rope. He generally tried to avoid anything that could accidentally get passed on to Keely. He scrubbed his hand over his face, and I noticed the stubble on his jaw was a little thicker now.

That had guilt settling in. Trace had been working around the clock to find something—anything—that would point us toward the culprit. "Sorry, T-money. I figured I'd be safe to rage-clean with someone out front. I'll be more mindful."

Trace blinked at me a few times before speaking. "One, did you just call me T-money?"

My lips twitched. "Maybe."

"Am I a rapper now?"

"I'm fairly certain you are far too much of a rule follower to be a rapper."

Anson choked on a laugh, knowing I was right.

Trace sent him a scathing look. "Hey. I'll have you know I drove five miles over the speed limit on my way here."

"Shit," Anson muttered. "Someone call his second-in-command. He needs to be relieved of duty."

"I hate you all," Trace muttered.

"No, you love us. But we give you gray hair." I ditched my cleaning gloves and moved into his space, swiping at the tiny flecks of silver at his temples.

"The insults keep pouring in."

I wrapped my arms around his waist and gave him a tight hug. "Sorry, T-money."

He hesitated for a moment and then hugged me back, hard. "I just worry about you."

"I know. And I don't handle that well."

Trace pulled back and stared down at me. "Who are you, and what did you do with my sister? You're all agreeable."

A laugh bubbled out of me. "You know, that's a little insulting."

One corner of Trace's mouth kicked up. "Insulting or accurate?"

"Both, damn it."

That only made him grin wider. "No one knows you like your siblings."

Wasn't that the truth? But as I studied him, once more taking in the presence of all three of them, the smile slipped from my face. "You found something."

Trace's expression shifted then, too. He lost some of the amusement, and his usual stoic mask slipped back into place. "Nothing concrete, but I brought Anson on board as a consultant."

Anson scoffed. "What he means is that he paid me a dollar and made me sign a contract."

"You accepted it," Trace shot back.

"Thank you," I cut in, meeting Anson's stare. I knew it cost him to put those profiler shoes back on. And he only did it for the people he loved. Because he'd fallen so head over heels for Rhodes, he'd do it for me.

"It's no big thing."

"It is a big thing. And I appreciate it," I said, steeling myself for whatever might come.

Trace shifted into official mode, his shoulders straightening, and his voice slipping into his no-nonsense tone. "We're working this one from multiple angles. I've got the local push. Anson's tackling the profile and connecting with his resources at the bureau, and Linc has provided some private resources."

My gaze cut to Linc. "Private resources?"

He met my stare and didn't look away. No part of him was intimidated by my challenge. I should've known as much. "I work with a security company out of Seattle. They have a different sort of resource network, along with a unique perspective on security systems and personal safety."

"The one Cope used to upgrade the system here? Holt Hartley's company, Anchor?" I asked.

Linc nodded. "Holt's a silent partner now. He's too busy running a search and rescue team in Washington."

"Yeesh. Hero complex, much?" I muttered.

Linc's lips twitched. "Not anymore. But he did design a new system for your workshop. The equipment already arrived. I've got an installer ready to go as soon as we finish clean-up in here."

That twitchy feeling took root again, the one that sparked the not entirely rational fear that held me hostage. I did everything I could to shove it down.

"Do you really think that will change anything?" I asked. "There was a system on it when someone broke in."

"That wasn't exactly a system," Trace cut in. "You have cameras and locks, but all it took was them cutting the external power source, and the cameras didn't do shit. All we have is that one shot. This system will be hardwired to the power grid, and those lines will be buried, just like they are at Cope's. We'll do the same for your house."

I battled not to argue. Logically, I knew it was the smart play. Knew I needed those precautions in place to keep me safe. But each new thing felt like a metal bar, and once they were all in place, I'd be in prison.

Linc moved in, reading my thoughts like a note scrawled on a page. "It's not forever. Just for a little while. We're going to find this asshole, and you won't have to worry anymore. You can play that noise as loud as you want in the middle of the night with all your doors and windows open."

"I'm gonna get a noise complaint from miles away," Trace muttered.

"It's good to have goals," I shot back. But the humor I searched for in those words didn't come.

Linc's fingers slid through mine, squeezing. "Just a little while.

Cope tried to hire a three-person bodyguard team, so be thankful I talked him down from that. The new system was our compromise."

I gaped up at him. "A three-person bodyguard team?"

"Pretty sure he suggested a dozen at first," Trace said.

"Jesus," I mumbled. "I'll take the security system."

Linc squeezed my hand and then released it. "See, told you she'd come around."

Anson's gaze followed the hand movement—the reassuring gesture, the release of it. I could imagine his genius brain putting all the pieces together, but I hated thinking about what he might find.

"Thank God for small miracles," Trace said.

I stuck out my tongue at him. "Hey, I'm agreeable now, remember?"

He chuckled. "Fair enough. All right, from my corner of things, we've got a deputy here while you are. They will be your tail for the foreseeable future. The county lab is still running trace analysis, but we're guessing the perp wore gloves in here. We haven't found a single print other than yours, not even on the broken items."

Damn. I was hoping whoever it was would be an idiot and leave a path straight to them. But that would be too easy.

"Anson?" Trace asked, tossing the baton.

I forced myself to look at the broody profiler but couldn't help but fear that he was about to lay all my secrets bare with his mental sorcery.

Anson met my gaze, and I swore he was trying to reassure me somehow. "We're looking at a progression in events, an escalation."

Even though Linc was no longer touching me, he was close enough that I felt him stiffen. As if the air around his body vibrated at a higher frequency due to the tension in his muscles. "Meaning this will keep getting worse," he surmised, his voice taking on a deadly air.

"It means that Arden isn't giving whoever this is the reaction they want. That can be a good thing or a bad thing."

I mulled that over, frowning. "That doesn't make sense. If this is linked to my past, it means someone's trying to silence me again."

Why not just take me out while I'm crossing the street sniper-style, or blow up my car? Why are they playing with me?"

A muscle in Linc's jaw fluttered wildly. "Could you please not talk about all the ways you could get dead?"

"Seconded," Trace mumbled.

"Sorry, but it's true."

Anson nodded. "You have a point. And it sometimes helps to approach it logically, not personally."

He was right. Because if I really let it sink in that someone wanted to hurt me—possibly kill me—after everything I'd fought through to get safe...I wasn't sure I could keep going.

"A couple of things," Anson went on. "We don't know for sure this is about your past. One of the things I wanted to talk to you about was if anyone has been paying closer attention to you lately. Anyone new in your life?"

"The deputies already asked me—"

"Quentin Arison," Linc spat, cutting me off.

Anson pulled out his phone. "Who is he?"

"A douchebag. But he doesn't exactly strike me as the type to get his hands dirty." I gestured around the space. "This took work. Quentin wears three-piece suits and thousand-dollar dress shoes."

Anson met my gaze as though he needed to know I was hearing him. "This takes rage, Arden. It's personal on some level, but that doesn't mean it will necessarily make logical sense to you or me. Someone whose mind has twisted on them can see something as slight as you not smiling at them as justification for this."

"She refused to go on a date with him. Refused to sell art to him before the auction," Linc cut in. "I had someone on my security team do a little digging. Family wealth, from Europe. Used to getting what he wants. His reputation is less than stellar."

I turned slowly to Linc. "You had a background check done on him because he asked me out?"

Linc shrugged as if it was completely logical. "I didn't like the way he looked at you."

Trace choked on a laugh. "And I bet that had nothing to do with him asking her out."

Oh, Jesus. I would never hear the end of this.

Linc ignored him and turned back to Anson. "You said you had a couple of things."

Anson nodded. "I talked with my old partner at the Behavioral Analysis Unit, and the agent who has the case. They haven't seen any movement."

"But?" I asked.

One corner of Anson's mouth tugged up the barest amount as if he was trying to smile but couldn't quite get there. "Whoever was pulling the strings back then stayed under the radar. We still have no clue who ordered the hit or who the second person in that hallway was. There are no phone records, no emails. We have no idea how they were communicating."

I knew all that. "If there's nothing, and I obviously haven't re-membered a damn thing, why would someone risk trying to hurt me now?"

"Arden, whoever had your parents killed uses people like pawns to get what they want. And they were smart enough to make it so we couldn't trace anything back to them. Even the few cases we know your dad threw don't have a common thread."

The reminder of what my dad had done felt like a stinging slap. He had thrown away his purpose and family for just a little bit *more*.

Anson pressed on. "Someone like that won't want any loose threads. They won't want to take that risk. They'll have been looking for you this whole time. And the kinds of people someone like that would hire for this type of work? Their brains don't process empathy the same way others do. Some simply disassociate from the fact that they're taking a human life. But others? They get joy from it and the hunt. And *those* people would play with you before they killed you. Just because it makes it more fun."

CHAPTER THIRTY-TWO

Arden

GRAY CLOUDS ROLLED IN, RIGHT ALONG WITH A CLAP OF thunder. It was the kind of stormy sky that sometimes meant rain and other times didn't. Which meant it was also the type that held the greatest risk of forest fire. As if there weren't enough threats in our midst.

Linc shoved a broken frame into a trash bag with enough force that it should've gone right through the heavy-duty plastic. He hadn't asked if he could help clean this time; he'd simply started stomping around, muttering to himself as he picked up detritus.

"You wanna talk about it?" I asked as I wiped the paste from the walls. It had cleaned a lot of the blood, but I would still need to paint them. Even then, I wondered if they'd ever be blood-free in my mind.

Linc picked up what looked like pieces of paintbrushes. "He shouldn't have told you that."

The statement had surprise lighting through me. "Who shouldn't have told me what?"

Linc straightened, finally turning his supremely pissed-off face to me. "Anson. Telling you there could be some psycho killer out there plotting your murder but deciding he wants to play with you first."

"Whether he told me or not wouldn't make the possibility any less true."

"But it would make you less fucking terrified," he spat.

"Linc," I said quietly. "Do I look like I'm cowering in a corner?"

His hazel eyes burned brighter. "You fight through the fear. You always have."

Damn him. He was right. I shoved the feelings down and soldiered on. But I knew something else, too. "When I have all the facts, it helps somehow. If I can name all the possibilities, it takes away some of the power." I held up my gloved hands, ticking off the options on my fingers. "One, unhinged hit man with a thing for the drama. Two, spoiled rich boy with too much time on his hands. Three, some unknown person I cut off in traffic, and they decided I was the spawn of Satan."

"It's not funny," Linc growled. A loud clap of thunder sounded as the sky darkened even more.

I pulled off the gloves and laid them over my bucket. "I know it's your instinct to shield the people you care about, but I don't want to be kept from the truth. The last time someone tried to do that, my whole world got ripped apart."

For a moment, I thought Linc might fight me and hold tight to the urge to shield me from everything, even truths I needed to know. But then he exhaled, his shoulders sagging in a mixture of defeat and understanding. He dropped the bag, not saying anything. He simply wrapped me in his arms and held on.

Maybe nothing needed to be said. Because Linc couldn't fix this, no matter how much he wanted to. He kept those strong arms around me as thunder rolled outside. Then, finally, his lips teased my hair as he whispered, "I'm sorry."

I held him tighter, my hands fisting in his shirt. "There's nothing to be sorry for."

Linc pulled back, searching my face. "I don't have a right to try to keep information from you. No one does."

"No. But I understand why you'd want to. I'd probably want the same if I were in your shoes."

Linc lifted a hand, his callused thumb skating across my jaw. "Trace's right. You've become agreeable."

I shoved at his chest, a laugh slipping free. "You all suck."

Linc grinned as he released me. "What do you think? More rage-cleaning, or are you ready for a break?"

I'd lost some of my mad over the past few hours as the sun sank lower in the late-afternoon sky. It was more a numbed sadness now. But as I looked around the room, I knew one thing. "I want every single thing that he touched in here tossed."

Linc's eyes flashed that brighter green. "Gettin' him the hell out of here it is." He met my gaze. "But please don't make my ears bleed."

The puppy dog look did it: I smiled for what felt like the first time in three days. "I can settle for some classic rock if you'll help me."

Linc leaned in, his lips brushing mine. "Deal."

We set to work as Jimi Hendrix played over the speakers. I worked on the walls while Linc tackled the floors. My poor couch would need to go to the dump. But my desk had survived. I didn't realize what we were circling until we slowed in the center of the room.

I stared down at the statue. The woman trying to break free was now beaten to hell and covered in blood. "I'm not sure she's salvageable."

"Why not?" Linc asked.

I gestured at the mangled piece. "Hand broken off. Face smashed in places. Dented."

Linc met my gaze. "She's been through hell and survived. Sounds like someone else I know. Bet you could find a way to make what she's been through beautiful."

My heart jerked in my chest, the urge to bolt lighting anew. But on its heels was something stronger: the need to stay. "Then let's get her up."

A grin spread across Linc's face. "Let's get her up."

We lifted her on a count of three. Whoever had toppled her must have been strong or fueled with a hell of a lot of rage because the two of us could barely get the piece upright. When we did, my brain started to run wild with ideas. I saw something new. Something better. Something fiercer.

"Oh, no," Linc started. "I know that look. But it's after eight, and you haven't eaten anything since breakfast. You can conquer statue lady tomorrow."

I gave him my best pleading eyes. "Just an hour?"

He huffed out a breath. "After you eat."

"Deal," I said quickly.

Linc stared at me for a moment. "I just got played, didn't I?"

"Maybe…" I singsonged.

He opened his mouth to say something, but his phone rang. He pulled it from his pocket and frowned. "It's Ellie. She doesn't usually call this late."

"Take it," I said. "I can start dinner."

"Are you going to poison us?"

I made a face. "I'm heating up one of Nora's casseroles. I think even *I* can do that."

Linc's lips twitched. "All right. I'll be in in a few."

"No rush," I said, heading for the door.

The outdoor lights flicked on as I stepped outside, eating the darkness like they always did. Gravel crunched beneath my feet until thunder drowned out the sound, but the lightning was still in the distance.

"Storm's coming," Deputy Allen said.

"I do love a summer storm."

"As long as we don't get a fire."

"As long as." I paused for a moment. "I'm heating up dinner for Linc and me. You want some?"

Allen shook his head. "Already ate. But thank you."

"Thanks for looking out," I called as I headed for the house.

"Just happy it's been boring as hell," he shouted back.

I laughed as I punched in my front door code and opened it to a waiting Brutus. His tail wagged, and he pressed into me. I gave him more scratches, bending down to press a kiss to his head. Brutus moved in and licked my cheek.

"I love you, too."

The simple admission made my eyes sting. Why did it come so easily with him, but was like pulling teeth with humans? Linc's face swirled in my mind, and the burning sensation in my eyes intensified. That battle of wanting something so badly yet being terrified to reach for it raged.

Linc thought hearing someone might be playing a sick and twisted game with my life would scare me? Hurt me? Nothing scared and hurt more than knowing the beauty of him and losing it.

A clap of thunder swept through the house, making the walls tremble. And as it rolled through, the lights went out.

The panic didn't come at first because I expected the electricity to flick right back on. It wasn't like there were high winds and torrential downpours. But the lights didn't return.

My heart rate picked up, the beats tangling with one another in an attempt to keep going. My hand fumbled, searching the pocket of my cargo pants as Brutus let out a low growl.

"It's okay," I wheezed. I felt for my phone and cursed when I realized I'd left it in the studio. The panic dug in.

My finger hooked around my keys, and a frisson of relief found me. But it vanished as I pressed the flashlight, and nothing happened. I tried again, my fingers shaking. Nothing.

The kitchen. There were flashlights in the kitchen. I just needed to get there. Only the hallway looked football fields long right now. I stumbled down it, struggling to stay upright.

My mom's voice flashed in my head. *"Stay here. No matter what you hear, do not come out. Do you understand me?"*

And then the image of her shoving me into the hidden closet rose. *"Love you to the ends of the Earth."*

The sound of a gunshot in my memory.

And then the darkness closed in on me even further.

CHAPTER THIRTY-THREE

Lincoln

MY FINGER SWEPT ACROSS THE SCREEN TO ACCEPT THE CALL. "Hey, El Bell."

"Hey, ConCon," she greeted, her voice soft.

I moved through the studio, clicking off the stereo and shutting doors and windows as I watched Arden make her way to the house. "Pretty late for you."

A fact that had my muscles winding a little tighter than normal, even as I tried to shove the worry down.

Ellie let out a small huff of air across the line. "You think I'm not going to check up on my big brother and his girlfriend after he tells me some creep smashed up her art studio?"

I shouldn't have told her, but she'd called just as I was finishing up with Trace. And Ellie had read me the way only little sisters could. She'd pushed, and I'd caved. "We're both good. Just spent all afternoon getting things back in working order."

Shutting off the lights, I stepped onto the back patio that overlooked the now-empty paddock and barn. With the storm clouds rolling in, you couldn't make out much of the moon, but it somehow still managed to be a beautiful night.

"Good," Ellie said, a little of the tension bleeding out of her voice. "That's good."

"What about you? How are things in New York?" I asked, just as a bolt of lightning streaked across the sky, illuminating the mountains for a split second before plunging the world into darkness again.

"It's New York. Same ole, same ole."

Thunder rolled, quicker this time. The storm was moving closer.

"I don't actually give a damn about New York. What about *you*?" I pressed. She was holding something back.

Ellie was quiet for a moment. "I don't know if I want to do it."

Everything in me froze. "Marry Bradley?"

More silence.

"El…"

"I feel like I'm scared to move," she croaked.

Fuck.

"Do you want me to come to New York?" I asked. I fucking hated that city, but I'd do it for Ellie. I'd have to convince Arden to come with me because I sure as hell wasn't leaving her here.

"No," Ellie answered quickly. In my mind, I could see her shaking her head, that mix of blond and brown swirling around her face. "I need to figure this out on my own. I just…I just needed to hear your voice for a second."

"I'm right here. Always. You should come stay for a while. Cope wouldn't mind."

Another pause.

"Maybe. I need to sort out my head first."

"El?"

"Yeah?" she whispered.

"Fuck everyone. Even me. Don't think about what anyone else wants but you. This is *your* life. Don't wake up twenty years from now and realize you wasted it living for other people. Find out what you want."

I heard short, harsh pants of breath and knew she was crying.

My hand tightened around the phone. I wished I had a wall to put my fist through.

Another bolt of lightning streaked across the sky. Way closer this time. The thunder that followed felt like it was practically on top of me.

"You need to go," Ellie rasped. "Sounds like you're in a storm."

"El—"

"I'll check in soon. Love you, ConCon."

She hung up before I could say another word. I pulled the phone away from my face and stared at the screen. An ache took root in my chest. I couldn't make the next choices for my sister. I just hoped she was strong enough to do what made her happy.

My gaze lifted, pulled toward the house, toward Arden. Sometimes, it felt like my entire body was attuned to her, subtly shifting in her direction at all times. A magnetic pull because of all she was.

But as I stared at the house, I realized something was off. The light by the door that was perpetually on wasn't now. And no lights glowed from inside.

I turned quickly, taking in the studio. While I'd turned off the overhead lights, I hadn't missed the two night-lights plugged into outlets on either side of the room. They weren't on now.

My mind raced, first fearing the worst and then realizing the storm must've knocked out the power. I was moving before I could stop myself, running toward Arden's house. The deputy must've seen me because he climbed out of his vehicle, his hand going to his gun. "Everything okay?"

I waved him off. "Power's out. Just want to make sure everything is okay in the house." I wasn't about to betray Arden's secret that the dark held all her monsters.

He seemed a little wary but nodded, climbing back into his car just as the rain started. It pelted against me in angry bursts until I reached the front door. Punching in the code, I hauled it open.

"Arden?" I called into the dark.

There was nothing. No answer. No light. Not a single sign of life.

Fear kicked up, clawing in ragged sweeps across my flesh. "Arden?

It's Linc." I flicked on the flashlight on my phone, and that's when I heard it.

A sound.

I froze. "Arden?"

It was so faint my ears could barely make it out. A whimper.

I moved toward that faint sound, heading down the hall toward the kitchen and living room. I heard it again.

Stilling, my gaze swept the room. And that's when I saw her.

Arden had shoved herself between a tall hutch and the wall in the far corner of the room, Brutus standing guard, his hair bristling at his owner's state.

As I strode across the room, Brutus growled. I muttered a curse, racking my brain for the terms Arden had used. "Freund, Brutus. Freund." I'd probably butchered the pronunciation. I'd taken one term of German in college, and that was it. But Brutus eased a fraction.

My hand dropped to his head, giving him a pat. "You did so good. But you gotta let me in there now. Okay?"

Brutus stared up at me as if considering my words and then subtly shifted back. I sank to the floor, moving in as close as I could to Arden. Her face had turned a stark shade of white, and her beautiful, gray-violet eyes were too wide. Her whole body trembled.

I wanted to kill whoever had put this sort of fear into her. And I wanted to do it slowly.

I didn't touch her. Not yet. I didn't know if she truly knew it was me. "Arden, can you hear me?"

She kept staring straight ahead, unblinking, as if seeing something other than what was right in front of her. "They're coming."

Agony twisted in my gut. "You're safe. I promise they're not getting anywhere near you. Deputy Allen is out there. I'm right here. You've got Brutus."

"They killed her," Arden croaked. "So...much blood. It's everywhere. It's seeping into the carpet. She's not breathing."

I scooted closer, my hands running up her calves and squeezing. "Arden, look at me. *See* me."

She blinked a couple of times as if trying to pull herself out of it, but she couldn't quite get there.

I squeezed her calves again, trying to give her something to anchor herself. "You hear my voice? You feel me? Come back. Come back to me."

She blinked again, faster now. Then her head moved, trying to find me. Finally, those beautiful, tortured eyes met mine. "Linc?"

"That's my girl. I'm right here."

"It's dark," she whispered.

"I know. But you're not alone in it. Not anymore." I swept the beam across the room to demonstrate that there was light, even in the dark.

Those beautiful eyes filled, and then she threw herself at me. I caught her, cradling her in my arms as huge, racking sobs took over. I held her to me, giving her the time to let it all out—everything she kept bottled up all the time.

"It was so real," she choked out. "Like I was back there. In that closet. Watching it all happen."

"I'm so sorry, baby. You're safe."

She shuddered against me and burrowed deeper. "So cold."

I moved then, grabbing my phone and shoving to my feet with Arden still in my arms. I might not be able to erase the memories that haunted her, but I could fix this.

Keeping Arden cradled against me, I headed in the direction of the bathroom, hoping the water heater was gas and not electric. I was just glad that I remembered Cope telling me the well water system had a small generator to keep things running during power outages. Brutus started to follow, but I held out a hand. "Stay. I've got her."

Brutus stared at me for a moment and then plunked his butt down.

At least I wouldn't be battling a dog, too. I navigated the furniture the best I could with only the light on my phone as Arden trembled against me more. Each vibration stoked my rage, building it into a fiery inferno. She'd been through too much. Had been traumatized. Threatened. Was living in fear.

I would've paid any price to take it all away. To end this for her.

Moving into the bathroom, I set the phone and Arden on the counter and started to release her, but her hands fisted in my tee and held tight. "Don't leave me."

Fuck.

My back teeth ground together, the rage nearly swallowing me whole. I dropped my forehead to hers, trying to shove the anger down. "I'm right here. Not going anywhere. Just going to turn the water on. Think I can do that?"

Arden was quiet for a moment. She didn't move, barely breathed. "Okay."

I moved as quickly as possible, turning the water on to warm and returning to her, the light from my phone casting us in a faint glow. I brushed my lips across her temple. "I'm right here. See?"

Arden's hand rose to rest on my chest, over my heart. "Right here."

She was killing me. Everything about this was slicing me open. All I wanted to do was erase every ounce of her pain, but I couldn't.

Instead, I kicked off my boots then shucked my jeans, socks, and tee, leaving only my boxer briefs on. If anyone was going to be cold in this bathroom, it would be me.

I ghosted a hand over Arden's face. "Would it be okay if I undressed you? Get you into that nice, warm shower?" Steam was already beginning to fill the bathroom in a way that promised endless warmth.

She nodded slowly, her throat working as she swallowed.

"Arms up," I said gently.

Arden raised them, and I moved closer to pull up her T-shirt. As I let it flutter to the floor, I took in her form in the sliver of light. She wore some sort of black lace bra I didn't want to look too closely at. My arms encircled her, fingers unfastening the hooks and letting that fall to the floor, too.

"Gonna lift you down now. Think you can stand?"

Arden nodded robotically. There was no life in the movement, no signs of the vitality that usually filled her.

I sank to my knees, my hands going to her left foot. I quickly untied the sneaker's laces. "Lift." She did, and I pulled the shoe and sock off, then repeated it with the other foot. I looked up to find Arden watching me. But it was as if she were peering through a looking glass or seeing something through some sort of distortion.

My fingers lifted to the button at her waist. "Almost there."

Arden's eyes went glassy. "Almost there."

I unfastened her pants and pulled them and her underwear down. She shivered, and I cursed, pushing to my feet. "Let's get you warm."

I held out a hand to test the water, adjusting it slightly before ushering Arden into the glass-enclosed space. I positioned her under the spray but facing away, toward me.

"Warm," she whispered.

"That's right. Gonna take care of you, all right?"

Those gray-violet eyes locked on mine. "You always take care of me."

The words were a beautiful knife to the heart, and I willingly took every ounce of the pain. "That's right."

My hands lifted to Arden's hair, searching for the rubber band that held those mountains of dark brown locks in a tangled mess atop her head. Latching on, I maneuvered it as gently as possible, letting all that beautiful hair free to fall into the spray.

I surveyed the shelf in the stall, trying to make out words in the near-dark. I found the shampoo and squirted a healthy dose into my palm. "Can you turn for me?"

Arden did, moving back a fraction. I rubbed my hands together to create suds and realized where Arden's cherry scent came from. This shampoo. Maybe this would give her back a little of herself.

My fingers dug into her hair, depositing shampoo across the strands. I massaged Arden's head, making sure every inch of her hair was cleaned. She hummed softly.

The small sound of pleasure erased a little of the memories of her whimpering. I wanted to give her only the good. So much of it that she wouldn't even remember the bad.

"Turn," I whispered hoarsely.

She did.

My fingers worked through her hair, rinsing the shampoo as I stared down at her. Arden didn't close her eyes—so trusting that I wouldn't get any soap in them. That trust was a gift, and I moved as if I were restoring the Mona Lisa.

When all the strands were fully rinsed, I repeated the steps with conditioner. Then, as Arden watched me, I reached for the bodywash. I squeezed soap into my palms and rubbed them together. My hands skated over her arms and torso, then moved up to cup her breasts, the perfect weight filling my hands.

Arden let out a soft moan, her nipples pebbling. My dick hardened in response, not giving a damn that this wasn't the time, and I still had soaked boxer briefs on. My thumbs circled the tight buds as Arden's head tipped back.

I released her breasts, even though it was the last thing I wanted to do. Sinking to my knees, I lathered bodywash over one leg, then the other. Arden's breaths came in quick pants as her fingers dug into my shoulders.

Water coursed over her, rinsing the soap free, but I still didn't move. She was so beautiful, a work of art in her own right. So strong, withstanding some of the worst this world had to offer.

Those gray-violet eyes found mine, brighter now. "Linc."

My whole body tightened in response to just my name on her lips. "What do you need?"

The violet flashed. "You."

A stream of curses flew through my mind. "I don't know if that's a good—"

Arden cut me off, bending to take my mouth, her tongue stroking in. The second her taste hit me, I was gone: cherries and mint and something that was only her.

She pulled back, tugging me to my feet. "Trust me to know what I need. And right now, I need to feel *you*. Everywhere."

My dick pulsed with that image and promise. I stepped back and saw a hint of pain in Arden's eyes at the perceived rejection. I quickly sat on the tiled bench in the shower and took her hand. "Take what you need, Vicious."

CHAPTER THIRTY-FOUR

Arden

MY WHOLE BODY TINGLED WITH THAT PINS-AND-NEEDLES feeling you get after coming in from hours in the cold. Muscle and sinew waking up. All because of Linc.

And it wasn't him just pulling me out of my haze. It was more. He woke things inside me that felt as if they'd been frozen for years.

It scared the hell out of me.

But I wasn't walking away. I was stepping into the fear without armor. No bleeding it into my art. No fighting it out on the mat. No riding for hours to drown it.

I was diving in.

Linc's hand curved around mine. "Whatever you need. Take it, Vicious."

My nipples pebbled, and my core clenched as the water fell on my back, just enough to keep me warm. My hold on Linc's hand tightened, and I moved it between my legs. My hand beneath his, I used his fingers to part me.

My mouth fell open in a silent gasp. There was power in this. In us being together. Moving as one.

I dragged his fingers over my slit, rocking into him. Goose bumps rose on my flesh as I guided him where I needed him the most. Together, our fingers circled my clit.

My breaths came in short pants now, and when my head tipped back down, I found Linc watching me with reverence.

"So beautiful, taking what you need. Owning your pleasure."

I shivered, but there was no fear here. Only heat. Just promise.

I dropped Linc's hand, pulling down the only thing between us—those soaking-wet boxer briefs plastered to his skin. My knuckles grazed his powerful thighs, making mine clench in response. Then I climbed onto the bench to straddle him. The hard, cool tile dug into my knees, but I didn't give a damn. Not when I was about to get what I wanted most.

My hand encircled Linc's dick, gliding up and down. He let out a moan, and his eyes fluttered closed for a moment before flying open again as I squeezed gently on an upward glide. There was fire in those green depths as Linc looked up at me, still not touching. Then he cursed. "I don't have a condom."

The reminder of what we were about to do had everything in me tightening in the perfect way. "I'm on the pill, and I've been checked."

"I have, too. I'd never take risks with you."

Invisible claws dug into my heart. "Linc."

"Tell me. What's my girl going to take now?"

"Everything."

"My vicious girl," he breathed.

I guided him to my entrance, sinking down slowly. My head tipped back as I took in the beautiful stretch, the one that flickered on the border of pain but reminded me that I was alive. That I could still *feel*.

Linc's hand found me then, gliding up my belly and between my breasts. He slid it higher, coming to rest where my neck met my jaw, his fingers tangling in my hair. "So fucking perfect."

His words echoed in the space, ricocheting off the tile like beautiful bullets. I let each one hit without protest, welcoming them.

I sank lower, taking all of him, feeling the power and pleasure surging. Linc rocked against me but didn't power up. His muscles trembled with the force it took to hold himself back. The gift he was giving me… Total and complete control.

I rose again and sank down once more, a little faster this time, more force behind my movements. That sense of power swept through me as Linc's other hand cupped my breast, his thumb circling my nipple. I arched into him as I rose and sank down again.

Giving myself over to it, I moved on instinct, in some nonsensical pattern all my own. And Linc let me find it—my way, my path. When my eyes met his, his fingers tightened in my hair. "There she is. Came back to me."

My walls fluttered around him. "Linc."

Those eyes burned, leaving brands.

"Let go," I whispered.

"Vicious—"

"Let *go*."

Linc gave me exactly what I asked for, what I needed, just like always. He let go.

His big body thrust upward, driving so deeply into me my eyes watered. The flicker of pleasure and pain mixed in the best way, reminding me this was just like life. You couldn't have one without the other.

But I didn't let Linc have his way alone; I countered each move, sinking down to meet him, my nails raking across his shoulders with a force I knew might've drawn blood. Linc's fingers tightened in my hair, pulling my head back as he powered into me again.

My walls fluttered around him as I teetered on the tipping point.

"Break with me," he growled.

I rocked, arching perfectly to bring him exactly where I needed him. Everything broke apart. Light and shadow mixed before my eyes as Linc moved through my orgasm, riding every wave, drawing each one out as far as they would go.

With one last thrust, he emptied into me, and a feeling of fullness I'd never experienced before surged. Because this was Linc, and he took me in every way, never settling for just the physical. He wanted it all.

As we came back to ourselves, Linc stroked my face, staring into my eyes as if trying to decipher my secrets. "Falling in love with you."

I stiffened, my muscles going rock-solid.

Linc's fingers stilled. "You run, it's really gonna piss me off."

Straight to the point. Like always.

"Not running," I whispered, fear wrapping around my vocal cords like a boa constrictor.

"But?"

"I can't say it back." It would be tempting fate. And I wasn't about to put Linc in the crosshairs.

His expression softened, and that thumb started stroking again. "Just because you don't say it doesn't make it any less true."

My mouth fell open. "Cocky much?"

Linc grinned, but it was almost childlike. "Not cocky. Sure. Sure of you. Sure of us. I'll believe for you for now. Until you can say the words."

My eyes burned, filled. "I'm not crying."

"Okay."

Tears slipped down my cheeks, and Linc wiped them away.

"That's water from the shower."

"All right."

"Why do you have to be so perfect?" I asked, a mixture of warmth and annoyance filling my tone.

"Because I live to piss you off."

I laughed, the sound sending vibrations through us both.

Linc cursed. "Are you trying to kill me?"

"Sorry." I pulled off him, wincing slightly.

Linc was on me in a second, hands gently cupping my face. "Are you okay? Was it too much?"

"It was perfect. You gave me exactly what I needed."

He bent and brushed his lips across mine. "Always will."

Linc shut off the water, but he wasn't done caretaking. He

wrapped me in a towel and dried every inch of me. His hand ghosted over my face again. "Are you okay?"

I knew he meant so much more than what we'd just shared. My fingers traced his tattoos, *truth* over one pec, *trust* over the other. The first time I'd seen them, I didn't know they were the things Linc valued the most. The two things he never got growing up. I might not be able to give him *I love you*, but I could give him those two words, the same way he'd given them to me.

"The lights went out, and my flashlight wouldn't work. I left my phone in the studio. It was so dark. And it was like I was back there, seeing it all over again. I freaked."

Linc wrapped his arms around me and pulled me against him. "I'm so sorry. It was a trigger. And with everything that's been going on, it's completely understandable."

"I miss her," I whispered. "Him, too. Even though I should hate him."

Linc pulled back. "He's your dad. He made mistakes, but that doesn't erase all the good."

My throat constricted, but I managed to nod. "I don't want to be scared anymore."

Linc's expression hardened, a coldness settling into his features. "I don't want you to be either. We're going to find this monster, and he's not going to hurt anyone else. Not ever again."

CHAPTER THIRTY-FIVE

Lincoln

I WANTED TO WAKE UP TO LAZY SEX AND MAKE ARDEN BREAKFAST in bed. Instead, I woke to loud, incessant knocking.

Arden rolled over and pulled a pillow over her head. "Make them go away. It's not even dawn."

It was well past dawn, given the sunlight streaming in through the half-open curtains. But my girl was dramatic when it came to mornings. Glancing at the clock, I was relieved to see the power had come back on sometime during the night.

I tugged the pillow off her head as the knocking continued. "Where's your phone?" Given everything that had happened over the past couple of weeks, checking her camera feeds wasn't a bad idea.

Arden scowled at me, trying to take the pillow back. "I dunno. In the studio, I think. Remember? If you ignore them, they'll go away."

"Or they'll break down the door because they think you've been kidnapped."

"Whatever." Arden pulled the covers over her head.

Apparently, I was on my own. Swinging my legs over the side of the bed, I stood and crossed to my duffel in the corner. I found a pair of sweats and pulled them on, heading for the source of the knocking, Brutus hot on my heels.

"Coming!" I yelled. "Keep your pants on."

Unlocking the door, I pulled it open to find Cope's annoyed face. That annoyance morphed into something more like anger as his gaze swept over me. "Why are you answering my sister's door shirtless?"

Well, shit.

Little Luca peeked around Cope, a look of confusion on his face. "Are you going swimming?"

Brutus let out a happy bark and went to the boy as I fought not to laugh. "Yeah, little dude. I'm going swimming."

"I'll go with you," Luca offered as he hugged the dog. "I love swimming."

Sutton, who was standing a step back, choked on a laugh. "Can never go wrong with a little swimming."

Cope whirled on his fiancée. "This isn't funny."

Sutton's turquoise eyes twinkled. "I don't know. It's a little funny."

"I'm missing something..." Luca mumbled.

"Why don't you guys come inside?" I offered, gesturing them in.

Cope stalked past me. "I don't need *you* to invite me into my sister's house."

"Geez," Luca muttered. "He's grumpy. Never knew he didn't like swimming that much."

I patted the boy on the shoulder. "Me either."

Sutton just giggled.

"Warrior," Cope growled.

"You don't get to dictate what I laugh at, Hotshot," she called.

Cope grumbled something under his breath just as a door slammed. Footsteps pounded down the hall, and a very rumpled-looking Arden appeared. "What the he—ck is going on?"

Cope looked from his sister to me and back again, taking in her wrinkled tee and sleep shorts. That thunderous look took over again. "I feel like I should be asking you that question."

Arden crossed her arms and arched a brow. "Should you, now?"

Oh, hell. Cope needed to abort mission now. It didn't matter that he was still healing from a gunshot wound; Arden would kick his ass.

Cope's shoulders straightened, and I didn't miss how much easier he was moving. "I fly down to check on my sister because"—he glanced at Luca, clearly not wanting to share what was going on—"I missed her, and I find my best friend and boss in her house, half-dressed."

Luca stared up at Cope. "He's going swimming. Whatya got against swimming? I thought you liked it."

Surprise lit Arden's features as Sutton stifled another giggle. Sutton wrapped an arm around Luca's shoulders. "Why don't we go make some scones for everyone?"

"Maybe a snack'll make Cope less grumpy," Luca mumbled, motioning for Brutus to come with him.

They moved toward the kitchen as Cope crossed into Arden's space. "What the hell is going on?"

"Oh, no, you don't," Arden shot back. "You do not get to come in here and act all overprotective-big-brother because you don't like who I have in my bed."

Cope made a gagging noise. "Dear God, stop. I do not need those mental images."

"You're the one who asked, so that's just karma."

I moved into Arden's space and wrapped an arm around her, pulling her against my side. Dropping a kiss to her head, I whispered, "He's just worried about you."

"Well, his caveman is showing," Arden whisper-hissed. "And the caveman is an asshole."

My lips twitched. "Fucking cute."

"I'm mad, not cute."

"You can be both." I gave her a quick kiss. "But maybe you can do that after you spend some time with your brother since he came all this way."

Arden sighed and looked back at Cope. "Are you okay? Your shoulder all right with the trip?"

Cope's gaze ping-ponged between the two of us before landing back on Arden. "Okay, who are you, and what did you do with my sister?"

"She's gotten agreeable," I said, humor lacing my tone.

Arden glared up at me. "I have not."

"Okay, agreeable when she doesn't get woken up before noon," I said, kissing her once more.

"Why are you kissing Auntie Arden?" Luca called from the kitchen.

"Yeah," Cope said, a mock glare on his face. "Why *are* you kissing her?"

I didn't think Cope or Luca would appreciate me saying, "*Because she tastes good,*" so I went with another truth. "Because she's my favorite."

Arden's gray-violet eyes softened as she looked up at me. "You're my favorite, too, Cowboy."

It might not be an *I love you,* but it was her version of it. And I'd take that and run.

Luca's face screwed up. "But not more favorite than me, right?"

Arden laughed, and it was the light and husky one. "No one could be more favorite than you. But you haven't even hugged me yet."

"I forgot," Luca yelled, running from the kitchen into the living room.

Arden caught him on the fly, hoisting him into the air, even though he was almost too big. She tickled his side, making him squeal and her laugh harder as she carried him toward the kitchen.

"Hell," Cope whispered, closer to me now. "You're gone for her, aren't you?"

I didn't look at my friend; I couldn't tear my gaze from Arden. Only it wasn't Luca she held in my mind; it was our little one. A girl with her eyes and smile. I saw a whole future in that moment, a life playing out in that hazy mist between reality and imagination.

"I've been gone for her from the moment she held that knife to my neck."

Cope cursed.

I forced my gaze from her and looked at my friend. Because he deserved my honesty. "I wouldn't have gone there if she didn't mean something to me. And now? Now, she means everything."

Cope stared at me for a long moment, likely taking stock of every micro-expression on my face. "You'll keep an eye on her?"

"I'll do whatever it takes to keep her safe." There was no doubt in those words, only complete certainty. Because if anyone tried to hurt a hair on Arden's head, I'd end them.

CHAPTER THIRTY-SIX

Arden

WHERE DO YOU THINK YOU'RE GOING?" LINC ASKED AS I stepped into the living room, finally dressed after a morning of my brother giving me the third degree. Thankfully, Luca and Sutton had managed to rein him in.

Linc sat in one of my overstuffed chairs, a tablet in his hands and looking too hot for his own good. He'd changed earlier, after one too many of Cope's *shirtless* barbs. Linc wore dark jeans, boots, and a worn Seattle Sparks T-shirt. No one would've pegged him as a tycoon now, and I loved the juxtaposition.

"You keep looking at me like that, and the only place you're going is back to the bedroom," Linc growled.

Heat flared between my legs. I didn't hate that idea, but I needed to get some things done first. "I'm going to The Collective."

Linc set the tablet down and pushed to his feet. "Why?"

"Because I need to check on things for the auction and show." After I'd finally grabbed my phone from the studio, I found more than a few worried texts from Farah, Isaiah, and Hannah—and some annoying ones from Denver.

"Can't Denver do that? Or whoever owns the gallery space? Shouldn't they be helping?"

I winced and then pointed at myself.

Linc's brows lifted. "You own The Collective."

It wasn't a question, but I answered anyway. "It was my first big purchase other than Wanda."

"Who the hell is Wanda?" Linc asked, confusion lining his features.

"My truck."

"Good name. Fits her." Linc moved into my space, his hand running over the side of my face. "Why wouldn't you just tell me you own The Collective?"

I shrugged. "I don't tell many people. My family knows. Denver, Isaiah, Farah, and Hannah. But that's it, really."

His roughened thumb stroked the line of my jaw. "Hates being the center of attention."

I made a face. "People don't need to know it's me."

"No, they don't. But I think what you've created is pretty damn amazing. And I bet the community programs were your brainchild."

My cheeks heated. I remembered when I'd gone to Denver with the idea. He'd thought it was a waste of time and money. I'd deflated but pushed on, and was so glad I had. Because those programs filled my cup more than anything else.

Linc dropped his head, his lips sweeping across mine. "You're incredible."

"Linc," I whispered, trying not to squirm.

"Okay, too much attention. Let's go to the gallery."

"You don't—"

Linc pinned me with a hard stare. "I go where you go."

"That means I'm gonna ogle you. You'll just have to deal with it."

Linc barked out a laugh. "I think I can handle it, Vicious."

We made the trip into town in Linc's Range Rover. I was shocked when he'd been okay with letting Brutus on the leather seats, but Linc had just leveled me with that stare and said, "It's an SUV. I think it can handle a little dog hair."

But that was Linc. He might have nice things, but he didn't worship at their altar the way my dad had. He enjoyed them but didn't protect them at all costs. And even though business clearly gave Linc a charge, he wasn't constantly looking for more, more, more.

Linc turned into a spot a block down from The Collective. The town was already full to the brim with tourists milling about, but that wasn't a bad thing. Hopefully, one or two would make a purchase in the gallery.

I hopped out of the SUV and moved to the back seat to hook up Brutus's leash and let him down. Linc met me at the front of the vehicle, wrapping an arm around my shoulders. It would've felt like a completely normal outing if not for the squad car that had followed us into town and parked a couple of spots down.

The deputy wasn't following us in, but he wanted to be close. That reminder of my studio and the rage had my stomach twisting. But I shoved it down. I wouldn't let the asshole win. I refused to live in fear.

"You good?" Linc asked as we walked toward the gallery.

I looked up at him. "I'm annoyed."

His lips twitched. "Still mad at Cope?"

"Well, his overprotective, alpha-male ass is annoying."

Linc chuckled, the sound skating over me in a pleasant shiver. "I don't know about alpha male. Overprotective? Yes. But I'm pretty sure he's just as protective of his brothers as his sisters."

I scowled at him.

Linc released me and held up both hands. "What'd I say?"

"You had to go and make a good point."

That made him laugh. "I'm so sorry. Never again will I make a good point."

"That would be the gentlemanly thing to do," I huffed.

Linc grinned at me as he opened the door. "Baby, I'm a lot of things, but a gentleman isn't one of them."

A shiver of promise raced through me, and I was pretty sure my eyes dilated as memories of last night swirled through my mind. I stretched up onto my tiptoes to whisper in his ear. "I don't know,

Cowboy. You let me come first. If that isn't the mark of a gentleman, I don't know what is."

"Vicious, if you make me walk into this gallery with a hard-on, I am going to spank your ass."

A fresh wave of heat swept through me as different images flashed in my mind.

"You like that idea," Linc rasped, his eyes going hooded.

My gaze cut to his, the hazel a darker green now. "I think I do."

"Gonna kill me," he muttered.

"But we'll have fun on the way out," I said, a smile lacing my tone as I stepped into The Collective.

As I moved inside, it was to find Farah standing there and fanning herself with a pamphlet about the gallery. "Would you two ever consider posing naked together?"

I choked on a laugh. "Farah."

"What?" she asked with mock innocence. "You're both hot as hell. We could do a whole show around it." She did a little jump. "I've got it! Tonight. Mood lighting. Wine. You two in the throes of passion, and me capturing it all."

"As flattering as that is, I'm gonna have to go with no on that one," Linc said, fighting a grin.

Farah made a wailing face. "You're raining on all my hottie-on-hottie dreams over here."

I patted her shoulder. "So sorry."

Her expression shifted, concern filling it now. "Are you okay? We heard someone messed with your studio."

Trace was doing everything he could to keep the details under wraps. The story we were going with was that it was a break-in and some minor vandalism.

"Someone felt like being an asshole is all. Probably thought there was stuff they could sell in there. Got mad when there wasn't," I lied.

"That's so scary," Hannah said, emerging from the office area with Denver in tow and looking worried. "But Trace'll get them. He always does."

Denver's expression was hard to read, but I saw the hint of a pout on his mouth. "You didn't think I might want to know about this? That it's something I *should* know about?"

I bristled at that, and I wasn't alone. Linc stepped up to my side, his already large frame somehow seeming more massive. "And why would that be?"

Anger flashed in Denver's brown eyes. "She's my friend." He paused for a moment, then continued. "And what if pieces for the auction and show were damaged? I'd need to know immediately."

There it was. The truth. Denver didn't give a damn about me. He just wanted more art.

How had it come to this? We'd been friends for years. Had grown up in the art world together in many ways. But it had been so much more. We'd cared about each other's wins and consoled the losses.

Now, I was nothing more than a cash machine to him. God, that sucked.

I lifted my chin and met Denver's stare. "You already have all my pieces for the auction."

Denver's jaw worked back and forth. "I'd still need to know about damage to other pieces."

"Because you might not have enough to sell?" I challenged.

A muscle fluttered in his cheek. "It's my job to manage your inventory. To know what's coming on the market and—"

"No," I clipped. "It's not. It's your job to manage The Collective and the pieces that come into the gallery. You don't get to dictate what I'm giving you or when. You don't even get to know what I'm working on. Because my art is just that. *Mine.* You can't control my creative process."

The room went silent for a moment. Hannah's gaze ping-ponged between us as she wrung her hands. Fighting and awkwardness were not her things. Farah, on the other hand, loved moments of honesty. She started clapping. "Preach it, sister. No one owns you."

Denver sent her a glare that should've had her taking a step back but didn't. "I'd watch it, Farah. I'm the one in charge of pushing your stuff, too."

She just rolled her eyes, unfazed. "Let's be real, Denny Boy. You don't put any effort into our stuff. Arden has always been your prize show pony."

Surprise streaked through me. Is that really what she thought? What they all thought? I sought out Hannah, whose gaze dropped to the floor as she tugged her lip between her teeth. She thought the same.

Hell.

I didn't follow much of what Denver did on the private side. The gallery space made enough to keep the building afloat, and that was all I cared about. But my lack of involvement had hurt the people I cared about. I really would have to fire Denver, which would hurt like hell.

Denver's mouth twisted into what almost looked like a snarl. "It's not my fault your work just isn't quite up to snuff."

Hannah's head snapped up, and I saw hurt blazing in her hazel eyes. "Denver," she whispered.

He just rolled his eyes. "Your watercolors are fine, but nothing that will spark real excitement in the art world." Denver turned to Farah. "And your mixed media is hit or miss at best. Without consistency, you'll never carry a show on your own." He flicked those ridiculous feathers in his hair over one shoulder. "At least Isaiah has something to say. It might be one note, but that's better than nothing."

"You're fired." The words were out of my mouth before I could stop them.

Denver's head whipped around in my direction. "You can't fire me."

"Can't I?" I asked as fury coursed through me. A good portion of that rage was pointed directly at Denver, but the rest was squarely on me. Because I hadn't seen what was going on. Hadn't seen it because I wasn't paying attention.

"You *need* me," Denver hissed.

Linc scoffed. "Does she? Arden has created something more special than you could ever dream of. What have you done other than get in her way?"

Denver's eyes narrowed. "Oh, and you're an expert on that now because you're fucking her?"

Oh, shit.

Linc stalked forward. "I'm giving you that one because you just had your ass handed to you, and with your lack of professionalism, I doubt you'll be getting another job anytime soon. But if you *ever* talk about Arden like that in front of me again, I will break your nose before you can blink. Then I'll take great pleasure in making sure every company you apply for a job with from now on knows exactly how shitty of an employee you are."

Denver opened his mouth, but Farah cut him off. "Oh, I wouldn't, Denny Boy. Linc here has the reach to ruin you."

Denver snapped his mouth closed, rage still swirling in his expression.

"Get your stuff," I said quietly, a heaviness taking over.

"You're seriously doing this?" he asked, delusional shock filling his words.

"What other choice did you give me?" I shot back. "The Collective is supposed to be about coming together to create something better than any of us could do alone. But you've been undermining that at every turn. And I've been too checked out to see it."

"I wasn't—"

"Get your stuff," I clipped. I didn't want to hear his excuses.

"Or I can help you," Linc ground out.

I did not want to see what that would look like. Brutus let out a low growl at my side as if to say, "*Move it.*"

Denver stomped toward the office area and grabbed some papers and his laptop before picking up a plant from the desk and a massive amount of snacks he'd probably bought with the company credit card. He looked ridiculous as he tried to move toward the front door.

"Here, let me get that for you," Linc offered in a sickly-sweet voice.

"Fuck off," Denver muttered as he stalked past.

"Don't let the door hit you on the way out," Farah called.

The door shut, and we all stared at each other for a long moment. I was about to speak when a ring cut through the quiet. Linc pulled his phone out and frowned. "It's my second-in-command."

"Take it," I urged.

"You sure?"

"Of course."

Linc answered, heading out the door as Isaiah strode in, looking more than a little rumpled. His clothes were wrinkled, his eyes red, and his hair messy. He looked around the room. "What the hell crawled up Den's ass?"

Farah's lips twitched. "Pretty sure that was Arden."

I scrunched up my nose. "Gross."

"No one wants up there, but I am into a little ass play," Isaiah said, giving me a wink.

Farah laughed. "That what you were up to last night? Don't think I haven't noticed you're wearing the same clothes as yesterday."

Isaiah grinned at her. "If I could remember what I did last night, I would be happy to share it with my favorite dirty bird."

"I'm gonna get back to my painting," Hannah said, her voice small.

"Wait," I said quickly. "I'm so sorry. I didn't know Den wasn't pulling his weight for you guys. I promise I'll find something better."

"Not your fault," she said quickly.

"It's not, really," Farah echoed. "Douchey Denny is his own problem."

"I still should've caught it." And I'd keep kicking myself about that for a while to come.

"Is someone going to fill me in?" Isaiah asked.

"I think that's a job for Arden. Hannah and I gotta work on our mediocre art," Farah said, wrapping an arm around Hannah and leading her toward the studio spaces.

I winced. It was Farah's way to make a joke out of everything, but that one cut.

A hand landed on my shoulder. "Ardy. What the hell happened?"

I looked up into Isaiah's warm, understanding eyes. "I fucked up."

CHAPTER THIRTY-SEVEN

Lincoln

I'M SORRY TO BOTHER YOU," NINA SAID ACROSS THE LINE. "I KNOW you've got a lot going on."

"That doesn't mean I'm not available if you need me," I said, stepping into the small garden in front of The Collective. It was clear that an artist had designed it. The narrow stone pathway formed an intricate design as flowers sprouted all around, leading to a mosaic bench in the center.

"It's your dad."

I stiffened, my hand tightening around my phone. "Is he going for another of our potentials?"

We'd locked down information even more after what had happened with Ice Edge, but it sometimes felt like my father had eyes everywhere.

"Not anyone we're considering." Nina paused. "I'm pretty sure he's going after the Sparks."

Everything in me stilled. My father *hated* that I owned a hockey team. Just like he hated that I'd played the sport in high school. It was beneath him. If I wanted to play a sport, he expected it to be from his list of approved endeavors. Tennis. Golf. He might've even been okay with lacrosse.

He said the violence of the game was beneath our station. But at least that was honest. Philip Pierce's violence was far more deceptive—a true snake in the grass. He would simply place the dominoes strategically and watch them fall. Just like he had with my mom.

"What do you know?" My voice was so tight I barely recognized it.

"I'm sorry, Linc," Nina said softly.

Her gentleness made it worse, but I battled not to bite her head off. "Not your fault. Just tell me."

She knew I needed her to rip off the Band-Aid. In a flash, she slipped into unemotional territory, her business mode activating. "I've gotten word from three different sources that your father is having some careful conversations with strategically placed individuals."

"Who?" I ground out.

"I've received confirmation of three specifics. Still working on the rest. Brent Lucie in substance testing. Carl Owens on the Board of Governors for the league. And Ewen Maxwell."

It got worse and worse with each name. Brent being up our asses with testing would be annoying, but I trusted my guys to play it clean. We made it clear there'd be no tolerance for anything less.

Carl was concerning because they could open an investigation if they had falsified proof that I was mishandling the team in some way. But Ewen was a knife to the back. He was one of the longest-standing members of the Sparks' board of directors. As far as I knew, we had a good relationship. He wanted to play things a little safer, but we usually met in the middle.

The fact that he hadn't shared that my father had contacted him was a betrayal. And it could be more. The start of a move to oust me as the team's owner. Because it was impossible to lead a team if no one believed in your leadership.

"I want a full list," I clipped into the phone. "And then I want to talk strategy."

"It might be time to go on the offensive. If you don't fight back, he'll never stop," Nina said quietly.

It was like a playground bully who wanted you to run or fight back. I kept thinking the best course of action was to simply ignore him, but maybe I was wrong. "I need to think about it. Give me a day or two."

The best business decisions were never made in the heat of anger or excitement, and they sure as hell weren't made with ego in mind. But the Sparks? That was my favorite company. Because it was so much more. It was a brotherhood. And I hated my father even more for trying to ruin that.

"Okay," Nina said. "I'll get to work."

"Thank you." I hung up before she could ask if I was okay because I didn't want to lie to my partner and friend. Instead, I shoved my phone into my pocket and raked a hand through my hair, tugging hard on the strands.

"That bad?"

I turned at the sound of Arden's voice, all smoky care. "Hey. You okay?"

She made a *tsk*ing noise. "You first."

"It's nothing—"

"Linc. You really wanna do this? Then it's give and take. Both of us."

"You just fired your friend—"

"And I can hold that *and* whatever you're about to tell me."

I sighed and pulled her into me, inhaling the scent of fresh cherries and letting it wash away the taint of my father. "We think my dad's making a play for the Sparks."

Arden reeled back, pulling herself from my hold and taking that scent of cherries with her. "What?"

I nodded. "Laying the groundwork in a variety of ways, just like he always does."

Arden's brows furrowed. "He's done this before?"

I lowered myself to the mosaic bench, dropping my head and

pinching the bridge of my nose. I didn't know how to explain it. Even coming from someone who'd lived through it all, it sounded unhinged.

The scent of cherries returned as Arden sat, moving in close. She stroked a hand across my back in soothing circles, the kind of comfort I hadn't gotten in well over a decade. "I'm here."

Such a gentle promise. But grounded, too. Just like Arden.

"My father has a need for dominance in all things."

Arden didn't say a word, just kept up those circles.

"With every hobby I had as a child, he had to show he was better or that the activity was dumb. Everything from building model rockets to playing piano." Countless memories swirled in my mind. Him accusing my mom of coddling me when she praised a painting I'd brought her. Stepping in during a piano lesson to show me *how it was really done*. I hadn't even realized that I'd started hiding the things I loved most from him in self-preservation.

"As I got older and saw who he really was, I pulled away," I went on.

"I bet he didn't like that."

My lips twitched. "No." My fingers gripped my knees, digging in. "My first serious relationship my sophomore year of college, I got an envelope by courier two weeks before we were supposed to move in together. Photos of him fucking her."

Arden sucked in a breath. "Linc."

"He always wants to take everything I care about. Won't be happy until I come home and toe the line. Let him control every last thing in my life."

"And that's what he does to Ellie, too, isn't it?" Arden asked softly.

I nodded, misery sweeping over me. "It's a little less overt with her. More strategic. But he knows I already know exactly who he is. So, he doesn't hide it. I think he actually gets a thrill out of me knowing."

Arden took my hand, lifted it from my knee, and slid one of hers beneath it while covering it with the other. "It sounds like he's sick."

I was sure he was. People didn't become that way in a vacuum. Maybe it was how my grandfather had been with him. But I wasn't sure the reason mattered anymore.

"Sometimes it feels like it'll never end. I keep thinking if I ignore him long enough, he'll just...stop and let me live my life. But it never ends."

Arden's fingers tightened on mine. "Think he'd accept my challenge for a jujitsu match?"

That startled a laugh out of me. "Gonna take him down for me?"

"Oh, I'd love to. Maybe go for a nice castration at the end."

My fingers curled, pulling our hands even tighter together. "Love you, Vicious."

A flash of panic flared in her eyes, but she fought it back. "I talk about castrating your father, and you tell me you love me?"

"Well, you do say the sweetest things."

Arden let out a soft laugh before sobering. "What can I do?"

"I don't think there is anything *to* do until I have more information."

"You'll fight it, though?" she asked, and I didn't miss the hint of hope in her voice.

"I'll fight it. I just don't want to stoop to his level in the process."

"Hey." Arden pulled our hands toward her, my attention along with them. "You won't. You just need to remember that fighting him doesn't mean you have to play his game. Just like a match. You don't let your opponent force you into their game, you keep playing your own. But that doesn't mean you don't fight back."

"You're wise, you know that?"

She leaned in, her lips brushing mine. "Damn straight. And I can't wait to watch you kick his ass."

I barked out a laugh. "My vicious girl."

Arden stood, pulling me with her. Not that it was much of a battle; I'd go anywhere with her. "Come on, Cowboy," she said, a smile playing on her face. "I'm taking you somewhere."

CHAPTER THIRTY-EIGHT

Arden

"YOU WANT ME TO GET ON THIS THING?"

The skepticism in Linc's voice had me biting back a chuckle. "It's not a thing. It's a horse. And her name is Stardust."

His gaze swept over the mare, lingering on the saddle and pack. "And what about me breaking my neck makes you think it will help me feel better?"

I couldn't hold back the laugh this time. "Stardust is as steady as they come. She won't spook, even if we come across a cougar."

Linc stilled, staring at me like I had two heads. "I don't think getting mauled by a cougar is going to help either."

I grinned back at him as I tightened the cinch on Whiskey's saddle. "Never ridden a horse before? I thought you were a secret cowboy."

Linc moved toward Stardust's head, letting her sniff his open palm before he stroked her face. There was an ease about the movement that was at odds with his earlier apprehension, which spoke of being around these animals before.

"My mom used to take me," he said quietly.

My gut twisted as guilt swept in. This might have been a big misstep. "We don't have to—"

"No," Linc said, cutting me off. "It'll be good. I think both of us could use a little time away."

He was right. Just a few days of having deputies trailing me every time I left the property and being perched outside my house and studio made me feel like I was suffocating. I could only imagine how Linc felt. It was as if his father had been tracking his every move for years.

I patted Whiskey and moved into Linc's space, leaning in and brushing my mouth across his. "A night under the stars will do us both some good."

One corner of Linc's mouth kicked up. "I wouldn't mind sharing a tent with you."

"What about a sleeping bag?"

"Even better." Linc lowered his head and took my mouth in a kiss that tipped hotter as his tongue stroked mine.

Stardust bumped Linc's back, forcing him to break the kiss. He turned, eyeing the mare. "It's not bad enough that I have one cockblock? Now, I have two?"

Brutus let out a soft bark as if he understood exactly what Linc had accused him of.

I scratched between Stardust's ears, where she loved it the most. "My girl's just ready to hit the trail."

"And now I have to hit it with a hard-on," Linc muttered.

"Have fun with that," I singsonged.

We mounted and headed for the trails that would lead us into Forest Service land. It was one of the things I loved about Cope's property. There was no need to trailer the horses somewhere to ride. I could just take off and go.

But I was still cautious. Emergency provisions. Sat phone. Extra supplies. Rifle, just in case. And Trace would've lost his mind if I didn't give him our exact route and camping spot. It had been hard enough to get him to agree to the trip in the first place. Safety first with him, always. Even before someone had vandalized my property.

But I understood why. When you grew up in situations where

safety was the last thought, it changed you. And in some ways, law and order had become the crutch Trace held on to. As though he couldn't be hurt again if he never colored outside the lines.

I guessed we all had things we thought would keep us safe and away from any more pain. But as I looked over at Linc, I knew those things were a lie. Because it only took one person crashing into your life to destroy every last wall you'd put up.

Icy claws of panic dug into my chest, but I shoved the sensation down. Instead, I focused on the man opposite me. The one who'd been there for me in all my darkest moments lately. I needed to do the same for him. Had to give him back a little of what he'd given me.

"It's so peaceful here," Linc said, his eyes shaded by a Seattle Sparks ballcap.

My gaze swept the high desert landscape, taking in the mixture of sage-filled plains and thick forests, all leading to Castle Rock and the Monarch Mountains. "The vastness of it always puts my problems in perspective."

He glanced over at me as Brutus ran ahead of the horses to sniff the trail. "You trying to give me that? Perspective?"

I shrugged. "Maybe. Or escape. A little reprieve to gather your strength to fight another day."

A muscle in Linc's jaw ticked. "I'm not sure he's someone I can ever defeat."

"Gotta find his weak spot. Same as sparring."

"Sometimes, I don't think he has one."

I stared at Linc for a moment, trusting that Whiskey would keep us on the path. "I know he does." Linc's gaze cut back to me, surprise lighting there. "He doesn't realize what's right in front of him. The incredible son. The amazing daughter. He's missing out on what he has in his quest for more. He can never take in everything that's been given to him because he's too blinded by trying to have it all."

Linc's throat worked as he swallowed. "I don't want to be like him."

Hell.

I guided Whiskey toward Stardust, close enough that I could

reach out and take Linc's hand. "You never could be. You're never blind to the world around you. Never turn away from someone who's hurting."

Linc didn't look convinced.

"You got Cope in with the best doctors and rehab specialists. And look how much better he's doing already."

"Maybe I just wanted my star player back," Linc challenged.

I rolled my eyes. "What about all you've done for me? Stepping in, even when I shoved you away."

Linc's gaze roamed over my face, feeling like a featherlight touch of fingertips. "Maybe I just wanted to get laid."

One corner of my mouth kicked up. "I guess that worked out well for you."

"I guess it did," Linc said, the dark green in his eyes flashing a little brighter.

"You can't hide from me, Cowboy. I see you. I see how much you care. You fight for the underdog every single time. The company that needs extra support. The sports team that was on an epic losing streak until you turned it around. Even paying the most attention to the quietest kid at art camp."

"Gracie?" Linc asked.

"Gracie." I squeezed his fingers. "You'll never be your father because you're uniquely you. You took all his ugliness and turned it into beauty. Like a living sculpture. So damn breathtaking."

"Vicious?"

"Yeah, Cowboy?"

"You say stuff like that, and I'm gonna need to fuck you. And the only thing that's around here are tumbleweeds and rocks. That does not sound pleasant. So, I'm gonna need you to stop being so amazing."

My mouth stretched into a wide smile. "I'll try my best, but amazing is kind of my default setting."

Linc barked out a laugh. "Damn if that isn't true."

The warmth of it all slid through me. Unfortunately, fast on its heels came panic. But I did what I always did and shoved that shit down.

CHAPTER THIRTY-NINE

Lincoln

POURING WATER INTO MAKESHIFT TROUGHS FOR THE HORSES, my muscles screamed in protest. I was in damn good shape, but apparently not the sort of shape I needed for riding.

I set the jug down and attempted a stretch, even though my muscles were not pleased with me. As I fought through the discomfort, I really took in our surroundings. I'd been many places in my life, but I'd never seen one as beautiful as this.

It was a hidden gem, tucked away from prying eyes by a dip in the landscape. The spot was nestled between Castle Rock and the Monarch Mountains, and if I thought my new property had good views, it had nothing on this campsite.

It was as if both rock formations towered over us, trees bordering us on the north side, and meadows on the south. A creek that gathered in a little dip ran through the landscape, forming the world's most perfect swimming hole. And the quiet…

It was a silence I'd never known before. Nothing but the sounds of the horses getting settled and the breeze rustling tree branches. Perfect.

But none of it was as perfect as the woman standing in the middle of our campsite, wind lifting mahogany strands of hair as she scratched Brutus's ears. When she straightened, those tendrils swirled around her, creating their own work of art.

She moved toward the swimming hole, kicking off her boots as she went. I had no choice but to follow. It was as if she had woven some sort of spell around me. Arden sat, rolled up her jeans, and sank her feet into the water. She tipped her face up to the sun, the rays making the apples of her cheeks glow.

I couldn't resist. I leaned over and pressed my mouth to hers. Arden's eyes opened, taking me in as I kissed her, not missing a moment.

"Thank you for this," I whispered against her lips.

Something passed over her face, but it was gone before I could pin it down.

"It's my favorite place," Arden said, turning her focus to the horizon.

I lowered myself to the bank of the swimming hole, then pulled off my own boots and slid my feet into the cold water. "I can see why."

"Sometimes, I come for a week. Bring my sketchpad and load one of the horses with supplies."

I tried not to think about Arden out here all alone or imagine all the things that could go wrong. "I bet you could create a lot of beauty out here."

A small smile played on her lips. "It definitely fills my bucket. And Brutus loves it."

I glanced over my shoulder to find Brutus passed out on one of the saddle blankets. He'd practically run the whole way here, so I could only imagine how tired he was.

A flicker of movement caught my eye. A dragonfly skimmed along the water and then floated up to rest on Arden's knee. Soft wonder filled her expression as she took in the creature that was a riot of color: pink, blue, and teal. "Well, aren't you beautiful?"

"In some cultures, they're supposed to bring good luck," I said quietly, not wanting to frighten it off. "That or be a sign of rebirth."

Arden's gaze flicked to me, emotion swirling there. "Rebirth." Her focus moved back to the dragonfly still resting on her knee. "Feels like I've been working toward that forever."

"Maybe she's telling you that you're already there."

Arden watched as the dragonfly took flight again, dipping and rolling before taking off into the wilderness. "Maybe she is." Her focus turned back to me, a smile playing on her lips. "This place really is magic."

"It is." I glanced around at the beauty engulfing us. "I wonder what trails I'll have off my property. You know, I think you can see it from up here," I said, turning and squinting into the distance.

"Really?" Arden turned, following my line of sight.

"See the creek that runs along the base of the mountains?"

"Damn, Cowboy. You got yourself a spot."

I pulled out my phone and tapped my photos. I knew I wouldn't have any service, but I'd already downloaded what I wanted to show her.

Arden leaned over and sucked in a breath. "Linc…"

"This is the first sketch of the exterior. Your brother has a gift."

"He does." Her gaze roamed the sketch, seeming to memorize every detail.

"Anything you'd do differently?" I knew I'd be lying to myself if I said I asked for any other reason than I hoped like hell Arden would be spending a lot of time there.

"It's perfect. The way it's just gonna settle at the base of the peaks. The way it's gonna meld with the golden grasses. I'm a little jealous, if I'm honest."

I grinned, locking my phone and setting it on the bank. "If you're really nice, I'll let you come visit."

She shifted slightly, her unease showing for the briefest moment. "What is it?"

She shook her head, strands of her hair lifting in the breeze again. "Nothing."

"Vicious," I growled.

She bit the corner of her lip. "How often are you going to use that house? Cope said it was just a vacation home."

I was an idiot. I hadn't once considered that Arden might think our situation had an expiration date. Hadn't thought she might need a little reassurance.

My hand slid along her jaw, and I tilted her face toward mine. "I can do my job from anywhere. I may have to fly to Seattle for meetings every couple of weeks, but I can *live* anywhere."

Arden was quiet for a moment, those gray-violet eyes searching mine. "Where do you want to live?"

"I'd live in that tiny-ass tent if that's where you were."

Her berry-stained lips parted on a sharp inhale. "Linc. You don't know that. You barely know me. I'm grumpy half the time, finicky about my space and art, and not exactly good at normal. You can't say that."

My hand shifted, sliding into her hair and holding tight. "You think I don't know I need to duck and cover if you get woken up before ten? Or that every time I get a little bit closer, you're going to try to shove me away? I know, Vicious. And I'm still here."

My fingers tightened further, making sure she paid attention. "But you're so much more than that. You're not afraid to tell me the truth. You see beyond the surface into everything beneath. You make me feel…not alone for the first time in years. And you make me want to reach for better, the kind of more that's all about being who you truly are."

Arden's eyes glistened with unshed tears. "That scares me."

"I know, baby," I whispered, dropping my forehead to hers. "But you're still here."

"I'm still here." She let out a long, shuddering breath. "Plus, leaving you unprotected in the wilderness would be rude."

I barked out a laugh as I released her. "That's very true. I need you and your switchblade to keep me safe."

Arden grinned at me. "Damn straight."

"How about some bourbon before dinner?" I asked.

"I wouldn't say no."

"Good." I pushed to my feet and headed for where we'd set up the drinks near a tree where we'd hoist our bear-proof container tonight. I rifled through the bottles of water and a few sodas until I found it. We didn't have ice, but we could set the glasses in the water. That'd cool it down quickly.

Pouring two healthy servings, I turned to head back and froze. Arden was nowhere to be seen. Not on the shore, not in the distance, not in camp. My pulse picked up speed as blood roared in my ears. Where the hell was she?

And that's when I saw it. The pile of clothes next to the boots on the shore.

A second later, a dark head of hair burst from the water's surface, sending droplets flying. Arden looked like someone who didn't have a care in the world as she treaded water in the center of the swimming hole. I, on the other hand, had just lost ten years of my life.

I stalked toward the water. "What the hell are you thinking?"

Arden's eyes widened in surprise. "I was thinking I was hot, and it was the perfect time for a swim."

"That water is barely above freezing," I shot back.

"Don't be dramatic."

My eyes narrowed on her as I set the drinks down. "Dramatic? Because I don't want you to get hypothermia?" That's when I zeroed in on her bare shoulders. "What are you wearing in there?"

Arden tried to swallow her laugh but was only half-successful. "What do you think I'm wearing, Cowboy?"

Fucking hell.

Just the mental image, the promise of what lay under the surface, had my dick stiffening. "Vicious, out of the water."

Those gray-violet eyes danced. It was the sort of mischief I hadn't seen from Arden in weeks. And damn, it was good to see.

She flipped to her back, her perfect breasts breaking the surface of the water. "What are you going to do about it?"

That challenge. The fire. My dick pressed harder against my zipper. "Spank that ass for scaring the hell out of me."

Arden's eyes flashed—a different kind of fire in them now. She flipped back to her stomach and swam toward me. "That sounds a hell of a lot more like a promise than a threat."

Everything in me tightened at the pure temptation swimming toward me. "Why don't you come out of the water and find out?"

Her gaze was liquid purple now as she swam closer to shore. She didn't stand, not yet. She seemed to be weighing her options and power moves. And it was hot as hell watching that beautiful brain work.

Arden's hands balanced on the sandy bottom. She was close enough now that I could see all of her, and the globes of her ass peeked out of the water. My hands fisted around nothing, wanting to touch her so badly.

She saw the shift. And that's when she stood, seeing that I was at my breaking point.

It wasn't slow or timid because that wasn't Arden. She stood in one fluid movement, beauty in motion. There was no bashfulness or hiding. Because that wasn't her either.

She stood in full ownership of her body as the water slid down her in what seemed like endless rivulets. Her hair slicked around the perfect breasts my hands ached to palm as those streams continued their journey, coasting down her stomach toward the tiniest dusting of hair at the apex of her thighs.

Thighs that were tan, curved with lean muscle, and dipped into calves painted the same. But it was her face that held me rapt. Those lips I knew tasted like cherries. Eyes that always welcomed me home. Ones I could lose myself in forever.

But now wasn't the time for tender. My girl wanted to play. And I always gave her what she wanted.

"On your knees."

CHAPTER FORTY

Arden

THE COLD WATER HAD ALREADY TIGHTENED MY NIPPLES TO THE point of pain, but at Linc's husky command, they twisted so tight my knees nearly buckled.

Linc's eyes darkened, the green turning stormy, practically swallowing the gold altogether. Like a lake in the middle of a hurricane. "I said, on your knees, Vicious."

A shiver racked me. But it wasn't one of dread, it was one of promise. My mouth curved. "Shouldn't you have to work for it a little harder?"

Linc took one step and then another, his powerful thighs straining against his jeans. "You don't think watching you sit on that horse for hours wasn't torture enough? Watching those breasts move with each step? Staring at those thighs clenching?"

My lips parted on an intake of breath.

"But you love knowing you torture me, don't you?"

My mouth curved. "Maybe."

Linc shook his head as he stepped closer, venturing into the water and not giving a damn that the bottoms of his jeans were getting soaked. He moved so slowly that I wasn't prepared when he struck with the speed of a viper, his hand sliding into my hair and pulling on the strands so my head was tipped back and my neck exposed.

Then his mouth was there, tongue running down the column of my throat. "You live to torture me. It's only fitting that I return the favor."

I could barely suck in a breath before Linc was moving again. He took me with him this time. I stumbled, trying to keep up with him, and it was just the off-balance upper hand Linc needed.

He dropped to the log near the shore, taking me with him and folding me over his lap, where I landed with an *oomph*. The air fled my lungs through force and excitement. My thighs pressed together as the air swirled against my overheated skin.

There was no warning before his hand came down hard on my ass cheek. A sting, then heat. Heat that pooled and spread. My thighs started to clench again, but Linc wrapped my hair around his hand, pulling hard as he made a *tsk*ing noise. "No relief for you. Not yet. A little torture before your pleasure."

My lips parted, a pant leaving them as wetness gathered between my thighs.

"That's my girl," Linc praised, his hand ghosting over the globe of my ass, coaxing a little more from that heat. "But you still have to pay for making me suffer through three hours of riding with a god-damned hard-on."

A soft giggle left my lips.

Linc's hand tightened in my hair. "Are you laughing at me?"

Before I could answer, his hand came down again, a little harder this time. My body bowed. The flicker of pain, the rush of heat, it was all so good I couldn't help the moan that slipped from my lips.

Linc's hand coasted over my ass to stroke between my thighs. "Fuck. You love it. Pussy's weeping already."

I shuddered against him. "Linc."

"So beautiful when she begs." He slid two fingers inside me.

My back arched as I pushed against him, so damn desperate for more.

Those fingers were gone in a flash, and Linc's palm came down in another strike. "My girl's greedy, too. Always ready to take what she wants. What she needs. But right now, you're going to take what I give you."

My head turned as I cast furious eyes on him. "Gonna give you blue balls if you're not careful."

Linc laughed, the sound full of mischief and heat. "You think I'm not already walking around in that permanent state because of you?"

My mouth curved, the power of that statement coursing through me.

Linc's eyes hooded. "You love that. Live to torture me. My vicious girl."

Those fingers were back, three this time, gliding in and out. I whimpered. They felt so damn good, but it wasn't quite enough. I pushed into Linc's hand, needing deeper, more.

My walls fluttered with the briefest shudder on the way to the edge. Then, Linc's hand was gone. I let out a sound of protest, and his palm came down on my ass again. It was almost enough to send me over the edge, the pleasure and pain. Linc gave me both.

He stood in a flash, bringing me with him as he released his hold on my hair. "Hands on the tree," he growled.

It was only two steps to the thick trunk, but each one had my skin burning hotter, the air feeling like a snowstorm in comparison. I didn't look back as my palms pressed against the rough bark, but I heard Linc: the sound of his zipper like a cannon in the quiet, the rustling of his clothes until his big body curved around mine.

Linc's hand twisted in my hair again, pulling my head back. "Tell me I can take you."

My core clenched as I pushed my ass against him. "Take me."

Linc slid his tip along my slit, teasing up to my clit until I whimpered again. He moved back to my opening, and that hand fisted my hair as he slammed into me. The force of it had my eyes watering and my mouth falling open. It was nothing but pure power and sensation. Nothing but everything Linc could give me.

The rough bark dug into my palms as he took me, but I didn't give him supremacy. I gave as good as I got. Met him thrust for thrust. Because the thing about me and Linc was that it was always a battle. We were never afraid to fight for what we wanted. And that made it beautiful—the honesty.

Linc muttered something nonsensical as he hit a spot that had light dancing in front of my vision. Those fingers tightened in my hair. "Need you with me. Always with me."

"I'm with you." The words were punctuated by gasps, my lungs stealing all the air they could get.

"Not close enough," Linc gritted out. "Finger on your clit. Find it with me."

My body obeyed without my brain stopping to consider the concession. One hand dropped from the tree and slid between my thighs. I let out a curse at the first sensation of my finger circling that bundle of nerves.

"That's it. So perfect," Linc praised.

My body sparked at his words.

"Tease it. Closer," he ordered.

Yet again, I obeyed. My body shuddered as sparks lit beneath my skin. Linc picked up speed, powering into me until I was all but lost.

"Fight for it," Linc growled. "I know my vicious girl battles like no one else. Fight for it with me."

And I knew he meant more than an orgasm. He meant he wanted me to fight for us. To make this something real. Something that could mean forever.

Terror swept through me, but I didn't stop fighting because he was with me. My finger circled tighter, sweeping across that most sensitive flesh and sending me spiraling. It wasn't a light and airy fall; it was a violent plummet. The orgasm racked my body with a fury that took us both down together in beautiful agony.

Linc cursed as he emptied into me, lengthening the fall with each thrust. But he never left me. We fell together. And as his forehead dropped to my shoulder, his breathing heavy, I felt all of him.

"Like nothing else, you and me. Like I can be whoever I need to, and you'll take me just as I am," he whispered hoarsely.

My throat constricted. "I know," I croaked. Because I felt the exact same way. And it scared the hell out of me.

"Do we have to leave?" Linc asked, pouting like a little kid as late-morning sunrays cast shadows over his face.

I couldn't help but chuckle. "We don't have to, but I think we'll be hungry by tonight," I said as I tightened the strap on the saddlebag, but the truth was, leaving was the last thing I wanted to do.

"Can't have my girl getting hangry on me." Linc stuffed the last of our camp's trash into the bag we were packing up.

I crossed to where we'd set up camp, bending to check my pack. Satellite phone, first-aid kit, snacks for the trip back, plenty of water. "You definitely do not want that," I said with a chuckle.

Linc moved into my space and wrapped his arms around me. "Thank you for giving me this. For knowing me well enough to give me exactly what I needed."

That foreign feeling in my chest shifted again. "I wish I could really fix it."

Linc brushed the hair from my face. "Well, you did offer to challenge my dad to a fight to the death. That's good enough for me."

My lips twitched. "I'd take his ass down."

"I have no doubt." Linc gave me a quick kiss and then released me.

I bent to lift the pack just as a crack sounded. It was almost like a tree branch snapping in the wind, only there *was* no wind today.

My brain tried to put the pieces together, reason out what it was, when Linc's body hit mine full force. Just as another crack sounded. And that's when I registered the sound.

Gunshot.

CHAPTER FORTY-ONE

Lincoln

I HIT ARDEN LIKE A LINEBACKER TAKING DOWN A RUNNING BACK, the force of it sending a sound of protest out of her. Or was it pain? Panic swept through me. Was she hit? Hurt? Something worse?

I kept her covered as another shot rang out. One of the horses whinnied, something snapped, and then Whiskey was running in the direction of Cope's property. *Hell.*

Brutus growled, then barked, and Arden yelled out some order in German. The dog instantly lay down, but the growling didn't cease. The shots did.

Other than Brutus's snarls and Stardust's sounds of protest, the world went eerily silent around us. No more shots. No nothing.

"Linc," Arden whispered.

"Not yet," I clipped. I wasn't exactly sure what I was waiting for. Another shot? Pounding hoofbeats, letting us know the shooter was fleeing? It certainly wouldn't be the sound of sirens, not out here.

That's when I heard it. The faint sound of an engine. If I hadn't been focused, I would've missed it. But it didn't sound like a car. More like a dirt bike or an ATV.

Still, I waited.

When the sound of the engine disappeared, I rolled off Arden, my hands instantly roaming over her in search of injuries. "Are you okay? What hurts?"

Arden started to nod, but then all color drained from her face, her skin bleaching white.

"What? Where are you hurt?" I didn't see any blood.

"I'm okay." Her throat worked as she swallowed. "But you're not."

It was as if her words sent feeling zinging back through me, and with it came the pain. A burning sensation took root in my side, and I glanced down. Blood bloomed on the lower right side of my torso.

It couldn't be that bad. I wasn't passing out or struggling to breathe. But the pain intensified as if to argue that point.

Arden was already moving. She hauled up the pack that had taken the brunt of our weight and began pulling items out of it. As she grabbed what looked like a phone, she cursed. The screen was smashed. She tried hitting a couple of buttons before giving up and moving on to something else and calling to Brutus. "Freigeben."

The dog ran over, licking her face and then mine. He was fine. No injuries. Just pissed as all hell on our behalf.

"We should move," I said, wincing with the words.

Arden sent a scathing look my way. "We're dealing with your wound, and then we'll move."

My gaze swept the campsite and the surrounding landscape. I saw no signs of movement, but that didn't mean someone wasn't out there, waiting. "How are we going to get home with only one horse?"

Arden winced. "We'll have to walk. Stardust can carry the supplies." She began pulling things from the first-aid kit. "Whiskey's smart. She'll run home. We just have to hope Cope or Sutton see her and send help."

If they didn't, the hike would take us all day. Who knew what could happen in that length of time?

"Lean against the tree and pull up your shirt," Arden ordered.

I did my best to shift back, the pain flaring, bright and fierce. I didn't miss Arden's panic as she saw my pained expression. Forcing a smile, I tried to keep my voice light. "You know, I really don't think now's the time for you to get lucky."

"You're not funny, Cowboy."

I leaned against the tree, wincing. "Come on, I'm a little funny."

Arden didn't laugh. Instead, she pulled some hand sanitizer from the kit and squirted some into her hands, rubbing them together. Then she donned gloves. "Lift your shirt."

I did as she ordered and cursed. There was definitely a bullet wound. "See? Not that bad. It's practically a graze."

Arden's gaze lifted to mine, fire flaring there. "You're not helping." She maneuvered so she could see my back, as well. "It looks like the bullet went through. That's good. But you're still bleeding. I need to clean the site and then pack the wound."

"Why does something tell me that's not going to feel like sunshine and rainbows?" I asked.

"Because it's not." She reached for a small bottle of hydrogen peroxide. "I'm sorry." And then she poured it over the wound.

A strangled noise left my mouth, and Brutus growled in response.

"Stay with me," Arden said, shifting so she could get to my back. She didn't wait for me to say I was ready, she just poured the peroxide there, too.

I didn't make a sound this time, but I bit down hard on the inside of my cheek—so hard I tasted blood. That probably wasn't the smartest move given the fact that I needed all the blood I could keep in my body. But there was nothing to be done about it now.

"Okay. Lean back," Arden instructed, helping me rest against the tree.

Pain pulsed through me, and my breaths came in shorter wheezes now. But Arden didn't stop. She rifled through the kit in search of something before cursing. Then she pulled something out of a zippered nylon bag.

I blinked a few times, trying to clear my vision. "Vicious," I mumbled. "What do you think I'm going to do with a tampon?"

Arden squared her shoulders. "You're not going to do a damn thing, but *I* am going to plug your wound."

I gaped at her. "With a...tampon?"

"That was how they were first invented. To plug bullet holes in the eighteenth century."

"Should I be scared that you know that?"

"Hey," Arden huffed. "I read."

She removed the tampon from the wrapper as I watched skeptically. But it wasn't as if I had a better idea. Arden's gentle fingers prodded the area around the wound, studying it. Then she looked up at me. "This really isn't going to feel good."

"Should I ask for the bourbon and a strap to bite down on like in the Westerns?"

"Linc. Please stop joking."

I saw it then, the true terror Arden was trying to shove down. "Vicious," I whispered, pulling her to me.

Arden's forehead dropped to mine, and she trembled against me.

"I'm going to be fine. You're going to patch me up, and then we're going to get the hell out of here," I assured her.

She pulled back a fraction, searching my eyes. "I think I should leave you with the rifle and Brutus. I'll take Stardust and ride for home as fast as I can."

"No." There was a slap to that single word, a finality.

"Linc—"

"No." I put even more force behind it the second time. "We stick together, you and me."

Those gray-violet eyes glistened, and Arden's jaw clenched with the struggle of holding back tears. "Don't want anything to happen to you."

"I'm pretty partial to you, as well. So, why don't we stick together and watch each other's backs?"

Arden nodded, a slight tremor in the movement. "Okay. Because I'm gonna be really pissed if you die on me."

I chuckled and instantly regretted it. "Don't make me laugh."

Arden winced. "Sorry." Her gaze swept over my face. "Ready to get the worst of this over?"

I swallowed hard. "Ready."

She pressed a kiss to my mouth and then stayed there for a second. "Close your eyes. That way you won't know it's coming."

I did as she instructed and focused on breathing. There was rustling, I felt Arden's fingers around the wound and then, without warning, blinding pain. The kind that stole your breath and made the whole world disappear around you.

All I could do was breathe—try to grab hold of air, over and over. Just as I caught that precious oxygen, pain flared in a fresh wave of white-hot agony. I kept breathing.

Some part of me was aware of Arden bandaging the sites, and then the pain dulled as if I could feel the disconnect between my body and mind.

"Drink this." Arden wrapped my hand around a small bottle.

"I hope it's bourbon," I croaked.

"You get home without giving out on me, and I'll give you all the bourbon you want."

My eyes flickered open. No bourbon, but the last of the orange juice. Probably not a bad idea to get a little sugar in the system. I tossed it back. "Hope this isn't leaking into my gut."

"Not funny," Arden growled.

"Easy, Vicious," I said, grabbing her hand. "Look where I was shot. Barely more than a graze. I doubt it hit anything vital."

Arden glared at me. "If you're not right, I'm kicking your ass."

"So grumpy when emotions are involved."

She rolled her eyes. "Do you want to try to stand, or do you need more time?"

I glanced at the sky. We were getting close to midday, which meant we *needed* to move. "Let's get me up."

"Okay. I want you to grab hold of my shoulders. I'm going to use my weight to lift you. Do *not* tense your stomach muscles."

I nodded, looping my arms around Arden. But even that caused a fresh wave of pain.

"Three, two, one." Arden leaned backward with all her might.

My mind went blank. It was as if all the nerve endings were

rioting, and everything just checked out. But maybe that was better, a mercy.

"Linc." Arden's voice, with just that hint of rasp, brought me back to the here and now. She pressed a hand to my cheek. "Are you okay?"

I nodded, needing a second before I spoke. "I'm good. I've got this."

She studied me, not looking all that sure of my words. "Okay. I'm getting Stardust, and then we'll go."

I just kept breathing, Brutus at my side. "You like me, don't you?"

The dog looked up at me, and I swore he let out a begrudging huff.

"Don't worry. I like you, too. Even if you are a cockblock."

"Should I be concerned that you're talking to my dog as if he's going to answer you?" Arden asked as she crossed to me, rifle in hand.

"He makes himself understood," I argued.

One corner of her mouth kicked up. "That's true enough." She bent to give Brutus a scratch. "You're looking out, aren't you?"

Brutus pressed into her hand in answer.

As Arden straightened, she scanned our surroundings. "Let's go."

I frowned. "Don't you need a lead rope for Stardust?"

She shook her head and made a clicking sound. Stardust moved right in our direction, packs in place.

"I'll be damned," I muttered.

"She likes to stay near her people. Plus, it's better if my hands are free. Just in case."

I knew what she meant. In case someone was waiting on our path home, and Arden needed to use that rifle in her hands.

"Let's move." The urgency of the moment bore down again as I started walking. Each step brought a new flare of pain, just like each rustle in the brush had me tensing. I just had to hope like hell that whoever had taken those shots was long gone.

Our progress was slow at best, and we had to take a longer route to stick to the edge of the tree line in hopes of protection—or at least something to dive behind if the shooter reemerged. But Arden was right, Stardust plodded along right behind us, and Brutus stuck to my side as if sensing something had happened to compromise me.

We were quiet as we moved, both of us continually scanning our surroundings. Stardust noticed it first. She shifted, letting out a soft whinny.

The rifle was instantly braced against Arden's shoulder as she swept the landscape in front of us. Movement flickered, and then a figure emerged from the trees, a gun leveled at us.

CHAPTER FORTY-TWO

Arden

I T TOOK MY BRAIN A MOMENT TO REGISTER THE PERSON IN FRONT of us. A count of *one, two, three*. And then I nearly collapsed, tears springing to my eyes at the sight of Trace on one of the sheriff's department mounts.

He was off his horse in a matter of seconds, striding across the distance and pulling me into his arms. "What the hell happened? I get a panicked call from Cope saying Whiskey came running home like a bat out of hell, but you guys were nowhere in sight."

Trace didn't wait for an answer; he simply turned and yelled, "They're over here." Then he was back, his gaze skimming over me.

"I'm okay. But Linc needs a hospital."

In a single heartbeat, Trace transformed from worried brother to law enforcement. "What happened?"

"Someone shot at us." Just saying the words felt ridiculous, implausible. Yet they were completely true. "Linc tackled me to the ground, but he got hit in the side. And I smashed the sat phone in my fall."

Trace's gaze snapped to Linc. "You saved my sister."

Linc smiled, but his face was too pale, and his brow was dotted with sweat. "Like I told Vicious, I'm kind of partial to her."

"Let's see the wound. I've got a first-aid kit—"

"Your sister already stuck me with a tampon."

Trace's brows rose as he turned to me. "A tampon?"

"Two, actually," I huffed.

Trace scrubbed a hand over his face. "Huh. Not a bad idea." He pulled a radio from his pocket and called in our location, asking for EMTs to meet us at the bottom of the trail, then looked back at Linc. "We're gonna get you in a litter. Carry you the rest of the way."

"I'm okay—"

"Lincoln Pierce, if you try to play the macho man right now, I will make your life a living, blue-balled hell. Do not argue with him," I snapped.

A cat-that-got-the-cream smile stretched across his face. "Your sister loves me."

Trace arched a brow, amusement teasing his expression. "Does she, now?"

"Big time," Linc said.

"I do not," I clipped, the panic and fear digging in. If I didn't love him, I wouldn't lose him. That was the rule I'd made in my head. It was completely ridiculous, but it was the only thing I had to hold on to.

Linc only smiled wider. "Keep telling yourself that, Vicious."

He tried to take a step toward me but stumbled slightly. Trace and I both surged forward. I ducked under Linc's arm, trying to prop him up. "Where's the damn litter?" I barked.

Just as I asked, Shep and Kye burst through the trees. Everyone talked over one another. Shep and Kye peppered us with questions, and Trace tried to answer them before barking out orders. But all I could do was focus on Linc: the way he leaned more weight on me, how his breathing had become more labored, shallower.

Terror dug in as pressure built behind my eyes. An engine sounded, along with shouts. EMTs had used one of Cope's ATVs to get up to us. They were moving now, taking Linc from me.

My ears buzzed as I watched them work. One of the medics,

a guy I recognized from town, looked up at me and grinned. "Nice thinking on the tampons."

I nodded numbly. "I can go with him, right?"

The smile slipped from the EMT's face. "Of course."

It didn't take them long to get Linc on the backboard and an IV in. As soon as they were set, I jumped onto the second ATV behind Shep. He followed the EMTs and Linc, but I couldn't take my eyes off Linc.

He was always so big and full of life. But now, everything about him seemed fragile. As if the slightest shift could pull him from this world.

As we got closer to Cope's property and my barn, I saw the crowd of people. Sheriff's department personnel, my family—too many all at once. They descended on us, but I didn't say a word, couldn't. I ignored every question and focused on following Linc.

The EMTs lifted him into the back of the ambulance, and I climbed in behind him, settling on the bench. One worked on Linc while the other slammed the doors and ran to the driver's seat. A heart monitor was hooked up, and I tried to focus on the beeping, the sound that told me Linc was still alive. But it wasn't enough.

"I'm okay, Vicious."

But nothing about Linc's voice said he was. It was too weak, raspy. As if he were fading.

I gripped the edge of the bench seat as the ambulance started to move, my fingers digging into the cushion. It took everything in me to force them free. I took Linc's hand, holding it as gently as possible.

"I know you're okay," I lied. I didn't know at all. But I held on anyway.

CHAPTER FORTY-THREE

Lincoln

IF YOU EVEN THINK OF GETTING OUT OF THAT HOSPITAL BED, I will tie you to it myself." Arden's voice cut through the incessant beeping and other annoying hospital sounds.

I turned on the edge of the bed to give her my most charming smile. "Kinky. I like it."

"Linc," she warned. And I should've taken that warning because the woman had been on the warpath for the past twenty-four hours. The second a flicker of pain showed in my expression, she was paging nurses. When a doctor showed, she peppered them with questions, listing off things she'd read in articles about abdominal wounds and all but threatening their lives.

"Vicious," I said, lifting a hand to beckon her over.

She didn't come. Instead, she crossed her arms in a way that thrust up those perfect breasts and pinned me with a glare.

"The doctor is signing my discharge paperwork right now. I can get up."

"He said you have to wait for a wheelchair."

"I don't need—"

"You had surgery," Arden snapped.

"Barely. They cleaned the wound and stitched me up. That's it."

A shadow passed over Arden's eyes, turning them stormy, and I knew it hadn't felt like nothing to her. *Hell.* "Come here."

She still didn't move.

"You don't come here, I'm coming to you, and you really didn't want me out of this bed."

Arden let out a soft huff of air and dropped her arms, walking slowly toward me.

The moment she was within arm's reach, I grabbed her T-shirt—the fucking adorable death metal unicorn one Fallon had brought in the change of clothes—and tugged her between my legs. I took her face in my hands, thumbs stroking the soft skin there. "I'm good. Barely in any pain. The doc told you at least five times that the bullet didn't hit anything important. No organs or arteries. The stitches will come out in a week. That's not even a bad gash."

Arden stared down at me, so much emotion swirling in those captivating eyes. "What if he's wrong?"

"Baby," I whispered, pressing a kiss to one cheek, then the other, then her forehead. "You bombarded him with eighty-two million questions. You talked to the surgical nurse, the anesthesiologist, and cornered an orderly. I'm good."

"I needed to make sure I was getting the full story."

My mouth curved. "I love you, Vicious."

"Linc." My name was a choked-out rasp as if her vocal cords were wrapped around the syllable, not wanting to let it free.

I dropped one hand from Arden's face and placed it over her heart. "You don't have to say it. Won't make it any less true."

Her eyes closed, squeezing as if in pain. "I'm trying to keep you safe."

My brows pulled together. "Keep me—"

"All right, you two lovebirds," a nurse said as she bustled into the room. "I've got your marching orders. The doctor would've brought them himself, but I'm just gonna be honest with you and say that he's scared shitless of this one over here." She inclined her head toward Arden.

Arden stepped back and out of my grasp, shaking off the pain in her expression. "I wasn't *that* bad."

The nurse arched a brow. "Honey, if he had the choice between you and a bunch of rabid dogs, he'd go with the rabid dogs every time."

Arden's jaw dropped, and I struggled not to laugh.

The nurse waved her off as she motioned an orderly in. "It's a good thing. We need our people to fight for us in the room we aren't in. That's you. A fighter."

Vicious to the bone. In all the best ways.

"Thank you for your help, Bess," I said as I stood.

Arden moved in as if spotting, and I pinned her with a look. "I'm not going to bite it."

Bess chuckled. "Precious cargo and all that."

This would get old quick. I lowered myself into the wheelchair. "I really can walk."

Bess made a *tsk*ing noise. "I'm not afraid to set the fighter on you, Mr. Pierce. You're going to take it nice and easy for the next week or two."

I was already twitchy. I wanted a run or a swim. Or better yet, a good fight.

"Good luck with that," a new voice said, stepping into the room. Cope grinned at me, but I saw the strain around his eyes. "We gotta stop meeting like this."

"You started it," I shot back.

"I think you both need to quit giving us all heart attacks," Sutton said as she moved into the room. "We could all use a nice round of boring."

"I could be into watching paint dry," I said. As long as Arden was with me.

Cope chuckled. "Well, you'll have plenty of time for your new hobby over the next couple of weeks."

"Week," I corrected him. "The doctor said I can start light workouts again when the stitches come out."

"I'm getting his credentials checked," Arden muttered.

Cope choked on a laugh. "She's still terrorizing the staff?"

"I'm pretty sure she made Dr. Mathison cry," I said as the orderly unlocked my wheelchair's brakes.

"My sister, the hero," Cope said.

"I hate you all," Arden grumbled. "Can we just go home?" Cope didn't answer right away, and Arden stiffened. "What now? Did something happen? Are the horses okay? Brutus?"

Cope held up a hand. "Nothing like that. It's just that Mom is in full mom mode, and the entire family is waiting for you."

Arden stared at Cope for a long moment before squeezing her eyes closed.

Cope patted her on the shoulder. "You almost got shot. I think you're going to have to deal with a little bit of hovering."

Arden's eyes opened again. "When I find this asshole, there's no one-ball castration for him. He's losing both."

Sutton looked back and forth between them. "I think I'm missing something."

"Trust me, you don't want to know," I muttered.

CHAPTER FORTY-FOUR

Arden

L INC SHIFTED ON THE COUCH, AND A FLICKER OF PAIN SWEPT
across his expression. I instantly leaned forward, reaching for
his pain medication, but Linc placed a hand on my arm to stop
me. "I'm okay."

Brutus lifted his head from his paws as if trying to see if Linc
was telling the truth. But I just scowled at Linc. "You winced. That
means you're hurting. And you could've taken your next dose for-
ty-five minutes ago."

Kye snickered from his spot in the chair opposite us. "You
thought getting shot was bad. It's got nothing on Arden riding your
ass afterward."

Fallon smacked his arm as she passed. "That's not funny."

"It's a little funny. And a lot true," Kye shot back.

I pinned him with my death stare. "Just remember this moment
when I let Fal glitter bomb your office at Haven."

The smirk slipped right off his face. "You wouldn't."

"Test me."

"Shit," Kye muttered.

"Swear jar," Keely said, looking up from her spot on the floor, where she was working on a puzzle with Luca.

Fallon's lips twitched as she held out her hand. "Yeah, Kye, swear jar. Pay up."

Kye leaned to the side and pulled out his wallet, scowling into it. "I only have twenties."

Fallon's dark blue eyes twinkled. "Sucks for you."

Kye smacked a bill into her palm but didn't let go. "I'll be checking the swear jar to make sure this was added, and you didn't use it to fuel your sweets addiction."

She laughed, tugging her hand free. "You'll just have to trust me."

Keely grinned at her. "If you get me some candy, too, I won't tell that it didn't go in the swear jar."

"Me, too," Luca cut in.

"Robbing me blind," Kye muttered.

"Like you don't deserve it," Cope called from his spot on one of the kitchen stools next to Sutton as Nora and Rhodes worked on some dinner concoction that smelled amazing.

Linc shifted again. He tried to hide the wince this time, but I saw the echo of it. My back teeth ground together as I leaned forward to grab the bottle of pills. "If you don't take one of these, I'm going to grind it up and slip it into your drink."

"I want to try to stretch at least another thirty minutes," Linc argued. "I hate that dopey feeling."

"Dopey is a heck of a lot better than being in pain," I shot back. "Arden—"

"Please." I wasn't above begging because seeing him like this was killing me. "I can't take it," I said, dropping my voice. "You're hurting because you were trying to protect me. Let me take care of you now."

Linc's hazel eyes flashed, turning more gold than green. "Vicious…"

"Please."

He grabbed my arm and pulled me into him until our foreheads were touching. "I'd take that bullet over and over again if it meant you were safe."

"Don't say that." Panic clawed at me, icy fear right on its heels. How many people had to be hurt because they were trying to protect me?

Linc's thumb traced my jawline. "You want me to lie to you?"

"I want you to be safe," I whispered.

Those hazel eyes swirled, and I saw confusion and worry there. But he didn't let go. Didn't let me fall into the pit of worry and fear.

"Are you gonna have a baby?" Keely's voice cut into my spiral, making me jerk back as a different sort of panic cut in.

"A baby?" I squeaked.

"You're all…"

"Mushy-gushy," Luca supplied, his nose wrinkling. "My mom and dad are like that *aaaaall* the time now."

It was the first time I'd heard Luca call Cope *Dad*, which had a different kind of pang lighting in my chest. But it couldn't drown out the panic and fear wrapping around my insides.

"Mushy-gushy, huh?" Shep asked as he strode in, Thea at his side.

Luca made a gagging noise. "The *worst.*"

Shep chuckled. "Sorry we're late." He glanced behind him. "*Someone* had to finish her gift for Linc."

Lolli bustled in behind them, holding what looked like a piece of art wrapped in brown butcher paper. "The artistic process cannot be rushed."

"I tried to explain that to him," Thea said, her lips twitching.

Lolli shook her head. "I'm really hoping you'll be a good influence on my grandson. Get him to loosen up." She paused for a moment. "You know, I'm working on a new blend of my brownies that helps in the mushy-gushy department. You and Shep should—"

"Lolli," Shep and half the room said at the same time.

She straightened, her countless necklaces jingling with the move. "What? Can't a grandmother offer her assistance?"

"Not in the mushy-gushy department," Kye said, struggling not to laugh.

Lolli let out a huff and crossed toward me and Linc. "I try to help, and all I get is grief." She stopped in front of Linc and extended the gift. "I thought you might need a little something to brighten your day after your ordeal. I worked round the clock to get it done."

A few snickers and smothered laughs sounded throughout the room. Linc glanced from Lolli to me. "Should I be scared?"

"Very," I told him honestly.

Lolli just scoffed. "Oh, just open it. You're gonna love it."

Carefully and methodically, Linc tore into the butcher paper. Dropping it to the floor, he stared at the piece of diamond art Lolli had created. His brows pulled together as he frowned. And then he saw it.

The glittering piece of art was set on a backdrop of ice. There was a pile of pucks, but the two at the top were artfully arranged into what looked like balls. Sprouting from them was a hockey stick with a very unique...tip.

All my siblings and their partners moved to circle the painting so they could see it. Rhodes choked out a laugh first. "Is that a diamond dick stick?"

"What's a dick stick?" Keely singsonged.

Kye held up both hands. "That's on you," he told Rhodes. "I'm not taking the fall when Trace wants to know where his kid learned that one."

Fal dissolved into giggles. "Diamond dick stick. Where are you going to hang it, Linc?"

Linc just stared at the piece for a long moment. "I think it's going to take me a minute to figure out the best spot."

"Smart," Lolli said, patting him on the shoulder. "You'll want it in the place with the best energy and flow. And I bet Shep can put in some custom lighting to make sure it really glitters."

"Oh, I can do that, no problem," Shep said, struggling not to laugh.

Linc's eyes narrowed on him. "Just as long as you do the same in your new place. I hear Thea has a dick-gourd painting that needs a place of honor."

The smile slipped right off Shep's face. "You fight dirty."

Linc chuckled, but his hand instantly went to his side. I shoved the bottle of pills into his hand. "Take one."

"She's right," Nora said, crossing to us and placing a steaming plate of lasagna and a salad on the side table. "You need to stay ahead of the pain, or you won't recover as quickly. Three bites of lasagna, the pill, then the rest of your dinner."

Linc sighed. "Okay."

I gaped at him. "I've been trying to get you to take this for the past thirty minutes, and you just cave when Nora tells you to?"

Linc grinned at me. "She's got the mom tone. You can't fight that."

"Dang straight," Nora said, lifting the painting from Linc's lap. "I'll just put this somewhere it won't get...damaged. And, Lolli, we need to have another talk about the appropriateness of your *gifts*."

"Dang it," Lolli whispered. "I knew I should've waited until she wasn't looking."

"Gotta work on the slyness," Kye told her.

"Always trying to harsh my buzz," she muttered.

Linc looked at me, amusement in his hazel eyes. "I love your family."

The warmth of those words swirled around me. I was glad we could give Linc some of what he'd missed growing up. He deserved that and so much more. But all I could think was that the more we all had, the more we had to lose.

CHAPTER FORTY-FIVE

Arden

A S DARKNESS SET IN, THE BOYS GOT TO WORK IN THE KITCHEN, cleaning all the dishes Nora and Rhodes had dirtied. It had always been that way with the Colsons. Whoever cooked never cleaned, and everyone pitched in to do their part.

Nora patted Linc's hand as she moved around the small space, tidying what didn't need to be tidied because she was never one to sit still. "You feeling better?"

"How could I not be after a meal like that one?" he asked, smiling at her with such warmth.

Nora beamed at him. "Nothing like a good meal to cure what ails you."

"Would've cured you better if you had some of my poppy tea with it," Lolli harumphed.

"What did I tell you about making that?" Trace asked, annoyance in his tone as he strode into the room.

"Daddy!" Keely yelled, leaping to her feet and charging at Trace.

He caught her on the fly, his face lighting in the way it only did for his daughter. "How's my Keely girl?"

"Good, but I missed ya. Luca and I did a puzzle and then went and helped feed Stardust and Whiskey. Supergran made Mr. Linc a diamond dick stick, and Grams didn't like it. Can Luca and I have a sleepover? He has to go back to Seattle tomorrow, and I'm gonna miss him."

Trace balanced her on his hip, his jaw going tight. "You've certainly had quite the afternoon."

Kye held up both hands. "I'm not responsible for the diamond dick stick, just so you know. That was all Rho."

Rhodes glared at him. "Traitor."

Trace pinned her with a stare that was a mixture of sheriff and big brother all wrapped into one. "Thanks for that."

She sent an exaggerated grimace in his direction. "It just popped out."

Lolli let out a huff. "There is nothing wrong with discussing the human anatomy. Or expressing through the medium of thousands of glittering gemstones. And maybe you'd be a little less grumpy if you used your dick stick a little more."

"Lolli!" half the room shouted.

"Jesus," Trace muttered. "I give up."

Sutton chuckled. "We'd be happy to have Keely for a slumber party. The bunk beds are all set up in Luca's room."

"Pleeeeeease, Daddy?" Keely begged.

Trace studied her for a moment and then caved. "All right."

"Yay!" Keely cheered before wiggling free and running back to Luca.

"I guess she didn't miss me *that* much," Trace muttered.

Sutton patted him on the shoulder before moving to gather the kids' things. "Get used to it. It happens more and more these days."

I looked at Trace, trying to read behind the easy mask he always wore. "Anything?"

There was a quick flash in those green eyes. "Let's talk about it in a minute."

My stomach twisted as Linc reached for my hand. They had something. Something Trace didn't want to talk about with the kids present. My gaze moved to Anson, who'd come in behind Trace and gone straight to Rhodes.

Rhodes had wrapped herself around him in a tight hug, knowing he needed her. Because it wasn't easy for Anson to slip back into those profiler shoes. Even though he did it for the people he cared about, there was always a cost.

"That's our cue," Nora said, gesturing for the crew to leave. And she was the only one who could've gotten them to do it.

Kye pinned Trace with a hard stare. "We want an update, too."

"I know. And I'll give you one tomorrow," Trace promised.

Kye didn't look like he was going to move, but Fallon tugged on his sleeve. "Come on. I'll treat you to a shake if you're a good boy and do as you're asked."

Kye's gaze cut to her. "Double chocolate with Oreos?"

"As if there's any other kind," Fallon huffed.

"Okay," he grumbled but then pinned Trace with a stare. "Tomorrow."

Trace nodded. The rest of the crew said their goodbyes, and it wasn't long before it was only Linc, Trace, Anson, and me. Even Rhodes had told Anson she'd wait in the car.

My small house suddenly seemed too quiet. It had felt too crowded all afternoon, and now it was far too empty.

"Gonna talk you through everything we know," Trace said, scrubbing a hand over his face. He looked exhausted.

Linc's fingers tightened around mine, assuring me he was right there.

"We found tire treads that fit an ATV on the trails just north of your campsite," Trace began. "And we found a sniper's nest. Where they lay in wait for their shot."

Linc's hand tightened more around mine, but I didn't think he was aware of it this time. "Did you get DNA? Prints?" he asked.

Trace shook his head. "Nothing yet. We found some fibers. Colors match hunting fatigues."

"Nest, camo, specialty vehicle. That takes planning," Linc surmised.

"It does." Trace turned to me. "Who knew you were going camping?"

My eyes flared as I put the pieces together. "Just you and Cope. I mean, I'm sure he told Sutton, but—"

"I already asked them. They didn't tell anyone. I know I didn't, which means one thing."

"Someone's watching," I whispered.

Linc didn't settle for simply holding my hand anymore; he wrapped his arm around me and pulled me into his uninjured side. But it didn't matter how warm he was, I was still freezing. Ice slid through my veins as I pictured someone with binoculars watching me through the lenses.

"Even if they were watching you from some vantage point here, they wouldn't have been able to keep up on foot. They would've had to know where you were going," Anson said, his voice devoid of all emotion. "Is this camping spot one you go to often?"

I nodded numbly. "It's my favorite one."

"Who knows that?" Trace pressed.

My head swam as I tried to think of everyone I'd shared that information with. "I—I don't know. Anyone I talked to about camping. It's a public spot, so I might've recommended it to a friend or even a stranger. I'm sure I've talked about going there. I just…I don't know to who."

Trace reached out and patted my knee. "It's okay. We're just trying to narrow the field. We'll figure it out. I've got deputies combing the surrounding property, trying to see if we can find a trail."

"But until then, we have to assume they're still watching," I whispered.

A muscle fluttered in Trace's jaw. "We do."

"But if they were watching, why not take the shot before? Why wait until we were in the middle of nowhere?"

"The distance was likely too great," Anson supplied. "Long-range sniper shots like that take a lot of skill."

"That should narrow down your suspects, shouldn't it?" Linc

asked. Only it didn't come out like a question, it was more of a demand.

"We're working that angle," Anson assured him. "My contacts at the bureau are putting a list together."

Trace cleared his throat. "The U.S. Marshals also wanted me to pass something along."

My gaze turned wary as I took in my brother. "What?"

"They want you to know that they'd be happy to put you back into WITSEC."

"No."

"It doesn't have to be for—"

"No," I said, putting all the finality I could into the word. "I'm not running. Not anymore."

"Arden," Linc said, pain lacing his tone.

I jerked and turned to him. "I'm not doing it."

"It would mean you'd be safe," he said, his voice dipping low.

Everything in me twisted. "Safe and alone. I'm done with that. I'm not letting this asshole and whoever is pulling the strings keep me from living my life. Not anymore."

Linc studied me for a long moment. "Okay."

I blinked at him a few times. "Okay?"

He nodded. "I'm not going to try to force you to give up your life. You've worked too hard to rebuild it. But I am going to be by your side every step of the way, making sure you're safe."

The panic was back. "Linc—"

"By. Your. Side," he repeated.

My heart hammered against my ribs, but I forced out one single word. "Okay."

Trace sighed. "I've got a deputy stationed outside. And we'll be making the rounds throughout the night. We'll do everything we can from a local perspective."

"Thank you," I whispered.

Trace squeezed my knee. "I'd do anything for my little sister. Even when she's being stubborn and annoying as hell."

One corner of my mouth kicked up as I tried to smile. "I'd be falling down on my job as your little sister if I wasn't being both of those things."

Linc let out a soft chuckle. "I *know* that's true."

"Well, you'd better get some rest because I know it's gotta take a lot of energy to be *that* annoying," Trace said, pushing to his feet.

I walked him and Anson to the door, but before Trace could leave, I gave him a quick hug. "Thank you. For everything."

He stared down at me. "Just please be careful. Nothing reckless because you're feeling hemmed in, okay?"

He knew me too well.

"I promise."

"Thank you."

"Drive safe."

"Will do."

I watched as he disappeared into the night, staring after him until there was nothing to see. Finally, I forced myself to shut the door. Letting out a long breath, I moved back to the living room.

Linc was already on his feet and holding out a hand to me. "You've had a long couple of days. You need a good night's sleep."

I did. But I doubted I'd find it tonight. Still, I followed Linc into my bedroom and got ready for bed. I'd lay there all night, staring at the ceiling, if I knew it meant Linc got the rest he needed to heal.

But when we turned out the light and Brutus settled into his dog bed, his soft snores filling the space, sleep tugged at me, and it wasn't long before it pulled me under. But my nightmares greeted me. My mom yanking me down the hall, shoving me into the hidden closet. The cold, cramped dark froze me to the spot, but when the gun went off this time, it wasn't my mom falling to the floor, blood seeping into the carpet.

It was Linc.

CHAPTER FORTY-SIX

Lincoln

YOU GOT SHOT AND YOU DIDN'T TELL ME?"

At the sheer volume of Ellie's shriek, I pulled the phone away from my ear. "It was really more of a graze."

"Lincoln Montgomery Pierce, did a bullet enter your body or not?"

I winced and this time it wasn't due to any physical pain. The truth was, at five days post-injury, I was only feeling a twinge when I moved too fast. I reached out a hand to stroke Stardust's cheek. "It entered and exited without harming anything important. I'm fine. I didn't want to worry you."

A sniff sounded across the line. "You promise you're okay?"

At the sound of tears in Ellie's voice, I gave myself a mental kick. "I'm totally and completely fine. Arden is like a drill sergeant with my care, and I'm back on my feet. I'm out with Stardust right now, actually."

There was another sniff and the sound of something rustling in the background. "How's my pretty girl doing?"

"She's great. I found out she has a fondness for watermelon," I said, glancing at the workers who were just finishing up installing a generator on the side of Arden's house.

"Really?" Ellie asked, a hint of amusement making its way into her tone.

"Stole a cube right out of my hand."

"You've been spoiling her with it ever since, haven't you?"

I chuckled. "Maybe."

Ellie sighed. "How's Arden holding up?"

I glanced toward the studio where Vicious had been locked away for hours on end the past few days. "She's dealing how she deals. Putting it all into her art."

Ellie was quiet for a moment. "Do you think you two should leave? Get some distance from Sparrow Falls and whoever this maniac is?"

It wasn't a bad idea, but I couldn't force Arden into that. "She's already lost so much, El. I can't make her leave her life again. Plus, if we go anywhere else, we wouldn't have this many people watching our backs."

"Please be careful," she whispered.

"I will. Promise."

"Thank you."

"How are things going with you?" I asked. The question was hesitant. I didn't want Ellie to feel any pressure from my corner. If she broke off her engagement, it had to come from her alone.

Sounds of more shifting came across the line, and I could picture Ellie curling into a ball like she often did, hugging her knees to her chest. "I told Bradley I needed a pause."

It took everything in me not to cheer out loud. "How did that go?"

"He told me to go to the spa for a week."

I blinked a few times as if that would clear the ridiculousness of Bradley's comment. "Seriously?"

"Yep," Ellie said, popping the P. "I tried to explain that I wasn't sure if I was happy. He told me it was just cold feet. That I should take a girls' trip and go shopping. Everything would be fine."

"El Bell."

"I know," she whispered. "How did I end up with someone who doesn't even know who I am? Who doesn't care that I'm not happy?"

"I'm so sorry."

"It's not your fault. I got myself into this mess. I need to get myself out. But it doesn't help that Bradley must've said something to Dad."

I stiffened. "What did he do?"

"Just called and reamed me out. Reminded me that a Pierce always follows through on their promises. That I needed to do the same or I'd regret it."

Rage blasted through me. "That's rich coming from him."

Ellie went quiet, and I realized my mistake, my anger getting the best of me and forcing something free that never should've left my mouth. "What do you mean?" she asked.

"Nothing. I—"

"Linc. Stop shielding me from everything. I'm not six anymore."

I snapped my mouth closed. *Hell.* She knew. Knew I was hiding things from her. She could feel it.

"Linc," Ellie whispered.

"I never wanted to burden you with any of it. You were too young and…"

"I'm not young now."

"But you'll always be my little sister."

Ellie let out an audible breath. "Have you ever considered that keeping things from me isn't protecting me?"

"You sound like Arden," I grumbled.

"Well, you're obviously not an idiot because you fell in love with a smart woman."

"I did, didn't I?"

"Tell me," Ellie said softly.

I gripped the fence rail with my free hand, letting the rough pieces dig into my palm as I tried to summon the words. My gaze went unfocused, the horses in front of me blurring as my eyes stung. "Mom tried to leave him. She wanted to take us with her."

Ellie sucked in air but didn't speak.

"She went to a lawyer to start the proceedings, but you know Dad. Eyes everywhere. He was waiting for her when she got home. Told her that if she tried to leave, he'd take every cent she had to her name and keep her from ever seeing us again."

"There's no way. It wouldn't have worked," Ellie argued.

"Wouldn't it have? You know how Dad is. He's got resources everywhere. Had a file of false evidence. And he made sure Mom knew it."

"She must've been so scared."

My rib cage tightened around my lungs, making it difficult to draw in a full breath. "She was."

"How?" Ellie whispered. "How did you know?"

"I overheard them." I could still picture everything as if it were yesterday, pressing myself against the wall next to the stupid priceless statue I'd wanted to smash into a million pieces. "He was cheating on her. Repeatedly. And after that day, he rubbed it in her face. Made sure she knew exactly what he was doing."

"Mom," Ellie croaked.

"I know," I rasped. "He beat her down, little by little. And that accident, on the bridge... El, there were no skid marks, no evidence that Mom tried to brake."

Ellie was quiet for a long while, and I gave it to her. Everything I'd just piled onto her required time to process.

"He killed her."

"Yeah. He did." Though it wasn't by cutting brake lines or sabotaging her engine. He killed her by stealing her life away, little by little.

More silence reigned. Finally, Ellie spoke again. "I need to go."

"El—"

"I'm okay. Maybe I'm finally seeing things clearly now. But I have some things I need to do."

"Let me help—"

"No, Linc. I need to do this myself. I've let too many people step in for me in my life. I need to handle this on my own."

I knew what Ellie meant. The life she'd lived had been one of privilege, but it didn't come without a price. And maybe she was done paying it.

"I'm here for you," I said. "You need a safe place to land, I've got you."

"Thanks, ConCon. I love you."

"Love you, too."

She hung up before I could say anything else. I pulled the phone away from my ear and stared at the device, hoping like hell I'd done the right thing.

CHAPTER FORTY-SEVEN

Arden

THE MUSIC PULSED AROUND ME, THROUGH ME, BLARING IN A way that would probably cause some permanent damage. But I didn't care. I needed it.

As if it cleansed my system, getting all that darkness to purge, bleed out of me and into the sculpture. The only problem was that it felt like I had a never-ending supply. Just when I thought I'd gotten it all, a new flood would rise.

So, I simply kept creating.

I should've been at The Collective, helping set up for the show and auction, but Farah had assured me she had it under control. And she was meant for the job. Ordering people around gave her a kick, and no one would be stupid enough to give her a hard time.

Maybe I'd ask if she wanted Denver's job. A pang lit just thinking his name. I hadn't heard a word from him since. And maybe that was for the best.

I lifted my blowtorch, binding one piece of metal to another and then stepping back. As the torch extinguished, I lifted my mask to study the woman battling her way out. Out of *what* was open to interpretation. And I wanted it that way.

Because we all had darkness we were climbing out of, things that held us captive. And this woman had fought to emerge from it. She was scarred and battleworn, but she was breaking free.

The music cut out, and I whirled, the stark change from chaos to silence almost too much for my ears to handle. "Son of a biscuit-eating monkey. Don't do that to me."

Linc's brows rose in amusement as he bent to scratch Brutus between the ears, setting a bag by the couch. "A biscuit-eating monkey, huh?"

I glared at him as I set the blowtorch down and removed my gloves. "Apparently, I get wholesome when someone scares the crap out of me."

He chuckled, but there was something beneath it. I saw shadows in those hazel eyes. The instinct was too hard to fight. I pulled off my mask and crossed to him. "What's wrong?"

Linc brushed his hand over my face as he held me to him. "You done running?"

A wash of panic swept through me, and hot on its heels came annoyance. "I'm not running. I'm right here."

It was a lie. My heart was running—terrified and ducking for cover. And when it wasn't running, it was building as many walls as it could, even though it was too late.

Linc held me to him, no judgment in those hazel eyes, but he wasn't buying my story either. "I've given you this play for the past few days. Can't give it to you any longer."

I tugged myself out of his arms. "You *gave* me this play? I decide what's best for me. And right now, it's this." I gestured to the statue behind me, the one currently saving my life as it took all the badness inside me and turned it into beauty.

"So, I'm just supposed to stand by while you work yourself to the bone, almost twenty hours a day? Only stopping to make sure *I've* eaten and taken my meds, but never once taking care of yourself?"

My mouth snapped closed.

Those hazel eyes flashed gold. "Yeah. I'm not going to stand by and let you slowly kill yourself. Because I love you. And despite the fact that it terrifies you, you love me."

The panic surged anew like some sort of back draft, the flames strangling me. "Don't." I threw my hands up as if I could ward him off.

"You love me." He took two steps forward.

I shook my head but couldn't get out a *no* because my body knew it was a lie.

Another step. "And I love you."

"Stop," I croaked. The panic was too much, clawing, trying to drag me under into the inky black.

Pain swirled in Linc's eyes. "Vicious," he whispered. "You love me."

I broke then, tears streaming down my face. "I love you." A sob tore free, and I nearly collapsed, but Linc was right there, catching me as I fell.

"I know," he said, lifting me in his arms and carrying me to the brand-new leather couch he'd had delivered.

"Your stitches," I rasped between cries.

"Are fine," Linc whispered, cradling me to him.

Sobs racked my body as I clung to Linc, terrified he'd disappear the moment I let go. Stolen because I'd had the audacity to love him.

Linc's hand swept up and down my back in soothing strokes. "Talk to me."

The words wanted out, but my body was battling to keep them in. "I-I was trying to keep you safe."

He pulled back, his eyes searching mine, trying to understand. "And loving me puts me in danger?"

I nodded. It was so stupid. Juvenile, even. But it was the only thing I knew to be true. The tears only came faster. "They weren't perfect, but I loved them. The only people I've ever really loved in this life. And he killed them. One and then the other. And it almost killed *me*."

I sucked in a shuddering breath, trying to keep the worst of the sobs down. "You know why I do jujitsu with Kye? It's not just so I feel safer. It's so I feel *strong*. Because I was so weak back then. I almost let it take me under. I wanted it to."

Linc's thumb traced my jaw, the rough pad assuring me he was there. "You were a kid. You were scared out of your mind and trying to make sense of it all, but your love didn't kill them. A monster did."

A hiccuped cry left my throat. "I miss them."

Linc wrapped his arms around me, holding me close. "Of course, you do."

My fingers twisted in his tee. "I can't lose you."

He held me tighter. "Baby, I'm not going anywhere. If you haven't noticed, I'm stubborn as hell."

A cross between a laugh and a cry bubbled out of me. As they eased, I pulled back and forced myself to look into Linc's eyes. "You almost died because of me."

He stilled, then his hand lifted to my face, brushing some loose strands of hair away. "And it reminded you of what happened before."

I nodded, that pain tearing at my insides again. "She was trying to protect me. She didn't get out in time because she was hiding me."

Linc muttered a curse and pressed his head to mine. "Should've seen that. I'm so fucking sorry. But I'm here, and I'm not going anywhere."

My throat tightened as I struggled to swallow. "I didn't want to love you. I didn't want to love anyone."

"I know."

My fingers tightened in his shirt, the cotton warping around them. "For so long, it was like I was living in exile. This weird in-between. My old life wasn't mine anymore, but I wasn't really living the new one either."

I pulled back, making sure my eyes met his so he could truly see. "You showed me the beauty of that in-between. Showed me I could blend them into something new—something where I didn't keep everyone at arm's length, if I was only brave enough to reach for it."

"Vicious," he rasped, holding me tighter. "I wish I could erase all the darkness that has ever touched you."

"You don't have to. You just have to be with me in it."

"Sure about that?" Linc asked, leaning to the side to snag a bag from the floor. "Got you something."

I took the bag, glanced at him, then opened it. "Cowboy," I croaked, pulling out a small key ring flashlight in a light purple. I traced the curves with my fingers.

"It's rechargeable. You just plug it in each night with your phone, and your flashlight will never run out of juice."

My tongue felt heavy, and my throat constricted as I pulled out a pack of four night-lights.

"These are solar, so they'll charge every day just by being out and light your house anytime it's dark. They turn on automatically."

I forced my gaze away from the lights to the man who cared enough to make sure I was never scared again. In every way he could manage. "Linc," I whispered.

"There's one more thing in the bag."

"Stop it."

His lips twitched. "What'd I do?"

"You're too amazing. It's rude."

He chuckled. "Pull out the pamphlet, Vicious."

I grumbled something indiscernible under my breath and pulled out what looked like instructions. Then I gaped at him. "You got me a freaking generator?"

"Best on the market. They'll service it every month to make sure it stays running, and it can power your whole house."

Tears pressed against the backs of my eyes. "Stop making me cry."

"Okay." Linc brushed his lips across mine. "Never want you to feel powerless. Not ever again."

I stared at him for a long moment, saying the only thing I could. "I love you." The words stirred a little less fear this time. Didn't strangle me quite as much on the way out.

"Say it again," Linc said, his lips hovering just against mine. "I want to feel it."

"I love you," I whispered, my lips moving against his with the words.

"Best gift I've ever received. Because I know the cost. Know how terrifying it is to let yourself step off that cliff."

It was terrifying. But now that I'd taken that step, the fear started to melt away. And it was because of one thing. "You're with me."

Linc slid his fingers through mine. "Always. And that will never change."

I pulled back and searched those hazel eyes. "Will you do something with me?"

Linc's gaze softened on mine. "Said I was with you, didn't I?"

"Yes, you did."

CHAPTER FORTY-EIGHT

Arden

MY TRUCK BUMPED ALONG THE GRAVEL ROAD THAT LED TO Colson Ranch, but Linc was behind Wanda's wheel now. I sat in the center seat, and Brutus was at the window. I'd been a little too shaky to drive and needed to be close to Linc. Had to remember that he was with me.

His fingers slid through mine like he could read my thoughts, and he twisted his head to kiss my temple. "Talked to Ellie. Told her everything."

I jerked back. "You did?"

Linc nodded, a hint of worry passing over his features.

"How'd she take it?" My stomach twisted for Linc's sister, for the rug I knew had just been pulled out from under her.

Linc stared hard out the windshield. "Said I've been shielding her for too long. And that it wasn't helping anything."

I pressed my lips together. Her words were so similar to the ones I'd given him.

He squeezed my hand. "Told her she sounded like someone else I know."

I leaned into Linc, trying to give him a little of the strength he'd given me. "It's not wrong to want to shield the people you care about. It shows how much they mean to you. You just have to pause and decide whether that shielding is actually the best thing for them. Sometimes, the best thing is just to let them know you're with them. Not in front of them."

Linc glanced down at me for barely a moment, but there was a lifetime in that smattering of seconds. And so much love. "With you."

I squeezed his hand hard. "I'm always stronger when you're at my side."

And wasn't that partnership at its core? Making each other better, stronger…more ourselves.

"I am, too," he said, pulling me tighter against him. "Even when you steal my last french fry."

My lips twitched as I remembered our meal last night. "You were too slow. And you're the one who gave me a taste for fries dipped in milkshakes. So, really, it's your fault."

Linc grinned at the road, shaking his head. "Adding insult to injury."

I leaned in, my lips ghosting over his ear. "How can you complain when you ate the rest of that milkshake off me?"

Linc cursed, and his grin shifted into a scowl as he pulled up in front of the ranch house. "Are you seriously trying to make me hard before seeing your mom? You're evil."

A laugh bubbled out of me. "The absolute worst. But you love me."

He turned and took my face in his hands, pulling it to his. "I do." And then he kissed me. It was one I'd never experienced before because it wasn't just one or two things. It was *everything*. Heat and comfort. Attraction and strength. Gratitude and promise. But most of all, it was love. The emotion that encompassed so much.

It wasn't a storybook kind of love. It was a messy one, imperfect with jagged edges, just like my statue. Because that love had been through a war. But it was stronger because it had come out the other side.

Linc pulled back, searching my eyes. "Ready?"

I swallowed hard. "Ready."

He waited for a moment as if making sure and then opened his door. I reached over Brutus to open mine, and he instantly jumped out. By the time I slid out, Linc was there, waiting. Just like always.

He pressed a kiss to my head. "I'll throw a ball for Brutus."

It was his way of giving me space and time. "Thank you," I whispered.

"I'll be here whenever you need me."

And I knew he would. It was a gift—one that still had a flicker of fear taking root. But it was a fear I knew I'd defeat. I wouldn't give it the reins again.

Glancing at my watch, I knew I was more likely to find Nora outside than in. So, I started toward the barn. But a flicker of movement caught my attention.

The vegetable garden. I should've known I'd find her there. It took over a chunk of her days from April through September. From prepping the soil to tending the seedlings to harvesting and keeping the plants healthy, Nora did whatever it took to care for them.

Just like she had for all of us.

The lump in my throat twisted, and my eyes stung as I watched her move through the space. She'd memorized where each plant was and what they might need but didn't let that stop her from taking her time to truly study them. Her hands were gentle and strong all at once, just like the woman herself.

Nora looked up, her green eyes flaring in surprise from under her wide-brimmed hat. "Arden." There was a flash of panic. "You didn't come over by yourself, did you? That's not safe. I—"

I lifted my hands. "Linc drove me. And Beth—sorry, *Deputy* Hansen—followed. I'm being careful."

The tension in Nora's shoulders eased. "Good. That's good." A smile teased her lips. "I know it's not easy for you to feel hemmed in."

I chuckled. "Not my favorite to be bound by rules and regulations."

"Never was," Nora said wistfully. "But since you're here, why don't you put those hands to good use? I've got more than a few weeds sprouting up."

I doubted it, given how meticulous Nora was with her garden. But she was giving me a task, something to give me time to say whatever I needed without being rushed. Just like when I was twelve, and she took me to the barn to groom Sunny. She never prodded me with questions, just gave me a chance to talk when I needed it.

Crossing to the garden, I lowered myself to the grass rimming the bed. "You know I've never had a green thumb. Not like Rho or Fallon."

"Oh, hush. You do just fine. You've kept those flowering succulents alive on your back patio for years now."

"Nora, I asked you to recommend plants I could not kill even if I tried. I don't think that's exactly a victory."

She grinned and lowered herself to a spot next to me—but not too close. "Hey, a win is a win. Don't sell yourself short."

Always pumping us up for every tiny success. God, I was lucky to have her. And I hadn't let her know what I'd felt: that she'd always given that gift to me.

A burn lit along my sternum, and I didn't shove it down this time. I let it come, let it mark me, and then, I let it pass. All the while, my fingers plucked minuscule shoots from the dirt that shouldn't have been there, piling them in a bucket Nora had placed behind us.

I wasn't sure how long it took before I was ready or how many weeds I'd plucked from the earth before the words made their way up my throat. "I love you, Nora."

The words were barely audible, but Nora froze next to me, then slowly turned. The expression on her face was the softest I'd ever seen. "Oh, baby, I know."

Tears gathered in my eyes. "But I didn't tell you."

"Didn't need the words. You gave me the actions. Showed me time after time."

"I was scared," I whispered.

Nora slid over and took my hand, covering it with hers, top and bottom. "I bet."

"I'm sorry."

"Don't you dare. Everyone expresses their love differently. Doesn't make it more or less; it just makes it unique to them."

My gaze swept over Nora's face, the lines there looking a little deeper. "You always know how each of us needs to be loved, supported, and cared for. You're the greatest gift for each and every one of us."

Nora's eyes glistened. "You make me cry, and we're going to have words."

"Well, apparently, I cry all the freaking time now, so you'll be in good company."

Nora's head tipped back, and she laughed full-out. Pulling me into a hug, she held on. "Love you, Arden. Exactly as you are. But also love that Linc's inspiring you to share a little more of yourself with all of us. Because *you*, my girl, are a gift, too."

I held on to Nora. "He's making me brave. Making me realize that this messy life is worth fighting for."

She pulled back but grasped my face in her hands. "It is. And you and your siblings show me that every single day."

"Thank you for giving me a safe place to land. For loving me just as I am."

"Arden," Nora croaked.

"I know it's late, but do you think—?" I paused, trying not to stumble over the words. "Could I call you Mom? I think my other mom…she'd love to share the name with the person who carried me through the dark."

Tears slid down Nora's cheeks. "I'd be honored to share any name with the woman who gave everything to save this most precious girl."

She threw her arms around me and held tight. "Love you more than the stars in the sky."

"I love you, too." We stayed like that for a long moment before letting go. When we finally did, I felt eyes on me. Not ones that made me twitchy but ones that gave me constant reassurance at the knowledge he was with me. And I was stronger for it.

Linc gave me bravery, boldness. A willingness to step into fear and find what lay beyond.

As I pushed to my feet, he crossed to me, Brutus at his side. It only took a handful of seconds for his arm to come around me and his lips to graze my temple. "Good?" he asked in that rough tenor.

"Better than good. Beautiful," I whispered.

Nora rose, her eyes still watery. "You've been good for my girl, and I'll love you forever for that. But if you fuck up, I'll be coming for you," she said, pointing her shears in his direction.

My eyes bugged out. "Mom, did you just say the F-word?"

She burst out laughing. "Sometimes, it's the only one that will do the trick."

"I'm with you there," Linc said, amusement coating his words.

"What's all the ruckus down there?" Lolli called from the back deck. "You're interrupting my Zen diamond zone."

I could only imagine what she was creating now. But I grinned up at her. "Mom said the F-word."

Lolli's jaw dropped. "Nora Leanne Colson, did you get into my stash?"

We all burst out laughing at that.

CHAPTER FORTY-NINE

Arden

I WRAPPED THE TOWEL TIGHTER AROUND MYSELF AS I SURVEYED my closet and scowled. The number of dresses I had was limited, to say the least. And I'd worn all of them at least twice. Mostly to little fundraisers at The Collective, and a few to the occasional family event that required them. None of them felt right for this.

For the first time since the night that had changed everything, I didn't want to fade into the background. I wanted to stand out. And nothing in this closet gave me that, save for the over-the-top unicorn onesie I had tucked away for Christmas Eve when my entire family wore them.

But, somehow, I didn't think that was the play for tonight.

"What did that closet ever do to you?"

I didn't jump at the deep voice that skated over my skin in a pleasant shiver. I welcomed it. My scowl battled with a grin as I turned. "It doesn't have what I need to wear."

Linc stepped into the small space, his heat seeping into me. "I think you look beautiful just as you are."

I arched a brow. "You think I should go to the fundraiser in a towel?"

"I don't think you should go at all. But I lost that battle."

We'd gone round and round about the fundraiser for The Collective. The risks and rewards. I'd come out victorious, but not without concessions.

"And how many security personnel do you have monitoring the event?" I asked.

"Twenty," he muttered.

I laughed, leaning into him. "It's called compromise."

Linc's fingers sifted through my freshly dried hair. "Does that mean we're grownups?"

"Never. But I think it means we get a gold star for a healthy relationship."

Linc's head dipped, his lips hovering over mine. "I do love a gold star."

My lips ghosted across his. "What do you want as a reward?"

"What do you think I want?" Linc moved, hoisting me up.

My legs instantly went around his waist, but I smacked his back. "Oh, no, you don't. We do not have time for any rewards. I have to get ready, and I still don't know what I'm wearing." Not to mention the fact that makeup wasn't exactly my strong suit.

"I might be able to help with that," Linc murmured against my ear.

I pulled back as he strode out of my bedroom. Brutus let out a happy bark, thinking it was a fun game. Linc carried me into the living room and then slowly lowered me to the floor. The loss of contact nearly had me giving in to the offer of forgetting the fundraiser and staying home with Linc.

Shaking off the lust haze, I turned and stilled. My jaw went slack at the sight. In the center of my living room was a rack of clothing. Mostly dresses, but with a couple of chic pantsuits mixed in. In front of the rack were more pairs of shoes than I could count. And on the couch lay a row of clutches in colors that matched or complemented the clothing options perfectly.

"What did you do?" I whispered.

"You've had a few things on your mind. Didn't think you'd have time to shop. And you need something special for tonight."

I turned back to him. "So you bought out a department store?"

Linc laughed. "I had a stylist send some options."

I moved to the rack, my fingers ghosting over each option. Linc's stylist had given me a rainbow of choices, including the typical artist's black. But I wasn't going for shadow tonight; I was going for light. No more fading into the background.

My fingers landed on a silky number. The dusky mauve color felt like a blend of earthiness and whimsical pink, and something about that called to me. It was a mixture of who I was and who I wanted to be.

Pulling it from the rack, I studied the dress. The shape would hug my curves in the perfect way. The spaghetti straps would expose my shoulders, tan from all my time with the horses, and the material would lean into a sultriness I didn't often own. It was perfect.

"This one," I said softly, holding it up for Linc to see.

"You don't want to try some on to make sure?"

I shook my head. "This is the one."

A smile tugged at his beautiful mouth. "Pink. Always full of surprises."

I opened my mouth to speak, but my doorbell rang, cutting me off. Brutus let out two quick barks to alert.

"Beruhigen," I said, giving him a pat.

"I've got it," Linc said, striding for the door.

A few seconds later, excited voices sounded. Familiar ones. They piled into the living room, all holding garment bags and carrying totes over their shoulders.

Rho was first, crossing the space and lifting a bottle in the air. "I brought champagne."

"I brought cupcakes," Sutton called. "And a massive makeup kit."

"I'm more excited about the cupcakes," Rho muttered.

Thea laughed. "I'm here for all three. It's been a minute since I've had an excuse to dress up."

"Sometimes it's nice to remember you're a girl," Fallon said as she laid her dress bag over a chair. "Oooooh! Is that what you're wearing, Arden? It's gorgeous."

Pressure built behind my eyes as I turned to Linc. "You did all this?"

He shrugged. "Thought it might be nice for you to have them."

How had he grown to know me so well in such a short period? He knew I'd be frustrated trying to find something to wear. Nervous getting ready on my own. And that my sisters would be the ones who could soothe those nerves best.

I rehung the dress and strode across the room. I reached up and grabbed Linc's face, pulling it down to mine. His scruff pricked my palms as my mouth met his. The warring sensations had me lost in a matter of moments. My tongue stroked his, and Linc's swiped back. I poured everything I had into the kiss, and when I pulled back, I gave him the words, too.

"I love you."

Those hazel eyes burned gold. "Gonna get you a rack of dresses every day of the week."

"Don't you dare."

Linc laughed. "Okay, once a week." I smacked his chest, and he kissed the tip of my nose. "You ladies have fun. We'll be back to pick you up at six-thirty."

He pulled away, and I felt the loss all over again, missing him instantly.

Fallon let out a hoot. "Good Lord, you two could melt Antarctica."

My cheeks heated. "Sorry," I mumbled.

"Don't you dare apologize," Thea ordered.

"Dang straight," Sutton agreed, arranging mini cupcakes on a tray. "There's not a damn thing wrong with that kind of love."

"Anson and I snuck off to a shed at his last jobsite," Rhodes offered as she snagged a cupcake.

Thea choked on a laugh. "Why am I not surprised?"

Rho arched a brow at her. "Not sure you're one to judge. I hear the barn at your and Shep's reno project sees a lot of action."

Thea's jaw went slack, and then she burst out laughing.

Linc had been right. This was exactly what I needed.

"Keep your eyes closed," Sutton instructed. She'd set up a makeup station at my kitchen island, and I'd never seen quite so many pots and palettes.

"I hate sitting still for this long," I grumbled.

Rhodes let out a chuckle. "*Noooo*, I never had any idea."

I reached out a hand from under the towel covering me and my precious dress and flipped my sister off. It only made her laugh more.

"Stop moving," Sutton ordered. "I'm almost done. Just a little more rose gold."

Nerves swept through me. "I'm not going to look ridiculous, right?"

"As if any of us would let you go out looking a fool," Fallon said from her spot on the couch.

"And I take my makeup very seriously." Sutton grinned. "Almost as seriously as my cupcakes."

"I think I need another one before we go," Thea said, sounding like she was crossing into the kitchen.

"All done," Sutton announced. "You can open your eyes."

I did as she instructed, my lids feeling a little funny with the false lashes at the outside corners.

Rhodes moved in and pulled the towel off me. "Time for the full impact."

I slid my feet into the strappy heels and moved toward the full-length mirror Fallon had hauled out of my bedroom. As I stepped up to it, I blinked a few times, trying to clear my vision. It was me, but not.

The silk fabric skimmed my body with a sultry touch. I took in the slight dip around my breasts, the slit revealing the smallest peek of thigh, the color that didn't let me hide in the background.

I felt…beautiful. Me. But more.

Fallon's hand curved around my shoulder, squeezing gently. "You look stunning."

"Linc's gonna swallow his tongue," Rho called.

Sutton laughed. "Or have a stroke."

"We need a picture," Thea demanded.

We all moved then, squeezing in as she tried to do a long-armed selfie. It wasn't perfect or posed, but it was a pile of happiness, all of us dissolving into giggles as we squeezed in.

The doorbell rang, and Brutus rose from his dog bed, letting out two quick barks. "I've got it, baby," I called, heading to the door.

When I pulled it open, I stilled. The man standing there was stunning in every way. Linc's deep brown hair was styled in one of those artful ways that was just a little messy. His scruff had been shorn so only a hint shone through. And his eyes burned a little more gold than green.

He wore a suit that matched my dress—a little more earthy than pink, but a clear correlation. It was a silent claiming. No, a *belonging.* Or more, a promise. That we belonged to each other.

"You match me."

There was no twitch of his lips or corner of his mouth tugging up. Linc's eyes burned brighter. "Wanted everyone to know that I was yours. How proud I am of all you do."

That pressure was back behind my eyes. "Linc."

"You look incredible. Everything you've always been but uncovered in a whole new way."

He understood what I was reaching for. Like always.

"But you're missing one thing," Linc said.

I frowned. "What—?"

Linc pulled something out of his pocket. A charm hung from a delicate rose gold chain. Not something over-the-top and covered in gems. Something that was me. The charm was an artist's palette stamped onto a rose gold disc. Simple. Beautiful. Me.

"It's perfect," I whispered.

Linc reached around my neck and fastened the clasp. As he stepped back, the necklace fell to the perfect spot. "Meant for you."

I lifted my gaze to his. "It is. Just like you are for me."

CHAPTER FIFTY

Lincoln

I COULDN'T STOP WATCHING HER AS SHE MOVED ACROSS THE space. The need was a mix of worry and captivation. Because Arden herself was a work of art. She always was, but tonight, it was as if she'd discovered a new palette to paint with.

Holt Hartley's company had provided the security for the evening. We had guards patrolling the entire block around The Collective, two positioned at every entrance, two checking IDs and running fingerprints at the check-in, and a handful more inside the party itself. Arden was safe.

I'd been telling myself the same thing over and over, yet my body wasn't getting the message. My fingers held tight to my rocks glass, the bourbon inside remaining untouched.

I swept the crowd again. Lolli stood talking to Walter, the older man who worked at Sutton's bakery. He had stars in his eyes, and I swore Lolli wore a hint of a blush.

Fallon talked with a man a few years older than her whom I didn't recognize as Kye glared in the man's direction, a clear threat in his gaze. Nora studied one of Hannah's paintings, pointing something out to Rhodes and Anson.

The reporter who'd given Arden a hard time was scribbling notes, glancing in her direction every so often as if salivating for a sound bite. Shep and Cope stood at the snack table, helping Keely and Luca plate tiny sliders as Trace scanned the area, just as on alert as I was.

A dapper-looking Isaiah charmed Thea and Sutton. Had they not both been taken, I had no doubt they would've caved as he explained the motivation behind his most recent sculpture.

Hannah wove behind the table housing the phone bank for the auction, making sure everyone was set up. And Farah snapped something at a caterer whose eyes went wide. I was fairly certain Arden had found her new gallery manager in that one.

A figure slid through the crowd. Even his movements were snakelike. Quentin Arison wore a three-piece black suit with a blood-red tie, his eyes fixed on only one person.

My grip on my glass tightened as I watched him slither up to Arden, not caring at all that she was mid-conversation with someone. Her smile was tight as she greeted him and made polite introductions to the person she was already talking to. But nothing about her demeanor said *welcome*.

"Are you going to do something about that?" a little voice asked.

I nearly jumped, not noticing my tiny friend approach. Glancing down, I took in Benny. I couldn't deny that he looked adorable. He wore a blue suit with a bow tie that had little paintbrushes on it.

"Well?" he pressed.

I grinned at him. "I think Arden's pretty good at protecting herself."

Benny scowled at that. "You don't fix it, I'm going to."

I couldn't help but laugh. "I guess a little rescuing never hurt anybody. What if we tag team?"

A grin stretched across Benny's face, and he held up his fist. "That's what I'm talking about."

I bumped my knuckles against his, and we started toward Arden's huddle. As we approached, she widened her eyes in a comical *SAVE ME* message. As I got within earshot, I knew why.

"My collection really is one of a kind. It's valued at over fifty million." Quentin's attention shifted from the man he was droning on at to Arden, his gaze sliding over her body in a way that had my hand fisting at my side. "Of course, I'm always on the lookout for new and promising talent."

I eased into the circle, my arm sliding around Arden's waist and lips dropping to her temple. "Everything good, Vicious?"

Arden melted into me, her hand going to my chest. "Just discussing the art we all gravitate toward."

Benny put his hands on his hips and glared at Quentin. "I don't think there's any art in Miss Arden's dress. You should look at the walls."

Arden ducked her head, trying to disguise her smile as the gentleman opposite us started coughing to hide his laugh. Dots of red hit Quentin's cheeks, but he scowled at the little boy.

"Out of the mouths of babes," I murmured.

Quentin's angry eyes flashed to me. "*Someone* should teach this child some manners. Where are his parents?"

"Someone should teach *you* some manners," Benny shot back, not intimidated in the least. "I know you don't look at a lady's boobies. My dad says."

This time, both the man opposite me and I lost it. The older gentleman wore a cowboy hat and shined boots, and as he turned to Quentin, his belt buckle gleamed. "The kid has a point. And all that money talk isn't the way we operate around here."

Quentin lifted his chin. "I won't apologize for my wealth."

"No need to," the man said. "Just like there's no need for you to shove it down our throats."

Quentin huffed out a haughty breath and turned to Arden. "I'll speak to you when you're not among such unsavory company."

He turned and stalked away before Arden could answer, but Benny yelled after him. "She likes her unsavory company. Savory sucks."

Arden covered her mouth to stifle her giggle.

Benny turned back to us. "What's unsavory anyway?"

She crouched down to give him a quick hug. "My favorite thing."

He grinned up at her as he rose. "I *knew* it."

A man who was the spitting image of Benny, just a few decades older, approached. "Benny, we talked about some thoughts staying inside." He glanced at all of us. "I'm so sorry."

I grinned. "Your kid is awesome."

The man chuckled. "Thank you. I think so most of the time, too. But right now, he's going to come get a snack with me."

Benny looked up at me, his eyes narrowing. "Just because you think I'm awesome doesn't mean you get a pass." He made a motion of pointing two fingers to his eyes and then at me. "I'm watching you."

"Benny," his father hissed, pulling him away.

We all burst out laughing as Arden melted further into me. "Benny, my hero."

"Hey," I whispered. "What about me?"

"You're always my hero," she said, brushing her lips across mine.

"Five thousand dollars. Do I hear six?" the auctioneer called from the small makeshift stage as he gestured to the large watercolor Hannah had done. "Going once, going twice, sold to the gentleman in the back with the admirable cowboy hat."

I glanced over to see my new friend, Howard, dipping his head in acceptance of his win. As I turned back toward the stage, it was to find Arden glaring at me. I couldn't help it, I smiled.

"She is going to kill you in your sleep," Kye muttered next to me.

I only grinned wider. "It'll be worth it."

"You're not wrong," Cope said, amusement lacing his words. "I really want to see that Quentin dude's head explode."

I'd purchased every single piece of Arden's artwork that had come up for sale. Quentin had run up the bids, but I didn't care. It was for a good cause. But the truth was, I couldn't stand the idea of him having any piece of Arden.

"Our final piece of the night. *Bleed to Bloom* by Arden Waverly," the auctioneer called as the crowd quieted. He pointed at the large canvas Arden had been working on the first time I'd walked into her studio. The one that had spoken to me from the moment I set eyes on it.

"He's glaring murdery daggers at you," Rhodes singsonged.

"Want me to use that new jujitsu move Kye taught me on him?" Lolli asked, her hands raising in some sort of made-up martial arts move.

"Oh, Jesus," Kye said under his breath. "You promised you'd never do that in public."

Lolli squeezed one of her biceps. "I know these guns are lethal, but that douche canoe deserves it."

"Mom," Nora whisper-hissed, pulling out the moniker she seemed to only use when she was really trying to rein Lolli in.

"Oh, all right, but you lot are always ruining my fun."

"Or trying to keep her from a permanent record," Trace muttered, squeezing the bridge of his nose.

"Let's begin the bidding at one thousand dollars," the auction-eer cut in. "Do I hear one thousand?"

Quentin raised his paddle. "Ten thousand."

The crowd murmured.

"We have a serious player in our midst, ladies and gentlemen. Ten thousand. Do I hear eleven?"

I raised my paddle. "Twenty-five."

Fallon let out a squeak behind me as the auctioneer's brows rose. "Twenty-five thousand. Do I hear twenty-six?"

Annoyance flashed in Quentin's dark eyes. "Fifty."

Arden's cheeks flushed as she wound her fingers together, glanc-ing nervously at her painting. I knew this one was special to her. To us. And I wasn't about to let Arison get his dirty little fingers on it.

"One hundred," I called with a raise of my paddle.

"One hundred thousand," the auctioneer called. "Do I hear one hundred and one?"

"One hundred five," Quentin called. He was losing steam, and it was time for me to go in for the kill.

I didn't wait for the auctioneer; I simply raised my paddle again. "One fifty."

The auctioneer grinned. "One hundred and fifty thousand dollars. Do I hear one fifty-one?"

Quentin dropped his paddle like a toddler having a tantrum. "She's not even worth twenty," he spat.

Anger surged inside me as Quentin stormed out of the gallery. *She*. Not the painting but the woman herself. He thought he could own Arden. But Arden wasn't a possession. She was a human being, one that could never be contained, one that lived fully only when she lived freely.

Benny leaned out the gallery's doorway, calling after Quentin, "See ya, wouldn't wanna be ya, buddy!"

The entire crowd burst into laughter as Benny's dad scrubbed a hand over his face. The auctioneer saluted Benny and then turned back to the rest of us. "One hundred and fifty thousand dollars. Going once, twice, sold to the gentleman in pink."

"It's mauve," I called back, the crowd descending into laughter again.

Arden leaned in to thank the auctioneer and then made a beeline to me. "What is wrong with you?"

"Duck and cover," Kye whispered.

Arden sent him a quick glare before turning back to me. "You bought every piece!"

"I did."

"Why? To play in some dick-measuring contest with a douchebag?"

"Ooooh, now that could be a fun game," Lolli interjected before someone hushed her.

"You said you hated the idea of your art being in his possession," I told her honestly.

Arden gaped at me, her mouth forming that perfect O. "So, you spent half a million dollars on things I would've given you for free?"

I moved into her space, my hands lifting to frame her face. "I'd spend every last dime if it meant you having ownership of your work. And it's a hell of a bonus that I'll live surrounded by your creations—by *you*—every single day."

"Linc," she whispered.

"Love you, Vicious."

"Love you, you over-the-top, ridiculous, alpha-male billionaire control freak."

I grinned down at her. "You say the sweetest things."

CHAPTER FIFTY-ONE

Arden

AN ARM SLID OVER MY SHOULDERS AS I MANEUVERED THROUGH the crowd. "Ardy, teach me your ways. That was a battle to the death," Isaiah said, a grin stretching across his face.

I shook my head, but a smile tugged at my lips. "I'm pretty sure there are more than a few women ready to catfight over you."

He made a show of shining his nails against his suit. "You're not wrong. Which just shows they have fabulous taste. But that fight would be unnecessary if you'd just marry me."

"Keep dreaming, clay boy," I said, slipping out from under his arm and making a beeline to the bar.

"You're breaking my heart," Isaiah called over the crowd.

I just waved without looking back, continuing on my path.

The bartender looked up from where she mixed a rum and Coke. "That was quite a show."

"Men," I huffed.

"You're telling me," she echoed.

"How's everything going here? Are you running low on anything?"

The bartender stepped back, doing a quick sweep. "I think we'll need another bottle of vodka and white wine."

"On it," I said. I turned around but stopped short when I came face-to-face with the reporter. I did my best not to grimace as I greeted him. "Mr. Levine."

"Sam, please."

"Sam," I amended. "I hope you enjoyed the event." I moved to the side to step around him.

But he mirrored my movement to block my path. "I did. How do you think it went?"

My smile grew a little more strained. "We'll see once the final tally comes in. If you'll excuse—"

"You know, I always find it curious when a subject is *this* reticent for an interview. Either they're putting on an act—a persona—in hopes of making their art more alluring, or they've got something to hide. Which is it, Arden?"

Annoyance melted into a touch of anger. "I guess that's your job to determine, isn't it? Good luck."

I moved quicker this time, not letting the jerkwad stop me. Slipping through the crowd, I made my way down the hall in search of the booze the bartender needed. I slipped into the first studio space and flipped on the light.

Hannah's space was always neat and tidy, so unlike Farah's, while Isaiah's was somewhere in the middle. I crossed to the closet in the corner where Farah had said she'd stashed the bar supplies. Opening the door, I turned on the light.

Even this space was organized. Hannah had covered the walls in a burlap material that fit the earthiness of her paintings. Stacks of canvases were lined up against the far wall, while brushes, paints, and other supplies lined the others.

Farah had cleared a spot to stash the alcohol bottles, plastic cups, and other bar supplies, and I wasn't surprised when I noticed we had far more liquor than we needed. Farah was always one to keep a party going.

Leaning over, I pawed through the bottles on the low shelves running the length of the closet. My hand closed around the bottle of vodka but as I lifted it, my bracelet caught on the burlap, pulling it back. I cursed, setting the bottle down and unhooking my jewelry from the wall covering.

Then I frowned. The burlap was loose, fastened only by hooks at the very top of the wall. And there was something behind it.

I gently pulled it back. Photos. Like some sort of massive collage. Only there was no artistic bent to it.

My mouth went dry as I tugged harder on the burlap. It fell in a whoosh, covering the shelves and spilling onto the floor. So many photos. They covered the entire wall, overlapping with one another.

They started with Isaiah as the subject. Him here at The Collective, around town, at his house. But there was one common thread. He clearly had no idea he was being photographed.

I moved deeper into the space, my stomach cramping as the photos turned from Isaiah to me. Except there was a different bent to these. Each one had angry Sharpie lines across them or even marks from what looked like a blade. My eyes Xed out. Face torn off. Words written across them.

Liar. Slut. Thief.

Holy hell. This was obsession. Rage.

"You bitch." The words were low but filled with so much anger. There was no soft airiness like I normally heard in Hannah's voice. There was only vitriol.

I whirled, taking in the woman I'd always thought of as a friend. Her red hair was piled on her head in an artful bun, her pale floral dress hugging her form. She looked beautiful, but there was nothing but hatred in her eyes as she filled the doorway. "Hannah, I—"

"You what? It wasn't enough that you made this whole night about you? You just had to invade my space on top of it?"

My jaw went slack. "No, I—"

"You just had to throw yourself at Isaiah for the millionth time?"

Shock zinged through me as I tried to put the pieces together. The photos of Isaiah. The ones of me. I dropped my voice, trying to gentle it as much as possible. "Isaiah and I are friends. That's all. I'm with Linc. You know that."

Hannah's eyes flashed with rage. "But he's not enough for you. You just have to keep Isaiah on the line. Give him just enough that he won't let go. So he can't see who else is right in front of him."

Nausea slid through me as memories swept through my mind. The way Hannah flushed anytime Isaiah paid her attention. How she was always offering to help him load sculptures or upload new listings to the website. How she seemed to hover around the edges of anywhere he was.

"There's nothing between us," I said calmly. "There never has been."

"You're right. And there never will be," Hannah muttered.

And that's when I saw it. The X-Acto knife clenched so tightly in her hand that her knuckles had turned completely white.

"Because you're going away for good." And then she lunged.

CHAPTER FIFTY-TWO

Lincoln

MY GAZE SWEPT OVER THE CROWD AS LUCA AND KEELY DID some sort of hopped-up-on-sugar dance in the middle of the gallery, joined by Benny and other faces I recognized from the kids' workshop. But I didn't see Arden anywhere.

I tried to pinpoint the last time I'd seen her in the crowd but, honestly, I wasn't sure. That had an unsettled feeling sweeping over me. Moving through the guests, I found Trace talking to an older woman I didn't recognize. "I'm sorry to interrupt," I said to the woman, then turned. "Trace, have you seen Arden?"

He was instantly on alert. "Not since you had that big show-down with the douchebag."

The woman let out a laugh. "Douchebag is the right term for him. Good job kicking him to the curb."

I forced a smile. "Happy to do it."

Trace placed a hand on the woman's shoulder. "It was good to see you, Louise. If you'll excuse me, I need to hunt down my sister."

She waved him off. "Of course, you boys enjoy your evening."

"You, too," I said, but I was already moving into the crowd, Trace at my side.

Isaiah looked up from chatting with two women. "Everything okay?"

"We can't find Arden," I said, my voice tight.

"I think she was going to check on the bartender."

I nodded, instantly moving in that direction. A female bartender worked the station, handing out glasses of wine, sodas, and mixed cocktails. I didn't even consider the rudeness of cutting a waiting patron off when I stepped up to the bar. "Have you seen Arden?"

The woman's brows lifted slightly. "She was going to get me more wine and vodka. But that was a little bit ago."

I shared a glance with Trace, my anxiety mounting. A muscle in his jaw ticked. "She probably got held up by someone she knows."

God, I hoped that was the case.

"What's going on?" Farah asked as she walked up wearing her usual artist's black. The only color present on her was the red slicked across her mouth.

"We're looking for Arden," I said, tension strangling my voice.

She grinned at me. "Man, you really are a goner, aren't you? Can't go five minutes without your girl. It's adorable, really. I—"

"Farah," I cut her off. "Have you seen her?"

"She went to get more of the booze I stashed in Hannah's supply closet."

I didn't wait to answer; Trace and I were already moving. We strode through the crowd and down the hall, coming up short at the doorway to Hannah's studio. As we stepped inside, I heard it. Voices.

"Hannah, let's just take a breath."

Arden's voice sent relief sliding through me, but not for long.

"I don't want to take a goddamned breath," Hannah snapped. "I want you to stop stealing all Isaiah's attention. I want you to stop being such a show-off. It's always about *you*. Your art. Your hatred of the press. Your stupid charity projects."

"I'm not—"

"But he falls for it every time," Hannah screeched. "He doesn't know who you *really* are. That you're manipulating him. That you're just doing it all so he'll fall for you. But it's not going to work."

He doesn't know who you really are.

The note we'd found on Arden's windshield flashed in my mind. *I KNOW WHO YOU REALLY ARE.*

That was what this was all about? Isaiah? The note, destroying Arden's studio, *shooting* at us?

Trace held up a hand, silently pulling a gun from the holster under his suit jacket. As he stepped farther into the main studio space, I followed behind. In a matter of steps, the closet's opening came into view.

Hannah's back was to us, Arden trapped inside, but it was the glint of silver metal that had my heart lurching. A knife.

My gaze connected with Arden's over the top of Hannah's head, and I swore relief swept through those gray-violet eyes. But it only made my gut tighten. Because there wasn't a damn thing I could do to help her.

And I wasn't sure Trace could either. The space was too tight. If he took a shot, it could go through Hannah and hit Arden.

"Hannah," Trace said, his voice taking on a robotic quality, one devoid of emotion. "This is the Mercer County Sheriff's Department. Put your weapon down."

The redhead whirled but kept the knife pointed at Arden. "No, no, no." Her free hand tugged at her hair in desperate jerks. "You can't be here. You can't. This is my place. Mine and Isaiah's. You can't be here. And *she* can't either."

Hannah lunged forward like a fencer, and Arden narrowly avoided the jab.

"Hannah," Trace warned. "Don't do that. You move like that again, and I'll have no choice but to shoot you. And I don't want to do that."

"You do want. You do." Hannah tugged harder on her hair. "Because then she'll have him. You'll kill me, and she'll take him."

"She doesn't want him." I spoke the words before really thinking them through. I knew you really couldn't reason with someone whose mind had warped in this way, but I had to try.

Hannah turned angry eyes in my direction. "I feel sorry for you. She's just fooling you, too. Pretending to be someone she's not. She's greedy. One is never enough for her."

"Linc is the only person for me," Arden whispered. "The only one I want, now and forever."

Everything in me tightened to the point of pain, ready to shatter into endless pieces. "Vicious."

"Love you," she croaked.

"LIES!" Hannah screamed the word, pulling harder at her hair. "Everything is lies. Even your art. Everyone thinks you're so good, but it's just scrap metal and bland paint. It's nothing. Just like you."

"Is that why you destroyed her studio?" Trace asked, his voice still remarkably calm.

"I destroyed her lies," Hannah spat. "Isaiah wouldn't stop talking about it that day. How *amazing* it was that Arden had organized all those workshops. How much the kids *loved* her. I couldn't take it. I had to let her know that I saw the real her, that she couldn't hide behind that do-no-wrong façade. She had to stop distracting Isaiah so he could see *me*."

Hannah jabbed the knife forward as if to punctuate the point. "I told Isaiah and Farah that I had a headache. That I had to leave. And I did. Her lies make me feel like my head's going to explode. I'd *never* lie to Isaiah. Not like *you*," she spat at Arden.

"What did you do, Hannah?" Trace asked softly, trying to keep her talking.

She let out a huff of air. "I know Cope has cameras, so I stole my brother's football pads, a hoodie, jeans, and that stupid mask he bought for Halloween last year. But it was good because I wanted you scared. It was a warning. But she just wouldn't listen. She's too damn selfish."

I tried to follow her thinking, but the logic seemed to be Hannah's alone, something that didn't quite fit. But she held on to it with a death grip.

"So, you tried to shoot her instead?" Trace pressed.

"She deserves to die!" Hannah cried.

Then she lunged again. Arden's eyes went wide, shock and panic filling them because she had nowhere to go. Hannah let out a scream that sounded more animal than human as Arden tried to evade her. But it was too late.

All I could see was blood.

CHAPTER FIFTY-THREE

Arden

I WINCED AS DR. AVERY RELEASED HIS HOLD ON MY HAND AND pinned me with a stare. "Are you sure you don't want those painkillers?"

I shook my head and leaned against the massive sectional in Cope's living room, Brutus at my feet. "The Tylenol's good enough."

Linc's frustration and anger hit me in waves from where he sat next to me on the couch. "Take the pills. There's no reason for you to be in pain. It's something *you* reminded *me* of not that long ago."

I twisted in my seat, resting a knee still covered in silk on his thigh. The poor pink dress had blood splatters on it now. I had a feeling those didn't come out of silk. "I'm okay," I promised him. "Need to brush up on disarming an opponent, but Kye'll deal with that."

I'd managed to grab Hannah's wrist and twist her arm behind her back, breaking her grip on the blade. But not before it clipped my palm. It wasn't horribly deep, but it had been a bleeder, which hadn't made Linc or Trace all that happy.

"Damn straight. We'll hit the gym as soon as the stitches are out," Kye said from the opposite side of the sectional. He was trying to keep it light, but I saw the shadows in his amber eyes. Fallon saw them, too, and was sticking close, making sure he didn't do anything stupid to try to bury those demons.

My whole family was worried—my friends, too—which was why we were currently piled into Cope's living space. I was doing my best to assure them that I was okay, but none of them seemed to believe me. All I'd ended up with was a slice across the palm while Hannah had landed in cuffs.

Isaiah scrubbed a hand over his face. "I'm so—"

"If you say you're sorry one more time, I'm going to attack *you* with an X-Acto knife," I clipped.

No one laughed.

"Come on," I pressed. "It's a little funny."

Linc leaned in, pressing a kiss to my head. "Gonna take a long time to see any humor in this, Vicious."

Farah shot me a grin. "I thought it was a little funny. But I also know that if I laughed, Isaiah would've smacked me, so…"

My lips twitched. "I can always count on you."

"To be inappropriate," Isaiah amended. His gaze gentled on me. "Let me say it one more time, and then I'll be done."

I let out a long breath. "Okay."

"I'm so damn sorry. I had no idea she was fixated on me like that. I thought we were friends. I just—I feel responsible somehow."

My stomach twisted as I thought of everything Isaiah was trying to parse through right now. And how violated he must feel. Because some of the pictures on that wall were of very private moments.

I leaned forward, making sure Isaiah saw my eyes. "None of this is on you. Hannah's mind is…broken, and it latched on to you as a life preserver."

A muscle along his jaw ticked, but he nodded.

"Good," I said, sinking back against the sofa and Linc.

Dr. Avery smiled at me as he rose from his spot on the coffee table. "Good to see your spirits haven't been dulled."

"Never," I said, returning his grin. "Thank you for coming all the way out here so I didn't have to go to the ER."

He patted my knee as he rose. "Happy to help. But let's stay out of harm's way for a while, okay?"

"I think that's an excellent plan," Nora said, walking into the space, Lolli behind her. "Here. Some tea." She rounded the couch and set the saucer on the table.

"I tried to slip the good stuff in, but my girl's too fast," Lolli groused.

Nora shook her head. "And I always will be."

"Remember to keep that hand dry for twenty-four hours," Dr. Avery called as he headed for the door. "Cover it in plastic wrap if you take a shower."

"I think I'll opt for a bath," I assured him. My muscles needed it anyway.

"I'll walk you out," Cope said, rising.

"You need to go, too," I pressed. "You should've left hours ago."

Cope, Sutton, and Luca were supposed to take Linc's plane back to Seattle right after the fundraiser so he could attend some important team meetings tomorrow.

Cope stared me down as if I'd grown a second head. "You were attacked. I'm not going anywhere."

"Barely," I argued.

"Did someone try to stab you or not?" Cope asked, exasperation coating his words.

"Please, don't remind me," Nora said, wringing her hands.

I sent my brother a pointed look. "They may have tried, but they failed. All I got was a cut that barely needed liquid stitches. I'm fine. Better than fine because the person who did all of this is in county lockup. I'm safe. I can breathe. And so should my family." I took a deep breath. "I love you all so much." The words burned as they made their way out of my throat, but they left beautiful scars in their wake. "I'm so lucky to have you. But I never want you to stop living your lives because you're worried about me."

Cope's shoulders straightened. "You said you love us."

"Because I do."

"I know," he croaked. "We all know. But you almost never say it."

My gaze flicked to Linc, staying there. "Someone taught me that it's important to say the words."

"Hell," Cope muttered. "I wanted to at least give Linc a black eye for hooking up with my sister, but he's good for you."

Linc chuckled, turning to Cope. "Sorry?"

"You should be. You stole my brotherly right."

Sutton crossed to Cope and wrapped her arms around him. "I think you'll live. But Arden's right. We should get back to Seattle. You're working too hard to get back on the ice to throw it away now."

Cope's eyes met mine. "You're sure?"

"I'm sure."

Just as they were about to get Luca from his movie fest with Keely, new voices sounded. Trace and Anson strode down the hall, coming up short at the full house that had gathered. They both looked...tired.

Trace no longer wore the expression he used to hide his fury. Instead, everything in his demeanor read resignation, maybe even a little sadness.

Linc's arm went around my shoulders, pulling me to him. "What's the update?"

Trace sighed. "Hannah was transported to county holding a few hours ago. We've been executing searches on her apartment and studio space. We found the mask she used in the break-in and her little brother's football pads to make herself look bigger in the video footage. It took us a little while to find her vehicle, but when we did, we found a rifle in the trunk. Matches the caliber of bullet found at the campsite."

My gaze moved to Anson. "Did you talk to her?"

If anyone could put together the broken pieces of Hannah's mind and understand her motivation, it was him. And I *needed* to understand.

Anson gave me a slight nod, and all the eyes in the room moved to him. "I haven't spoken with her long enough to diagnose her— even if I did still have my credentials. But Hannah's life hasn't been an easy one. She hasn't been shown a lot of kindness." He glanced at

Isaiah. "You were kind to her after an especially nasty dustup with her parents. She latched on."

A war of emotions flashed across Isaiah's face. "I wasn't the only one who was kind to her. So were Farah and Arden, even Denver."

"It's not always logical," Anson explained gently as his focus shifted to me. "Just like it's not logical that she blamed you for not getting what she wanted. But that doesn't mean there isn't a root."

"And what's the root here?" Shep asked, leaning forward as Thea rubbed his back.

"Isaiah represented kindness and respite when Hannah didn't have much of that in her life." Anson cast a quick look at me. "Arden had so much of what she wanted but didn't have. More acclaim and notice for her art. A family that loved and supported her. Isaiah's attention."

I curled closer to Linc, wishing I could disappear into him. His lips ghosted over my hair. "It's not your fault."

"He's right," Anson agreed. "It isn't on either of you. It's not even on Hannah's shoulders. That's what makes it so damn heartbreaking."

Farah's eyes flashed. "You guys are being a little too kumbaya about this. She's been stalking Isaiah. She *attacked* Arden. And who knows what else?"

I suddenly felt so exhausted I could barely keep my head up. "She's sick, Farah. And that's nothing but sad."

Farah made a disgruntled noise in the back of her throat. "Leave me to my angry-girl ways."

One corner of my mouth kicked up. "We all have our methods of processing."

Trace shifted, his arms crossed over his chest. "The prosecutor will want to know how hard you want to press."

If only I had been hurt, I'd be begging for the least possible punishment. But it wasn't just me. She could've *killed* Linc. I looked up at him, those swirling hazel eyes gazing down at me with so much love.

"She can't hurt anyone else," I whispered before forcing my gaze away from the man who held my heart in his hands. "She needs help, but she also needs to be somewhere she can't do any more damage."

Trace nodded. "I'll talk to the prosecutor about requesting a se-cure mental health facility as opposed to prison." He glanced at Linc. "You good with that? You're the one she shot."

Linc held me tighter. "I'm good with whatever Arden wants."

"And what she is too nice to tell us all right now is that she wants some alone time with that hunk of hers," Lolli said.

Kye made a *psh* noise. "Arden isn't too nice about anything."

Fallon smacked his arm. "She is too nice. You should know that by the fact that she let you slide with that sloppy takedown the other day."

Kye whipped around in Fal's direction. "My takedowns are never sloppy."

Fallon arched an amused brow at him. "You *sure* about that?"

He frowned. "I want a replay."

"Sure, you do, fight boy," Fallon said, pushing to her feet and dragging him with her.

Everyone slowly began making their way to the door. Cope squeezed my shoulder. "You sure you're okay with us leaving tonight?"

"I'm sure. I'm going to take a bath and go to bed. I need to sleep for a week."

"Vampire," Cope muttered, dropping a kiss to the top of my head.

"Love you, pucker," I called.

"Love you, too."

Nora gave my arm a pat. "Call if you need anything. I'll drop some food at your place tomorrow afternoon. Any requests?"

I looked up at her, a smile playing on my lips. "Mexican casserole?"

She chuckled. "You've got it."

"Thanks, Mom."

Her eyes misted. "Get some rest."

Neither Linc nor I moved as everyone left. We listened as car doors slammed and engines started. But neither of us said a word until silence reigned for a few solid minutes.

Linc brushed hair away from my face. "My heart stopped when she dove for you."

I curled into him more. "I'm sorry. I'm right here. Not going anywhere."

He pressed a hand over my heart. "Just going to need to remind myself of that for a while. I hope you don't mind a clingy boyfriend."

My mouth quirked. "Boyfriend, huh?"

Linc chuckled, the sound skating over me. "Ridiculous term. But it'll have to do until you let me have *husband*."

Everything in me seized. "Linc."

"Not yet." He dipped his head, brushing his lips across mine. "But soon."

My stomach flipped, and I waited for the fear to creep in, the kind that made its home because I knew just how much someone meant to me, and how much it would cost if I lost them. But it didn't come. We'd made it through too many battles for it to win now.

"I love you," I whispered across his lips.

"I know."

I laughed, pushing off his chest. "I want to take a really long, hot bath," I muttered.

"Want to do it in my room here? Tub's bigger."

He was right about that. Cope had gone so ridiculously over-the-top in every bathroom in this place. But tonight, over-the-top relaxation was exactly what I needed. "That sounds good. Can I borrow sweats to change into?"

"You know I love you in my clothes."

"Possessive."

Linc grinned against my mouth. "With you? Always."

A cell phone ring filled the air, and Linc cursed, pulling it out. "It's Ellie."

"Answer it," I urged. "Can you take Brutus out with you so he can do his business?"

Linc nodded, getting to his feet as the phone continued to ring. "Come on, B-man. She's kicking us to the curb."

I just shook my head as Linc led Brutus into the backyard. As

I started up the stairs, I could feel the strain in my muscles. A bath would be good. But as soon as my hand healed, I was getting my ass back in the gym. If the dustup with Hannah had shown me anything, it was where I was weak. And I'd attack those weaknesses with a single-minded focus.

Making my way down the hall, I stopped at the room Linc had been half-staying in. Cope had decorated each spare room with one of our siblings in mind. This one had been for Shep. The artwork on the walls was a series of stylized architectural drawings, and the furniture had a rustic air to it that matched Shep's tastes.

I moved to the dresser, searching for a tee and some sweats. My fingers ghosted over the soft cotton of a worn Seattle Sparks T-shirt, so I pulled it out and tossed it onto the bed. Then I found sweatpants I knew I would drown in but figured the drawstring might save me.

Crossing to the bathroom, I flicked on the light. It felt brighter than necessary, and I couldn't help but study my hand. The liquid bandage stuff Dr. Avery had used had done the trick. The angry slice across my palm was nothing more than a red line now.

But it would scar. And that scar would remind me of tonight. Of all Linc and I had been through. I found I wasn't sorry about that. Because it would also be a reminder of all we'd overcome and how strong we were when we stood together.

I lightly traced the line, feeling gratitude instead of pain and letting that sink in.

Finally, I dropped my hand and moved toward the massive tub. But as I reached for the faucet, I was plunged into darkness.

Panic flashed hot and bright, digging into my muscles. *Breathe.* I gave myself the command over and over as I cursed myself for not having my phone or keys—the ones with the new flashlight Linc had given me.

Dark spots danced in front of my vision as I gripped the side of the tub. *No.* I wouldn't let this fear win either. It was just a stupid power outage, probably caused by record-setting temperatures earlier in the day.

I forced myself to straighten, focusing on keeping my breathing even. Linc was downstairs, right outside. I'd find him, and we'd be fine.

I slipped into the bedroom, and that's when I heard it. Footsteps. Not hurried ones the way Linc's would be if he knew the power was out, but slow and measured. Deliberate. And then I heard a voice.

"Let's play a game, Sheridan. You hide, and I'll seek. I'll even give you to the count of ten. Run while you can."

CHAPTER FIFTY-FOUR

Lincoln

I JUST GOT YOUR MESSAGE. I'M SO SORRY. MY PHONE WAS ON silent. I should've checked it sooner. Are you okay? Is Arden okay?"

"El Bell, breathe," I said, stepping out into the night and gesturing for Brutus to head past the landscaping to do whatever he needed.

"You said some woman attacked you and Arden! Breathing is secondary at the moment."

I couldn't help it; a small chuckle slipped free, and, God, I needed that.

"This isn't something to be laughing about, Lincoln."

Shit. I knew Ellie was seriously pissed if she was calling me Lincoln. "I'm okay. Arden's okay. She's got a cut on her palm, but that's it. She disarmed the assailant, and the woman's in jail now."

An audible exhale came across the line. "Good. That's good. Can you guys stop with all the life-in-danger stuff? It's getting a little old."

I laughed full-out this time. "Noted. I'll try to keep things nice and boring."

"Thank you."

"How are you doing?" I asked, watching as Brutus caught the scent of something, chasing it into the underbrush.

"You and the love of your life nearly get knifed, and you're asking me how *I'm* doing?" she asked incredulously.

"Just because I have a lot going on doesn't mean you don't. I can hold both."

"You were always so good at that." Ellie's voice went tight as if she were trying to keep a sob from erupting.

"Hey, what's going on?"

"It's nothing. It's just…long few days. Talked to Dad."

I couldn't help the curse that slipped free.

"That about sums it up," Ellie muttered. Then she went quiet for a long moment. "You were right. I knew he wasn't the best dad, but I don't even think he looks at us as children. It's like we're possessions."

"I didn't want you to have to know that the way I do," I said softly.

"I was so blind to it," she whispered. "So blind to it that I ended up engaged to someone who sees me the same way."

"Ellie—"

"It's true. And what's worse is that I don't like the person who did that. Who let herself just go along with being treated like nothing more than an accessory."

My gut hollowed out. "You're so much more than that."

"I don't know if I am. But I'm going to change that. I told Bradley I couldn't marry him tonight."

"Seriously?" As much as I'd hoped my sister would break free, I knew that blowing up a years-long relationship wasn't exactly easy.

"Yep." I heard a refrigerator opening—or maybe a freezer—then ice clinking into a glass.

"How'd he take it?"

"About how you'd expect a spoiled, overgrown toddler to take anything he doesn't like."

"Ellie—"

"It's fine. But I think I should probably put some distance between us for a while."

"Come here," I said instantly.

"ConCon. You're in the honeymoon phase. You've had a lot of drama. You don't need your little sister on your doorstep."

"You're exactly who I need. It'd do me some good to have you around. Who knows, maybe you'll like it here."

Ellie was quiet for a moment. "Arden did say I could be a cowgirl if I wanted to be."

A laugh bubbled out of me. "Are you having some sort of quarter-life crisis?"

"Probably. Gonna get a cowboy hat to prove it."

"You come to Sparrow Falls? I'll get one for you."

"Gonna hold you to that. Just like I'm going to make Arden give me some riding lessons."

God, I loved the sound of that. My sister, my girl, the warm embrace I knew the Colsons would give Ellie. We needed it. All of it. And maybe that's what Sparrow Falls would give us both. A chance to start over. To build the family we always should've had. The one our mom had never been able to give us the way she wanted to.

"I can't wait," I said softly, turning toward the house. But as I did, I froze. It took me a second to realize what was off about the image that looked back at me. The lights. Or the absence of them.

My head jerked in the direction of Arden's place. Two windows still glowed down there. It was just Cope's place that was submerged in darkness.

Panic grabbed hold, but I was already running, calling across the line. "Call the sheriff's department. Tell them something's wrong. The power's out. It's wrong. Everything's wrong."

I just didn't know how right I was.

CHAPTER FIFTY-FIVE

Arden

MY BARE FEET HIT THE RUNNER ON THE HARDWOOD FLOOR, and I couldn't help but remember another rug all those years ago—one that had been so precious to my parents, only to be stained with my mother's blood. I wasn't about to let history repeat itself.

The footsteps behind me continued to climb the stairs as my gaze jerked around, and I tried to find my best hiding spot as pools of moonlight lit my path. Or better yet, somewhere that might house a weapon of some sort. But there were no kitchen knives or letter openers up here. And even if there were, whoever this was could have a gun.

"Sheridan," the voice singsonged.

It was clearly female. And familiar somehow. Panic lurched in my chest as an image of Hannah with that knife flashed in my mind. But she was in county lockup. It couldn't be her.

"Come out, come out, wherever you are. I just want to play a game."

Every fiber of muscle and sinew in me wound so tight it felt like they would all snap with the barest touch. Because I *did* know that voice.

My mind whirled as I yanked open the door to the hall closet. Linens on one side, cleaning supplies on the other. I frantically searched for something, anything to defend myself with. But nothing except maybe the mop would help.

"Time's up, Sherry baby," the voice called. "It's too boring if you don't play."

The footsteps picked up speed, running up the last few stairs. I had no choice. I slipped into the closet and closed the door behind me. I'd thought it was dark before, but I was wrong. Out of the closet, there was at least some light from the moon—enough to make out my surroundings. But in here, there was nothing but blackness, the faintest glow emanating from the seam of the door.

My heart hammered against my ribs, each inhale twisting and tripping as each tried to get to the next one. I squeezed my eyes shut and tried to force my breathing to slow. It was no use. And if I wasn't careful, I'd end up passing out by the time this asshole got to me.

So, I did the only thing I could think of. I focused on Linc.

Somewhere along the way, he'd become my grounding force. More than just a feeling of safety but something that helped me step into my strength.

I pictured his face in my mind. His dark brown hair and hazel eyes. The scruff I loved tracing with my fingers. The way those eyes saw right to the heart of me and reminded me exactly who I was.

"What's the matter, Sheridan? Don't want to join Mommy and Daddy in the great beyond?"

My eyes flew open, my breaths no longer short pants but deep, pissed-off inhales. The more she spoke, the more I was certain. And the betrayal felt like a knife to the gut.

Farah.

But it didn't make sense. She was maybe a handful of years older than I was. She certainly couldn't have been involved in what'd happened to my parents all those years ago. But she knew exactly who I was. And she wasn't here for a slumber party.

My mind reeled, thinking about the day a few months ago when she'd shown up at The Collective. She'd told me a story about being an artist looking for fresh inspiration. Her self-deprecating demeanor and brash jokes had lowered my walls. And it wasn't long before I invited her in.

Only now, I could see those conversations in a different light. The way she'd slip in the occasional question about my past. How she talked about losing her mother in an attempt to learn more about how I'd ended up with the Colsons. I'd just never realized why.

The footsteps changed tone, from shoes on hardwood to carpet. Muted. Only punctuated by the occasional clack as she searched room after room.

I braced, my hands searching for something—anything—that might help me. I stilled, my gaze locking on the faint shadow of a spray bottle. I lifted it, trying to bring the label into the faint moonlight coming in from the seam in the door. *Warning: keep out of eyes.*

Perfect.

I gripped the cleaning spray, my fingers tightening around the trigger. The footsteps slowed. Not right in front of the closet but close.

A sigh sounded. "This is growing old, Sheridan."

I shuddered at the name. Because it didn't belong to me anymore. I was Arden in every way that mattered. And more than that, I was a Colson.

"Hmmmm," Farah said dramatically. So like the woman I'd grown to know but different. Because there was a coldness beneath it that I'd never heard before.

"Where could the scared little artist be hiding? I wonder…"

The door to the closet flew open, and I didn't wait. I sprayed the cleaning solution like there was no tomorrow. Farah jerked back, a strangled sound leaving her throat. "You bitch!"

There was no time to waste. I kicked out, my foot connecting with Farah's stomach. Like I was, she was still in her dress from the event, but she'd changed her footwear. Gone were the spiky stilettos; in their place were combat boots. It gave her an edge over my bare feet, and she didn't waste it.

Farah struck out, her fist glancing off my jaw in a stunning punch that she followed with a hook to my ribs. I doubled over, the pain stealing my breath. She moved in, quick as lightning, but I knew if she got ahold of me, that would be the end.

I forced myself upright, using the force of the movement to fuel my uppercut. My fist connected with Farah's diaphragm, and she wheezed out a curse. I didn't miss the moment of opportunity. My knee came up and connected with her chin.

Farah doubled over, but it was almost as if she were immune to the pain. She simply kept moving. Her leg snaked out, sweeping mine out from under me and sending me slamming into the floor. The force of it stunned my entire system, a mix of pain and shock flooding me.

It was only a matter of seconds before I got my bearings, but it was too late. Farah straddled me, her entire weight pinning me down as she pressed a knife to my throat. "I wouldn't if I were you."

My chest heaved as I struggled to suck in air without pressing my neck into the blade—its sharp edges glinting in the moonlight. Farah's dark hair was pulled up into a tight knot now, and there was pure glee in her blue gaze.

"I really have to thank ole Han for her flair for the dramatic. Our little innocent wildflower isn't so innocent after all. It's going to make killing you and pinning it on her all the more fun."

"She's in jail," I wheezed.

Farah grinned. "Is she? Because I think *someone* pulled some strings and got her out on bail tonight. An hour ago, actually. Just enough time for her to get over here, short-circuit Cope's security cameras, and stab you a few dozen times. They'll find the knife with her prints on it in the flower pot by her back door. Just like they found that rifle in her trunk."

"You," I whispered, my mind whirling, trying to connect dots and strings to pull together a picture of the truth.

"I didn't have time to get fingerprints on that one. But it wasn't necessary. Hannah's so batshit, I think she'd have agreed to murder you and wear your skin as a suit."

My breaths came quicker as my brain jumped from one thing to another. "You shot Linc."

Farah winced. "Wasn't supposed to. That boy really does have a hero complex. It was getting a little annoying."

"How?" I croaked.

"Sheridan, really? It's quite easy. Point, aim, fire."

"How did you know where we were?" I pressed. Time. I needed time to get the upper hand again. My palms pressed into the carpet, the right one smarting where it had been cut. But I just let the flare of pain fuel me.

A laugh bubbled out of Farah, one so joyful it was slightly terrifying. "I have been infiltrating your life for months, babe. I've had a lot of marks over the years, but you might be my favorite. So mistrustful but always centering that suspicion on the wrong people. Poor Denver was just out for a buck. And you missed me and Han."

A different sort of hurt flared. The kind born of betrayal.

Farah's smile widened as she leaned closer to me. "Remember when I asked you if I could use your phone to look up The Mix Up menu? Mine was dead, poor me. You just handed that sucker over. Easy as one, two, three, getting that spyware on your device. I could read every text message and email."

It was a violation—the knowledge that she'd been reading every communication coming in or out of my phone. But it was also so much worse. "You saw the message I sent Trace about where I'd be."

"I did," Farah said, grinning wider. "Had to steal an ATV from one of your neighbors. That was inconvenient. But I have to say, I didn't mind the show you and Lincy Boy put on. Hot. It just would've been better if you'd ended up in a body bag."

My stomach roiled, acid churning as rage swept through me. I braced to buck my hips when a new voice entered the chat.

"Stop playing with your food, Clarissa."

That voice. It was so cold. So devoid of emotion. But it was also familiar. And had me hurtling back fourteen years. To that night. The man who had stayed in the shadows. The one who had ordered my mother's death.

"Aw, but it's more fun this way," Farah pouted.

"Get her up. We need to move quickly. Lincoln won't be on that call for long," the man snapped.

As if Farah's leash had been jerked, she moved in a flash, leaping off me and yanking me up by my hair. She pulled my back to her front and pressed the knife against my throat again. "I told you we should've gotten him out of the picture long ago."

"I'm not going to kill my son, no matter how much of a disappointment he is. But I will kill you, Sheridan. It's long overdue."

Son.

Blood roared in my ears as a wave of dizziness swept through me.

Son.

The man took two steps forward into the glow the moon cast through the window. I had the voice. One I'd never forget as long as I lived. But now, I had a face. One I'd seen before.

Cold. Calculating. No kindness or gentleness.

And the last time I saw it was in the family photo Linc had shown me in my studio.

CHAPTER FIFTY-SIX

Lincoln

I RACED INTO THE HOUSE, SKIDDING TO A STOP AS I LOOKED around. Cope's place was too damned big. And with the staccato pattern of darkness and moonlight, there were too many places for someone who wanted to do harm to hide. I didn't have the first idea where to start looking. But then I realized it didn't matter. I just had to get to Arden.

She was all that mattered.

I started toward the steps, picking up to a jog. But then I heard it. Voices.

Stilling at the bottom of the steps, I strained to listen.

"I'm not going to kill my son, no matter how much of a disappointment he is. But I will kill you."

Each word was like a blow from a heavyweight champ wearing brass knuckles. Because I knew the owner of that voice, the wielder of that cruelty and vitriol.

My father.

Everything swirled in a mixture of confusion and fury. My father was here. Threatening Arden. None of it made sense. I knew he hated me. But enough to kill the woman I loved?

A soft growl sounded next to me, and I glanced down to see Brutus. My fingers latched onto his collar instantly, holding him back. Not until it was time.

I kept my grip on Brutus but began creeping up the stairs, straining to hear every word.

The sound of Arden's voice was a sweet relief, but the words she spoke nearly brought me to my knees. "You killed my parents."

My father scoffed. "*I* have never killed anyone. Did I touch a weapon all those years ago? No. Have I used this gun in my hand? It's only for protection. I'm a man with jealous enemies, after all."

"You pulled the strings. That makes you just as guilty," Arden snapped.

"Does it, though?" he cooed. "I'm just a man who likes to make sure the job is done *right*. Likes to see the blood of his enemies pour from their veins. The life drain from their eyes."

"And what did my parents ever do to you? My father didn't want to keep going with your sick game? So what?" Arden's voice trembled with fury or fear, maybe a mix of both. I wasn't sure.

"Such a promising colleague, with an impressive legal brain and a gift for finding all sorts of loopholes in the law. You can imagine my disappointment when he suddenly decided to end our association. I'm afraid he ultimately proved to be nothing more than a weak waste of space. He wanted to be a part of my world and run in the circles of the true *elite*, but he wasn't willing to pay the price. Wanted the prize but never the payment."

I reached the top of the stairs, pressing myself against the wall to keep Brutus and me hidden. Hugging the corner, I could just see around the wall, and the image cast in the moonlight had fury burning through my veins.

Part of my brain recognized my father, his back to me, a gun gripped in his hand. But at the same time, he was completely unrecognizable, a monster of nightmares. And those nightmares were Arden's.

"He paid the price," Arden rasped. "He would've paid anything. He just didn't want to keep throwing cases."

I couldn't see her, not yet. I just needed to take another step or two without getting my father's attention.

He made a *tsk*ing sound as he cocked his head to one side. "Now, Sheridan. My clients trust me to fix things for them to secure a certain outcome. The trade of a stock with insider knowledge. A child gaining admission to the appropriate university when their grades aren't quite up to snuff. The tipping of a case one way or the other for completely justifiable reasons. How are they going to trust that a judge who suddenly grows a conscience will keep his mouth shut?"

I climbed one step then another, trying to keep a hold of Brutus's collar. But the moment I reached the second to last stair, I only had eyes for Arden. Her already-blood-spattered dress had a couple of tears in it now, and someone had her in a tight grip, a knife pressed to her neck.

My body jerked slightly as I recognized *who* had Arden. Farah. I flipped through my memories, trying to remember everything I could about the woman. An artist from New York who'd come to Sparrow Falls seeking new inspiration and a change of pace. Not exactly someone I could see teaming up with my dad.

But the New York tie… That was something. And maybe Farah wasn't an artist at all. I'd never seen her create pieces that required technical skill. Had never heard her discuss her friends' creations with any deep knowledge. Maybe it had all been a lie. A façade.

"He would've stayed silent," Arden whispered. "To keep my mom and me safe. He would've kept your dirty secrets."

My father laughed at that as if she'd told him some hilarious joke. "But your mother already knew, didn't she? Why else would she have offered me money the way she did that night? She *knew* your father had betrayed me. He stole from me in a way. And I can't stand for that."

What he couldn't stand for was anyone having power over him. Anything that could cost him even a sliver of his kingdom.

"How does it feel, Farah?" Arden ground out. "Knowing you'll take the fall for this greedy prick?"

Farah gripped Arden's hair harder, giving her a good shake. "I don't take the fall for *anyone*. I line up the dominoes for someone else's demise."

"Not this time," Arden rasped. "He's lying to you. He knows they won't believe Hannah did this on her own. Cutting the power takes planning, and Hannah's been in lockup."

Farah's gaze snapped to my father as if a flicker of doubt were creeping in. "Don't even think about screwing me, Philip."

He held up a hand in an attempt to placate her. "That's not how I work. And why would I want to sacrifice my greatest weapon? How many enemies' lives have you infiltrated for me? How many secrets have you stolen?"

Like a child preening at his words, Farah's whole demeanor softened. "We do have the most fun together, don't we?"

My father's head turned slightly, just enough for me to see the sick smile spreading across his face. "We do." His gaze flicked to Arden. "I have to say, I've grown a little attached to you. All the hours I've put into finding you. The artists' age-progression renderings. The investigator following every lead. But it wasn't until you moved that money that I found you."

Confusion lit in Arden's eyes. "Money?"

"All that money your parents left you, just sitting in the bank, and you never once touched it. But four months ago, you moved it from one bank to another and logged in from your home computer."

The color drained from Arden's face. "You tracked me from a computer."

"Well, *I* didn't. I have people for that. A well-placed network. It didn't take me long to get Clarissa—I'm sorry, I mean *Farah*—in place here. I needed to know if you remembered more than my voice and those damn shoes."

"Talk about a boring assignment," Farah muttered. "'Watch her. See if you think she's remembering anything new.'"

"You were so determined to survive, I honestly thought about letting you live, just to keep things interesting. But then you had to get involved with Lincoln."

Hearing my name on my father's lips had sickness roiling in my gut. In that moment, I would've carved his blood from my veins if I'd had a knife. I wanted to burn out any pieces of him in me.

Arden's jaw clenched, her fists along with it.

My father tapped his fingers against his thigh. "What were the chances? You ending up with a foster brother on that godforsaken hockey team? Kismet. Destiny. But I couldn't let you get close to my son. Risk that you would somehow recognize me from a photo or video. Hear my voice and send me straight to prison."

"My brother," Arden growled.

My dad cocked his head in confusion.

Arden's fingers dug into Farah's forearm. "Not my *foster* brother. My *brother*."

My father's head fell back in laughter. "So attached to that fake family of yours. It's such a shame they'll lose you." His gaze hardened as he looked at Farah. "Do it."

I didn't wait. There was no time, no perfect moment. I released Brutus and charged around the corner, going straight for my dad, knowing that Brutus would see Arden in danger and go for her.

I hit him with all the force and power I could muster, but my father twisted at the last moment, avoiding the worst of my tackle.

A shriek of pain sounded, distracting me for a moment. Just long enough to register Brutus's teeth sinking into Farah's calf. Enough time for my father to clock me with the butt of his gun.

I stumbled back a few steps, trying to get my bearings.

Arden's fist lashed out, connecting with Farah's cheek in a brutal blow. Brutus didn't miss his opportunity. He leapt in the air, his teeth sinking into Farah's arm. The sound that came out of her this time was more animal than human. Her fingers released the knife as if all the tendons holding them in tension had been severed. And maybe they had.

Arden kicked the blade away as Farah fell to the floor, screaming in pain. "*Halten!*" Arden yelled to Brutus who promptly sat on Farah, using his full weight to pin her to the floor, his teeth lightly pressing against her neck.

It was all I could see before my father surged forward. I circled him as sirens pierced the air, my hands moving into a guard position as if that would protect me from a bullet.

My father let a slew of curses free as his eyes, so similar to mine, lit with rage. That fury was unlike anything I'd ever seen. As if that cold mask had finally been pulled.

"I should've known you would be my ruin," he sneered.

"That's on you, old man. You're the one who poisons everything you touch."

My father's lip curled in a half snarl. "You know, I wanted to give you a chance to come to your senses. Just needed to strip everything from you first so you'd come crawling back, begging for scraps like the mongrel you are."

I rolled to the balls of my feet. "You should know by now that I'll never come begging for anything from you. I'd starve before I took a single scrap from your tainted table."

My father grinned, the motion twisted just like he was. "Give your mother my best."

And then, he fired.

Everything swirled: the moments, the sounds, the images in front of me.

Some part of my brain was aware of law enforcement calling out from below. Another caught hold of a scream behind me. But it all came apart as some force hit me from the side, taking me to the floor as another shot sounded.

I hit the carpet and hardwood with enough force to knock the air clean out of me. And then all I could see was Arden. Her mahogany hair a tangle around us, her beautiful eyes wide with shock.

My father screamed in pain as it sounded like some deputies took him to the floor. But all I could see was Arden.

"Cowboy," she whispered.

"Vicious." I rolled us so she was beneath me. "Are you okay? Are you—?" Everything stilled, the barked orders around me turning to nothing but a faint buzz. Because there was blood on Arden's dress—way more than had been there before. And it was pooling on her belly, spreading across the fabric.

"Help!" I screamed the word, desperate for someone who could stop this from happening.

"Pressure," Trace clipped. "Pressure on the wound."

My hands moved without thought as I leaned my weight onto Arden. "Why?" I croaked, my eyes filling, tears falling and mixing with all that blood.

"Because I love you."

And then I lost those eyes, the ones that had held me hostage. The ones that had saved me. They were gone, and there wasn't anything I could do to stop it.

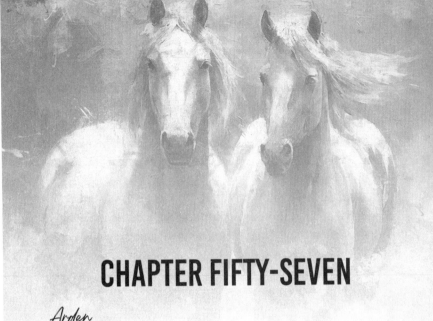

CHAPTER FIFTY-SEVEN

Arden

NORA HELPED ME EASE ONTO THE COUCH AS MORE THAN HALF a dozen people hovered. Shep and Thea from their spot by the island where a mound of food was piled. Kye in the corner, a hard look on his face that hadn't left since I'd woken up in the hospital. Rhodes and Anson in chairs opposite, concern even making its way onto the stoic ex-profiler's face. Lolli and Fallon in the kitchen, working on more food we didn't need. And Brutus right by my side, like always.

I understood why. Getting shot could get your family riled. Having to undergo a splenectomy on top of it didn't help. And almost a week in the hospital made us all twitchy.

"Do you need water? Juice?" Rhodes asked, bracing to stand.

"How about this new CBD iced tea I've been perfecting?" Lolli asked hopefully.

Shep sent her an exasperated look. "I don't think now is the time for Arden to be your taste-tester."

"Why not?" Lolli asked, her hands going to her hips and making the bedazzled pot leaf on her shirt stand out more, along with the script that read: *I'd Hit That*. "We'll know if it helps pain."

"We're not mixing your experiments with Arden's *prescription* medication, Mom," Nora clipped, her voice taking on that final air.

Lolli's gaze cut to me. "You just let me know if you need a little something extra."

I grinned at her. "I think the shower was good enough for me. Best drug around after nothing but sponge baths for a week."

Linc's movement at the windows was slight, an infinitesimal tightening of his jaw, but I didn't miss it. And the agony from that tiny movement was far worse than the pain in my side. He glanced at his watch and then strode into the kitchen, spilling a single white pill into his hand. Moving to the fridge, he pulled out some of the lemonade Thea had made, knowing it was my favorite.

In a matter of seconds, Linc was lowering himself to the coffee table in front of me and handing over the glass and pain pill. "It's time."

"I think—"

"Doctor said to stay on top of the pain for at least these first few days."

Linc's voice was so bleak, I couldn't bear it. I took the glass and pill, swallowing the medicine down. I knew I had about thirty minutes before it made me feel fuzzy. I both hated and welcomed the sensation. I hated not being aware. Welcomed not having to see all the ways Linc was pulling away.

He was physically present, but emotionally? He might as well have been on a different continent.

It was like he couldn't process it all, and learning all the ways our lives had been inextricably linked before we even met would be a mind fuck on a good day. But finding out that his father had been responsible for killing my parents and terrorizing me had been more than he could take.

Linc had stayed by my side every moment in the hospital, but that almost made it worse. His quietness and the way he turned inward were a constant slice to my skin, far worse than anything Hannah or Farah had inflicted.

Now that we knew Hannah hadn't been responsible for Linc's shooting, she had a better chance of getting the help she so desperately needed. Trace had worked with the county prosecutor to get her into a mental health facility with the appropriate security.

Farah—or Clarissa, as she was really known—was sitting in county lockup and had been denied bail. Her DNA had been linked to two other murder-for-hire cases, and her fingerprints to the theft of a priceless heirloom that had belonged to one of Philip Pierce's business rivals.

That man was far more twisted than anyone could've imagined. He'd begun pulling strings for his own betterment and power but found he had a knack for it. Blackmail, intimidation, murder, all to get the rich and powerful what they wanted most. He was a broker of sorts, and there was nothing he wouldn't do and no lines he wouldn't cross.

The FBI was still putting the pieces together, but it appeared as if my dad had met Philip at a political fundraiser. Philip had sensed an opportunity: a judge in his pocket in Boston was something he'd be more than happy to use.

But as the cases Philip asked my father to throw got more serious, Dad got cold feet. Philip didn't handle the change of heart well, and he wasn't a man who left loose ends to chance.

"Arden?" Linc's voice cut into my swirling thoughts like a blade.

He hadn't called me Vicious once since I'd woken up, and I found I hated the sound of Arden on his lips.

"Sorry," I muttered.

"You okay?" he asked. The question was gentle. *Everything* about Linc was gentle these past few days. And I hated that, too.

"Fine," I lied. "The meds just make me loopy."

Linc nodded, and I could see his knowledge of my lie in his hazel eyes. He pushed to his feet. "I need to make a call real quick. I'll be back."

There were lots of calls, along with the gentleness. I knew they were necessary. He had countless fires to put out with the press getting wind of Philip's arrest and again when the charges were filed. But as I watched him walk away, I couldn't help but wonder if we'd ever get back the closeness we once had.

"Don't let that boy push you away," Nora whispered.

I turned, taking her in as she lowered herself to the couch next to me. "I can't force him to talk to me. Can't force him to let me in."

"I don't know about that," Rhodes said. "Mr. Anti-Color over here was pretty pushy when he wanted to be."

Anson, who was indeed dressed in only gray and black, glared at her. "I just showed up, and you threw yourself at me."

Rhodes let out a huff. "Fal softened me up for you."

"You're welcome," Fallon called from the kitchen.

"He's been through hell," Nora said softly, her gaze moving to the patio where Linc stood, phone pressed to his ear. "Never seen anyone more ravaged than him when you were wheeled into that trauma bay. Never seen anyone more lost."

That was Nora, my mom, the woman who could never resist a lost sheep. She always had to bring them into the fold. And more than that, she wanted her kids' happiness. I reached over, laying my scarred hand over hers. "I love you, Mom."

Her eyes misted. "Love you, too. And I've fallen in love with Linc through you. So, don't let him run in some misguided attempt to be noble."

"Okay. But I need one thing first."

"Anything," she whispered.

My lips twitched. "I need some help getting off this couch because it's really freaking hard to stand with these stitches."

"I got you," Kye said, his voice gruff as he strode across the room, scarred motorcycle boots eating up the space. He offered his hands, his larger palms engulfing mine, strong fingers hoisting me up.

"Thanks," I said on an exhale.

Kye met my gaze, the ink on his neck flexing, the wings of the sparrow there almost seeming to flutter with the tension. "Give him hell, Killer. He needs someone who will go into battle with him and not be scared of the demons there."

It was almost as if Kye were speaking about himself *and* Linc. And I wanted that for him. I just had to hold on to hope that we could both find it.

CHAPTER FIFTY-EIGHT

Lincoln

THANKS, NINA." I SCRUBBED A HAND OVER MY FACE, THE stubble tipping into beard territory now. "I really appreciate you handling more than your fair share these past couple of weeks."

Nina had single-handedly sniffed out the traitor in our midst, a VP in acquisitions who had been more than happy to take my father's bribes. He'd been fired and reported to the police. My company and the Sparks were safe, but that didn't bring with it the relief it should have.

"Linc," Nina said across the line. "It's what family does. And we've been family since our two misfit selves found each other in undergrad."

A burning sensation lit along my sternum as I struggled to keep breathing. "Love you, Neens."

"Love you, too. Now, go take care of that girl who stole your heart."

That hurt worse. Knowing what Arden was to me. What she would *always* be. But also knowing there was no way she could be mine. Not anymore.

"Will do." I hit end on the call before she could say anything else because I couldn't take it. Not when I was this close to breaking.

I shoved my phone into my pocket and stared out at the landscape I'd fallen in love with. Stardust and Whiskey grazed in their pasture, completely at peace. We'd gotten closer the last couple of days as I'd taken over feeding and mucking their stalls. It was as if they could sense everything weighing on me and did whatever they could to bring comfort.

A throat cleared, and I whirled, my nervous system still not back to normal.

"Sorry," Trace muttered. "I thought you heard me."

I ran a hand through my hair, tugging on the strands. "In another world, I guess."

He nodded. "Talked to the prosecutor. He's been working with the other jurisdictions to figure out who's going to try your father first."

"Don't call him that." The words were out of my mouth before I could stop them.

Trace winced, a hint of empathy flooding his eyes. "I get that. Trust me. I get it more than you'll ever know."

Hell. I guessed we all carried scars, and some were more similar than we could've imagined.

"Mercer County is going to try Philip first. The case is the freshest and strongest. Attempted murder and conspiracy to commit murder. Not to mention, breaking and entering, illegal wiretapping, and a host of other things."

"Good." And it was. Philip would go to prison. I just hoped like hell he rotted there.

"He's not going to breathe free air again," Trace promised.

"I hope you're right."

Trace stared at me for a moment.

His silence set me on edge, evident in the quiet tightening of all my muscles. "Something else?"

"Ellie."

Surprise had my brows lifting. My sister had raced to Sparrow

Falls after that night. She'd gotten meals, handled calls to our lawyer, and done anything she could to help. "What about her?"

A muscle in Trace's jaw began to flutter as his green gaze went stormy. "She's got a black eye. Thinks we can't see it under the cover-up, but it's there."

The tension eased from my shoulders. "She was frazzled after Rhodes called her to tell her what had happened. Hit herself with her suitcase getting it out of her closet."

The strain didn't leave Trace's expression. "You sure about that?"

"Ellie doesn't lie. Not to me," I clipped.

He held up both hands. "Okay. I was just checking."

I nodded. I knew he was trying to help. He was a protector through and through. I just didn't have the energy to explain Ellie's sometimes klutzy ways.

"Trace, can I have a minute with Linc?"

Her voice was like the most beautiful sort of agony, a husky musicality that wrapped around me like a vise-grip.

Trace's gaze moved to Arden. "Of course. I'll be inside if you guys need anything."

Neither of us said anything as Trace headed for the back door. I didn't even turn around. Arden's voice was bad enough, but seeing her? I'd crumble.

But she took no prisoners, like usual. My vicious girl.

Arden rounded me, coming to stand between me and the pasture so I had no choice but to look at her. To see her beauty. Her fierceness. Her strength.

Those gray-violet eyes flashed with anger, sadness, and frustration, all in equal measure. "Are you done?"

"With my call?"

Her stare hardened. "Playing the idiot isn't a good look on you."

I knew it. But I couldn't find anything else to say. Because there *wasn't* anything. Nothing left but the brutal truth. So, I finally spoke it into existence.

"How can you even bear to look at me?" I rasped out.

Those beautiful eyes flared in shock. "Linc—"

"His blood runs through me. The man who cost you *everything*. His eyes are *my* eyes." I knew the sentiments weren't completely logical, but it was all my mind had grabbed on to these past eight days. Tortured and tormented by all the ways Philip Pierce and I were the same.

Arden moved in then, getting right up into my space. Her hand lifted, fingertips ghosting over my brows, around, and then down to the sensitive skin beneath my eyes. "Your eyes could never be anything like his. Because they look at the world with kindness and wonder. They look for ways to help, not harm. They see beauty when all he sees is ugliness."

"Arden," I croaked.

One hand dropped to rest right over my heart. "The blood that runs here is yours alone. So uniquely you, it could never belong to anyone else."

That featherlight touch burned me. "You'll never be able to forgive me."

Her eyes flashed a brighter purple. "You're right." A single fraction of a pause. "Because there's nothing to forgive. He was a monster to us both. But we slayed that dragon."

"Vicious," I breathed.

"Vicious for all the things that matter. And you will always matter most."

I stared down at her with a mix of wonder, pain, and gratitude.

"I'm not scared of the dark. Not anymore. Because you gave me the light. Please, don't take that away."

My arms wrapped around her, more of that beautiful agony sweeping in. "I won't."

"Promise?" she breathed, tipping her head back.

"With everything I have. Everything I am."

"Good, because I'd hate to have to kick your ass."

A smile curved my mouth for the first time in over a week. "And I know you could do it, too."

EPILOGUE

Arden

YOU'RE SURE?" I ASKED, GAPING UP AT DR. AVERY.

He smiled, the lines around his mouth deepening. "The test doesn't lie."

"I just—I—I'm supposed to be getting my stitches out," I said dumbly.

Nora moved in next to me, her hand taking mine and squeezing. "And they're out. This is just a bonus."

A bonus.

The slightest flicker of fear lit something deep in the darkest parts of me. But then I remembered the light. Not the one that came from the sun or the bulbs over my head, but the one that lived inside me. The one that Linc and I had created together.

My hand went to my belly. And this little one was a part of it. A baby. A being that was me and Linc.

"What if I'm no good at this? What if—?"

Nora cupped my face in her hands. "Arden. You were made for this. I've seen it more times than I can count. Your kindness. Your fierceness. It's the perfect blend. And this baby is so lucky to have you."

I gently pressed my hand against where the baby lay, growing. "I love him or her already."

Nora's eyes misted. "Me, too."

I was glad she had come with me today. Linc had a meeting he couldn't get out of—there'd been quite a few of those lately. He'd gotten everything back in order for the Sparks and had even managed to rescue a skate company in Minnesota that Philip had targeted because of him.

We were healing in all ways. But right now, I was thankful for Linc's many distractions because it was Nora I needed most in this moment. Someone who'd been down this road in infinite ways. Someone who was everything I wanted to be.

My gaze flew to Dr. Avery. "What about the surgery? The shooting? Is the baby okay? How do we know? Are we—?"

He cut me off with a small smile. "Everything we've gotten back from your labs looks great. But why don't we take a peek and see how your little one is looking?"

"Now?" I squeaked.

"You can come back with Linc if you'd prefer," Dr. Avery assured me.

I worried my bottom lip, going back and forth in my mind. "Could we do both?"

Dr. Avery chuckled. "Of course, we can."

Nora helped me lay back as Dr. Avery rolled over a machine. Pulling up my shirt, I waited. Nora took my hand in reassurance as the doctor squirted on some gel and began moving the wand over my stomach. But all I could think about was everything I'd been through these past few weeks. All this *baby* had been through. I squeezed my eyes closed, hoping with everything I had that he or she was okay, safe.

And then I heard it.

A rapid whooshing. But I *knew*.

"It's my baby," I croaked, my eyes flying open as he moved the wand again.

Dr. Avery grinned so wide it looked like his face might split in two. "Babies. *Plural*. There are two in here."

Nora let out a strangled sound. "Twins?"

Dr. Avery nodded.

Nora chuckled. "Go big or go home. Isn't that what the kids say?"

"Twins," I whispered.

Nora squeezed my hand. "You okay?"

I looked at the doctor. "Are they okay? Both of them?"

"Everything looks great. We'll get you in with a specialist to confirm, but they look like happy, healthy little ones to me. You're around nine weeks."

My head spun. "Linc did say he wanted a football team."

Nora held the door for me, and I stepped out into the sunshine, my mind still reeling. I was leaving with a referral to an OB-GYN, two weeks' worth of prenatal vitamins, and approximately eighty-two pamphlets on pregnancy.

"So much for birth control," I muttered.

Nora chuckled as we headed down the sidewalk. "Sometimes, life just finds a way."

"Are you comparing my babies to *Jurassic Park*?"

She only laughed harder. "Hey, it's a good movie."

"You and Kye," I muttered. They couldn't watch it enough.

My steps faltered as I saw a familiar figure headed down the street. His attire was a little more subdued than normal—no feathers in his hair or hipster hat—but it was Denver all the same.

Nora touched my elbow. "Want me to run interference?"

I shook my head. "It's time."

Denver had sent flowers to the hospital and cookies to my house, but we hadn't spoken. The truth was, I'd been putting him off, unsure of what to say.

"I'm going to pop into the bookstore," Nora said softly. "Find me when you're ready."

I nodded, somewhat aware of her disappearing into the closest shop, but my gaze was on Denver. His pace slowed until he stopped in front of me. "God, it's good to see you. How are you doing?"

"Just got my stitches out." It was all I could muster.

Denver stared at my torso as if he could see where I'd been wounded. "I'm so damn sorry, Ardy. For everything. I just—I got caught up. And it wasn't good. I didn't treat you right. And I wasn't there when you needed me because of it."

"Den. This"—I gestured to my stomach—"isn't on you. None of us saw it."

He scrubbed a hand over his face. "Isaiah's really twisted up over it. The Hannah stuff has him tweaked. But Farah? That's fucked."

Denver wasn't wrong, and his words had me realizing I needed to have Isaiah over to do a check-in. "We'll get through it," I promised.

"We will." Denver's gaze swept over my face. "Is there anything I can do for you? I know it's too little too late, but if I can help with anything, just say the word."

"Could you come back to work?" I asked.

I hadn't planned on asking him, but it felt right. Maybe early pregnancy hormones were making me ooey-gooey, but I just wanted all the people I cared about close. And Denver might've messed up, but I cared about him and knew he cared about me.

Denver's brown eyes widened. "Seriously?"

"We need to do things differently this time."

He nodded quickly. "I know. There won't be any pushing you to do things you don't want to do. I'm taking your lead. And I actually have some ideas for the kids' program. I think we should do a clay workshop with Isaiah. Kids love getting messy."

I laughed. "I love that idea. Why don't we meet next week? We can talk it out. I actually got some funding recently that will help." I was finally going to put that trust my parents left me to use. And we were going to do a world of good with it.

"I'd like that," Denver said quietly, then winced. "Did you see the article?"

I just smiled and shook my head. Sam Levine had gotten the scoop of the century. A reclusive artist, who turned out to be a young

girl who'd been hidden away in witness protection. But I'd give him
this, he still wrote about the kids' program and gave ways to donate.
He even connected my past with my need to give children that outlet.
It had made the checks and online contributions pour in.

"It could've been worse," I told him. "And honestly, it's nice not
to have to hide anymore."

And that was true. There was a lightness to me I hadn't had before. No looking over my shoulder. No wondering if someone was
staring for too long. I was free.

Nora's SUV pulled to a stop in front of my house. She put it in park
and turned to me. "You going to be okay?"

My mouth curved. "I'm better than okay. But Linc might pass
out when I tell him."

Nora laughed. "That man's made of stronger stuff. He's going
to be so happy."

"You think?" I asked, the nerves setting in.

"I *know*," Nora said, giving my hand a squeeze. "I see the way he
looks at you. There's nothing he wants more than to build a life with
you. This is just that."

"Maybe just a little sooner than expected."

"Time is relative. Pretty sure you've lived a lifetime these past
few weeks."

She wasn't wrong there.

"Okay." I said the word on an exhale and reached for the door
handle. "Now or never."

Nora released her hold on me. "Text me later. I need updates."

"Love you, Mom."

"More than all the stars in the sky."

Holding that love tightly, I stepped out and crossed to the house.
The sun cast it in a beautiful glow, and I heard Brutus's happy bark

from inside. I twisted the knob, eager to see my boy. We didn't lock the door anymore. There was no need. And that felt like freedom, too.

Brutus bounded over to greet me, letting out more happy barks. I laughed as I gave him a good rubdown. "I'm sorry, but you're not allowed in doctors' offices. But I missed you, too."

"How'd it go?" Linc called from down the hall.

I followed the sound of his voice deeper into the house. I found him perched at the kitchen island, which had become his part-time office. The sheers were pulled across all the back windows, which wasn't typical, but maybe the sun had been causing a glare on his computer.

"So?" Linc pressed, sliding off the stool and crossing to me.

"Picture of health," I said, a nervous smile taking root on my face.

Linc stilled just before he reached me, his eyes narrowing. "Something's wrong. Was it the blood test? Do you have an infection? Are there additional internal injuries? Do you—?"

"I'm pregnant." I blurted the two words, and Linc went stock-still. Well, everything other than his eyes widening to saucers.

"What?" he rasped.

"Pregnant. Preggers. Knocked up. Bun in the oven. Eating for two." *More than two.*

Linc moved into my space then, into me. One hand slid along my jaw and into my hair, tipping my head back. "Tell me again."

"I'm pregnant," I whispered. "Twins."

Those beautiful hazel eyes flared wide again. "Twins?"

A giggle slipped free. "It's honestly your fault. You must have super sperm to make this happen."

A grin spread across Linc's face; the kind that made the whole world stop. "We're having babies."

"You okay with that?" The nervousness slid back in. "We weren't planning—"

"Vicious." His hand slid to my belly, and he lightly pressed his palm there. "There's nothing I want more than to make a family with you."

My eyes misted at his words. "Mom said you'd say something like that."

"She's a smart woman. I love you, Arden. You changed me. From the moment you walked into my life, nothing was the same."

"Because I almost killed you?" I asked, tears mixing with my smile.

Linc barked out a laugh. "You do know how to make an entrance."

"I love you," I whispered.

"More than anything in this life and the next. Even if you steal my thunder."

I frowned. "What do you mean?"

Linc took my hand and led me toward the back doors, Brutus following behind us. Pulling back the gauzy curtains, he opened the door and guided us out.

I came up short. It was my back patio, but also…not. Because the entire space had been filled with wildflowers. Rustic bins and vases filled to bursting with every color under the sun. It was like stepping out into a sea of blooms.

"Linc," I rasped.

He tugged me forward to a small cocktail table also covered with wildflowers. But there was something else on its surface. Drawings. No, plans.

Linc squeezed my hand. "Shep finalized the plans. I wanted you to be the first to see. We can change anything you don't like. But—"

"It's a studio," I croaked.

"Of course, it is." Linc's finger traced the outline. "These three walls will be glass. And I had him put skylights here and here."

"A barn."

"Gotta look after my girls," Linc said with a smile. "And there's enough room to get a few more horses if you want. Plenty of grazing space."

"The house…is massive."

Linc frowned. "Now that we know we've got two coming, I think we might need to add—"

"Cowboy," I chastised.

A grin tugged at his lips. "I want it to be you and me. Us blending our lives. Making something more beautiful together."

"We already are," I whispered.

"Marry me."

The two words weren't a question or a demand. They were a simple truth.

Tears filled my eyes. "I'll bind myself to you in every way I can."

Linc's hand slipped into his pocket. "You told me once that you sometimes have to bleed to bloom. You showed me that the deepest beauty can come through the worst pain. You saw me through the dark. You gave me beauty from hardship. You showed me how to create that."

He slid a wide gold band onto my finger. The ring was breathtakingly unique—like my art come to life. There was no massive center stone, but an array of tiny ones. Inset red diamonds encircled by glittering white ones. It looked like a trailing vine of flowers. Almost like that first painting he'd influenced.

"Linc," I breathed.

"I knew it couldn't be bulky with your work. And I wanted it to be you. Wanted it to be what you gave me, too."

I looked up into those hazel eyes that had become my home. "It's us."

"One more thing."

"Anything," I whispered.

Linc's callused fingers teased around the ring. "When we get married, I think we should both change our last names."

"What did you have in mind?"

The gold in his eyes blazed brighter. "Colson."

Nothing could've been more perfect.

For an exclusive bonus scene, scan the code below and join Catherine's newsletter. The scene will be delivered to your inbox instantly. Happy Reading!

https://geni.us/BtflExlBnsScene

CAN'T WAIT TO SPEND MORE TIME IN
SPARROW FALLS? READ ON FOR A LOOK AT

Chasing SHELTER

I SET THE FINAL BOX IN THE LIVING ROOM AND SURVEYED THE space. As vibrant and quirky as the outside of the bungalow was, the interior was fairly...bland. Furniture in neutral tones with the occasional hint of color in the form of a throw pillow. It reminded me too much of my bedroom growing up, as well as the apartment I'd shared with Bradley and the aesthetic my design firm favored.

Rocking from my toes to my heels, I started envisioning what the space *could* be. The colors and textures I could use to bring it to life. The only problem? I wasn't sure what I wanted my life to be. And I'd gone so long without color that I wasn't sure what my favorites were anymore.

Color wasn't the only thing I'd gone without. I'd missed out on so many things. But I could only change one thing at a time.

I slid my phone out of my jeans pocket and moved to one of the bags from the massive haul I'd gotten at a catchall store. Grabbing a portable speaker from the bag, I hooked up my cell and opened my music app. It only took a couple of minutes of scrolling before my lips tugged up.

Boy Band Bangers.

I hit play, and *NSYNC's *Tearin' Up My Heart* filled the room. My preteen heart soared.

Sayonara, silence.

I lost myself in unpacking everything I'd purchased for my rental over the past few days and the suitcases of personal items I'd brought from New York. I'd left behind a closetful of clothes Bradley was likely shredding out of spite.

It didn't matter. That wardrobe was just as bland as the walls of my apartment. I'd get new clothes that fit the me I didn't quite know yet.

By the time I finished getting the bulk of my new belongings settled, I was a starving, sweaty mess. But Backstreet Boys were keeping me going with *Everybody*. I swung my hips to the beat as I made my way to the kitchen.

Looking around the room, I tried to decide what the easiest thing to make would be. Definitely nothing that required steps and assembly. Maybe I could take a cooking class for that.

I crossed to the fridge, opened the freezer, and grinned. Arden knew me well. The compartment was filled to the brim with frozen lasagna, bags of veggie stir-fry, and an array of other meals. But moving required one thing and one thing only.

Pizza.

Grabbing a veggie lovers from the top of the stack, I read the instructions. Seemed simple enough. I crossed to the oven that looked older than the Backstreet Boys bop currently playing from the speakers. I turned the knob to bake and set it to four hundred and twenty-five degrees. I quickly cut the pie out of the plastic wrapping and set it on the rack, which had certainly seen some use over the years.

After making sure the preheat light flashed on, I headed for the stairs. While the lot for my rental was large, the house was fairly small. It had two bedrooms and one and a half baths, with a tiny living room and office downstairs. But it was all I needed and more—because it was mine.

I snagged a fresh change of clothes from my room and headed for the shower. Turning on the water, I peeled off what I'd been wearing and left it in a pile on the floor. A smile that probably looked more than a little unhinged spread across my face.

I could leave my clothes in that pile all week if I wanted to.

There'd be no arched eyebrows or wrinkled forehead and look of disgust from Bradley. No sharply barked command from my father that no daughter of his would be a slob. I could pick them up whenever I damn well pleased.

And as if *NSYNC could read my mind, *Bye Bye Bye* came on the second I stepped into the shower, seeping up through the floorboards. I belted out the lyrics as I shampooed my hair and washed my face. By the time I was ready to turn off the water, I felt better than I had in years, maybe ever.

Quickly toweling off and getting the excess water out of my hair, I reached for my underwear and grinned. They were totally ridiculous. An impulse purchase at one of the big-box stores I'd hit up in preparation for my move. I was pretty sure they were a kids' design, but I didn't give a damn.

The rainbows decorating them reminded me of what I'd wanted to be back when I wasn't afraid to reach for it. I pulled them on and then reached for my bralette. The lace was a creamy white, but I'd find some brighter ones. There was a small boutique in town that might carry some things. If not, I'd order online.

Before I could dream up what colors to buy, an angry beeping blared so loud it resembled a tornado warning.

Did they get tornados in Oregon?

I didn't have the first clue, but I was already racing out of the bathroom. And that's when I smelled it.

Smoke.

"Shit, shit, shit!" I raced down the stairs toward the kitchen. Smoke billowed out of the oven in angry waves, and I tried to remember if this was the sort of fire I could put out with water. I spun around, trying to see if there was a fire extinguisher or a pitcher of some kind, as the blaring warred with the nineties pop.

I swore I heard something else, too. A banging. But I was too worried about potentially blowing myself up to seek out the source.

I should have.

Because I was frantically opening cabinets one second, and the next, a dark god of fury was striding into my kitchen. I gaped as the man hauled open the oven and sprayed something inside to douse the flames.

As he straightened, I took in the details I couldn't grasp before. Dark hair still damp from a shower. Green eyes like the hues found deep in the forest. Scruff dotting a jaw so sharp it could cut glass. And a worn Mercer County Sheriff T-shirt, the kind that was perfect for sleeping in.

"Trace?"

ACKNOWLEDGMENTS

This book made me cry more than once. And not just the *oh, I'm emotional and in my feels* tears. Also, the *is this book a dumpster fire* feels. I went back and rewrote large sections twice during the first draft, which I have never done in the history of twenty-five books. Usually, I save that pain for developmental edits.

But in my gut, I knew there were things that needed changing. The problem is that when you start tweaking at that stage (at least for me), you lose all perspective. So, I finished the book on a wing and a prayer and hoped like hell it was decent when I picked it back up again.

I swear I read through the first few pages with one eye closed, and then...I laughed. I cried (in a good way this time). I fell in love with Arden's fearlessness and Linc's tender heart. But I still held my breath as I sent it to betas, just hoping that *maybe* they'd also not think it was a steaming pile of garbage.

Spoiler alert: They loved it. Their encouragement and enthusiasm were everything I needed after a particularly rough patch of self-doubt (hello, writer over here!). They also gave me ways to make it better, as all the best betas do. So, the first thanks have to go to them. Glav, Jess, Jill, Kelly, Kristie, and Trisha, thank you from the bottom of my heart for giving me the words I needed and always helping me find the path.

The next thanks have to go to the one and only Elsie Silver, who made sure this book actually got done when I was rocking in a corner. She talked me through spicy scenes I didn't want to write and told me I was a boss bitch who could finish this book.

Samantha Young, who listened to endless plot voice memos when I was stuck. Encouraged me when I was feeling down. And who always has my back. Here's to our granny house in the country with our caretaker.

Laura Pavlov, the one who can *always* make me cackle-laugh, even in the worst of times. And who is always there to celebrate the peaks and valleys. Just remember, trust my gut, Rocky.

Rebecca Jenshak, who is the recipient of more spiraling voice memos than she ever thought she would be when I conned her into this friendship, and who is always there to talk things through when I need her.

Willow Aster, who will send me Elton and Winston animal pics every time I need them and laugh with me when we're feeling punchy, but most of all, who's the most tenderhearted and encouraging of friends.

Kandi Steiner, the best cheerleader a girl could ever ask for. She's always down for a T-Swift jam sesh or a heart-to-heart, and I'm so grateful for both. Also, I finished this the day before Rosie came! And I know our girl is going to be just as fierce as Arden!

The Lance Bass Fan Club: Ana Huang, Elsie Silver, and Lauren Asher. Thanks for the endless *NSYNC giggles, the advice, and the cheerleading, but most of all, your friendship.

Jess, who listened to endless spirals about whether I screwed something up, reread passages multiple times, and offered to help in a million different ways. I'm so lucky to have you in my corner!

Paige B, my warrior, my meme queen, my Swiftie sister. Thanks for cheering me on to the finish line of this book and supporting me in all the ways. I'm so grateful.

To all my incredible friends who have cheered and supported me through all the ups and downs of the past few months, you know who you are. Romance books have given me a lot of things, but at the top of that list are incredible friends that I am so lucky to have in my life. Thank you for walking this path with me.

And to the most amazing hype squad ever, my STS soul sisters, Hollis, Jael, and Paige, thank you for the gift of true friendship and sisterhood. I always feel the most supported and celebrated thanks to you.

The crew that helps bring my words to life and gets them out into the world is pretty darn epic. Thank you to Devyn, Jess, Tori, Margo, Chelle, Jaime, Julie, Hang, Stacey, Katie, Jenna, and my team at Lyric, Kimberly, Joy, and my team at Brower Literary. Your hard work is so appreciated! To my team at Sourcebooks: Christa, Gretchen, Katie, and so many others, thank you for helping these words reach a whole new audience and making my bookstore dreams come true.

To all the reviewers and content creators who have taken a chance on my words…THANK YOU! Your championing of my stories means more than I can say. And to my launch and influencer teams, thank you for your kindness, support, and sharing my books with the world.

Ladies of Catherine Cowles Reader Group, you're my favorite place to hang out on the internet! Thank you for your support, encouragement, and willingness to always dish about your latest book boyfriends. You're the freaking best!

Lastly, thank YOU! Yes, YOU. I'm so grateful you're reading this book and making my author dreams come true. I love you for that. A whole lot!

ABOUT THE AUTHOR
CATHERINE COWLES

Writer of words. Drinker of Diet Cokes. Lover of all things cute and furry. *USA Today* bestselling author, Catherine Cowles, has had her nose in a book since the time she could read and finally decided to write down some of her own stories. When she's not writing, she can be found exploring her home state of Oregon, listening to true crime podcasts, or searching for her next book boyfriend.

STAY CONNECTED

You can find Catherine in all the usual bookish places…

Website: catherinecowles.com
Facebook: catherinecowlesauthor
Facebook Reader Group: CatherineCowlesReaderGroup
Instagram: catherinecowlesauthor
Goodreads: catherinecowlesauthor
BookBub: catherine-cowles
Pinterest: catherinecowlesauthor
TikTok: catherinecowlesauthor

ALSO AVAILABLE FROM
CATHERINE COWLES

The Tattered & Torn Series
Tattered Stars
Falling Embers
Hidden Waters
Shattered Sea
Fractured Sky

Sparrow Falls
Fragile Sanctuary
Delicate Escape
Broken Harbor
Beautiful Exile
Chasing Shelter
Secret Haven

The Lost & Found Series
Whispers of You
Echoes of You
Glimmers of You
Shadows of You
Ashes of You

The Wrecked Series
Reckless Memories
Perfect Wreckage
Wrecked Palace
Reckless Refuge
Beneath the Wreckage

The Sutter Lake Series
Beautifully Broken Pieces
Beautifully Broken Life
Beautifully Broken Spirit
Beautifully Broken Control
Beautifully Broken Redemption

Standalone Novels
Further to Fall
All the Missing Pieces

For a full list of up-to-date Catherine Cowles titles,
please visit catherinecowles.com.